PENGUIN BOOKS

The Coronation Party

Norma Curtis was born and brought up in North Wales, where she formed part of the Girl Guides' guard of honour at the investiture of Charles, Prince of Wales. Since writing her first short stories for a teenage magazine, she has gone on to write seven novels. A former chairman of the Romantic Novelists' Association, she met Queen Elizabeth II at a reception at Buckingham Palace. She now lives in North London.

D0262745

The Coronation Party

NORMA CURTIS

PENGUIN BOOKS

PENGUIN BOOKS

UK | USA | Canada | Ireland | Australia
India | New Zealand | South Africa

Penguin Books is part of the Penguin Random House group of companies
whose addresses can be found at global.penguinrandomhouse.com

First published 2023
001

Copyright © Norma Curtis, 2023

The moral right of the author has been asserted

Set in 12.5/14.75pt Garamond MT Std
Typeset by Jouve (UK), Milton Keynes
Printed and bound in Great Britain by Clays Ltd, Elcograf S.p.A.

The authorized representative in the EEA is Penguin Random House Ireland,
Morrison Chambers, 32 Nassau Street, Dublin D02 YH68

A CIP catalogue record for this book is available from the British Library

ISBN: 978-1-405-95628-4

www.greenpenguin.co.uk

Penguin Random House is committed to a
sustainable future for our business, our readers
and our planet. This book is made from Forest
Stewardship Council® certified paper.

For Joe and Dani,
and to Paul, with love

I

The air in the small Welsh town was sweet with birdsong and the wide black Dee glittered under the old stone bridge as the steam train pulled out of the station, trailing smoke like speech bubbles. It was mid-April and in one of the white houses that made up Little Green Street, forty-five-year-old Tad Jones was preparing to hold a meeting.

Tad's given name was Thomas Kelly Jones, but a long time ago when he was a young poet who took himself seriously he had chosen Tad as his pen name, seeing himself grandly as a father of words. Although to begin with it was a source of gentle mockery, Tad became the name he was known by to everyone, even his wife.

Tad wanted to hold the meeting to discuss plans for a Coronation party in the street on the second day of June. He had decided to take his neighbours into the dining room, because it seemed to him to be more official to sit around a mahogany table, and he had placed a writing pad at the head of it for notes. The notepad also contained his inaugural speech as self-appointed chairman of the Coronation Party Committee. Restlessly, he straightened his tie, smoothed his springy dark hair flat as best he could, and looked at the time. 'They're late,' he said anxiously to Helen, his English wife, eight years younger than him.

She slid her headscarf from her fine, fair hair, took off

her floral apron and folded it carefully. 'No, your watch is fast, Tad,' she reminded him fondly.

It was true, Tad always kept his watch five minutes fast so he could be sure he was never late for anything. But as a result he was quietly resentful of anyone not on Tad time – in other words, the rest of Wales.

Tad put his flat cap over his dark wild hair and went outside and down the path to stand on the pavement, looking for signs of life behind the net curtains in the windows and resisting the urge to check the time again.

He tucked his hands in his pockets, rolled his weight to and fro on the balls of his feet. It was a lovely afternoon and the sky was a cool, pale blue, smudged with cloud. His gaze drifted along the curve of green hills that surrounded the town, and settled on the grey ruins of Crow Castle that stood guard over it. The history that castle had seen! And now history was being made again. 'The Coronation of Queen Elizabeth the Second,' he said aloud in wonderment, feeling the majestic words on his tongue.

'What's that now?' asked a stern voice behind him, startling him. 'Talking to yourself, Tad? That's a bad sign.'

It was Emlyn Kremlin, his neighbour from across the road, a staunch socialist with a Teddy Boy quiff, which Emlyn claimed was natural because he'd inherited a cowlick from his father. As his father had gone bald in his early twenties there was no one to say otherwise.

'Come on in, Emlyn! I was beginning to wonder if everyone had forgotten about it.'

'Why would you think that? I'm three minutes early, I think you'll find.'

'Is your mother coming?'

'No, she asked me to tell you sorry, she doesn't feel up to it. But really she just doesn't want to come.'

Emlyn's mother, Old Mrs Hughes, was known as a straight talker who had got increasingly eccentric in her old age. She lived next door to Emlyn and would, Tad thought regretfully, at least have made up numbers if no one else showed up. Mrs Evans two doors down had said that while she was very interested in the party, with five children to look after she had enough on her hands and couldn't possibly get involved.

He glanced down the quiet road one last time, and said, 'You'd better come on in then.'

No sooner had they sat down than there was a knock at the door and to Tad's relief he heard Harry and Mai Lloyd, his immediate neighbours, greeting Helen in the kitchen. Harry was a big man whose small face rested comfortably on the pillows of his neck. His wife, Mai, always wore her brown hair twisted in a neat bun and studied local history, or that's how she liked to describe it. She knew everything about everybody, and some things that they didn't even know about themselves.

'Come in, come in!' Tad said, pleased to see them. 'Put your trilby on the dresser, Harry. That just leaves Nancy still to come.'

The neighbours all glanced at each other quickly before looking away.

Nancy was a law unto herself, but she was Helen's closest friend in Little Green Street; blonde and sexy in a slightly dishevelled way, she enjoyed life tremendously – a little too much at times, Tad feared. But as she was younger than they were, Helen had insisted she be invited onto the committee to add some glamour.

Nancy arrived just as Helen was putting the tea tray on the table. She had styled her blonde hair in big curls around her face, like Marilyn Monroe, and she was wearing a red check shirt-dress like a cowgirl from a Western.

'Perfect timing!' she said, congratulating herself with a smile.

'Take a seat,' Tad said, eager to get started. He worried that Nancy was a bad influence on Helen. Putting the thought aside, he opened his notepad and started the meeting. He kicked things off by establishing that the Coronation Party in Little Green Street was his idea and on account of that, he felt he should be the one to chair the committee. Also, it *was* his house after all, but he left that out.

'Nonsense,' Emlyn Kremlin replied immediately, 'it's not your idea. Every street in the country is having a Coronation Party. Is it mostly for the children, are you thinking?'

'Well, yes, it's an important occasion for them,' Tad said.

'In that case, I'm not interested, as I haven't got any,' Emlyn said matter-of-factly, getting to his feet.

'It's not *just* for the children,' Tad said quickly, bearing in mind his daughter Lauren was going on fifteen, 'it's for all of us, to celebrate this great moment in the history of the British Isles.'

'Fair enough.'

As Emlyn sat down again, Tad glanced at his notes. He decided to carry on with his speech regardless, because he'd been practising it at the end of the garden where

Helen couldn't hear him and he didn't want it to go to waste. He liked to think of himself as an orator, but she wasn't so sure.

He took out his wallet and extracted a newspaper clipping from *The Times*. Once he'd smoothed it flat on the table, he announced, 'I'm going to start by reading these words of Churchill's about the young Queen. It's a speech he made in the Commons, which I feel sums up the mood of all of us around this table.' He cleared his throat. '"A fair, a youthful figure, a Princess, wife and mother, is heir to our traditions and glories. She is also air to our united strength and loyalty. She comes to the throne at a time when tormented mankind stands uncertainly poised between catastrophe and a golden age. Let us hope and pray that the accession of Queen Elizabeth II may be the brightening salvation of the human scene. (Cheers.)"'

'Hear, hear.'

'What do mean, "Cheers"?' Emlyn asked.

Tad looked at the cutting more closely. 'That's just what it says here. Cheers, in brackets. That's what the members of the House of Commons did when they heard the speech. To be honest, I expected a few cheers from around the table.'

'Hurrah!' Emlyn said obligingly with a grin.

Tad continued, 'It was Lloyd George himself who gave me the idea for a party.'

Harry roared with laughter and slapped the table. 'Lloyd George? Come off it, Tad.'

Tad backtracked. 'I mean Major Gwilym Lloyd George, the Minister of Food.'

'Oh, Gwilym, was it? Then why didn't you say so?'

'I would hardly mean David Lloyd George, would I, Harry? Unless it was a seance.'

Emlyn was looking at Tad suspiciously. 'And when did Major Lloyd George confide in you? You kept that quiet.'

Tad could feel his wife's cool gaze settle on him. She could see right through him which disconcerted him at times.

'I heard him on the wireless,' he admitted. 'He was talking about ration concessions for Coronation parties. An extra meat allowance.'

Harry perked up. 'Forget meat, let's have chocolate cake,' he said.

'And sherry,' Nancy suggested, nudging Helen with her elbow, 'as it's a party.'

'No, we're not having drink,' Mai said disapprovingly. 'People will get up to all sorts!'

'We have to have a glass of something,' Nancy said, 'for the royal toast.'

'It's called the loyal toast,' Helen said automatically.

'What? Why isn't it a royal toast?'

'Because we're showing our loyalty to the Queen.'

'We could just as easily show our loyalty with tea,' Mai argued.

'You can't toast Her Majesty with *tea*,' Emlyn said scornfully, siding with Nancy. 'It's better not to toast her at all.'

Tad raked his fingers through his dark wiry hair and puffed out his cheeks. Emlyn had a point. He felt torn, which was unlike him, as he normally knew his own mind. He was veering from one side of the argument to the other. He did very much like the idea of a loyal toast, and being the one to propose it. But he didn't want Coronation Day to end in a rumpus, which it was likely to if there was alcohol involved. He turned the page in his notebook, wrote down *toast/tea?* and put his pen down.

'And we want singing,' Emlyn said.

'Singing goes without saying, Emlyn. I was getting to that. I think we should ask the choir to come and sing the national anthem, all five verses. And whoever wants to stay afterwards can join us for a bite to eat.' Tad was choirmaster and, seeing Harry frown, he added: 'Maybe your Rhiannon would play "God Save the Queen" on the harp, to accompany the choir?'

That settled it for Harry, although chocolate cake alone would have done it, and he clapped his hands together. 'Rest assured.'

'We could buy Union Jacks and hang them in our windows,' Helen said. 'They'd look pretty and so patriotic, going all the way down the street.'

Tad caught Helen's eye and she smiled coolly back at him, resting her cheek in her palm and playing with her pearl earring, a habit of hers. She hadn't mentioned this idea to him beforehand and he wondered why. Sometimes she made him feel like a boy, which wasn't always a good thing. He could look at his wife for long moments at a time, with her fair hair, her slender figure and her distant gaze, and have absolutely no idea what she was thinking, whereas he was the very opposite – he tried never to let any of his thoughts go unspoken.

Suddenly, watching her curl a strand of fair hair around her ear, he forgot about his speech. He wanted more than anything to make her laugh.

She hadn't laughed much since her beloved father was suddenly taken ill fifteen months earlier. He had died before she could get to her parents' home in London. The fact she'd not been there with him to say goodbye weighed heavily on her and the period of national mourning for the death of King George VI on the same day had been overshadowed for Helen by her own private grief.

Tad had done his best to support her, but it seemed as if a gulf had grown between them and she remained elusive, a little out of reach.

But she'd also seen the young Queen's response as a yardstick for her own sorrow, and now with the Coronation only six weeks away, she'd told Tad just that morning that she too was going to look to the future with courage.

He felt a rush of love for her. He knew that when she was growing up in London her family enjoyed celebrating state occasions, that they had meant a lot to her and her family when her father was alive, and while this party was for the whole street to enjoy, in his heart it was mostly for her. 'Yes, of course we shall have flags in our windows,' he declared warmly. 'Good idea!'

Helen gave a small smile and nodded pointedly at his notebook. He picked up his pen and wrote it down.

'We could wear fancy dress,' Nancy said suddenly. 'I could dress up as the Queen, and wear a crown and sash and a slinky gown.' She stood up and posed, one hand on her hip.

'Yes! Let's all dress up,' Emlyn said, his eyes lighting up at the thought of Nancy's gown. He also had a marvellous idea of his own. 'And I'll go as a—'

Mai interrupted. 'A slinky gown, Nancy? It's a coronation, not a beauty pageant!' She disliked beauty pageants almost as much as alcohol. 'I could probably fit into my lace wedding dress again, I've lost so much weight with rationing. It's white lace, very royal-looking and not slinky at all. It belonged to Harry's mother, you know. I'd make a purple crown, to denote royalty.'

'Loyalty you mean, Mai,' Nancy corrected.

Tad blinked and scratched the back of his neck doubtfully – the only queen that Mai looked like was Queen Victoria.

'Oh!' Helen said with a start, 'I forgot about the tea!' She took off the tea cosy, knitted from scraps of brightly coloured wool by Old Mrs Hughes, and rested her palm against the china pot. 'It's not so hot now. I'll make a fresh one.'

'I'll help you,' Nancy said quickly, scraping back her chair.

Tad watched them leave the room. He heard them laughing in the kitchen. Helen sounded happy and Tad was pleased they were getting involved in the Coronation Party. It was what he'd hoped for. A celebration was a source of joy.

In the interlude, Harry took a cigar out of its case, ran it under his nose to savour the aroma and leant back in his chair with a deep satisfaction as though all the problems of the world had been solved.

Emlyn lit a cigarette and picked a flake of tobacco off his tongue.

Mai stood up and poured milk into the bone china cups. She had an ulterior motive for being helpful because

Helen was proud of the tea service and Mai wasn't quite sure whether it was quality or not. She held the last cup to the light before pouring the milk, and then she turned it upside down and read the stamp. 'Royal Crown Derby,' she said. 'Fancy!'

'Loyal Crown Derby, you mean,' Emlyn added with a smile, looking towards the kitchen as he heard Nancy's delicious laugh.

When Nancy had first come to the town to visit her daughter Flora, an evacuee staying with Old Mrs Hughes and Emlyn back in the days when they had the farm, there had been a general expectation that she would fall for Emlyn, a single man. It was assumed that her husband had been killed in the war, although this remained unverified by Mai even after some serious probing, because Nancy told her firmly that she never talked about him.

In the end, despite high hopes from the rest of the town, the romantic relationship between Emlyn and Nancy had never got off the ground, but they both knew perfectly well about the gossip that had surrounded them and gently teased each other about it.

Helen came back from the kitchen with the fresh teapot, followed by Nancy, and poured the tea. Harry rested his cigar in the ashtray and Emlyn stubbed out his cigarette.

Once the sugar bowl had been passed round, and the hot tea stirred, blown on and sipped, they were ready to continue with their plans.

'We haven't talked about the practicalities,' Harry pointed out. 'We'll need tables and chairs for everyone.'

'We could borrow them from the church hall,' Mai suggested.

'Mai, it's a long way to carry them from the church to here,' Emlyn warned. 'And Harry's got his knees. We've got our own tables and chairs,' he pointed out sensibly. 'We can bring them out for the tea party and take them home at the end of the day. Same with plates and silver-ware. Have you written that down, Tad? Don't forget to say it was my idea. I don't want you taking all the credit.'

As Tad put his teacup down and reached for his pen, it occurred to him belatedly that he should have appointed a minutes secretary. It took him a few moments to get it all down.

'And now to the question of food,' he said. 'I propose that we each bring enough for ourselves and a bit extra to share. And Harry, you'll have to bring bigger portions than the rest of us. We know your appetite.'

Tad meant this perfectly seriously, but everyone laughed.

Harry patted his stomach fondly and agreed. 'Do you hear that, Mai? Bigger portions.'

Mai tossed her head and a hair grip fell out of her bun. She felt for it on the chair and tucked it back in. 'You and your stomach, Harry,' she said.

'We could make bunting, to decorate the street,' Nancy suggested. 'We've all got sewing machines. Flora will help, I know she will. She's good at needlework.'

'Splendid!' Tad said, jotting down *Bunting*. He wondered about his own daughter, who was more dreamy than practical, and looked at his wife. 'What will Lauren do to help, do you think?'

'She'll write a poem about it, I expect,' Helen said with a wry smile. 'I suppose she could make food for the children, like those little party snacks from the Ministry of

Food leaflets. I kept them all, I had a feeling they'd come in useful one day.'

'Wonderful! Mai? How about your Rhiannon?'

'If Rhiannon's playing the harp for the choir, I should think that's enough of a contribution, don't you?' Mai said briskly, folding her arms. 'She's got practising to do. She hasn't got time for fun.' She and Harry had great ambitions for Rhiannon on the music front and they wouldn't let anything get in the way of parental pride, especially not a party.

'Of course, of course, quite right,' Tad agreed soothingly. As a music teacher, he applauded single-mindedness where practising was concerned.

'Anyway, what about Garth?' Mai asked him. 'You haven't mentioned him. He ought to have something to do. He's always out with our girls.'

Garth lived with his widowed mother at the bottom of Little Green Street. When his father drowned whilst fishing, his mother Barbara became a recluse and refused to leave the house for any reason, so Garth did the shopping, the gardening and the outside windows and generally looked after himself as unobtrusively as possible.

Tad was poised with his pen above his notepad and looked around the mahogany table, eyebrows raised in query. 'Any suggestions for a job for Garth?'

'I think Garth's got enough on his plate as it is,' Nancy said, looking in her handbag. She took her gilt powder compact out, opened it with a click and studied herself in the mirror for a moment before tucking a curl of blonde hair behind her ear. 'Don't you, Mai?' She said it so sweetly and kindly that it couldn't really be taken as criticism.

And yet ... Mai opened her mouth to argue, and changed her mind.

Harry glanced at his pocket-watch. 'Look at that! It's nearly time for supper!'

Emlyn laid his hands flat on the table. He looked round at his neighbours. 'Haven't we got a lot done! Well, now that that's all sorted, I'll be off,' he said, reaching for his scarf. 'I've got to see a man about a dog. Same time next week, Tad?'

'Hasn't time flown!' Despite his disappointment the meeting was ending already, Tad felt a burst of organisational satisfaction at the way it had gone. 'I hereby bring the proceedings to a close!'

Everyone else got up too, and after seeing his guests to the door, Tad said to his wife, 'I don't know, Helen, they're a handful, I can tell you,' but he looked very happy nevertheless.

It was true, they hadn't resolved everything, but it didn't matter. There was going to be a next time.

2

Fourteen-year-olds Lauren, Flora and Rhiannon were sitting on the ancient stone bridge, one of the Seven Wonders of Wales, dangling their legs over the thrilling, roaring, foamy black waters of the River Dee, while red-headed Garth was towering above them on the bridge wall, one hand holding tightly on to the black lamp-post to steady himself, acting as lookout for signs of life from Lauren's house.

Suddenly he had news. 'They're leaving! The door's opening! I can see Emlyn Kremlin talking to your mam, Flora.'

'How do they look?' Lauren asked anxiously, because she'd heard Tad planning his Coronation Party speech down the garden by the rhubarb and she had been hoping, for his sake, it would go well.

'Hard to tell.' Garth shielded his eyes from the sun. 'They just look normal to me,' he said. 'Harry's following them, Rhiannon. He's smoking his cigar and saying something to Tad. Now Mai's waving to Helen.'

'Yikes! I'm supposed to be doing music practice, she's going to kill me,' Rhiannon said. 'Help me off, Garth, will you?'

Garth didn't need to be asked twice. He jumped down onto the safety of the pavement and held his arms out to catch her. Rhiannon grabbed his hand and shrieked, blinded by a flurry of her long brown hair as she stumbled against him.

'Garth! I nearly fell in then!'

'It's all right, I would have dived in and saved you,' he said boldly.

She laughed. 'Would you?'

'Like a shot!'

'Liar!' Flora was kicking her legs against the bridge wall, looking down at the tumbling river, holding her blonde hair away from her face. 'Have you ever jumped in, Garth?' she asked mischievously.

It was something that the boys did in the summer holidays, standing above the river daring each other, scared to death, choosing their spot carefully so as to drop with a splash into the deep glossy waters, to emerge cold, wet and elated before climbing up the rocky bank to pavement level and joining the dripping, shivering, thrilling queue to do it again.

Garth had a visceral fear of drowning, which was a good reason for not doing it. For a moment his face tightened, but then he said, 'No, but I'm going to one day.'

'I wouldn't,' Rhiannon said firmly. 'I'm scared of depths. I'm all right with heights, though, I can look up at things for ages and it doesn't bother me.' She laughed at her own joke. 'I'd better go home before I get into trouble.'

'Your parents treat you like a little girl,' Flora said. She swung her legs around and brushed her blue skirt down. 'You should ignore them.'

Rhiannon bit her lip. 'It's all right for you, Flora. Your mam's easy-going.'

'We'll walk back with you. I want to find out what's happening.' Lauren sympathised with Rhiannon. Tad wasn't as strict as Harry and Mai, but he was definitely a lot stricter than Flora's mother Nancy, who was glamorous and full of fun and who thought the most important thing in life was to be happy.

Lauren would desperately like to be a rebel like Flora. She only behaved herself because she didn't want to upset her parents, especially not now. Her mother had been in mourning for a year and a half and it seemed to have lasted for ever. She hadn't said anything, nor cried much at all, but it was like seeing the reflection of a candle in a mirror – she'd lost her brightness.

Lauren knew it was for her that Tad wanted the Coronation Party to be such a success, so that, like the Queen, her mother could put her grief behind her and have something wonderful to think about instead. He wanted her to remember the Coronation with joy, in the same way as the Queen would remember her special day. 'What will we wear to the party?' she asked suddenly.

'I'm going to wear red, white and blue,' Flora said. 'It's patriotic.'

'I'll do the same,' Lauren said quickly.

'Me too,' Rhiannon said.

'What about me? I haven't got anything red or blue,' Garth said. 'Only my school shirt is white.'

'There you go! That's a start, Garth! You just need a bit of red and blue and you're all set.' Rhiannon was always kind.

They walked with Rhiannon back towards her home in Little Green Street so that she could practise her music, and she fluttered her fingers in the air to limber them up and get them in the mood.

Nancy was coming towards them in her red check dress, swinging her handbag in the crook of her elbow. She fluttered her fingers back at Rhiannon. 'The Coronation Party is on, and I'm going as the Queen,' she announced as she passed them.

Why hadn't they thought of that?

'What is my mam going as?' Rhiannon asked, but Nancy didn't turn round.

There was a quick way to find out, as they were nearly home, so they said goodbye and arranged to meet later.

Lauren's parents were in the kitchen when she arrived home. Her mother was at the sink, peeling potatoes in her apron, and Tad was hunched over the table writing up his notes on the meeting.

Her mother turned and smiled, and Lauren's heart melted as she put her arms around her from behind, and kissed her shoulder. Her mother felt warm under her cotton shirt. 'We just saw Nancy and she says she's dressing as the Queen.'

'So is Mai, as long as she can get into her mother-in-law's wedding dress.' Helen's eyes gleamed with amusement. 'You know Mai. She feels hers looks more royal.'

Lauren grinned. 'Are we all supposed to be going as queens? We were going to wear red, white and blue, to be patriotic. Are you going as the Queen, too?' Helen rinsed the potatoes in the pan and left the peel in the colander, ready for the compost heap. As she dried her hands, she turned to Tad almost shyly. 'I'm wearing my bluebell-blue dress,' she said, and as she caught his eye she blushed, as if he wasn't her husband of many years but someone that she had only just realised she'd fallen for.

'You look beautiful in that dress,' Lauren said.

'It goes with your eyes.' As Tad looked at his wife, his serious face lit up, as if he was seeing an awe-inspiring and life-changing vision. He opened his mouth to speak, but the words didn't come out – it seemed to Lauren that his loving feelings came soaring out of his brown eyes instead.

Embarrassed by the display of affection between her parents, Lauren tried to lighten the tone. 'What else did you decide on?' she asked.

Tad checked his notepad. 'Food, music and bunting, and I'm going to hand out flyers to everyone in the street, on behalf of the committee. I've nominated myself to do it.' His dark wiry hair was standing on end, as if he'd had too much excitement.

Worst luck, Lauren had inherited that hair, which went mad if she was caught in the rain. People would look at her in surprise when she tried to straighten it and tell her they wished they had naturally curly hair, but she knew for a fact they wouldn't appreciate it if they did.

'Anything else?' she asked hopefully.

'We're having Union Jacks in all the windows,' her mother said.

'That was your mother's idea, credit where credit's due,' Tad said fondly. 'On Coronation Day itself, the choir's going to come and sing the national anthem, all five verses, and we'll have the loyal toast, with tea or sherry, and then whoever wants to can join us for the party. You're going to help with the children's food.'

'Okay! I can't wait!' Remembering she had school work to do, Lauren picked up her satchel. 'I'm going to get on with my geography,' she said, and hurried upstairs to sit on her bed with a feeling of relief as she took it all in.

Her mother only wore her favourite blue dress on very special occasions, and she hadn't put it on since her father died.

Lauren saw it as a sign that things were good again and her mother was going to be happy.

She had been sad herself when her grandad died, but her sadness seemed neatly packaged in the corner of her thoughts where she would only come across it now and then. For instance, when she received a birthday card containing a ten-shilling note with *Love from Grandma* on it, seeing just one name instead of two had made the tears come out of nowhere, and they smudged the handwriting and her mother kissed her head and gave her Tad's blotter to dry the card with.

But her mother's sadness had been too big to be tucked in the corner. It took up all the space in her mind so there wasn't much room for anything else, especially not for loving them. And she and her father had got used to that.

Lauren had tried to understand how she was feeling. At night, lying in bed with the light off and her whole room turned to grey, she'd imagined what life would be like without Tad in it, without his energy, his passion and his words. It was like looking into a bottomless pit, nothing there but space, and it terrified her so much that she had to switch the light on again and read an ancient Enid Blyton to calm herself down.

She went over the scene in the kitchen and mention of the bluebell-blue dress. Mum's feeling better, she thought. Her prayers had been answered and the answer seemed like a beautiful gift. She clasped her hands under her chin and closed her eyes and said a fervent thank you to God.

3

Emlyn hadn't gone straight home after the meeting. He headed to his mother's house first because he'd been struck by a marvellous idea for a staggering costume for the Coronation Party, but he would need her help.

He was greeted at the gate by his mother's Pembrokeshire corgi, Waffles. The little dog was short enough for a cow's kick to pass right over his head, and dutiful enough to ensure the herd was kept together at all times. The dog was the last evidence of the family's farming days, and the herding instinct was in his veins to an infinite degree.

These days, for want of cows, Waffles kept the residents of Little Green Street together by going from house to house to check on their whereabouts, probably in his working dog's mind regretting the fact that they were not half as intelligent as the animals he was used to, and nothing like as obedient.

Emlyn's mother, Old Mrs Hughes, was sitting in her parlour, bathed in the mellow glow of polished horse brasses. She was knitting a hat from brightly coloured scraps of wool, some of which had found their way into her grey hair, where they dangled like ribbons.

'Well, Emlyn, is it going ahead?' she asked him doubtfully.

Emlyn glanced in passing at his reflection in her ornate brass mirror and smoothed back his dark quiff. He was, if truth be told, the best-looking man in the street. 'It is indeed,' he confirmed. 'Tad tried to make a speech, to convince us, even though we were convinced already. Said he's got the idea from Lloyd George.'

'No!' Old Mrs Hughes exclaimed. 'I thought he was dead long ago!'

'Not him, his second son, Gwilym.'

'Gwilym? Why didn't you say?'

'I'm just telling you what Tad said.'

'Lloyd George, indeed,' Old Mrs Hughes scoffed. 'Tad's too clever, sometimes.'

Emlyn felt his mother had put her finger on it. 'It's going to be fancy dress,' he added. 'Nancy's going as the Queen.'

'Heavens! I don't think the Queen would like that. Sunday best is good enough for anyone.'

Emlyn himself had no objections to seeing Nancy clothed in the slinky gown of his imagination, and as the Queen was busy herself on that day he didn't think she would mind either.

'Oh, I don't know. I think it's a tribute to enter into the pomp and ceremony of the occasion. Where's your button box?'

Old Mrs Hughes stopped knitting with her needles in mid-air as though bracing herself for a shock and looked at him suspiciously. 'What are you up to, Emlyn Hughes?'

'I'll tell you what I'm up to. I'm going as a Cockney Pearly King, if we've got enough buttons.'

Old Mrs Hughes's puffy eyes widened. 'That *is* a good idea. The button box is in my sewing cabinet. Fetch it to me, Em.'

Emlyn opened the cabinet and took out the button box, which had a vaulted wooden lid like a small treasure chest and was gratifyingly heavy.

His mother put her knitting to one side and placed the box on her lap. She unfastened the latch and opened the lid.

Emlyn had never had cause to look in the button box before but he was impressed by the orderly interior which was divided into sections, depending on size and colour. Even better, what gladdened his heart was that by far the bigger portion of the box was taken up with mother-of-pearl shirt buttons which women in the Hughes family had cut off diligently and saved for just an occasion such as this.

The idea of being a Pearly King had come to him in Tad's dining room at the committee meeting in a flash of inspiration.

'How many buttons do you need?' Old Mrs Hughes asked him.

'All of them, I should think.'

'Dew! That many? That will be some sewing, Emlyn.'

Emlyn had had the good fortune of seeing a Pearly King up close in London when he went to pay his respects at the King's funeral the previous year. It was a rainy day and he had walked from Euston to King's Cross Station to join the crowds for the arrival of the royal train.

That day, Euston Road had bloomed with umbrellas that flourished in the intermittent rain like fungi, and Emlyn had smoked to pass the time, and now and again looked idly up at the office windows with people's faces pressed to the glass, and watched workmen perch precariously on ladders, fighting off all boarders with curses and threats. But time and again, with nothing to do but wait, no matter where Emlyn looked it was the Pearly King that drew his eye.

The Pearly King was wearing a pearly hat covered in white ostrich plumes, and a costume covered in pearl buttons. Emlyn had eased himself sideways through the crowd to get a closer look at the man's finery, and saw that the mother-of-pearl buttons were arranged across the back of his jacket in the design of an ornate crown, with embellishments.

A subdued murmur had run through the crowd and he hurriedly put out his cigarette. As the cortege approached, Emlyn held his breath. He saw the royal crown glittering poignantly in the rain on top of the flag-draped coffin, then the solemn figures of the Duke of Gloucester and the Duke of Edinburgh following the carriage, both wearing dark coats and carrying black silk hats.

Immediately the gun carriage drew level, the Pearly King took his cap off with a dramatic flourish and held it over his heart, the gesture so sincere yet so extravagant that in that moment Emlyn, despite being a chapel-goer, would have killed to have been him. He had never coveted anything so much in his life as that outfit. His own black coat and the trilby pressed to his heart seemed a very sorry affair in comparison.

Now, looking at his mother's button box, it seemed to him that the first step before anything else was to have a design. Apart from the crown, he would like something additional to represent Wales. His immediate thought was to have a red dragon, but that would be a challenge created out of white pearl buttons, so a daffodil or leek might be better. He could even have both, one either side of the crown.

Once he'd created the design, he would put his mind to a hat. 'Before I go, I don't suppose you have any ostrich feathers?' he asked his mother hopefully, as if it was the kind of thing that people sometimes had hanging around the house that you didn't notice until you wanted them.

But to his surprise, his mother said that she was fairly sure she had got some somewhere, and she would keep an eye out for them.

That sorted, Emlyn clapped his hands together. 'Right then,' he said cheerfully, getting to his feet, 'the sooner we get started, the better,' and he went to his own house to unearth his funeral suit.

Harry Lloyd also had an idea of what he would wear on the day.

He had an enduring memory of the previous coronation, that of King George VI, which had taken place in 1937 when he was twenty-nine years of age and Mai and he were just married. He and his parents had been sitting in the kitchen, listening to the commentary on the radio, when he heard the 'Crown Imperial' march for the first time. Sitting with his elbows on the Formica table, Harry had unexpectedly found himself moved to tears by the music. The triumph and the fanfare had swept him up into a different world, and he had leapt to his feet, roused into action. Unable to contain himself, he had thrown himself into conducting the orchestra with his teaspoon.

His parents had been startled – the cups rattled in their saucers, his mother patted her heart to get it going again and his father told him sharply to stop playing the fool, but the memory thrilled him even now.

The man in charge of the orchestral music, Adrian Boult, came from Chester, just a train journey away, and Harry realised he might well have seen him around in person at some time whilst shopping, without knowing it.

To Harry's great joy, this very same man – Sir Adrian Boult as he was now – had been invited as guest artist to the town's musical festival for the past two years running. Both times, Harry had sat in the audience utterly mesmerised by the famous conductor's economy of movement, his grace, the elegant way he used his baton. He wielded it like a wand, magicking the spirit of the music out of the air so that it swept you away. He came to a decision. He was going to go to the Coronation Party dressed as his hero.

There was no need to go to any expense either, he reflected, which was an important consideration. All he needed was his suit and tie, and a baton for conducting. He remembered Adrian Boult sporting a lavish brown moustache, and it occurred to him that he might be able to grow one in time for the party, if he put his mind to it.

Mai had gone upstairs to try on his mother's wedding dress. His mother had lent it to Mai for their wedding, but she'd left the other guests in no doubt as to who carried it off better, so Harry was very glad it was getting a second outing all these years later without his mother being present.

Harry went up the stairs and tapped on the bedroom door.

'Don't come in yet!' Mai said quickly. 'I'm not ready! Is it done up, Rhiannon?'

'Most of it,' Rhiannon said. 'Can you breathe?'

'More or less.'

Harry raised his eyebrows on his side of the door. Being able to breathe in a frock seemed to him to be a minimum requirement, but he didn't know much about ladies' fashion.

'Ready!' Rhiannon announced. 'Come in!'

Harry went in and for a moment felt as if he was seeing his wife just as he'd seen her eighteen years before. 'My word!' he said happily. 'I'm a lucky man!' Which is exactly what he'd felt on his wedding day.

'Undo it, Rhiannon, I'm going to pass out!' Mai said frantically, flapping her hands, and as Rhiannon unfastened the dress she gulped for air as if she'd been under water. 'It's a bit tight,' she confessed, and her voice was flat with a combination of breathlessness and disappointment.

'You could leave it undone and wear a cape to hide the back,' Harry suggested kindly.

'Harry Lloyd, get away with you!' Mai said, flapping her hand at him, shocked to the core. 'Leave it undone?' But she went to the mirror and looked at herself in the lace dress. Her face softened and she turned to Harry again. 'A cape?' she asked hopefully. 'What sort of a cape?'

Harry waved the general shape of a cape in the air. He knew better than to carry on talking. He kissed her fondly on the cheek. It was sometimes better to let Mai think about things in her own time, so he went downstairs to put on his recording of the 'Crown Imperial' and find some-thing suitable in the cutlery drawer to conduct with.

4

The Hand was a historic white-stuccoed hotel built high on the banks of the River Dee, near the parish church at the end of a narrow road of white-stuccoed cottages and quaint shops. It was where the Dee Male Voice Choir met every Thursday evening for choir practice.

Harry, Emlyn and Tad were sitting at a table by the window in the cosy, nicotine-yellow, smoky bar. The grey pewter tankards hanging above the bar gleamed, the spirit bottles glittered, and an empty pint pot sat on the piano for tips. They liked to get there half an hour early so that they could have a beer before the rehearsal began, to lubricate their voices.

After finishing his first pint, Emlyn cleared his throat and did a few vocal exercises to limber up. He sang '*Lolo-lolohhhhh*' in a deep bass, as if he were singing down into a canyon, and graduated through the scales to a chilling falsetto of '*Leeleeleeleeleeeeee!*'

'You need oiling, Emlyn,' the landlord observed soberly.

'It's true, I do,' Emlyn replied happily, picking up his empty glass. 'Same again, Billy, please.'

Seeing Emlyn stand up, Harry finished his off quickly and asked for the same again, and make it quick, too, before Mai turned up. His wife usually arrived at five to seven, just for the singing, and drank a small, sweet sherry piously as if it was communion wine.

'We'll start with "God Save the Queen",' Tad said, 'to get into practice.'

At that, Harry stood up with alacrity and nearly knocked the table over with his wide girth.

'Where are you going?' Tad asked him, taken aback.

Harry looked surprised to be asked. 'I'm standing for "God Save the Queen".'

So Tad stood up too and as Emlyn returned, he was pleased at their formality when all he'd done was get another round in.

This was a big year for Tad, not only because of the Coronation but because the Dee Male Voice Choir had been practising since last summer for the International Musical Festival that took place every year for one week in July. As choirmaster and conductor, he felt they had a good chance of winning, even though they were up against male-voice choirs from all over the world. This year was going to be particularly special because the Queen and the Duke of Edinburgh were attending the festival as part of their tour of Wales in July.

The festival was a magnificent event dreamt up by a local man after the war to make the broken, war-torn world whole again through song. Their motto was: *Where Wales Welcomes the World*. Everyone in the town got involved. The contestants arrived by train or by coach, travel-worn and weary, from Denmark, Germany, Norway, Italy, Canada, Spain, Yugoslavia, the USA, all of them laden with bright costumes – including surprising hats with tassels, and shoes with pom-poms – and the townspeople were there to greet them with cups of tea and a warm welcome. They took them into their houses, and communicated through the language of gestures and smiles, and gave them a clean bed and hot meals and made them feel at home. When the visitors competed, their hosts were their supporters, and they went to watch and cheer them on.

It was an ambitious endeavour, to unite the world, there was no doubt about it. But for one week every July since 1947, the miracle happened. The town needed it, because there were times in life that only a miracle would do. The Dee Male Voice Choir had lost almost half of its good lads to the world war. For those men that were left, it had taken them some time to have any heart to get together and sing. But now, eight years on, they presented as full and powerful a group of singers as anyone could wish for. Being a music teacher, Tad considered himself perfectly qualified to say that.

For now, as they weren't immediately practising 'God Save the Queen', they sat down again.

Harry quickly managed to get a quarter way through his second beer, and was in a hearty mood. 'You know, it's thanks to Wales that the Crown Jewels stayed safe during the war,' he said. 'I have it on good authority that they were hidden in a slate mine towards the coast.'

'Whose authority? Mai's?' Tad asked sceptically.

'A policeman, a local, told me,' Harry replied. 'In confidence, like.'

'It must be true then,' Emlyn said, straight-faced.

'The royal wedding rings are made of Welsh gold too,' Tad pointed out.

'And Queen Victoria's bed, that one they made for her and Albert in Penrhyn Castle, was made out of Welsh slate. It must've been like sleeping on a billiard table,' Emlyn said cheerfully.

'How would you know, Emlyn?'

'He's thinking about his misspent youth,' Tad said. 'Passing out in the pub after a long night.' With all these close links between royalty and Wales, they felt practically related, and it left them with a warm glow of satisfaction by the time the women turned up.

The women made up the audience in the rehearsals. They drank sherry, shandy or plain lemonade, and had a convivial night of it, and when the men took a break the women sang their own songs sometimes, if they were in a singing mood, and Nancy kept time by clapping along because she didn't have a voice for singing and didn't know the words either.

Helen hadn't been to choir practice for over a year because of her bereavement, so, as Tad finished his drink, he was surprised and gratified in equal measure to see her appear in the doorway, pale and ethereal. Her fair hair was freshly curled back from her clear face and her navy coat was slung loosely over her shoulders. She smiled when she saw him and came over to his table, to him, and rested her hand briefly on his shoulder. It felt light, barely more than a shadow falling on him.

'I'm going to sit in the corner with Nancy,' she said into his ear.

Her soft cheek brushed his for a moment and as Tad watched her join her friend, he was aware she had left the scent of her Côty perfume behind. He breathed it in, glad she was here. This year, the atmosphere at choir practice had an added focus and now she wouldn't have to take his word for it – she would be able to hear the difference for herself, because there was nothing quite as powerful as music for reviving a bruised spirit.

Harry was three-quarters through his second pint so that when Mai arrived he could let her assume he'd just had the one. He gulped it too fast, and burped. 'Beg pardon,' he said.

'Granted,' Emlyn replied automatically, smoothing back his quiff before they got started.

Tad took up the conversation where he'd left off. He had a talent for that. 'We'll start with "God Save the Queen", because we need to practise for the Coronation Party,' he repeated for Emlyn's sake.

'You've already said that,' Harry pointed out. He took out his cigar and looked at it thoughtfully for a moment before putting it back in its tube. 'Let me ask you something, Tad, which I've been wondering about lately. Who voted for you to be the choirmaster?'

The question seemed to come out of the blue. Tad looked at him blankly, ran a hand through his wild dark hair and cast his mind back. 'To be honest, I don't remember a vote, as such,' he said after a moment. 'I took over from Vaughan Reid when he retired.'

'But why?' Harry persisted. 'Why you?'

Tad thought about it. 'I don't think anyone else was interested,' he said truthfully.

'I see. But what if they were?'

For a moment, Tad felt uneasy. 'I suppose they would have mentioned it at the time,' he said.

Truth be told, if Tad had wanted he could, as a music

teacher, legitimately claim a certain professional aptitude, whereas Harry worked for the Electricity Board, and the only music he encountered in his working life was the hum of electricity along wires.

'I think we should take it in turns to conduct,' Harry said. 'What do you think, Emlyn? Do you think Tad should hand over the baton now and then?'

'He doesn't use a baton,' Emlyn pointed out.

'His metaphorical baton,' Harry said patiently. 'You know what I mean.'

Emlyn rubbed his chin thoughtfully and mulled it over. 'It depends,' he said at last. 'If we win the Male Voice Choir category this year it's obvious we should keep Tad on. We'd be fools not to! But if we don't win, maybe it's worth trying your idea and giving someone else a chance. I'm very willing to take a turn myself next, to keep it fair.'

'Yes! Being fair! That's what I'm talking about.'

Tad was looking at Harry, perplexed. They were old friends, they'd known each other all their lives, from babies in prams, to school, to marriage and children, and all the way through till now. But there was a gleam in Harry's eyes that reminded him of a calf called Paddy that had belonged to Mrs Price from White Gap Farm years ago. They used to cut across her fields, he, Harry and Emlyn, to take a shortcut home from school, but one day as they were messing around throwing burrs at each other, trying to get their school caps furred like a guardsman's busby, they heard a warning bellow and realised that the calf had grown into a bull. Its large, gentle brown eyes were by then small, mean and focused, sending malevolent dark beams of irritation at them.

And that was how Harry's eyes looked now.

It wasn't just his eyes, either. His face was different, somehow. He hadn't shaved his upper lip. It looked odd, as if it were speckled in smuts.

Out of the corner of his eye, Tad saw Mai in the doorway and gestured the fact to Harry. With a last, pointed glare, Harry got to his feet and went to the door to escort Mai in because his wife would rather die than come into a bar by herself and she'd give him hell if he didn't. He called to the landlord to give her a sherry and Nancy sauntered over to invite Mai to join them. She was wearing some kind of swirly skirt that seemed to billow as she walked.

'Two shandies, please, Harry,' she said cheerfully.

'Right you are,' he replied. 'Pass this sherry to Mai, will you, while you're waiting.'

The room was getting crowded. Oswald, the organist, was standing by the piano sorting through his sheet music, and the conversation increased in volume to a roar. Tad got to his feet and went over to the piano to tell him the plan. Oswald was a tall man. 'I don't have to stand up for "God Save the Queen", do I?' he asked. 'Only I won't be able to reach the keys if I'm standing. I've got short arms.'

'No, no,' Tad said, still distracted by the conversation with Harry.

The bar was now full, and the men lined up in two rows along the wall opposite the window. Tad stood in front of the enthusiastic choir and gestured to Oswald to begin playing.

Some of the choir found themselves singing 'God Save

the King', as old habits die hard, but Tad halted the singing and they began again.

Tad started off as he usually did, with just his index fingers tick-tocking like a metronome, and as the choir warmed up he used his hands, flicking his wrists.

And as the singers under his instruction achieved the deep-throated harmony he was looking for, he threw more and more of himself into it, using his wild arms and barrel chest to finish with a glorious crescendo, stretching the final 'Queen' out until his arms wouldn't stretch any further, and then bringing the whole thing to an end with a double-handed chop.

The echo of the men's voices seemed to hang in the air with the blue cloud of cigarette smoke.

Helen, Mai and Nancy looked at each other.

'It's coming on, isn't it?' Mai said, impressed.

Nancy giggled. 'You know, Helen, when Tad conducts, he puts me in mind of a ship's captain fighting to stay upright in a terrible storm.'

Helen was loyal to Tad and pretended not to hear. 'You're right, Mai, it is coming on,' she agreed. 'It's going to be quite a party.'

'Harry thinks they've got a good chance at the festival, too.'

'Do you think they've got any chance of winning? And what's the prize, anyway?'

'Fifty pounds,' Mai said.

'To *share*? It doesn't seem much.'

'I wouldn't say no to a share of fifty pounds,' Nancy said.

'I suppose not, when you put it that way.'

'And it's not about the prize, it's about the honour. Imagine knowing you are the best male-voice choir in the world! It would make their year,' Mai said fondly.

Helen nodded. Tad had never spoken to her about how much he wanted the choir to win, but she could see the ambition burning in his eyes on Thursdays as he got ready for choir practice, and the way he hummed to himself around the house.

If he wanted this, then equally, she wanted it for him. She loved his enthusiasm for life. It was one of the things that had attracted her to him when she first saw him on a soapbox at Speakers' Corner in 1937, a serious, good-looking young man of twenty-nine, aware of the unsettling rise of Adolf Hitler and the Third Reich, preaching about Moral Rearmament to a congregation of tramps and pigeons.

Passion such as this was the complete opposite of what she was used to. Her mother, in contrast to her gentle, loving father, viewed feelings as dangerous things which should be subdued at all costs until they gave up the fight. She showed her displeasure by becoming arctic cold until you couldn't stand the chill any longer and gave up.

Helen had recognised her father's warmth and generosity in Tad, and loved him for it.

At her father's funeral, her mother had seemed to be carved out of stone. And when Helen had taken out her handkerchief to dry her eyes, her mother told her sternly to pull herself together. But Tad, on the other side of her, had heard the whisper and taken her hand and nestled it in his own, using his warmth to comfort her.

Across the little table, Nancy opened her handbag, took out her compact and reapplied her lipstick. The light flashed across her face as she pouted at her reflection and patted her hair, satisfied. 'Shall we have another?' she asked.

Mai placed the flat of her hand over her sherry glass with alacrity. 'Not for me,' she said firmly.

'Thanks, Nancy,' Helen said. 'I'll have a lemonade.'

'Don't thank me, I'm not the one who's buying them,' Nancy winked.

She left her bag on her chair and walked through the crowded bar with an easy sway of the hips which didn't escape anyone. Sure enough, moments later she was back with two drinks, very pleased with herself.

Oswald struck a chord on the piano, the choir readied themselves, and they sang 'Guide Me, O Thou Great Redeemer' with lots of stops and starts and repetition, until Tad felt that they'd got it right.

Usually during choir practice, the non-singers felt free to talk quietly amongst themselves, but tonight there was something electric about the singing. The volume and the resonance coming out of the bar caused guests of the hotel to stop as they were passing, and pop their heads around the door to find out what was happening, maybe thinking it was a gramophone playing loud. When they saw it was coming from the small band of men, they edged in to watch, and listened, struck immobile with admiration and appreciation. At the end of the hymn, there was a stunned silence.

During the silence, the choir was looking at Tad as if he was not the choirmaster, but the alchemist.

He bowed to them, moved to tears, and as one, the choir returned the bow.

The little audience burst into applause with a stomping of feet and banging of tables. A couple of guests who had come in late from an evening stroll along the river path and were still wearing their trilbies threw them into the air. One of them hit an electric candle on its sconce and knocked the shade off.

Tad was still trembling with emotion as he, Harry and Emlyn made their way to join the women at their table, pulling up stools.

'What did you think?' Tad asked his wife hopefully.

'You did yourselves proud.'

Tad only wanted to make *her* proud, that's what mattered to him. 'You enjoyed it!' he said.

'Yes. I thought you were wonderful. And so did the choir.' Helen's face creased in a smile. 'Twenty pairs of eyes looking straight at you,' she said.

'To be strictly accurate, nineteen and a half,' Emlyn said, moving his seat closer to Nancy. 'Hugh Pritchard lost an eye in the Somme. It hasn't affected his singing, though.'

'In the Somme? I heard he lost it playing darts in the dark,' Harry said.

'Don't ask,' Mai cautioned Helen, but it was impossible not to.

'Why was he playing darts in the dark?'

'For a bet.'

'Did he win it?'

'No.'

Outside, night had fallen. The town had lost its definition and the river had become invisible.

38

Helen and Mai reached for their coats and got ready to leave.

Billy rang the bell for last orders, and asked Oswald to straighten the lampshade while he was passing.

The men who had work tomorrow shuffled out into the starry darkness, and the retired men with rosy faces leant on the bar and asked for one for the road.

Nancy and Emlyn decided to have one for the road, too.

Harry seemed his usual self again. He put on his jacket and Tad helped Helen on with her coat. They left the bar in a chorus of goodnights.

Outside in the cool spring air, even the river seemed to rush by quietly out of respect for the lateness of the hour.

Helen took Tad's arm as they crossed the stone bridge and squeezed it close. 'I do love you,' she said.

Tad looked at her in surprise. Her face was pale and vague in the moonlight. 'I know,' he said.

She laughed. 'Do you? You're modest!'

He didn't laugh back. 'But I *know*,' he said seriously. 'And I love you too.'

'Well then.' She nestled her head against his shoulder. 'Good.'

The lamp-posts threw yellow circles of light on the pavement and they watched their long black shadows shrink and stretch before them as they walked.

Behind them they could hear Harry humming the same phrase over and over, his shoes beating time on the pavement.

'Give it a rest, Harry,' Mai said.

'I'll have to, I've forgotten how the rest of it goes. I tell you, Mai, that was singing!'

Tad chuckled softly. 'Listen to them.'

The lights were still on in the railway station, like an invitation to go somewhere else, but why would you? Tad wondered. This town was where they belonged. It was home.

5

Lauren was lying in bed in the empty house, eyes wide open, fully clothed, listening out for her parents to come back from choir practice. On the wall opposite her bed there was a print of flowers in a vase. Looking at this picture, she sometimes saw faces in the petals, vague and indistinct. Her mother sometimes told her she had too much imagination, but she couldn't help it. It wasn't something she'd chosen, it was just the way she was made.

When she was alone at night, and it was dark, she sometimes noticed too that the proportions of the house seemed to change. The rooms would grow larger and noises would echo in the unfamiliar space.

She got up and went to the bathroom and noticed that all the bedroom doors were ajar in what felt a sinister manner, revealing nothing but more darkness.

She went back to her room and tried to distract herself by starting to read an Agatha Christie. At ten o'clock, she gave up, closed her book and went out onto the landing. The staircase led down into darkness too. At the bottom of the stairs, she felt she sensed something waiting.

Holding her breath, she stood very still, listening.

She hurried back into her room, closed the door, knelt on the bed and looked across at Flora's house. It seemed to glow white but the windows were in total darkness. Maybe Flora was already asleep, and dreaming.

Lauren rested her arms on the cold windowsill and wondered what kinds of things Flora dreamt about. She herself dreamt about exams that she hadn't revised for, being asked to hand in homework on subjects she'd never heard of, or going to school naked by accident and kissing Garth on purpose.

But she had a feeling that none of these things would bother Flora's dreams at all. And one thing she was re-assuringly certain of was that Flora wasn't scared of the dark.

The four of them had spent a couple of hours that evening at Rhiannon's, planning their red, white and blue outfits for the tea party. Garth said he was going to wear a red, white and blue tie, he was pretty sure his mother could manage that.

Garth's mother lived in the end house of the cul-de-sac, the one with a triangular-shaped garden. She didn't like going out, but it wasn't snobbery or anything like that, it was just that she found the open air intimidating. She was a slight woman with brown hair and nervous, jerky movements.

Garth said that when she'd read Tad's flyer about the Coronation Party it worried her no end, because she was nervous of things like that.

'How can she be nervous of a party?' Flora had asked him incredulously.

Garth said she just was.

The way he said it, it sounded to Lauren like something he'd made his peace with.

'If your mam can't sew you a tie, I'll do it,' Rhiannon offered.

Lauren had also thought about offering, but was put off by the thought of Flora teasing her.

But Flora hadn't teased Rhiannon. She was wondering what qualities made Rhiannon less teasable than herself when she heard the sound of voices in the street. She cleared the condensation from the window and saw her parents and Harry and Mai coming home, laughing.

Her parents were walking arm-in-arm, like a courting couple.

Lauren closed the curtains quickly, glad to see they were almost home and that they were happy. She realised that she'd been entirely wrong about the house. There was nothing wrong with it at all; it was safe and cosy and warm. She hurriedly undressed and put her nightdress on, and hung up her school clothes and jumped into bed just as she heard the front door open.

Her mother came upstairs and popped her head in. 'I saw the light on,' she said, 'so I came to say goodnight.'

Lauren faked a yawn. 'How was choir practice?'

Helen smiled. 'Rather wonderful, actually.'

Lauren propped herself up on her elbow. 'Was it really?'

'Yes, really.' Helen came in and kissed her forehead.

'You smell nice, Mum.'

'Goodnight. Sweet dreams.'

'Goodnight, and say goodnight to Tad.'

As her mother switched the light off and closed the door, Lauren lay on her back in her soft bed and sighed happily. Her mother was her old self again. All was right with the world.

*

At school the next morning, Mr Jones the headmaster announced in assembly that there was going to be an end-of-term competition for the best Coronation poem written in the form of praise poetry.

Mr Jones was a stern, middle-aged man, dark-haired, lean, with a booming voice that put his pupils in mind of impending disaster and the wrath of God. 'By that I mean nothing subversive,' he announced, just to clarify it for the jokers. His dark gaze swept the hall, which was otherwise used as a gym, and smelled of sweat and blood.

Here he paused and as an afterthought he added, 'And no limericks. The winner will be crowned—' he dropped his chin and lowered his voice to a spectacular hush '—School Bard.' And he left the stage promptly with his black academic gown flapping around him like a crow's wings.

There was a hubbub of resentful protest once he'd gone. As they filed out of assembly and jostled in the corridor, Flora grumbled that in her opinion the competition was impossible. 'How can we write a poem about something that hasn't even happened yet?'

Lauren liked the idea of being School Bard. 'We know some things that will happen, though. The Queen will have a crown put on her head for a start,' Lauren said. 'And she'll get to the Coronation in a stagecoach.' Even as she said it, it didn't sound quite right and she screwed up her nose. 'Or is that what highwaymen used to rob?'

'She'll have ladies-in-waiting, too,' Rhiannon added.

'Yeah? Waiting for what?' Flora asked curiously.

'To obey the Queen's whims.'

Garth laughed. 'Standing around like fielders on a cricket pitch, waiting for the whim to come their way.'

They had maths first lesson, with John Fred Owens. He had a temper and his favourite punishment was to hit a pupil on the knuckles with the edge of his ruler. He was a master in torture. For a lesser misdemeanour, he would just throw the board duster at them, which was made of felt and wood and left a tell-tale imprint of chalk dust on a navy blazer that their parents would see, which meant a double punishment because the chalk dust was very hard to brush off.

Rhiannon was quiet, clutching her battered satchel to her chest, because she didn't understand maths and she dreaded John Fred's lessons.

'Are you thinking about the poetry competition?' Garth asked her, hanging back.

'A bit.'

'Praise poetry is about qualities, isn't it?' Garth said thoughtfully. 'What a person is like.'

Lauren was lost in a daydream. She could imagine writing a wonderful poem of tribute and admiration. It was so vivid a vision she could almost feel the weight of the crown when the headmaster put it on her head, and her modest words of thanks.

She was jerked back to reality.

'Garth, Lauren, Rhiannon, stop loitering!' John Fred barked from the door of his classroom, and the day carried on in the same old way.

6

A few days later, Flora, Rhiannon and Lauren went to the market to choose material for their Coronation dresses. Flora was consulting the instructions on the Simplicity Miss Petite pattern and reading them aloud. 'We need lightweight to medium-weight fabric, cotton, cotton lawn, linen, that kind of thing.' They had chosen the pattern together. It was the New Look: a fitted bodice with a full skirt and a cummerbund around the waist for definition.

The market was lively with people, dazzling with colour and loud with stallholders. Women with their baskets full collided with them like bumper cars in search of a bargain. 'Not two and six!' Jones Pots was shouting, 'Not one and six!'

'How about a penny!' shouted a small boy, running past, dodging the crowd.

'Not a shilling!' Jones Pots yelled, and the women waited eagerly. 'Give me sixpence!'

The haberdashers' stalls were at the back. They considered themselves a cut above the fly-by-nights. They didn't have to shout to attract customers, the customers came to them. Mr Lewis's stall was at the end, and he was sitting on a wooden fishing stool wearing a straw boater and tilting his face to the sun, half hidden behind vivid bales of cotton and moygashel, velvet and tulle, muslin and linen.

'Beautiful!' Rhiannon said.

'I love the smell of new,' Flora said, sniffing the air, 'don't you?'

'So are we going to have a bodice of one colour, the skirt of a different colour, and a sash in the third colour?' Rhiannon asked. 'I forgot what we decided.'

'We decided to come and see what he's got,' Flora said, feeling the cotton between her finger and thumb.

'Which colours are you looking for?' Mr Lewis asked, listening to the conversation without opening his eyes. He continued sunning himself. 'I've got a yellow seersucker, beautiful for summer.'

'We don't want yellow, we're making dresses for the Coronation.'

'For the Coronation! You'll be wanting red, white and blue, then,' he said. 'I've got some lovely striped here.'

He got up off his stool and hefted the rolls around, dropping them with a whump, until he found the one that he wanted, which he unrolled for them to admire.

The red and blue stripes were very vivid against the white background.

'I love it.' Flora took the Simplicity pattern out of her shopping bag and with narrowed eyes the three of them used their imagination to superimpose the stripes on the illustration.

'It's nice, isn't it?'

'Stylish.'

'Sophisticated,' Rhiannon said.

'There's words!' Mr Lewis said admiringly.

They consulted the pattern again and calculated how much fabric they would need, plus extra for Garth's tie.

There was a certain amount of argument involved about how to pay for it, because Lauren would need most because she was tallest, and Rhiannon was the smallest, and Flora was somewhere in between. Mr Lewis pointed out that there was only an inch or two between them, but he would serve them individually with what they needed to save bothering with fractions.

Their houses would soon be filled with the rhythmic beat of the sewing machines as they made their dresses for the party.

On Saturday morning as Helen was reading the paper, Tad called her urgently to come upstairs to see something strange. When she joined him at the bedroom window he pointed to Harry's garden next door. 'Look!'

Harry was standing on the lawn in his paisley burgundy dressing gown, vigorously sawing a branch off the willow. It was difficult to see what was wrong with that particular branch from this angle. It seemed no different from the rest of the tree and it was too thin to be dangerous.

That was interesting enough but more was to come.

When he'd sawed it through, Harry picked it up and whipped the air with it energetically, as if he was swatting flies. The silk of his dressing gown flashed in the morning light.

'What's he doing?' Helen whispered, horrified and fascinated, even though there was no way he could hear her through the closed window.

Whatever Harry was doing, he wasn't satisfied, because he threw the branch down in contempt and went over to his birch tree. He stood contemplating it for a few minutes, and then turned and went inside his shed.

Moments later, he came back out with his stepladder and set it down next to the birch tree. He picked up his hacksaw and a few minutes later, he had a fresh branch to swat with. After he'd swatted the air a few times from the top of the stepladder, he climbed down and stripped the leaves from it, and then he held it out at arm's length, like a magician. He stood, poised, motionless for a minute and then swung round, as if he could sense he was being watched and wanted to catch them at it.

'Duck!' Tad said.

They crouched by the windowsill, feeling ridiculous.

'Did he see us?' Helen asked.

'I'm not sure.'

They crept out of the bedroom and went back downstairs to look casual, just in case there was a knock at the door and it was Harry. They waited, but as the time passed they relaxed.

'I'm worried about him, you know,' Tad said thoughtfully, pouring the tea. 'He had a very cold expression at choir practice last week, and there's his moustache. Have you noticed it?'

'Can't miss it,' Helen said.

'Exactly. I've known him since he was a boy, and he's never shown any ambition to grow a moustache before.'

'He couldn't have grown one when he was a boy,' Helen pointed out logically. She frowned. 'Oh no, I'm turning into Emlyn.'

'Heaven help us!' Tad glanced at the clock and got to his feet. 'Dear me, if I don't get a move on, I'll be late.

Find out what you can from Mai,' he said as he kissed Helen goodbye. 'She'll know what's going on, if anyone does.'

'I'll do my best,' Helen promised.

As luck would have it, Helen and Nancy were meeting at Mai's at ten-thirty, in the front room. This was dominated by Rhiannon's harp and Helen noticed that the gilt music stand held the sheet music for 'God Save the Queen' arranged by Thomas Arne.

They had bought a few yards of cotton fabric in red, white and blue, and they were spending the morning cutting out triangles for the bunting. It took a bit of concentration to get them the right size, even with the template, but as they busied themselves with this, Helen couldn't get the image of Harry in his silk dressing gown flailing at thin air out of her mind. She was desperate to know what it was all about, and waited for Mai to bring up the subject of Harry's odd behaviour in the garden.

Mai hadn't mentioned Harry at all though, which was strange as she lived for gossip and she could talk cheerfully about people and their little foibles all day, real and imagined, so it was doubly surprising that she was keeping quiet about her husband.

It was Nancy who helped her out in the end. 'What's it like kissing Harry now he's got the beginnings of a moustache?' she asked Mai.

'Nancy Hall! What a question!' Mai said indignantly. Then she sighed. 'It's a bit bristly, to be honest, and I can't get on with it. I like a man to be clean-shaven.'

Nancy laughed. 'Why don't you tell him?'

'I have. He told me not to interfere, because it's none of my business. Ooh!' she added in a burst of furious energy, 'He does make me mad!' Mai illustrated the strength of her feelings by cutting the point off a blue triangle, and she put her scissors down and went to the kitchen to put the kettle on.

Helen and Nancy exchanged wide-eyed glances of surprise at this evidence of matrimonial discontent, and listened to Mai clattering around with the crockery, expecting to hear a smash any minute.

When Mai came back with the rattling tea tray, she took the conversation up heatedly from where she left it. 'None of my business? If it's not my business, whose is it? I'll give him what for! I don't know what's possessed him! It's that moustache, it is!' She took a few deep breaths to compose herself, and in a normal tone she added, 'Help yourselves to sugar.'

Unfortunately for Helen, who was still desperately curious to find out about Harry's activities in the garden, Nancy swiftly brought the conversation round to neutral territory by asking Helen what she was going to wear to the tea party.

'My blue tea-dress,' Helen replied. 'How about you, Mai? Did you fit into your lace wedding gown?'

Mai was staring rather miserably into thin air. 'More or less,' she said. 'By which I mean it won't fully do up. Harry said I could wear a cape.'

'That's a good idea!'

'Not really. I haven't got a cape.' Mai replaced a hair grip more securely in her bun, and got up and went over to the music stand as though to remind herself what the

51

occasion was all about. She hummed the opening notes absently.

'Why don't you go and try the dress on now, and we'll see what we can do,' Helen said to cheer her up. 'Maybe we could add a panel to it or something, with hooks and eyes.' She started to gather up the coloured triangles.

'I'm not in the mood now. And we still need to hem these, don't we.'

Helen didn't see the point in hemming each piece all around. 'We just have to make a channel for the string. They only need to last a day, after all.'

Nancy was knee-deep in triangles too. She yawned, and studied her index finger. 'Look, I've got a blister from cutting. That's it for me. I think we've done enough for today.'

'Yes, I agree,' Helen said, seizing the opportunity to bring the subject back to Harry in the garden. 'And I've got some urgent pruning to do. Our garden is looking so overgrown.'

'Urgent pruning?' Mai asked, perplexed. 'What do you want to prune now for, Helen? Wait till autumn. Which trees need pruning, anyway?'

Helen waved her hand vaguely in the direction of the garden. 'Umm, I'm not sure. I thought Harry said it was a good time . . .'

'No,' Mai shook her head. 'You must have misunderstood. He wouldn't have told you that. Anyway, you want to let Tad do it. Give him something to do,' she said with some finality.

'Yes, thanks,' Helen said. She found herself at a conversational dead end, so unless she revealed that she and Tad had been spying on Harry from the bedroom, there was nothing for it but to drop the subject.

Nancy was folding up her fabric.

Mai was still all for hemming each piece all round, but Nancy sided with Helen, they only had to sew a channel at the top for the string.

Although it went against the grain for Mai not to do a job perfectly, she agreed that she could see the sense in it, because the bunting would have to stretch all the way down Little Green Street and there was plenty more sewing to do before the job would be finished. Her capitulation was a rare enough event for Helen and Nancy to exchange glances. As they said goodbye and walked down the path, carrying their bundles of fabric, Nancy raised her eyebrows. 'Pruning, Helen? Something's going on, isn't it?'

'Shh! Was it that obvious?' As they reached Helen's gate, she confided: 'Tad and I saw Harry acting oddly this morning. He was in his dressing gown thrashing the air with branches. Funny Mai hasn't mentioned it, don't you think?'

'Maybe she doesn't know.' Nancy looked at her for a moment, her forehead furrowed. 'It's something to do with Harry's moustache, mark my words. He's like a different man! Even Waffles has noticed it. One way or another, this Coronation Party's bringing out a different side to all of us.' She looked across at Emlyn's house and added with a conspiratorial smile, 'And maybe that's no bad thing!'

7

At the next meeting of the Coronation Party Committee on the twenty-fifth of April, both Emlyn and Harry had an air of suppressed excitement about them as they took their places around Tad's dining-room table.

Harry had taken to smoothing his whiskers with his index finger, but in any case, all eyes were on the moustache without him needing to draw attention to it. It had grown quite long and now dangled over his upper lip, but oddly there were a few bare patches where no hair had grown at all.

Emlyn regarded Harry with folded arms and shook his head regretfully. 'Now that it's past the bristle stage, you look very dubious,' he said.

'What do you mean, dubious?'

'Well, it's a bit mangy, isn't it? To be truthful, Harry, and it pains me to say this, you look like a ne'er-do-well.'

'Give it a chance.' Harry frowned. 'It's got a lot of growing to do yet.'

'I've got mixed feelings about it, too, to be honest,' Mai added, throwing her weight behind Emlyn.

'Mai!' Harry said sharply. 'Let it rest, woman!'

They all looked at him in astonishment.

'Steady on, my boy,' Tad said. 'She's just giving her opinion. You've always been keen on free speech.'

'No, I haven't,' Harry said.

Helen thought of Harry in the garden in his dressing gown sawing branches off and stabbing the air. She wondered if the moustache had wrought some kind of personality change in Harry, or whether it was a sign of an incipient nervous breakdown, and he would decide to grow a beard to match and hit the open road and come back years later and remember nothing about it.

Harry had obviously come to the conclusion that some kind of explanation was called for, because he said, 'If you must know, it's part of my costume for the party. And that's all I'm telling you.'

Tad said thoughtfully, 'You're not coming as Charlie Chaplin, are you, Harry?'

'No, of course not, why would I?'

'It's just that there aren't many costumes that require an obligatory moustache, that's all.'

'Well, rest assured, I'm not.'

'There we are then,' Tad said, anxious to keep the peace. 'I'm sure I speak for us all when I tell you we will look forward to the revelation. Now then, I think we should turn our minds to discussing the food.'

'We discussed it last time,' Emlyn said. 'Check your minutes. We're each bringing something for ourselves and some to share.'

'I don't need to check my minutes,' Tad said smoothly, 'I remember it perfectly well. What I mean is, we don't all want to bring spam sandwiches for instance, do we? It would be nice to have some variety. If everyone decides what they want to bring and we compare notes, we can make sure there's no overlap.'

'How about an ox roast?' Emlyn asked. 'The Ministry

of Food is granting permission for ox roasts, if it's a local Coronation tradition.'

'Emlyn, man, it will take days to roast an ox!'

'Is it a local tradition here?' Helen asked hopefully, because she liked the idea.

'Indeed not. Ox roasts!' Harry said scornfully. 'This isn't the Wild West, Emlyn. We need chocolate cake, that's what we need. I said that last time, too.'

'Be quiet, will you, about your chocolate cake!' Mai's top knot wobbled in exasperation. 'Tad's got it in his minutes.'

'"Chocolate cake",' Tad said in a soothing tone. 'Here. It's already written down. See?' He showed Harry the pad.

'All I'm saying is, you can't have too much chocolate cake at a Coronation Party.'

'Very true.'

'I'm doing cucumber sandwiches,' Helen said.

'I'll do egg,' Emlyn offered.

'Taken to keeping chickens, have you, Emlyn?' Harry asked him drily.

'No. Why?'

'You've got feathers on your jacket.'

Emlyn looked startled. 'It's quite windy out,' he said quickly. 'They must have blown on me.'

Nancy picked one off and handed it to him.

Tad raised his eyebrows.

Emlyn took the feather in his hand. It was long, pale and spidery. He put it carefully in his top pocket, which was the respectful way to behave in someone else's house, otherwise it would be littering, but he made it look a bit like a love token.

'Anyway,' Harry said, 'what about you, Tad? What are you going to wear for the Coronation Party?'

'My best suit,' Tad said modestly.

'Pathetic! Where's your ambition? Enter into the spirit of it, man! Get a bit of flamboyance in your life! You've got the personality for it!'

'For goodness' sake, don't encourage him,' Helen said with a smile.

Mai raised her hand. 'What about if it rains, Tad? What will we do then?'

Tad frowned. Rain hadn't featured at all in his vision of the party. It was all blue sky and sunshine, he had taken that for granted. 'We can bring umbrellas to keep the sandwiches dry.'

'I was thinking more of Rhiannon's harp, to be honest. It's Victorian, and it doesn't take well to damp. And with the choir coming, unless they're happy to sing *a cappella*, it would be a bit of a washout without it.'

Dismayed, Tad ran his fingers through the wild thicket of his hair and squeezed his eyes shut.

'How about this,' Emlyn said, coming to the rescue. 'If it rains, Rhiannon and the choir can perform from your front room with the windows and the door open, and we can join in from under our umbrellas.'

'Wonderful! All those in favour of the choir singing from Harry and Mai's house if it rains?' Tad asked. 'Right then.' He checked his notes to see what was next. 'Bunt-ing! Ladies?'

'All in hand,' Mai said. 'We're meeting for another sewing session on Monday evening.'

'Excellent. Any other business? No? Let's have a cup of tea.'

8

After the committee had disbanded, Tad was left feeling particularly restless about the subject of costumes. He was forced to admit that Emlyn was right for once. He *should* wear a costume, he *did* have the personality for it. It seemed unduly modest now to think of wearing a suit for such a splendid occasion as a day of royal pageantry. Emlyn was more perceptive than he'd ever given him credit for.

He saw his guests to the gate, and went to the kitchen to tell Helen he was off to stretch his legs for five minutes. Putting on his tweed cap, he headed towards town, crossed the bridge and walked down to the river to get his thoughts straight.

As he went past the mill, the river widened, surging and foaming around flattened grey rocks. The canopy of green trees on the opposite bank reached out over the water, trailing their branches into the current, and Tad climbed down the bank to the water's edge and jumped precariously from one rock to the next until he was right in the middle of the roaring Dee, king of his own small island. He watched the smoke from the steam train rise thick and white behind the trees as it pulled out of the station and he felt he was making a journey in his own life, too.

Tad was not a man given to envy, but he had felt the emotion strongly once in his life, and probably because it was so rare an event, the feeling had never quite left him.

It was on the occasion of the marriage of Prince Philip to Princess Elizabeth.

He had studied the splendid photographs in the news-papers over the following days for a long time. As a music teacher and poet, Tad wasn't ashamed to admit he was a romantic, and they looked to him like the model of a perfect couple. The princess was shy and radiant, and Prince Philip, in his naval officer's dress uniform, was the handsome hero by her side. Tad felt, from certain angles, he had a touch of Prince Philip about him, with his fine features and upright stance. There was a sensitivity, too, common to both men. He wanted very much to be Helen's hero, and to have her look at him in the same way Princess Elizabeth looked at Prince Philip. Helen's grief had made her distant, but recently, the days she was happy were beginning to outnumber the times she was sad, and the Coronation would be a culmination of the promise of a new era for them both.

The only major difference was the hair. Prince Philip's, from all the pictures he had seen of him, was very well-behaved: flat, with a side parting and a high shine. But it was a shine that could only be down to one thing – Brylcreem.

Keep your hair shipshape – Brylcreem your hair!

And, talking of ships, there was Prince Philip's naval uniform, in which he looked particularly splendid.

Tad had been ten years old when the Great War ended. When he was a youth, he had loudly cursed his bad luck at being too young to fight. But in the years that followed, on Armistice Day, when the names of the dead from the town were read out, he knew exactly where his name would have fitted if things had been different.

At the declaration of the Second World War he had been thirty-one, and registered for National Service. But he was a miner working down the pit, which was a reserved occupation, and by then his attitude towards war had changed. In the pitch-black heat, by the gleam of his lamp, he thanked God every day that he had never been called on to fight; never been caught wanting for courage, or a brave heart, never suffered trench foot, never had to kill, never dodged bullets or been plagued by night terrors and remorse.

But if he *had* joined up, if mining hadn't been a reserved occupation, he would have joined the navy.

Seeing Prince Philip on his wedding day, in his dress uniform with gold buttons and gold braid, the peak of his white cap glossy and shining, Tad had been struck by a yearning for what might have been.

And there was one detail that stood out in his mind: as a wedding gift from King George VI, His Royal Highness Prince Philip had been given the title of Earl of Merioneth, a place that was close to Tad's heart because it was where his mother was born.

'Earl of Merioneth,' he said aloud, raising his voice over the booming water just to savour the taste of the words in his mouth.

He couldn't fathom now why he had been content to settle for wearing his best suit for the party. It showed a terrible lack of imagination.

But now he was giving it free rein. There was an army surplus store on the outskirts of the town which he had never before had a reason to enter. He had a good reason now, but there was something else he needed to do first.

Energised with fresh enthusiasm, and with Prince Philip's short back and sides foremost in his mind, Tad leapt back across the rocks. He'd made up his mind. He was going to get a haircut.

The barber was John Williams, choir member, bass, a sincere man who greeted Tad warmly with a gleam in his eye because he liked a challenge.

Tad took off his cap and sat down in the leather chair.

'The usual trim?' John Williams swivelled him round like a fairground ride and considered Tad's vertical hair from all angles. 'I'll get my lawnmower,' he said.

On the shelf, out of the corner of his eye, Tad could see a row of red Brylcreem pots lined up. 'Now then, John, I've got a question to ask you. Do you remember the royal wedding?' he asked. 'From a professional point of view, I mean?'

'I remember the general gist of it. Why do you ask?'

'I'm thinking of Prince Philip. Remember his haircut?'

'I do indeed. Short back and sides, hair combed back.' John Williams's eyes met Tad's in the mirror with only the faintest trace of alarm. 'Is that what you want? Short back and sides?'

'And smoothed flat.'

'Smoothed flat?' John Williams rubbed Tad's coarse hair between his finger and thumb thoughtfully. 'I'll have to use the hairdryer on it, to get it straight. And Brylcreem, to keep it flat and give it a shine.'

Tad took one last look at his old self with his wild, schoolteacher's hair. From now on the face in the mirror would be that of a military man.

John Williams led Tad to the wash basin, shampooed him and then took him back to the chair and draped him in towels. And he began to snip.

Forty minutes later, John Williams was done.

It was strange what a difference a haircut made to a man, Tad thought, leaving the barber's with a red jar of Brylcreem in his pocket.

He felt a lot lighter for a start, although his hair must have weighed practically nothing at all.

When John Williams handed him the mirror, Tad had seen a stranger looking back, and now as he glanced in the chemist's window he saw that same stranger walking along the road in step with him.

For the first time, he wondered what Helen would think about his transformation. If she didn't like it—

It will grow, he consoled himself.

He walked through the town and turned right towards Corwen.

The army surplus store was set back off the road. It looked deserted. A battered mannequin stood guard outside it in battledress and a camouflage net, and as Tad entered he could smell canvas and boot leather and, he fancied, sweat and dust.

'Can I help you?'

Tad turned to see Dennis Hill behind the counter, younger than himself, with piercing blue eyes and a regimental tattoo on his bicep.

Tad explained his mission, to look like Prince Philip for the Coronation Party, bringing in more detail than was truly necessary.

'You're wanting an officer's uniform,' Dennis said, as if it was the kind of thing he was asked all the time. 'Follow me.'

The navy uniforms were in the back of the shop, on rails, in no discernible order that Tad could see.

Dennis rattled the hangers and found what he wanted. 'Now this here is a lieutenant commander's tunic, which is the closest I've got. It's got a little wear to it, but it's in generally fair condition. See? It says it on the label, "Fair condition". Have a look.'

The tunic was heavy, solid. The brass buttons gleamed like gold, and the red and gold braid seemed particularly royal, somehow. He took it off the hanger and Tad tried it on.

As he stood in the dim shop, a feeling of unreality came over him, as if he'd stepped into another life and become someone else entirely.

'I've got a ceremonial sword I can sell you, if you're interested too,' Dennis said diffidently, as if it made no difference to him either way.

Tad looked up from fastening the buttons, and nodded. 'It won't harm for me to take a look at it,' he said reasonably.

Dennis opened a cupboard behind the counter, moved a few things around while cursing to himself, and produced the sword, embellished with a gold tassel. He handed it to Tad.

'Nice, isn't it? So you've got your hilt, made of gold-plated brass. You've got the lion pommel here, and the rawhide scabbard,' he said. 'It's a bit scuffed but you can buff that out with dubbin and elbow grease. Gold-plated mounts.' He shrugged. 'That's it, really.'

Tad held it in his left hand, as Prince Philip had done on his wedding day, and looked at himself in the mirror.

He was lost for words. He'd never realised that inside the old him there existed a different person altogether, this military man.

And also, he observed, there was a third person involved: Narcissus.

It was unexpected because he'd never been a vain man; never had any cause to be. But the feeling he had now reminded him a little of being in love. He wanted to keep looking at his new self. He was finding it difficult to tear himself away.

'I'll take them,' he said hoarsely.

'Righty-ho.'

Tad handed him the sword, and reluctantly took the jacket off.

'Are you all right for trousers?'

Tad had always felt that if a thing was worth doing, it was worth doing well, and he didn't see any reason to deviate from this belief right now, although he felt light-headed from what he was about to spend.

And yet, nothing in the world would have persuaded him to leave the army surplus store without his costume even if it put him into debt for the rest of his life and he had to sell the house.

Dennis took the sword and tunic to the counter, and picked out a couple of pairs of trousers for Tad to hold against his waist for size.

And when he'd decided, Dennis wrapped up all the purchases in brown paper and string, including the sword, and Tad paid.

He wasn't as shocked by the price as he'd expected, and when he left the dimness of the shop, he was surprised to find it was still daylight, and that life outside was going on very much as it had before he'd gone in.

He'd done more shopping in one day than he'd done since the war ended.

His packages were heavy and he was trying to keep the sword balanced on top when he saw Harry coming out of the Post Office.

'Harry! Give me a hand would you for a minute?' he said.

'Me?' Harry looked at him warily. And then his face showed absolute astonishment. 'Tad?'

'Watch it! It's going to drop!'

Harry grabbed the sword without looking at it. 'What happened to your hair?'

Tad answered the question with a question. 'Who do I remind you of?'

'No one. I would swear on the Bible I've never seen you before in my life,' Harry said seriously.

Tad was both thrilled and anxious by this admission. 'It's for the party,' he said.

'Ahhh!' Harry nodded, understanding. 'I see. Well, good for you. I'm of the same mind, Tad. You just wait! I've got a surprise in store for you all for the Coronation.' He tapped the side of his nose.

'So have I,' Tad replied.

'I feel we owe it to the Queen to make an effort. You can't go wrong if you make an effort, that's my feeling.'

'It's my feeling, too,' Tad said. They looked at each other in a bond of mutual understanding and brother-hood, and headed home.

9

Helen was writing out a shopping list when Tad came in through the door, and she said hello without looking up. He went upstairs to hang his purchases in the wardrobe, but the thrill of them was too much. He tried the trousers on, put the tunic back on, unwrapped the sword and admired the result purely objectively, as if he were a stranger.

And then he had the idea of surprising his wife. Smiling to himself, he went back downstairs into the kitchen, and stood by the table where she couldn't avoid seeing him.

But when Helen looked up he didn't quite get the reaction he had hoped for. She screamed such a shrill and violent scream that he was alarmed at what the neighbours would think. Dropping the sword he rushed to her, covering her mouth with his hand, only to be bitten by her.

'Dammit, woman!' he shouted, shaking the pain out of his hand.

'Tad?'

'Of course it's me,' he said crossly. 'Who did you think it was?'

'What's got into you, frightening me like that?' she said indignantly, now that the adrenaline was subsiding.

'I didn't mean to frighten you,' he said, 'I wanted to surprise you. It's my costume for the party.'

'Ohhh.' Her face cleared. Once she was calm again, she looked at him with growing interest. 'You look absolutely and entirely different,' she said in her beautiful English accent. 'You look like Prince Philip.' Her eyes were wide and shining. 'You're going to go as Prince Philip, aren't you!'

'That's correct,' he confirmed shyly, and he had never loved her more.

'Your hair!' she exclaimed, as if she'd only just noticed and was taking him in, bit by bit. 'My word, Tad.' She got up from the table and put her arms around his waist.

Tad nuzzled her blissfully and she raised her pale face to his, offering herself to his kiss.

The back door opened and they sprang apart guiltily.

'Mum!' Lauren said in alarm. 'What are you doing?'

'It's me!' Tad said quickly. 'It's my costume for the tea party.'

Lauren stared at him. 'How did you get your hair flat like that?'

'I called on John the barber,' Tad said.

'It looks completely straight,' she marvelled. 'Who are you being?'

'Prince Philip, Earl of Merioneth,' he told her.

'Oh.' She frowned. 'But Tad, Nancy's going as the Queen.'

'So is Mai,' Helen told her.

'Yes, but if Tad is Prince Philip, you should be the one to go as the Queen, shouldn't you?'

Helen looked at Tad, and then back at her daughter. 'It's true,' she said. 'I decided I'd wear the blue dress. But I can see now that it's not very patriotic to take that attitude. I mean, if the Queen took that attitude she would probably just put the crown on her own head and go back to feeding the corgis and—' she waved her hand vaguely

'—planning what to say to heads of state and that type of thing. And if we've already got two Queens coming to the tea party, then we might as well have three.'

It was a very simple argument, nicely put in Tad's opinion, and the spontaneity of her reaction to his outfit thrilled him to his core.

Lauren smiled dreamily and rested her chin on her hand. 'What will you wear as the Queen?'

'I think I'll wear my wedding dress,' Helen said, 'same as Mai. It's the most regal gown I've ever owned. I will ask my mother to send it. And of course I shall wear my pearls.'

She went to get her black leather writing case there and then, so as to catch the next post, and sat down to write a letter to her mother, asking her to send the wedding dress as soon as possible, and explaining that she was going to wear it at their Coronation Party on the second of June, which she was attending as the Queen.

She signed it, *Your loving Helen*, sealed the envelope, and put it in her basket so that she could visit the Post Office when she did her shopping this afternoon.

Little did she know that the letter, with its innocuous request, would change the course of events for all of them.

10

At the third meeting of the Coronation Party Committee, Emlyn came through to Tad's dining room, now referred to by all as 'The Boardroom', and did a double-take as he saw a strange man sitting in Tad's place, Tad's notebook and pen in front of him on the table. He stared at Tad in amazement. 'What's happened to your hair?'

'It's for the party,' the neighbours chorused.

'Oh.' Emlyn understood immediately and tapped the side of his nose. 'Say no more.' Still, he marvelled at the change in Tad. The celebration was bringing out a side of them all that they had never encountered before. It was like a rebirth.

Emlyn, Harry and Tad had known each other all their lives and didn't expect surprises, but these secrets that the three men were keeping from each other added a thrill to everyday life. Part of the sweetness was in knowing and respecting that they had their secrets, and the sense of anticipation at the butterfly-like revelation when the great day came was all the more exciting for it.

Having said that, Emlyn, whose natural black cowlick quiff was nurtured with care, couldn't begin to fathom why Tad had decided to flatten his hair. Apart from being distinctive, he hadn't realised until now that it had added a good three inches to Tad's height. Now he looked smaller, and younger, like a choirboy. Like Harry's moustache, it was going to take some getting used to.

But, Emlyn reflected, his own new secret alter ego took some getting used to, too.

His mother, Old Mrs Hughes, had produced two separate sets of ostrich feathers. One was black and attached to a velvet tam-o'-shanter that had once belonged to her aunt, and the other was slightly off-white, being part of the feather duster that she used for cobwebs.

In his mind's eye, Emlyn remembered that the Pearly King he had seen at the King's funeral had had white feathers in his cap. He'd imagined white, and wondered if the black feathers were a little funereal.

'Try it on, Em, before you judge,' his mother had encouraged him.

He shouldn't have been surprised that the hat fitted him, because the one thing he remembered about Auntie Ginny, its previous owner, was that she'd had a lot of hair.

'Now,' his mother said, handing him her silver mirror, 'imagine it covered with white pearl buttons. It will give it a lift, see?'

He tried sweeping the cap off his head respectfully. It had a good weight to it. It wasn't surprising, he thought, that ostriches couldn't fly.

And he didn't want to be an exact imitation of the Pearly King. It was more a representation, really.

His mother had him try on his funeral suit, now transformed by the mother-of-pearl buttons into a garment of lively glamour, to see if it went with the hat. Not much imagination was needed to conclude that it did.

'I hope nobody dies between now and June the second,' Old Mrs Hughes said, clasping her hands together, 'after all this effort.'

'It's champion,' he said appreciatively. 'You've worked miracles.'

'Get away with you!' she said happily.

Emlyn was smiling as he relived the moment. It was a long time since he'd asked his mother for anything. These days, he did things for her.

But he realised now that there was nothing quite so satisfying to his mother as being needed, and he needed her now, because he would never have painstakingly sewn all those buttons on his jacket himself to create the look that he hankered after. He would have put that dream on the shelf and let it fade. Giving her all that work to do had made her very happy.

'Emlyn?' Tad asked sharply. 'Are you with us?'

Emlyn looked at Tad's newly innocent choirboy face. 'I was just marvelling at the difference in you,' he said, which was only one word away from his true thoughts and didn't count as a lie.

'We're going to discuss the menu.' The meeting was to be devoted entirely to the question of food, a subject dear to all their hearts ever since the beginning of rationing in 1940, but especially Harry's. For the first time since the war, fresh eggs were back on the menu instead of powdered, cream was legal to sell again, and sweets and chocolate were no longer subject to restrictions.

'Chocolate cake,' Harry said gleefully. 'Now that chocolate's not rationed, we can have plenty of it.'

'It's all very well for you to keep asking for chocolate

cake,' Mai pointed out to him, 'but we're all going to enjoy it, and I think in view of that, we will probably need three or four.'

'That enough for you, Harry?' Nancy asked him, tongue-in-cheek.

Harry didn't argue.

'I can make a chocolate cake with butter icing, the one you don't have to cook,' Helen said.

Nancy offered to make a chocolate gateau. 'Mine has to be cooked for an hour at a low temperature but if you make one too, Mai, we could share the oven.'

'That's a good idea.' Mai opened her shopping bag. '*People's Friend* magazine has a recipe for Coronation Chicken, which the Queen is apparently having at her banquet.' She took the article out of her basket to show them, via the illustration, what the finished dish would look like. They passed it round, until it came back to Mai again.

'What's in it?' Emlyn asked, to save the bother of reading.

Mai read out the list of ingredients. 'Chicken, curry paste, mayonnaise, cream, tinned apricots, fruit syrup, and blanched, flaked almonds.'

'All mixed up in the same dish?' Harry asked in alarm.

'It sounds like two dishes to me, Mai,' Tad declared. 'Apricots, cream and almonds for pudding, and for the main, chicken with curry paste and mayonnaise.'

'That does seem a very peculiar dish, if it combines chicken and apricots,' Emlyn said doubtfully. 'Maybe it's been printed wrong.'

'No, it hasn't. Listen to the method. Cook the chicken, cut it into cubes, drain the apricots, mix the mayonnaise with the curry paste, cream and apricot syrup from the tin, add the apricots, sliced, and sprinkle on the nuts like jewels in the crown. That's Coronation Chicken.'

'It sounds easy enough,' Helen said. 'You men don't have to have it, but if it's good enough for the Queen to have on her Coronation Day, I think we should have it too.' She said it forcefully, as if she was defending the Queen's sense of taste.

Mai, who had gone to the trouble of bringing in the magazine, agreed wholeheartedly, and Nancy said that it sounded absolutely delicious and she had a good mind to make it on a regular basis once the weather got warmer.

Tad said he thought jam tarts might be nice on the day as the Queen was the Queen of Tarts.

'You're thinking of the Queen of Hearts, on a playing card,' Harry said. 'There's no such thing as the Queen of Tarts.'

Tad opened his mouth to argue, but then thought better of it.

'Jam tarts are always nice,' Helen said, feeling generous again now that Mai was getting her own way about the Coronation Chicken.

Tad was writing all these things down and when he'd finished he looked at the list with satisfaction. 'There will most definitely be enough food to make it a celebration. In fact, the party is beginning to take on the generous qualities of a banquet.'

'We're going to carry on with the bunting today,' Helen said, 'once we've bought more twine. Won't the street look festive!'

II

The ruins of Crow Castle sat on a green hill high above the small town, crumbling and atmospheric and plagued by the evil spirit of Gogmagog, who, according to legend, hid his treasure there.

It was a steep climb, and there was nothing to do once you got there except admire the view of the green, humped slopes of Barber's Hill, Bryniau-bach and Pen-y-Coed that curled around the busy town like sleeping dragons. The Eglwyseg Cliffs and Offa's Dyke stretched into the fading blue wild distance and courting couples used the castle walls as a convenient bed-head to lean back on.

It was a good place to write poetry in peace, too, up in the clean air with only the mild bickering of sheep to disturb them, and Lauren, Garth, Rhiannon and Flora struggled and stumbled, school bags bouncing on their backs, as they panted their way over the springy grass and then scrambled over the shale near the top, their hearts thumping with effort and the joy of being away from the insanity of their elders.

'I didn't even recognise your Tad without his hair,' Garth said to Lauren, catching his breath while they waited for Rhiannon and Flora who had trailed behind. 'I walked straight past him in the street! He looks as shiny as a Mormon.'

'Putting a brush through his hair used to be like getting the knots out of barbed wire, but now he can do it with a comb in two seconds flat.' For a moment, Lauren looked at Garth, slightly troubled. 'But he doesn't look like Tad. I don't like things to change,' she admitted. 'It makes me happy when everything stays the same.'

Garth nodded. 'There's too much excitement in the air at the moment, that's what my mother says. She's very sensitive to vibrations. That's why she doesn't go out. She can tell when there's a storm coming.'

Lauren looked up at the blue sky. A little group of flat-bottomed white clouds sat together, very still, putting bits of the town far below into shadow. 'But not today, though,' she said.

'No, not today.'

Below them, Rhiannon and Flora were still climbing and occasionally clinging to each other, giggling and sliding as they reached the shale.

Garth was smiling to himself, watching them. His hair blazed red in the sunlight.

'I didn't know you worried about things like that, too,' Lauren said.

His smile turned crooked. 'Didn't you? I worry about everything,' he said ruefully. 'I worry about my mother. I worry about another world war. I worry about having to fight, and being killed, what my mother would do without me.'

Lauren nodded. Garth's mother had lost her mind to grief when Garth's father John had drowned on home leave towards the end of the war, whilst fishing. Before that, she had been a perfectly normal person, with a normal person's trust in the goodness of life. When her husband didn't come home for tea, she sent Garth to look for him, and when they found his fishing rod and stool it seemed to them both that he must have been called on some unknown but urgent errand.

But a few days later, John Pugh had floated to the surface, swallowed up by the pond and then regurgitated, and that was the day Mrs Pugh's trust in life lay in ruins around her.

'Let's have a walk around while we wait for the others, and see if there's anyone else up here,' Garth said, and he shook himself like a dog after a swim.

They always looked out for dropped money too when they came up here, not the hidden treasure of Gogmagog, but change that had fallen out of boys' trouser pockets at night as they lay down with their girls to look at the stars.

By the time they'd done the circuit of the ruins, and found no money and nobody but a sheep chewing in a hollow, Flora and Rhiannon had reached the top. Hearing their voices, Lauren and Garth decided to hide and give them a fright.

But Flora and Rhiannon guessed what they were going to do and crept around the other side, and in the end they all scared each other to death because the anticipation had put them on edge.

'So are we all going to write a Coronation poem together?' Flora asked hopefully.

Lauren chewed her lip at this dilemma. She was good at poetry, a talent she'd inherited from her father. Lauren could imagine the pride on his joyful face if she brought home the bard's crown.

It wasn't the same for Flora. Her mother wouldn't care one way or the other. Nancy thought it was more important to be happy than to be clever.

'Don't know. How would we share the crown, anyway?'

'We could keep it for a month each,' Flora suggested.

Flora hadn't been brought up on poetry like the others had. Poetry was the rhythm that was always in their words, and secretly Lauren didn't think that Flora had the slightest chance of winning, but she liked Flora and felt mean for thinking it. 'Tell you what, we could – I could help you, if you like,' she said.

Flora smiled. 'Yeah? I know what I want to say. It just won't sound like poetry. Could you make it sound like poetry for me?'

'Yes.' Lauren was getting her exercise book out of her school bag, because she had a few ideas, too. 'You write down everything that you want to say, and we'll make a poem of it afterwards. Let's give ourselves an hour and spread out and meet back here.'

It was a wonderful place to write about majesty, being on the very top of the hill, sitting on a castle wall. It gave Lauren a feeling of superiority to look down on the quiet world. Far below, a shiny black car moved as lethargically as a beetle along a grey road, and along the canal a brightly coloured narrowboat was being pulled along slowly by a plodding, silent-hoofed horse.

This, she thought, must be how the Queen felt looking down on her subjects. Strangely enough, from this high up, subjects looked more like objects. She scratched her head with her pencil and wondered if she was experiencing a poetic revelation or simply a misuse of language.

Mr Evans, their English teacher, deplored the misuse of language. She wondered if he would be judging the poems, or the headmaster. They should try to find out, because it would make a difference.

She wrote down the title: 'The Coronation'.

How would the Queen feel on Coronation Day? she wondered. Scared, or powerful?

The Queen was powerful, she was certain of that. She could have people put to death for treason with a snap of the fingers, if she wanted. They did that a lot in the olden days. Henry VIII had his wives killed when he went off them, instead of just breaking up with them like any normal person.

Lauren wondered what constituted treason. What if the Queen tripped up, and her crown rolled off, and people laughed behind their hands? Just imagine, Lauren thought, if she had them all put to death for that. While it was definitely imaginative, it was not exactly praise poetry, although praise poetry did often include warriors and rivers flowing red with blood and that kind of thing.

Surely a person was only powerful if they used their power. Did powerful people get scared of losing it? The Queen would be Queen until she died and then her little boy, Prince Charles, would take over, so she had nothing to worry about really.

Lauren lay back on the grass thinking profoundly and staring at the sky. She could feel the world turning. Birds flew over, fluttering playfully, and she closed her eyes. The warmth of the sun shone red through her eyelids.

She woke to find a shadow had fallen over her, and Rhiannon nudging her with her foot.

'Have you finished?' she asked.

Lauren's mouth was dry. She sat up and her exercise book fell off her lap. 'No, not yet. I'm still thinking.'

'Flora's finished hers all by herself in the end.'

'Really?' Lauren shielded her eyes with one hand and tried to make out Rhiannon's expression. 'Is it any good?'

'Well . . . It sounds like Flora, if you know what I mean.'

'How did you get on?'

'I thought I'd write it about the first verse of "God Save the Queen" and I got stuck at "send her victorious, happy and glorious". I don't understand it. Send her where?'

Lauren found that she couldn't remember the words so she had to go over it in her head. ' "Long to reign over us".'

'Send her long to reign over us?'

'It means send her to reign over us for a long time.'

'But she's already here. She doesn't have to be sent any-where. When you look at it line by line, I don't think it's very good as poetry,' Rhiannon said. 'But when you sing it, you don't think of the words, luckily.'

Lauren got up and brushed the grass from her skirt. They walked back to the meeting point and sat down next to Flora and Garth.

'I've finished mine,' Flora said happily. 'Why don't we all read them to each other?'

'Mine's not finished yet,' Garth said.

'I haven't even started.'

'I started but I've made it too complicated,' Rhiannon confessed. 'I'm nervous, that's what it is, about playing the national anthem at the Coronation Party. I wish I could just enjoy myself.'

'Why don't you tell Tad you don't want to do it?' Lauren asked her.

'The choir would have to sing by themselves, unaccompanied.'

'So what? We could join in. We probably will, anyway.'

'I thought you liked doing that kind of thing, playing the harp and things,' Garth said, and he swivelled round so that he could see Rhiannon better. But her long wavy brown hair was blowing in her face, and he moved it away delicately, letting it fall over her shoulder, and looked at her curiously. His face flushed suddenly. 'What?' he asked, realising they were watching him. 'Well, I did!'

'It makes my father happy,' she said. 'That's why I do it.'

Garth nodded. 'If I still had a dad, I'd want to make him happy too,' he said.

Flora sighed. She was staring silently into space, her eyes narrowed, wisps of her fair hair flying in the breeze.

'Read us your poem, Flora,' Lauren said.

Flora stood up and opened her exercise book, looking proud and self-conscious at the same time:

> 'The Queen, long dress and sash, the proud
>   crown on her head,
> knowing she's Queen because her father is dead.
> Having a feast fit for royalty,
> with lords and ladies toasting to loyalty.
> At the end of the day she sits on her bed.
> Long live the Queen. The King is dead.

'That's it,' she finished.
'It's good,' Lauren said.

'Yes, it's really good,' Garth agreed.

'See? You've written a poem!' Rhiannon said. 'Honestly, it's better than the national anthem if you ask me, and I'm not making that up.'

Flora shrugged and sat down again, hugging her knees.

'Shall we carry on writing, as we haven't finished yet?' Garth said, resting back on his elbows and looking at the sky. 'The trouble is, I'm not bored enough to write at the moment. I have to be really bored before I can think. There's too much to look at up here. If I was at home, trying to keep quiet because my mother was in the armchair having forty winks, my imagination would be running riot all over the place.'

'Why doesn't she go to bed for her forty winks?'

'She worries about dying in bed in the daytime. What people would think.'

It seemed to Lauren that she had learned more about Garth today than in the last fourteen years. Everyone seemed to have accepted that Garth's mother was a bit of a recluse since, *you know*.

But Lauren knew what it felt like to worry about what people thought. Like when she'd been told off and been sent to her room and nobody had come to look for her to see if she was ready to apologise. In those circumstances, it was hard to know when to put her pride away and come out again and apologise of her own accord. Now! Now! But instead, she would just lie there feeling miserable and alone, waiting for the right time and worrying it would never come.

'We should get your mother to come to the Coronation Party,' she said. 'Just to see if she likes it.'

'She won't.'

'But we could try.'

'How?'

'We could ask her to come for five minutes, for a piece of chocolate cake,' Flora said.

Rhiannon nodded. 'My dad can't wait for the chocolate cake, it's all he talks about.'

Garth plucked a piece of grass and chewed the root thoughtfully. 'I might be able to get her to come for five minutes,' he said at last.

'We could put her at the end of the table, nearest to your house, so she won't have far to walk if she's not enjoying it. We could reserve a seat specially for her, with a reserved sign.'

The three of them looked at Garth with enthusiasm.

The blade of grass waggled in his mouth like a cigarette as he sat with his blue eyes narrowed, looking out at the whole wide world from the top of the hill, considering the plan.

'Okay. There's no harm in trying,' he said.

12

Helen had been looking out for the postman because she was waiting for the wedding dress to arrive from her mother's.

Instead, he delivered a letter one morning at the beginning of May and Helen experienced a moment's foreboding when she recognised her mother's sloping handwriting. She propped the unopened envelope up against the blue china teapot and looked at it thoughtfully while she sipped her tea. Something had happened to the dress. (Moth? Theft? Lost in the postal system?) It was disappointing, but no matter, she told herself, she would think of something else to wear to live up to Tad's new persona.

She smiled. It was a strange feeling, sharing a bed with a man who looked so different from her husband. Their relationship had suddenly taken on the quality of the start of a love affair, all the excitement without the guilt, and with this new rush of love she'd wanted to wear the wedding dress really quite desperately.

Taking a deep breath, she slit the envelope open with her butter knife and took out the letter. It read:

Dear Helen,

I have not asked you for much, and I was surprised to receive your letter asking me to send your wedding gown so that you may wear it at a street party in honour of the Coronation.

Naturally I assumed that you, Tad and Lauren would be
coming here for that momentous weekend to watch it in person
rather than trying to emulate an occasion of great historical
significance in your street, two hundred miles away from where the
event itself is taking place.

I haven't seen you since my birthday when you visited briefly for
two nights, and even then you came alone as if coming as a family
would involve too much effort for your recently widowed mother.

You must recognise how difficult it is for me, being a widow,
and I have tried not to burden you in any way with the depth of
my loneliness, being aware that you have your own life and have
chosen to live it about as far away from me as you can get.

I have prepared the bedrooms for you to stay and in view of
this, I will not be sending your wedding gown as you shan't be
needing it. I would appreciate it if you could let me know the date
and time of your arrival. I don't feel it is too much to ask for you
to spend a little of your time in the place you were once happy to
call home.

Love,

Mother

Helen's heart clattered anxiously in her chest. She had
the sudden sensation of being rushed along, tumbled in a
wave of her mother's emotions.

One line spoke to her louder than the others and took
her breath away: '*Naturally I assumed . . .*'

She'd always believed her father had been the driving
force behind their enjoyment of royal events. Helen had
thought that with his death, that particular part of their
lives, the cheering and the applause, the proud patriotism,
the excitement of being in a large crowd as subjects of the

realm, would be over, finished, consigned to the past. But she'd been wrong. She carried on reading: '. . . *that you, Tad and Lauren . . .*' It moved her to tears that her mother had imagined the four of them celebrating the Coronation together.

Since she'd first taken Tad home at the beginning of their courtship, they hadn't become one big family but had remained two small ones: Helen, Albert, Dorothea, and Helen, Tad and Lauren. She'd thought it was the way her parents preferred it. They were refined, polite, and Tad was – well, he was Tad: loud, jovial and opinionated. She loved them in entirely separate ways, defending Tad from her mother's coolness and her parents from Tad's boisterous tendencies. But what if she'd been wrong all this time?

Helen folded the letter up quite deliberately and put it back in the envelope, blushing shamefully with guilt.

Needing to talk to someone, she hurried across the road to Nancy's. She tapped on the door and went straight in.

Nancy was sitting in the kitchen wearing a hair-net to keep her blonde curls in place, and a slinky pink house-coat. She was looking through a magazine, smoking contentedly and tapping her ash into a saucer.

'Oh, hello,' she said with a smile, closing her magazine. She looked at Helen. 'What's wrong with you on this bright and sunny day? You look as if you've lost a pound and found a penny.'

'I've just received a letter from my mother, that's what.' Helen put the letter down on the table. 'Here.'

'Do me a favour and put the kettle on, then,' Nancy said. She opened the letter and took her time reading it.

When she finished she smoothed it out on the table. 'Well, doesn't she sound a sweetie!'

'What am I going to do?'

'Find something else to wear, of course. You don't have to wear a wedding gown, do you? The Queen won't be wearing a wedding gown because it's not a wedding,' she said logically. 'And neither am I. You can embellish something you've got with lace or a bit of ribbon and look just as good as royalty.'

'I don't mean about my costume. I mean what am I going to do about my mother? She's expecting us to go, isn't she?'

Nancy took her hair-net off and shook out her blonde curls. 'I honestly don't see how you can go. Tad has organised the party and if your mother had wanted you all to go and stay, she should have mentioned it before now. You're not a mind-reader! Tell her you'll all go and see her after the Coronation. It will be the school holidays then, and you could stay for a week if you wanted to.' The kettle whistled. She jerked her head at it and smiled. 'Be a love and make us a brew, will you, while you're up?'

Helen took the kettle off the heat, feeling close to tears. If only it was as easy as that. She rinsed a cup for herself, made the pot of tea and came to sit down opposite Nancy, resting her cheek in her hand.

'I suppose you're right. I feel awful about it, though.'

'I don't blame you for not going,' Nancy said cheerfully. 'She sounds a complete tartar.'

'She is, rather. But . . .' Helen's voice softened, 'she's my mother.' She sighed. 'I don't know what Tad's going to say about it all.'

'Don't tell him,' Nancy said, pouring the tea. 'What's the point? You'll just get him worked up for nothing. It's only a month away and if it's a straightforward choice between your mother and Tad, it's obvious who you're going to choose. You can say you changed your mind about the dress.'

'Yes, I could do that, I suppose.'

'Go as something else. And then – forget about it.'

'You make it seem easy,' Helen said. 'The truth is, I've neglected her.'

'She'll live. People like that always live the longest, have you noticed that? Whereas the sweetest people in the world, who you'd happily be friends with for ever, die young with a smile on their face, and we're just left with the sour ones.' She pulled a face and crossed her eyes.

Helen forced a smile. 'She's not that bad. I suppose I could go as Britannia. Fashion a sheet into a robe and make a shield and trident, and maybe some kind of helmet. It's about as patriotic as one can get. You're right about the wedding dress, it's no loss, really. And I'd be up against Mai in hers, and she'll get a few digs in because she thought of it first. Better to wear something completely different.' But the gloss had gone off the plans now, at least a little.

Before she could voice her thoughts any further, Nancy looked at her wristwatch.

'Look at the time! I'd better get dressed,' she said, finishing her tea quickly. 'I've got things to do.'

'So have I.' Helen put the letter back in the envelope and finished her tea. 'Thanks for the advice. See you later.'

*

Back home, Helen propped the letter behind the clock on the mantelpiece in the front room, a room they hardly used. She picked up her sewing box and went upstairs to the blanket box, took out a white sheet and draped it around herself. It just needed stitching around the shoulders, and a belt to cinch in the waist. She would make a shield out of cardboard, and paint a Union Jack on it. And as for the trident, she was sure that Tad had a pitchfork in the shed with three prongs. Which just left the helmet. A cereal box and tinfoil might do the trick, she thought, with a plume of red crêpe paper and a bit of creative imagination.

As she went down to the garden shed to look for the pitchfork, she caught sight of Harry coming out of his workshop, blowing dust from what looked like a small doorknob.

He looked up when he saw her, and put the piece of wood in his pocket. 'Good morning!' he called out. 'Another fine day, isn't it!'

'Yes, indeed.' She hadn't seen him to speak to for a couple of days, and she was surprised at how bushy his moustache had become. It was as thick and brown as a yard brush, bristling in the sunshine.

Harry patted it with his index finger and looked at her curiously. 'Doing a bit of gardening?' he asked, glancing at the fork.

'It's for my costume.'

'Ah.'

'And you've been doing woodwork?'

Harry looked startled. 'How did you know that?'

'You've got sawdust in your hair.'

'Oh. Yes.' He hesitated before adding shyly, 'I'm working on my costume, too.'

A little thrill of excitement passed between them over the hedge.

Helen went back to the house, and gave up trying to work out what kind of costume involved woodwork.

She glanced at the time. Tad would be home soon from his day's fishing in the Dee and Lauren would be in for tea. She propped the pitchfork outside the back door and put the letter from her mother to the back of her mind as she peeled potatoes, scraped carrots, sliced leeks and simmered the mutton in a large saucepan, until Tad came home.

'What's this fork doing outside the door?' Tad asked as he took off his wellingtons.

'Oh, that! It's for my costume. I'm going as Britannia and that's my trident.'

'What about your wedding dress?'

Helen skimmed the brown scum off the top of the simmering pan. 'I've changed my mind,' she said as she tilted her cheek to be kissed.

'But why?' Tad was disturbed by the news. 'Don't you think it will look a bit odd, me going as Prince Philip and Mai going as the Queen?'

'It doesn't mean anything, Tad, it's just a party for fun, that's all.'

'Only I liked the idea of the two of us together going as—' He hesitated, and collected himself. 'As you wish, of course. You will make a fine Britannia.' He raised his eyebrows suggestively. 'She had a bare breast as I remember from my textbooks.'

'Get away, Tad Jones!'

'It caused quite a stir in our history lesson.'

'She's not half naked on a ha'penny, I would have noticed.'

'Are you sure?'

'Certainly!'

'Are you *really* sure?' He caught her by the waist and just then, Lauren came in and Helen turned around and stirred the stew, flushed with laughter.

Lauren dropped her bag on a chair and looked at them doubtfully. 'What are you two laughing about?'

'Your mother is going to dress up as Britannia for the tea party.'

'Oh?' Lauren waited for him to say more. When he didn't, she said, 'Guess what, Garth is going to try to get his mother to come.'

This was news indeed. 'Is he now?'

'And we promised that she could sit at the end of the table nearest her house so that she can dash off if it gets too much for her.'

Tad nodded. Barbara Pugh's grief had been over-whelming and enduring. They would never know what had caused John Ivor to go in the water once he'd put his rod away. Shell shock, some said. In the days following his death, Tad had walked to the pool and found himself star-ing at the shining water in the still of the evening, overcome by the beauty and calm and wanting to not just be an observer but to overwhelmingly belong to it, to be absorbed in it, to walk into the pond's cold embrace. Get-ting his shoes wet had brought him to his senses. Tad had avoided the pool ever since, out of respect and a sense of superstition that he would never admit to.

'Good,' he said. 'Good.' He'd had qualms about giving up on Barbara for these past years but she had said she wanted to be left alone, and they had respected the request. Maybe, he thought now, they ought to have persevered with her. That would have been the kind thing to do. 'He's a nice boy, Garth.'

Lauren went to wash her hands and came to sit by the table.

Helen served the Welsh mutton in bowls and Tad said grace, and they ate in silence until they were full and slightly drowsy. Every so often, Tad would catch his wife's eye and their gaze would hold for a moment, as it had when they were courting.

Tad had never really felt he deserved Helen in his life. When he'd been standing on that soapbox by the privet hedge before the war, preaching about Moral Rearmament, she'd stayed to listen, or to watch. As soon as he saw her, he found himself preaching to her alone about the Four Absolutes: absolute honesty, absolute purity, absolute unselfishness, absolute love.

In reality he really had been preaching to her alone, because apart from a group of small boys who had jeered every speaker in turn with a strict sense of fair play, there was no one else there on that windy day but pigeons.

In the intervening years he had stopped being active in the movement but he still tried to live his life by the Four Absolutes, which seemed to be an important signpost to guide him.

Later that night, before bed, as was his habit, Tad went around the house winding up the clocks. When he came to the clock in the front room, he noticed a letter in a blue envelope propped up behind it on the mantelpiece, and picked it up.

He recognised his mother-in-law's handwriting and he looked at the date on the postmark.

That was strange. He wondered why Helen hadn't mentioned it. Curious, he turned it over in his hands. Reading his wife's letters was a very low thing to do in his opinion, and he would go so far as to say it was unforgivable. Nevertheless . . .

'"*Love*, Mother"?' Tad repeated incredulously once he'd read it, shaking his head. He went to rake his fingers through his wild hair, but his new hairstyle prevented it, and he sat down in the armchair with the letter on his knee. 'I wouldn't have thought it of her,' he said softly. 'Blackmail, that's what it is.' He started to read the letter again. He only saw the reproaches and they went against his sense of fair play.

He tucked the letter back behind the clock and wound it up. He wondered uneasily why Helen hadn't mentioned it, but he understood now why she was going as Britannia and not as his Queen. It should have reassured him. And yet, the guilt it stirred up was dark and muddy as silt.

He put the clock back in its place with the brass key tucked under it.

He stared out of the window at the quiet street. Tonight at choir practice they'd be practising 'Jerusalem', 'Men of Harlech', 'Myfanwy' and 'Guide Me, O Thou Great Redeemer' for the festival. Whenever he happened to pass Harry's house at six o'clock in the evening these days he could hear Rhiannon playing the national anthem, and to his ears the delicately melodious sound seemed to emanate from angels. Harry was right to be proud of her.

Thinking of Harry, Tad wondered again about the purpose of his moustache. It had grown long enough to hide his mouth and it moved most disconcertingly as he talked, as if it was taking on a life of its own. Now that Harry had proved he could grow facial hair with relative ease and efficiency, Tad wondered if he might graduate to a full beard and sideburns, but to date there was no sign of expansion.

This set him thinking about Barbara Pugh, who possibly might venture a few yards along the street from her home to the Coronation festivities. That was interesting in itself, and something of a miracle, but then he was forced to reflect on the emotional loneliness of grief, and his thoughts went fleetingly to his mother-in-law and veered away again.

And then there was Emlyn, showing up with mysterious strands of feathers on his jacket he hadn't really explained with any credibility. Tad's thoughts looped full circle back to his wife tucking a reproachful letter from her mother behind the clock without mentioning it.

What did it all mean?

The people he'd known all his life had become oddly unpredictable recently, and it unsettled him.

He could simply ask Helen about the letter, but then it would bring the subject out into the open, where they would be forced to look at it together from all angles.

As he went upstairs to the bedroom, he sensed that Helen gave a little jolt as he entered, as if she had suddenly remembered something important. He looked at her quickly but her face was blank and shiny with cold cream so he went to the bathroom to brush his teeth and wash his face, and then he got into the cool bed, creaking the springs. He switched the bedside light off and they lay silently side by side in the dark. For a moment it seemed as if the letter was intruding, creating a space between them.

Tad put his arm around her and he could hear the river as a muted roar.

Helen turned to look at him, and he felt her minty breath on his face.

'Tad?' she began hesitantly.

'Yes?' he replied.

He waited for her to carry on, but she was silent for a few moments and then she turned away from him.

'Never mind. It doesn't matter. Goodnight.'

'All right. Goodnight, then.' Tad lay awake until his thoughts stilled at last. Presently, the river stopped its roaring, and he fell asleep.

13

Emlyn had been summoned round by his mother, Old Mrs Hughes, to try on his Pearly King outfit. When he got there, the pearl-button-covered jacket was draped in the armchair, arms outstretched in all its ethereal glory as if it owned the place.

Emlyn picked it up carefully and noticed it was twice as heavy as it used to be, but in appearance it was nowhere near as depressing as its previous guise. 'Dear me, it's got a weight to it,' he marvelled.

His mother got up from her chair and helped him on with it as meticulously as a valet.

'There! How's that? No, wait! Don't move! I've got a surprise for you!'

She went out of the room and came back carrying the velvet hat with the black ostrich feathers. There was very little hat to be seen because it was a blizzard of pearl buttons, as if the wearer had been caught in a haberdasher's dream of a snowstorm.

Emlyn held back his quiff and eased the cap carefully onto his head. It felt, he thought, as heavy as a crown, and it forced him to stand perfectly upright, instead of his usual Teddy Boy slouch. And then he went to look in the mirror over the mantelpiece. He could only see his head and shoulders but that was enough to twist his guts with excitement. 'Well, I never!'

'It's turned out well, hasn't it?' Old Mrs Hughes said.

'I should say!' He looked at himself sideways, from both angles, impressed at how impressive he looked. 'It's better than I ever imagined! The Pearly King I stood next to at the King's funeral procession wasn't a patch on this, and I think the black ostrich feathers are much better than the white would have been, even if we had managed to get the cobwebs off. You have done well!' He took his mother's hands in his, and felt how rough her fingers were from the stitching. He tried to think of words to show his gratitude. 'Thank you,' he said fervently in the end.

'Get away with you,' she said, pleased. And then she added, 'Won't everyone be surprised!'

He turned back to the mirror, proud and confused.

He was a working man, a passionate socialist, always had been, and yet here he was unexpectedly finding he had aspirations towards greater things.

He felt as if someone had opened a door into his firmly working-class soul and found it contained an array of riches – it was both impressive and embarrassing in equal measure. 'You know, I hardly recognise myself,' he said, shaking his head in disbelief. The plumes bobbed and tapped on his hat. 'I could conquer the world in this.'

I could date Nancy in this.

The glorious thought shone in his head like a gleam of sunlight.

He had always believed that Nancy was out of his league.

After the war, once the land girls had left and labour was hard to come by, his mother had sold the farm which would have been his inheritance, and he had gone to work for the Milk Marketing Board. Without the farm, he had nothing to offer Nancy. He had instead settled for what they had – an easy friendship that sometimes bordered on flirtation after a few drinks.

He had always thought that their friendship was enough for him.

Until now.

The future seemed once more to be waiting for him, open-armed with possibilities.

His mother, standing behind him, seemed to sense a change had come over him. 'I'll put the kettle on,' she said softly and reverentially, as if she was in church, and she tiptoed off into the kitchen.

14

In school on Monday, after assembly, Flora stayed behind in the corridor, bracing herself against the flow of pupils to hand her poem to the headmaster personally. 'Excuse me, please, Mr Jones. This is my Coronation poem for the competition.'

The headmaster's black academic gown settled around him and he looked at the sheet of paper in surprise, and took the poem with a frown. When he finished reading he said, 'Is this all your own work, Flora Hall?'

'Yes.' She added quickly, 'And it rhymes,' in case he hadn't noticed.

'Well, well, well, well! It's *poignant*,' he said. He looked at her sternly for a moment, and then he smiled.

It was a strange smile, mainly because it was such a rare event to see. What Flora noticed most was that he had a lot of teeth.

'Well done, Flora,' he said. He folded the paper in half and walked up the corridor, trailed by the billow of his robe.

'I got four wells in a row,' Flora said to Garth, who had waited for her so that they could go to maths together.

'Well, well! That makes six,' Garth said, and Flora nudged him with her elbow and laughed.

Flora and Garth were bound together by their lack of a father, and although they never spoke about it, it singled them out, somehow, in a mutual bond of understanding. It was harder to hate an only parent than to hate a pair of them. What would they do without them?

Garth couldn't hate his mother anyway because she was miserable enough as it was. But he couldn't rely on her, either; he could only rely on himself.

They were aware it was a more precarious existence, having one parent rather than two.

'He said it was poignant,' Flora told Garth, with her mind still on the headmaster.

'Yes. I thought that, too.'

It was the first time that Flora could ever remember being pleased about schoolwork she'd done. School to her was more of a social thing, and studying just got in the way. A lot of the subjects she didn't see any point in anyway. They bore absolutely no resemblance to her world. In any case, she wanted to become a hairdresser, and there was no point in learning about the Romans for that.

At break time, Flora, Rhiannon and Lauren were discussing their dresses for the party.

Flora curled a strand of hair around her finger. 'I've nearly finished making mine,' she said. 'I've just got to hem it. How are you getting on?'

'Awful. Have you done the buttonholes?' Rhiannon asked. 'I'm no good at buttonholes.'

'Me neither,' Lauren said. 'I'm using hooks and eyes, it's easier. I'm no good at needlework.'

Flora looked across at Garth who was kicking a deflated football to get rid of his energy. 'It's my favourite subject. I might start making Garth's tie once I've finished.'

'Will you help me with my outfit after you've done Garth's tie, Flora?' Rhiannon asked her.

'Yes, of course, how far have you got with it?'

'Just the bodice so far. I haven't got much time really, what with the harp and Dad's moustache.'

Flora and Lauren exchanged surprised glances and then burst out laughing.

'What's your dad's moustache got to do with anything?' Flora asked.

Rhiannon looked serious. 'There's ructions in our house because my mother can't stand it – it's made my father very furtive. And Waffles can't stand it either. He seems to think he should get rid of it somehow.'

While the residents of Little Green Street had their own reasonably good-humoured opinions on Harry's moustache, Waffles had reacted to it badly. When he saw Harry, he stood stock still and his serious eyes became very focused. He seemed to have made it his mission to see the moustache off as he would any other trespasser. In the beginning, speculation was that the dog thought it was getting rid of a centipede underneath Harry's nose that he was unaware of, but as the moustache grew longer, they wondered if he suspected it was a field mouse, and eventually, possibly a rat.

Harry fended off the dog, playfully at first but getting increasingly more annoyed.

It didn't take long for the intelligent dog to work out that he was going to have to act with stealth. His damp, twitching nose would appear by the door of the bar, then his eyes and the white fur around the neck of his tawny coat, and conversation would stop in anticipation.

Harry grew wise to it pretty quickly, and went on the alert any time it was quiet, bracing himself, because although he was a big man, Waffles was strong.

'To be fair, it is funny to watch,' Rhiannon admitted. 'But Dad's being very secretive about his costume because he says he wants to surprise my mam. And,' she added, 'he's been whittling a lot.'

'Whistling?' Flora asked.

'No, whittling, whittling wood. He never used to whittle before growing his moustache.'

'Whittling wood,' Flora repeated, baffled. She had no idea what that meant.

'Anyway, what with one thing and another, it's hard to concentrate on sewing.'

'I know! I haven't even finished my poem yet, have you?' Lauren asked Rhiannon.

'No. I'm going to have to start again because it's about the national anthem and it doesn't really make sense. To be honest, I think it was a bad idea to draw parallels with the national anthem. My mother said I was just being clever. And I was, I suppose.'

In Little Green Street there was no greater insult than to be accused of being clever because it was basically showing off.

To Rhiannon's relief, the bell rang for the end of break, and all her problems were deferred until lunchtime.

15

In the junior-school music room, Tad was taking recorder class, his ears jangled by an aviary of shrillness. He was trying not to wince. Being a music teacher was an awful job if faced with too many pupils who couldn't hold a tune, he thought. He himself wouldn't have trusted the children with anything more complicated than a triangle.

In his opinion, while any instrument played badly was an offence to the ear, there was nothing quite as offensive as a badly played recorder. The tune they were learning was 'All Through the Night', but it was absolutely impossible to identify a melody amidst all the toots and squeaks. However, he couldn't fault his pupils' enthusiasm for throwing themselves into making a noise. Some of them were using the recorder as a whistle and not bothering with finger exercises at all.

Dear heart alive! he thought to himself, and he rapped the desk with his ruler. 'Stop! Stop!' Gradually the din died down and he picked up his own recorder. 'Now listen, class. I want you to hear what it's supposed to sound like. Pay attention.'

His class nodded obediently. They were very good at making a show of obedience; there was no faulting them for that. Their inability to carry it out was the problem.

Normally, he would close his eyes, but he didn't dare take them off the children – he had to be constantly watchful. But he played melodiously, with feeling, going over the lyrics in his mind . . . *hill and dale in slumber sleeping, I my loved ones' watch am keeping* . . .

The words taunted him to his very soul.

He could hardly keep watch over his loved ones by ignoring danger, could he? And the danger had come looking as innocent as the devil in the form of a blue envelope tucked behind the clock.

He remembered that heartfelt sigh that Helen had given in bed last night. He frowned. There was no doubt about it, it was a very harsh letter to receive, and not at all helped by the fact that the accusations were not inaccurate.

He suddenly realised he had stopped playing mid-tune. The recorder was resting on his lower lip and his class was looking at him with bright-eyed interest, wondering what was going to happen next. Tad gathered his wits together. 'So now you can understand how it's supposed to sound, can't you?' he said. 'It's a lullaby, to send a baby gently to sleep. Now! What would happen if we played it loudly and shrilly, do you think?'

'The baby would cry!'

'Scream!'

'Scream its head off!'

'Have nightmares.'

Each child trying to go one up on the other.

'Exactly!' Tad said. 'So what we're going to do is try playing the same tune again, but this time we will be play-ing it softly and sweetly so the baby will have happy dreams.'

The result was no more musical than before, and some pupils seemed to be blowing diligently into thin air – he could feel the gusts of their breaths like a light breeze – but it was definitely quieter.

'Very good!' he said happily, because he was of the opinion that a little encouragement went a long way.

He had also come to a decision.

They would invite Dorothea here. Who knew, once she got used to the idea, she might enter into the spirit of things and enjoy herself. It was the perfect answer. Helen would be happy and Dorothea would be assured of a warm welcome. The town was good at that.

16

Emlyn went to call on Nancy that evening, hurrying through the rain without a coat and holding his black umbrella over his head. He radiated the smell of Old Spice and Brylcreem.

Flora answered the door. She was holding a yellow pencil between the V of her fingers like a cigarette. 'Hello, Emlyn,' she said, and she gave a little smile.

Emlyn found himself surprised to see her, even though she lived there of course. 'Oh! Hello, Flora. Is your mother in?' he asked politely.

'No, she's not back from work yet. What do you want her for?'

He was taken aback by the question. 'Nothing much. I just fancied a quick word, that's all. Don't worry, I'll come back later.'

'All right.' Flora blew an imaginary stream of smoke right at him. 'Or you can come in and wait if you like, out of the rain.'

Emlyn looked up at the broad canopy of his umbrella. The raindrops seemed to hit it musically, like a refrain, and dripped, clear as crystals, onto Nancy's red-brick doorstep. 'No, you're all right. I'll go and meet her,' he said, 'save her getting wet.'

'Is it urgent?' Flora asked.

'It is and it isn't,' he said cryptically. It had seemed a

matter of great urgency, as he was getting himself ready, to ask Nancy out before the courage endowed upon him by the power of the Pearly King's costume wore off and he was back to feeling ordinary again. 'Thanks, anyhow. See you later,' he said.

'Alligator,' Flora prompted with a cheeky tilt of her head.

For a worrying moment he thought she was referring to him, but they'd had American visitors in the town the year before who had charmed them with their catchy American slang.

'In a while, crocodile.'

Nancy worked at Cuthbert's seed factory, which was situated in Upper Dee Mills, and as Emlyn walked there with the rain drumming on the silk of his umbrella, he began to whistle with happiness. Even the relentless grey of the seed factory, combined with the grey of the rain and the grey faces of the shopfloor workers carrying their overalls in their bags, was not enough to dent his mood.

Emlyn saw Nancy at once, sheltering in the doorway. With her blonde hair and her red lips, she looked like the star of a musical, glowing in the limelight, casting the rest of the workers into the shade.

'Nancy!' he called, lifting up his umbrella so she could see him properly.

She waved and put her handbag over her head and ran to him.

He held his umbrella over her.

'Emlyn, am I glad to see you!' she said, tucking her arm into his. Under the umbrella's canopy she smelled feminine, of face powder and lipstick. 'Where are you off to?'

'I'm off to right here to meet you,' he said cheerfully.

'Aww, Emlyn!'

They walked together in step, and as well as the orchestral rain on the umbrella, his left shoe had developed a squeak from the damp. He tried his hardest to rectify it before Nancy noticed.

'Are you limping?' she asked him in a voice full of concern.

'No, I'm trying to get rid of the squeak,' he confessed as they crossed the road, and Nancy giggled.

When Nancy giggled, it always gave him confidence. 'Come on a date with me,' he said quickly as they stepped on the wet pavement.

'A date?' she repeated. She didn't look at him.

'It's not too soon, is it?' he asked anxiously.

'Too soon?' she asked, perplexed.

'After losing your husband, I mean. I realise that some people never get over their loss. Look at Barbara Pugh. Nine years and she's a broken woman still and whatever glue of human kindness might exist that could fix her, we've yet to find it.'

Nancy bit her lip. 'Emlyn,' she began, 'it's not that.' She stopped talking for a moment and then went on softly, 'What would your mother say?'

Emlyn frowned and watched the rain bounce on the slick black pavement as they walked. It hadn't occurred to him to factor his mother into it. It seemed to be a private thing, just between the two of them, his asking Nancy on a date. But there were no such things as secrets in Little Green Street, and he realised he'd been very short-sighted because he hadn't thought about what he'd do if Nancy said yes.

It was true that Old Mrs Hughes was known for plain-speaking and was quick to condemn, but she was a kind soul deep down, and when Flora had first moved to the town and lived on the farm with her as an evacuee, compassion had softened her heart. Any criticism of Nancy was purely superficial, relating mainly to the height of Nancy's heels, the yellow of her hair, and the length of her dress.

There was no point in mentioning that, so Emlyn cast around for something positive that his mother might have said about her and blurted out the first thing that occurred to him. 'She admires your whites on the washing line,' he said.

'Does she? Did she tell you that?'

'Yes, many times.' Emlyn began to be aware that in the dark shelter of boned silk over their heads, his damp sweater was competing with his Old Spice aftershave and he was smelling of sheep. Luckily the rain eased off its noisy drumming and diminished to a few occasional notes, like a musical box running down. He lowered his umbrella like a shield and saw that the nature-washed day was bright again, and the leaves and the grass and the hills were glittering like emeralds. 'It's stopped,' he said in surprise.

'It would, wouldn't it, now that we're home,' Nancy said as they entered Little Green Street. She laughed and disentangled her arm from his and he flapped his umbrella as wildly as if he was struggling with a turkey, to get the worst of the wet off it.

'Thanks for walking me home, Emlyn,' Nancy said. She looked at him, and her eyes were warm and very blue.

They had walked too quickly. He'd not known the distance to ever be that short, even though he'd lived in the town all his life. 'Where did we get to in our conversation? I've forgotten,' he said, so that he could stay in her company for a few seconds more.

'You were asking me on a date.'

'So I was. How about it?'

'Yes. Let's go somewhere nice.'

For a moment, he stared at her blankly. She was smiling at him and then he realised – it was as simple as that. He smiled back. 'Somewhere nice. I'll put my mind to it. Goodbye.'

17

Mai was dusting the windowsill in a desultory manner. She, who knew everything there was to know about everyone, was feeling out of sorts these days because she didn't know what her own husband was up to. And the worst of it was, she couldn't admit it to a soul, or else her reputation as the local historian would be in jeopardy. All she knew for sure was that his change of mood was something to do with his moustache. He was a different man with that moustache, very much like Sampson before Delilah shaved his head. She had never had cause to sympathise with the perfidious Delilah before, but she could perfectly understand now how that life-altering trim came about.

She had been looking out of the window to see if the rain had stopped when she'd been distracted by the sight of Emlyn struggling wildly on the pavement with his black umbrella, his quiff drooping in the damp. Following him had been Nancy, smiling as if he was doing something worth smiling about.

Mai had quickly put two and two together: Emlyn had walked with Nancy in the rain. *And him without a coat on!*

She had stepped back from the window and carried on watching more discreetly, wondering if Nancy would invite him into her house, but to her disappointment they had parted ways. Still, this was news, and when she heard both their doors close she hurried out of the house in the drizzle and went two doors down to Helen's, full of excitement.

Helen was wearing a floral scarf around her head and her apron was smeared with flour and chocolate. 'Am I glad to see you!'

'You'll never guess!' Mai said. 'Emlyn and Nancy!'

'Emlyn and Nancy what?'

'I've just seen them walking out together!'

'Oh, is that all? Come in and taste this chocolate cake, Mai. I'm testing out the recipe.'

'I shouldn't,' Mai said, but she came in and tasted it anyway, and after she'd swallowed a mouthful she ran her tongue over her chocolate-coated teeth thoughtfully. 'Is this the one that you're not supposed to cook?'

'Yes.'

'It's a bit wet. Put it in the oven for twenty minutes, that's what I would do.' She was eager to get back to the subject at hand. 'But Emlyn and Nancy! Did you know about it?'

'What is there to know about?' Helen asked sharply.

It was not at all like her to be sharp and Mai was taken by surprise. 'Ah, it's nothing really I don't suppose,' she said, feeling deflated.

She was about to leave when Helen asked, 'Are you feeling all right, Mai?'

'So-so.' Mai turned back to look at her friend. She recognised the troubling currents in an instant. 'Are you?'

'Have you got time for a cup of tea?'

'I have. I was only dusting when I saw them, and looking at the rain.'

Helen slid the scarf from her hair and untied her apron. She made the tea and poured them a cup. 'Come into the Boardroom,' she said. 'The smell of chocolate's making me feel sick.'

They sat opposite each other in the dining room, looking curiously at each other across the mahogany table.

'You go first,' Helen said.

'All right.' Mai took a deep breath and her bun wobbled uncertainly. 'It's Harry and that moustache of his. It's changed him beyond recognition. Normally he would consult me about this kind of thing but he grew it all by himself, furtively. He's very secretive these days and I don't know what to do about it.' She folded her arms. 'There! I've said it!'

Helen agreed. 'You're right, it has changed him. Even Tad's noticed it, and he's not the most perceptive man in the world.'

'I've even been wondering if I could shave it off while he was asleep.' Mai was only half joking, and testing the idea out as a possibility.

Helen laughed. 'It's a bit drastic, Mai. And it would ruin his fancy dress for the Coronation Party, whoever he's going as. Has he told you?'

This was another bitter blow to Mai, and she shook her head. 'Not yet. Has Tad told you who he's going as? I'm only asking because Harry saw him walking past the Post Office with a sword all wrapped up in brown paper.'

'Ah, the sword. Yes, he has told me, but he's not telling anyone else, he wants it to be a surprise.'

'Is it St George and the Dragon? That's what Harry thinks, on account of Tad's hair looking very English.'

'That's funny! English hair! No, it's not St George and don't ask me anything else because I'm no good at keeping secrets.'

Mai was puzzled. 'Why would you want to? Secrets are for sharing.'

'Hmm. I'm not sure I agree. I can tell you my problem though, if you like,' Helen said after a moment. 'My mother wants me to go to London for the Coronation.'

'Does she? Has she got an invitation for Westminster Abbey?' Mai asked avidly. 'Or would you be in the stands?'

'No, we'd just be lining the street with everyone else.'

'Waving flags!'

'And cheering. If it wasn't for the party, I would have said yes, but . . .' Helen shrugged.

'So you're not going?'

'I suppose not. I haven't written back yet because I know she will be upset and I feel bad about it.'

Mai sipped her tea, deeply gratified that Helen was thinking of choosing the tea party over a trip to London. Quite right, too. London! She and Harry had been on a Whit Sunday coach trip there once, and after a day of sightseeing – St Paul's, the Tower of London, Trafalgar Square – they'd had trouble finding the coach again and when they finally did find it, they were hot and bothered and late. Worse, all the seats in the front had been taken, and as they walked down the gangway to the back of the coach there was a lot of discontented grumbling from the passengers who'd got there early and been forced to wait for them for almost twenty minutes.

She didn't envy anybody who lived in London, but it was impossible not to admire them.

'What does Tad say about it?'

'That's the problem. I haven't told him.'

'Oh? Why not?'

Helen looked up with tears in her eyes and brushed her fair hair away from her face. 'Because he's so happy about everything, and I don't want to spoil it.'

Mai propped her chin on her fist and looked at Helen with great interest, and a bit of envy too. 'You actually like your husband!' she said, almost accusingly.

'Well, yes,' Helen said, looking confused. 'I *love* him.'

'Well, of course you love him, he's your husband and you're obliged to,' Mai said dismissively. 'But liking him is a different matter altogether.' Mai wasn't sure that she liked Harry. She had until recently, but she wondered now if the beauty of him had worn off, like silver plate, and she was down to the base metal underneath.

Helen was smiling. 'You are funny, Mai,' she said. 'And I feel better about the cake now, I'm not sure why. It might have set a little more solidly since we've been talking. Perhaps you could take a slice for Harry and see what he thinks. It's no use my asking Tad because he'll say it's lovely no matter what, whereas I know Harry won't spare my feelings.'

'No, he's not known for that.'

'And I've been thinking. You could pretend to like him with his moustache for a few days and see if it makes any difference. He might not be so defensive about it.'

To Mai's mind, pretending to like it was more radical than doing a Delilah. 'I suppose I could try. And I'll tell him you need his verdict on your chocolate cake. That will cheer him up. I'd better go, I stopped in the middle of my dusting.'

They went back into the kitchen and Helen put a slice of the cake on a tea plate. At least she tried to, but it stuck to the knife and she had to use another knife to get it free.

'It's still a bit stodgy, I'm afraid,' she said.

Back at home, Mai applied her Coral Island lipstick, tucked a few stray strands of hair back into her bun and waited for Harry to come home from the Electricity Board. The kitchen was as dark as evening from the rain, and it was too early to switch the light on.

Even though she'd been talking about the moustache just now with Helen, when he came into the gloomy kitchen through the back door in his damp macintosh it was still a surprise to see it, looking like a hedge that had been planted between the two halves of his face, curving into the foothills of his round cheeks. It was very lavish now. It had lost some of its coarseness and become as sleek and glossy as an otter, despite the rain.

'It's wet out there,' Harry said.

As he hung his coat up, Mai noticed her husband was smelling strongly of Brylcreem. He pulled a chair out, sat by the kitchen table and took his wallet out of his pocket. Out of the wallet he took a miniature tortoiseshell comb and groomed his moustache gently with a distant look in his eyes.

Mai watched him incredulously with folded arms and then reminded herself she was going to try liking it. 'It's coming on a treat, Harry,' she said.

He stopped combing and looked at her, trying to weigh up the meaning behind the words. And then he put the comb back in his wallet and tucked it away. 'How has your day been?'

'Very nice, thank you. I went to Helen's. She's sent you a slice of her chocolate cake to try after your tea.'

'Chocolate cake?' Harry's small eyes gleamed. 'Never mind after my tea! I'll have it now.'

Mai uncovered it, put it in front of Harry and fetched him a cake fork.

Harry dug in, having to open his mouth wide so as to bypass his moustache. He worked his jaw thoughtfully as he ate, sucking in his cheeks and raising his eyebrows in surprise. He seemed to be having trouble swallowing. Then he frowned. 'It's a bit—' he began saying around the mouthful, and then he fetched himself a glass of water and swilled it around his mouth '—sticky,' he finished hoarsely. 'It hasn't been cooked long enough.'

'It hasn't been cooked at all,' Mai said. 'It's a special recipe to save on heating.'

Harry sat down again with his glass of water in front of him, folded his arms and looked at the cake with an expression of deep disappointment. 'It's not how I remember it. I like yours better, Mai. This doesn't taste like yours at all.'

It was the nicest thing he'd said to her in ages. 'Doesn't it?' she asked, with a show of innocence and hiding a smile.

'Not a patch on it. I don't think this one's worthy of the Queen's Coronation, and I don't mind telling Helen so myself. She'd expect me to tell the truth.'

'She does, but don't be too hard on her. I'll tell you what, Harry,' Mai said, resting her hand affectionately on his broad shoulder, 'I'll bake you one of mine this evening.'

'Oh, Mai.'

He said it so happily and so sweetly that her heart melted. She sat down next to him and patted his hand.

'You'll never guess,' she began in this moment of intimacy, lowering her voice although there were only the two of them there, 'Helen's widowed mother wants her to go to London for the Coronation.'

'No! What about the party?'

'She thinks she'll say no to her when she's got the courage, but she hasn't told Tad about it.'

'Why hasn't she told Tad?'

'She doesn't want to worry him.'

'Why should it worry him if she's not going?'

Mai realised she was definitely losing her touch, because she hadn't thought of wondering that herself. But her eyes gleamed. 'That's a good point. I don't really know, to be honest, Harry. And I don't think Helen does, either.'

It was a long time since they'd spoken to each other confidentially like this. It seemed to Mai that they had been drifting apart slowly, carried on separate currents out of arm's reach, and she hadn't expected them to suddenly snap back together like this, in a flash. She was surprised but, more than surprised, she was relieved, because she had been miserable lately without him.

Harry was looking at her with eager eyes. 'I'm going to let you in on a secret,' he said, 'about my fancy dress. But you must promise not to tell a soul and if you make me a promise, you have to keep it. Be honest about it now, Mai,' he said, tapping the table for emphasis, 'because if you can't keep it then I shan't tell you.'

Mai covered her face with her hands and in the darkness of her palms she thought about the thrilling nature of secrets. Sharing them gave her the same feeling as buying sweets now that rationing had ended; it was a feeling of simple joy. But she knew that when she had a secret and passed it on saying it was a secret, it was a secret in name only. This was going to be a real one, just between her and Harry, and strangely enough, that was a thrill in itself.

She took her hands away. 'I promise. Who are you going to be?'

Harry sat up straight in the chair, took a deep breath and raised his heavy chins momentarily off his chest. 'Adrian Boult!' he announced grandly.

It was an anti-climax, to be honest, and for a moment Mai wondered if Adrian Boult was somebody he worked with – the name seemed vaguely familiar. 'Fancy!' she said, playing for time.

'Stay there! I've got something to show you.' Harry grabbed his raincoat and hurried outside into the drizzle, which had just started back up. Mai saw him pass the window and she stood up and watched him head to the shed.

'*Adrian Boult*,' she muttered to herself.

Harry came back into the kitchen with a stick in his hand and mud on his shoes. He stood on the doormat and waved the stick at her. 'You see?' And as he waved it he started humming the national anthem.

Of course the name made perfect sense now it was accessorised and she felt weak with relief.

'Sir Adrian Boult!'

Harry nodded modestly.

'Sir Adrian Boult,' she repeated, remembering his grace, the elegance of his movements at the music festival. 'You're the absolute spit of him!'

This wasn't entirely true, as Sir Adrian was older than Harry, and thinner, with different hair. But the big moustache was identical. And there was the baton, too, as an additional clue. She wouldn't have got it without the humming and conducting, but it didn't matter because at least she'd got there in the end.

'Think how he felt, conducting the royal wedding!' Harry said, marvelling.

'And we've seen him with our own eyes! Mostly from behind,' Mai added truthfully.

'Here,' Harry said, handing her the baton. 'Have a look at this. I made it myself.'

Mai admired the baton generously and wholeheartedly, because she'd feared the worst and the explanation was wonderfully pure and simple, after all. 'So this is what you were doing in the shed! I couldn't imagine what was going on! And all those branches!'

'It had to be straight, you see? No use having a crooked baton. Unless the choir was standing around a corner,' he added with a grin that made him look like his old self. 'Feel the balance, Mai!'

She felt the balance by wafting it around the kitchen. 'Marvellous! All you need now is a choir!' It was meant to be light-hearted, but Harry seized on her words.

'It's true, Mai,' he said passionately. 'That's all I need! I have suggested we take it in turns to conduct, because after all, fair's fair, and Emlyn agreed with me, too, but there's no budging Tad.' Harry's grin faded slowly and was lost behind his moustache.

For a moment they sat in silence. Mai looked at Harry fondly and saw the boy in him, the boy she loved and wanted to please. 'Unless . . .' she began.

Harry raised his eyebrows hopefully. 'Unless?'

'Tad decides to go to London with Helen.' And on that note, Mai got up in the drizzle-dark kitchen to put the kettle on.

18

As usual, Tad, Emlyn and Harry got to the Hand early that evening to prepare for choir practice, and they entered the smoky bar in good spirits.

'Whose turn is it to get them in?' Harry asked, rubbing his hands eagerly.

'Yours,' Emlyn said. 'I got them last time, remember? You were trying to get an extra one in before Mai came and you sent me up to get it.'

'I don't remember any such thing,' Harry said. 'This is how I remember it. You asked me if I wanted a pint, and I did. It was a gift, I thought, otherwise I would have said no.'

Billy did a double-take and folded his arms over his large chest. 'Out with you! No riff-raff,' he said. 'Oh, it's you is it, Harry? I couldn't see who it was behind the moustache.'

'Three pints of the usual, please.'

The barman reached for a pint glass. 'One day someone will ask for the unusual.'

'And what will you give them?'

'The Hand cocktail,' he said. 'It's savoury based: Bacardi, bitter lemon, tomato juice—'

Harry put up his hand and stopped him. 'Sounds like soup. We'll stick to the usual, if you don't mind.' He waited for his pint, pulled up a stool and contorted himself to look at his elbow. 'Billy, this bar is all wet.'

Billy the bar handed him a towel. 'I know, I've just wiped it down.'

'I can see that but I'm feeling a bit hard done by all the same. Have you got a reduction for a wet elbow?'

'Harry, you're incorrigible.'

'He's maligning me with his long words,' Harry complained, taking out his wallet reluctantly. 'One for yourself?'

'Not just yet,' Billy said. 'Ask me when you're on your second. I like to keep on a par with my regulars, and so far you haven't partaken. Get it? There's a pun for you!'

'Not charging for puns now, are you?'

Once Billy had pulled the pints, they took them to their usual table.

'Now then,' Emlyn said when they had settled themselves. He glanced over his shoulder to check whether anyone was listening, and, satisfied, he turned back. 'I can't abide gossip so I'm getting this out in the open.'

'What's the difference between getting something out in the open and gossiping, out of interest?' Tad asked.

'Because this is about me. You can only gossip about other people. When it's about yourself, you're passing on information.'

'True enough. I'm not arguing,' Tad said.

'That makes a change.'

'I was curious, that's all.'

'I've always thought that about you. Anyway, I'm taking Nancy on a date.'

This was a turn-up for the books, and both men looked at him in surprise.

'Are you?' Tad asked cheerfully. 'Does she know?'

'Yes, she does, and she's asked me to take her some-where nice.'

'You're besmitten,' Harry said, chuckling, 'you've got a shine to you.'

Emlyn ignored him. 'And my question is, where's nice? It's the kind of thing two married men like you will know, which is why I'm asking.'

'The Boat Inn is romantic, if you're after romance, and you can sit out in the summer and look at the river,' Tad said.

'*If* I'm after romance? As opposed to what?'

'Mind you, where there's rivers, there's midges,' Harry warned.

'Stay inside and look at the river through the window then,' Tad said. 'It's always a treat to go to the Boat Inn. Ask Helen, if you don't believe me.'

'Ah! Talking of Helen . . .' Harry said slyly, drawing invisibly on the table with his finger.

The way Harry said it made Tad look at him closely. There was something in his tone that unnerved him. Tad felt he wasn't going to like it, whatever it was. 'What about Helen?' He put his hand around his glass, feeling the cool-ness of it. The chill seemed to spread through his veins and up his arm, until even his armpit felt cold.

'Never mind,' Harry said, shaking his head. 'It doesn't matter.'

'No, go on, out with it, man. Say whatever you began to say.'

'If you insist.' Harry took a few strong sips of his pint and put it down square on the beer mat. And he looked up at Tad with his small, bull-like eyes. 'I think you ought to know she's in something of a dilemma. Dorothea wants her to go to London so she'll have company for the Coronation.'

For a moment, Tad didn't respond. Then he said hoarsely, 'I know she does.'

His immediate alarming thought was that his wife had confided in Harry, but he realised that that was unlikely. 'I suppose Mai told you, did she?'

'That's right. She said Helen doesn't want to worry you by mentioning it.'

'I'm not worried.' Tad tried to sound nonchalant to hide his uneasiness. Why had Helen found the need to talk it over with Mai, rather than with him? 'I'm not worried in the slightest,' he said more firmly. 'She's not going to change her plans now, with the party just a month away. She's looking forward to it as much as the rest of us.'

'She's told you that, has she?' Harry downed the rest of his pint in one, dabbed the froth off his moustache with his handkerchief and put his empty glass down heavily. 'She's torn. And her mother's a widow,' he added darkly. 'You have to see it from her point of view, Tad. It's understandable that she and her mother would want to share the Coronation experience together. Just think if it was your own mother.'

'Torn, is she?' Tad rubbed his hand across his forehead. He hadn't thought of it like that. He'd assumed she'd refused the invitation without his help.

'It's true, Harry,' Emlyn agreed. 'It's awful to think of her mother spending the day alone. Take my mother. She wouldn't miss sharing this celebration with us for the world.'

'Exactly!' Harry said. 'You've put your finger on it, Emlyn! All I'm saying is, just because Helen's torn, there's no need for you to be, Tad. I can take over the choir for you and I'll be glad to do it, for the sake of matrimonial harmony. Another pint, boys?'

Just as he was lifting his hand to indicate Billy could get pumping the ale, Emlyn voiced his opinion, putting a stick in Harry's spokes.

'Or why don't you invite her mother here to the party?' he suggested.

Tad thought of the scathing tone of the letter and he scratched his chin. 'I don't think she'd come. She's right there in London, on the spot, where it's all happening.'

'Exactly! Do you hear that, Emlyn? She's right on the spot!' Harry echoed.

Emlyn was undeterred. 'But in London she won't be any more involved in the ceremony than she is here, will she? It's all about the spirit of the Coronation. And the spirit is not confined to one place. It will be just as strong here as it is there. And Helen's mother can sit with my mother,' Emlyn said. 'They'll be about the same age and they'll have a lot to talk about.'

'Such as?' Harry asked irritably. 'You mean like philosophical arguments on knitting? Come on, Emlyn, I challenge you to name one thing they've got in common!'

'That's true.' Tad's eyes widened. Dorothea and Old Mrs Hughes? He tried to visualise this anticipated conversation, without success. It was difficult, even for a man of his imagination, to think of anything that they had in common.

But Emlyn hadn't finished yet. 'Look at it this way. If you invite her, you'll be able to take the moral high ground even if she turns you down.'

The moral high ground had always held appeal for Tad, and he brightened. 'I think you've got something there, Emlyn,' he said. 'If it's company she wants, she'll have plenty of it. And it's easier for one to travel than three.'

'True,' Harry conceded, 'but—' He cut himself off as though something had occurred to him that he was reluctant to share. Then he gave a little shake of the head, as if he'd decided against saying it.

'But what?'

'Think about it, Tad. Be fair.' Lowering his voice like a concerned doctor, Harry went on, 'Isn't she getting on a bit? Isn't it a bit far for her to travel?'

'A bit far? It's as far as it's always been,' Tad replied. 'I don't know what the distance has got to do with it. She's not walking here, is she? She'll be sitting down in a railway carriage for a few hours doing nothing, legitimately, and you can't beat that, in my opinion.'

'To be fair, it's a strenuous day's work for you, Harry, sitting down doing nothing,' Emlyn said with a grin.

Even as hope dawned bright in Tad, Harry's face flushed with irritation as he glared at Emlyn. They were two men on an emotional see-saw.

'Some people ought to keep their noses out of other people's business, Emlyn,' Harry declared crossly, getting to his feet and knocking his stool over. 'I'm going out for some fresh air. I don't like the atmosphere in here.'

His anger seemed to come out of the blue. Not for the

first time, Tad wondered what was troubling Harry these days and he glanced at Emlyn, but he was lighting a cigarette, his mind on the present moment. 'We've just got time for another one before the hordes arrive,' he said happily. 'Your turn to get them in, Tad.'

19

Flora was lying on her mother's comfy eiderdown with her hands behind her head watching her mother get ready.

Nancy was putting her make-up on before she took her curlers out of her blonde hair. There was the click of the gilt powder compact, the dab of the sponge, the red of the lipstick, the Marilyn Monroe pout.

'Where are you going?'

'To the Hand. It's choir practice.'

'Is that all? Why are you dressing up?' Flora asked suspiciously.

Nancy turned on her pink velour dressing-table stool. 'Emlyn's asked me out on a date and I want to look nice.'

'Emlyn Kremlin?' Flora asked in surprise, even though they only knew one Emlyn in the world.

When the bombs were dropping on Liverpool and they first moved to the small safe town in a green valley hugged by gentle hills, she used to worry that her mother would marry Emlyn. He was always coming round to the house to fix things that Old Mrs Hughes had been happy to live with, like leaking taps and the garden fence. Even though he looked a bit like a film star with his black Teddy Boy hair, or as near as you could get to one in the small town, Flora wasn't sure she wanted a man coming to the house to fix things all the time. It made her nervous and fearful all over again.

But then everything did get fixed, and Emlyn stopped coming to the house. And Flora missed him because she'd got used to having him around. He never tried to make conversation, for a start, and he'd never ever asked how her schoolwork was going. She hated it when people asked that. It wasn't as if they cared about the answer, it was just because they couldn't think of anything else to say.

'Emlyn's all right,' Nancy said with a faint smile.

'Is that your date? Choir practice?' It was a bit disappointing.

'He's going to take me somewhere nice another night, with music and dancing and Babycham. Tonight is just choir practice, but I want to look nice.'

'You look beautiful,' Flora said.

'Do I? I feel old, sometimes.' Nancy turned back to the mirror and looked at herself closely.

'You're not old, Mum,' Flora said quickly. She knew that her bright glamour and her smile were something that she put on deliberately to hide how she really felt. But she was fiercely glad her mother was like that. The alternative was being like Garth's mother, hiding fearfully away from the world, and that was much worse.

She got off the bed as her mother started taking her curlers out. Her hair formed blonde, springy tubes which smelled of Sta-Blond shampoo.

'Leave it like this,' Flora said, laughing and patting her mother's hair.

'Wouldn't they be surprised!' Nancy said and ran her fingers through the curls.

'Let me do the back for you.' Flora wanted to be a hairdresser one day, and for a moment she put her face next to her mother's, both of them framed, cheek to cheek, in the reflection.

Nancy patted her face gently. 'Get on with it then,' she said. 'I don't want to be late.'

'I might come with you.'

Billy let the youngsters into the bar sometimes on choir practice night, to make up the audience. All the men from the town seemed different when they were singing. She liked the low, powerful rumble of the bass section, and the way they all concentrated as if nothing else in the world mattered except for the music. But mostly she wanted to see whether Emlyn seemed any different now that he'd asked her mother on a date.

She brushed the back of her mother's hair gently, softening the curls. 'Hair-spray, madam?'

Nancy laughed. 'Yes, please.'

A quick spray, and Nancy was done. She got to her feet.

'How do I look?'

'Wonderful! I'm going to Lauren's. See you later.'

Lauren came to the door wearing her Coronation dress. 'Come in, Flora, I'm glad it's you. What do you think? I feel like there's something wrong with it.' She did a twirl. 'Ow! I just got stabbed by a pin.' She looked down at her waist. 'Is there blood?'

'Stand still! No, no blood. It looks all right,' Flora said, smoothing it straight. 'Once you've hemmed it you're done, more or less.'

'I have hemmed it,' Lauren said.

'Have you? They look like tacking stitches.'

'I know, I did it in a rush. Look at my fingers, they're covered in pinholes!'

'Lauren Jones, the human pincushion. You could join a circus. I'll collect the money and play the trumpet to announce you.'

'I'd love to join the circus, wouldn't you?' Lauren said dreamily. 'I'd travel around and see the world.'

'Before you go, come to choir practice with me first. Emlyn's asked my mother out on a date and I want to see if he blushes when he sees her.'

'Emlyn and your mum?' Lauren giggled and covered her mouth with her hand. 'Emlyn's in love!'

'He'll have red hearts flying out of his hair like confetti!'

'Everybody's happy,' Lauren said, 'and it's because of the Coronation, isn't it? From now on we're all going to live happily ever after!'

'About time, too.'

'Yes. About time. Wait there while I get changed.'

'Don't be long.'

Flora listened to Lauren hurrying up the stairs. We're all going to live happily ever after, she said to herself. But in her mind a cloud went over the sun and she shivered. She hadn't thought about her father for ages, but she thought about him now, about the one time she met him, the sound of him when he came into the house, the slam of the door, the thud of his boots, the scraping of his chair, and about the smell of him, a fog of tobacco and beer, and her mother crying. He belonged to a different world made of grey streets, rubble and smouldering wood.

I'm only thinking of him now because I'm happy, she told herself. It was as if happiness made her brave. But she stopped herself from being too happy, just in case it was taken away from her.

Suddenly propelled out of her chair by a rush of anxiety, she touched the wooden table for luck and felt her way along the cold, solid wall of the hall, let herself out of the front door and hurried down the path, running her hands along the dusty, prickly hedge. She looked up and down the street to reassure herself that it was all still there, the solid white houses, Old Mrs Hughes's squat, pebble-dashed bungalow, everything the same as it had always been, and nothing had changed.

The upstairs window opened and Lauren leant out. 'Flora, wait for me! I won't be long!'

'I'm just going to get Rhiannon,' Flora said, because it was the best reason she could think of on the spur of the moment.

'Fetch Garth as well!'

Lauren closed the window abruptly with a bang, like a Juliet breaking up with her Romeo, and Flora went to call on Garth and Rhiannon.

By the time the three of them got back to Lauren's, she was closing the front door and they linked arms and took up the whole pavement as if they were royalty as they walked to the Hand Hotel.

20

Now that he had a plan, and partly because he was enjoying his second pint, Tad felt a lot better about the evening, and was getting some of his confidence back.

'Stop worrying that moustache, Harry,' he said jovially. 'You're petting it like a sick dog.'

Harry had regained some of his optimism, too, on the grounds there was plenty a slip betwixt cup and lip. Tad might invite his mother-in-law but it didn't mean she would necessarily come.

'A sick dog? Look at you and your hair,' Harry replied playfully, 'which has gone one step further and got rigor mortis. How did you get it to play dead like that?'

'Brylcreem.'

'Marvellous stuff!' Harry lowered his voice. 'Between you and me, I'm using it on my tish.'

'Tish, is it now?'

Emlyn chuckled to himself and shook his head. 'Boys, boys.' And he turned towards the door, not for the first time, keeping an eye out for Nancy.

'Swap seats with me, Emlyn,' Tad said, 'before you strain your neck.'

'There's no need,' Emlyn said, but he stood up and they swapped seats anyway and got comfy again. 'There's no saying that the ladies will come tonight.'

'I bet you ten shillings they will,' Harry said, taking out his wallet.

'You've got insider knowledge! Put your money away.'

'Here they are now!' Tad said, and on account of good manners he and Emlyn stood up sharpish. Harry was less sharp because of his knees, and he raised himself a couple of inches off his stool and sat back down again because Mai wasn't looking at him anyway; she was deep in conversation with Helen.

Nancy came in behind them and smiled in their direction.

The smile was at the same time both shy and dazzling.

'She certainly looks happy to see you,' Tad observed.

Emlyn looked like a young man who had seen the girl of his dreams, blonde and fresh and beautiful. He made a deep noise of appreciation at the back of his throat.

'You're purring,' Tad said fondly, clapping him on the shoulder. It had always seemed a shame that Emlyn hadn't found himself a good woman and it wasn't for want of trying. He had spent a small fortune on engagement rings in his youth, but none of the future Mrs Hugheses had managed to hold their own against the current Mrs Hughes, his mother. By the time she moved into the bungalow and became Old Mrs Hughes, he'd run out of eligible women to take out. Excluding Nancy, of course.

'I'll sing my heart out tonight,' Emlyn promised him.

'Quite right, too,' Tad said, but immediately he was distracted by Mai. She and Helen had finished their conversation, and Mai was now looking their way. No, not their way – she was looking directly at Harry with what could have been the trace of a conspiratorial smile. He glanced at Harry, and Harry was semaphoring back to his wife with his eyebrows.

Only Helen was as ethereal and as cool as usual, and although logically he knew she was only looking round for a seat, he felt she was avoiding him and he wondered again why she had confided in Mai, of all people, before she confided in him.

The men from the choir were arriving now and the volume in the bar had increased. Oswald the organist was towering above them, like a heron amongst pigeons. Oddly enough, his height didn't get him served any quicker, as bar staff always caught sight of his chest and then looked beyond him to people more on their eye level.

For a moment Tad imagined grabbing hold of Helen and taking her outside into the hush of clean air to somewhere they could be quiet, like the churchyard. Sitting on a stranger's cold memorial in the blue evening shade of the yew trees he would tell her what he had so far found out from every source apart from her, and ask her to put this right.

'It's packed tonight. Word's got out,' Emlyn said.

'Word's got out? What word?'

'That the choir is singing "God Save the Queen" for the Coronation.'

'Well, I never!' Tad said, although he understood perfectly that there were times in people's lives when celebrations could only be expressed en masse, through singing and cheering and coming together. It was very hard to celebrate as just one person, alone. It was a good thing to have an audience there to listen. It made a big difference to their voices to sing to someone, to be listened to. 'That's grand, and they won't have long to wait. We'll get started in five minutes,' he said with relish. 'We'll give them full value for money tonight.'

21

As the sun tilted slowly towards the hills, taking with it the warmth of the day, Rhiannon tagged behind the little group of Flora, Lauren and Garth as they headed to the Hand for choir practice. She had cut the 'Age 13' label out of her skirt which her mother had let out, and was scratching the small of her back where the stub of it itched.

'Listen!' Garth said suddenly, holding his arms out to stop them in their tracks. The roar of conversation in the Hand could be heard all the way from Castle Street. He laughed. 'If a stranger came to the town looking for the place, it would be easy enough to find. "Follow the noise," I'd tell them. My mother thinks I'm noisy, sometimes. I wish she was here. She'd think I was a mouse after that.'

'Just imagine if they start singing now. It will be like a musical box,' Rhiannon said. 'We'd better hurry or there won't be time for them to get us drinks before they start.'

'I had a shandy at choir practice once,' Garth remembered.

'How come?'

'Someone left it on the table and I drank it. I feel bad about it now, to tell you the truth.'

'Did you feel tipsy?'

'I thought I did, for a moment, but it might have been the guilt.'

He ran his fingers through his red hair. 'I'm going home for my swimming trunks and a towel. I'll go right now. I'll see you on the bridge.'

They watched him run, and when he turned the corner out of sight Flora said, 'He won't, you know. We'll wait and wait and he won't come back. He'll say his mother needed him.'

'He'll end up like Emlyn Kremlin,' Lauren said. 'He'll have to look after his mother for the rest of his life.'

'There's nothing wrong with Emlyn Kremlin,' Flora said quickly.

'I know. I'm just saying. That's who he'll end up like.'

'He *might* come.' Rhiannon wound her hair around her hand.

Back at the bridge, a small crowd had gathered to watch the boys jump down into the foaming black water of the Dee. Flora was talking to one of them, Peter Thomas, and Lauren was staring up at the castle on the hill.

Rhiannon dragged her hand along the stone wall and looked down at the wrinkling river. Jumping off the bridge into the Dee was safe as long as you aimed for the right place, not the foaming part but the glassy pool, because it was true, she thought; still waters run deep.

Rhiannon leant over the bridge wall. She recognised one of the boys as the one Flora had said was Paul Baker, *rather rough*, and she pulled her blowing dark hair away from her face and sidled through the watching people.

Her heart jumped as she saw Garth climbing onto the bridge in baggy black shorts, holding on to the black lamp-post for balance, the international flags above his head snapping loudly like wet towels. Against the shadowy hills he was white and skinny and the evening sun lit up his hair like a match.

'Go *on*, mun,' Pete Thomas was saying to him. Pete shook his wet head like a dog, scattering cold black drips all around him. 'Remember to push off though – you want to jump out, not down.'

Rhiannon watched Garth edge along the wall until only the tips of his fingers still touched the lamp-post. Then he edged further, his arms wide and trembling, until he was facing the part of the river that was smooth as black ice. He swung his arms, ready to go, and then steadied himself.

Rhiannon felt her stomach muscles clench. Her heart started beating as hard as if she was on the wall.

Garth lifted his arms again, and wobbled, the sinews dancing on his feet like piano wires.

'Go *on*,' Pete said loudly, as though he was speaking for the whole crowd of people. 'Go on or get down.'

'Shut up, I know,' Garth said between clenched teeth.

Rhiannon watched the breeze tugging at his shorts, and he swung his arms again and went up on the toes of his long white feet.

Rhiannon felt the crowd thickening around her, settling against the wall like a people-drift, murmuring, nervous for him and longing for him to jump and all ready to sigh with relief – or grief – when he landed.

She felt sick from his indecision. What if he didn't jump out far enough? What if he hit the rock in the middle? It was a big rock, a sacrificial rock worn smooth by the current.

'Do it!' Pete said, all charged up by the size of the audience and eager to jump again before they lost interest.

'Ffff—' Garth began irritably but he saw Rhiannon.

'*Don't* do it,' she said, and her voice was high-pitched. 'It's stupid.'

Garth grinned at her. 'I know,' he said. He looked down at the black river and he stretched out his arms in a big gesture (maybe his last gesture, Rhiannon thought), and his arms stopped shaking as though his mind had suddenly released its hold on his body, leaving him free to step out into the long drop without thinking about it. He dropped without kicking; a skinny white blur.

Rhiannon heard the crowd sigh as he hit the black water. It cracked and foamed around him, and a long time passed before he rose back to the surface again, assisted by his air-filled shorts ballooning around his legs. He broke the surface and swam to the rock, and when he climbed onto it he rolled over and stared up at the sky. Rhiannon watched him, laughing, her hair whipping in the wind. She was amazed at how friendly the rock seemed now; completely harmless after all.

Garth got to his feet and paddled in the shallows to the bank. He was climbing the wooden steps, obliterating Pete's drying footprints with his own, when Rhiannon went to meet him. Her wavy hair was flying around her and she tried to hold it back as he stared at her, dripping.

'Mr Jones said we're not supposed to jump off the bridge,' she said.

Garth stepped gingerly onto the pavement and stood on one leg to brush the stones from his sole. He shrugged.

'Are you going to jump again?'

'Yeah.'

'I couldn't jump off the bridge, not in a million years. I was nearly too scared to watch, but I forced myself to,' she said, skipping sideways so that she could walk and watch him at the same time.

This was the most personal thing she'd ever said to him. She waited for him to say something back but he was staring at the crowd parting for him, making way for the hero; and they didn't want to get wet.

He stood under the flags and unzipped his sports bag and took a faded blue towel out which he draped casually around his neck.

Garth wiped his face with the corner of the rough towel.

His gaze drifted to the river where the currents tangled together in white torrents, by-passing cracked rocks in which bird-dropped seeds had taken root and leafed. White houses lay along the curve of the river, backdropped by green trees and hills. Behind them was the blank blue stare of the sky, clear as the eye of God.

Garth threw his towel onto his bag. He straightened up and, with his arm, he shielded the sun from his eyes as he looked towards the hills. Suddenly he jumped up onto the bridge wall and stretched out his arms. Then he jumped, legs kicking, hitting the chill river like a fist, sinking, rising, his pale shape materialising in the dark waters, swimming, emerging pink-skinned from the sting of the water as he dragged his belly onto the warm rock.

He rolled over onto his back and laughed at the sky. He felt entirely different now: triumphant and strong. He was fine, he hadn't drowned. He'd confronted his worst fear, head on, and beaten it.

He let only the smallest remnant of doubt cast a shade over his happiness as he wondered what his mother would say when she found out.

22

A few days later Garth was in the kitchen doing the dishes, up to his elbows in soap bubbles with his shirt cuffs getting dangerously wet. He was looking out at the hazy world behind the white net curtains with hunger. He'd always felt detached from it, but now he was eager to get out there in the spring evening light and be part of it. Devour it, even, because he had found out that he had an unexpected taste for danger which had started with the bridge jump.

He'd always been a cautious lad by nature, it was just the way he was.

To some boys, maybe most, rough-and-tumble came naturally. At the drop of a hat they wrestled in a flurry of limbs with cheering spectators in the noisy schoolyard, in public on the disapproving street, in private rolling over half-buried bricks and dandelion seeds on waste ground, energy erupting for no known reason.

But not him. He tried to avoid it by hanging out with girls, which had recently brought its own problems – he would never have done the jump if Flora hadn't talked him into it.

But they'd been a constant in his life so it wasn't that, it wasn't them, he concluded. It was him. He'd grown taller, and his school trousers, frugally purchased too large to leave room to grow into, were now too short around his ankles. He'd grown into them and then swiftly grown back out of them again.

And he had a chest. Logically, he knew it had always been there covering his ribs, but it had been so narrow and insignificant that he'd never taken much notice of it until his school shirts were tight around the buttons.

And he felt different in his head. All the worries that had troubled him for what seemed most of his life now looked manageable, and even welcome, like challenges to be undertaken and beaten.

There was no denying it, he concluded. He'd grown up.

He gave a shiver. It gave him great satisfaction to realise he'd found his courage without looking for it. It had just happened. He shook the froth from his hands and picked up the tea cloth to dry the crockery.

He'd been putting off talking about the party to his mother because he was waiting for a good time to do it, but the truth was there was never a time for her that was better than any other.

Too much time, and she would have longer to worry. But he was also aware that he couldn't leave it too late and spring it on her, because she needed to get used to it.

He took a penny out of his pocket, blew the fluff off it, tossed it, caught it. Heads it's now, tails it's later.

He lifted his hand.

Tails.

He was disappointed and prepared to toss again when he realised that this was the right time and the penny's only purpose was to make him come to the decision for himself.

He put the penny back in his pocket, put the plates

away in the cupboard and the cutlery in the cutlery drawer, and went quietly into the parlour in case she was sleeping in her chair.

She wasn't asleep, she was sitting up straight and looking out of the window. Her newspaper lay on the arm of the chair and her brown hair was sticking up at the back like a wren's tail.

'There's Waffles, doing his rounds,' she said, watching the corgi going into Helen's to check who was in.

Garth sat on the tapestry footstool by her feet and while he was there he lifted her blue plush slipper back on her heel.

She thanked him with a faint smile. 'That's nice of you.'

'I've been thinking, Mam. It's not long until the Coronation Party.'

Her smile faded. 'I know.'

'I want you to come,' he said gently. 'We're reserving you a place at the head of the table, just for you and you only have to stay as long as you're enjoying yourself.'

Although she was sitting still, her hazel eyes seemed to skip around in her head, not looking outwards at anything but looking inside at her frantic, scattering thoughts. 'Not the head of the table,' she said quickly, 'no, no. It's a responsibility, Garth.'

'Sorry, the foot,' he corrected himself. *Stupid.* 'The foot of the table.'

'Oh, the foot?'

'Out of respect for the Queen,' he said.

His mother's anxious face softened. '*There's* responsibilities,' she said, curling her fingers into the cuff of her beige cardigan. 'Coming to the throne, and her so young with everybody's eyes looking at her, wanting the experience for themselves and she can't stop them, can she? And she can't hide. Fair play to her. I'd run away, I would, Garth. I'd run to the hills.'

He hadn't really looked at the Queen in this light before. He'd always imagined she'd be happy to show off and be admired. That seemed to be one of the perks, in his opinion. 'Yes,' he said. 'It's true. Even if she's not in the mood when she wakes up on Coronation Day, she'll do it anyway.'

In the silence that hummed between them it suddenly seemed that he wasn't only referring to the Queen.

His mother seemed to think so too. She rested her forearms on her knees and looked down at him intently. Her eyes didn't seem as full of thoughts as usual. 'I'm beginning to think I ought to come,' she said at last, her voice lifting with surprise. 'Not because I want the fun, you understand.'

'No, I know.' Garth had the breathless sensation that he'd been blowing up a balloon and that this was the moment he should stop blowing because one puff more and the whole thing was likely to go pop, leaving him with a sorry knot of tattered rubber between his fingers.

As it was, he would let it bounce around so they got used to it.

He heard a rasp of heavy breathing at the door and Waffles looked in on them, his sturdy body swaying, happy to see that Garth was on his level. He nudged him with his hard head and let himself be patted by each of them in turn. Satisfied, he left to continue his rounds.

Garth unfolded himself from the footstool, stood up and stretched.

'Dew, I can see your ankles,' his mother said. 'Good job it's the holidays coming up or you'd be going to school in shorts again!'

Garth laughed. 'Everything's got too small for me all of a sudden.'

'You're going to be as tall as your dad.'

He shifted his weight awkwardly, as they didn't usually talk about his father. 'Anyway,' he said, 'the kitchen's neat and I'm going out for five minutes. Do you want anything before I go?'

'I'm fine, thank you.'

'See you later, then.' He was by the door when he heard her call him back. He wondered if he could ignore it but reluctantly, for love of her, he went back into the parlour. 'Hello?'

'You're champion,' she said.

23

On Saturday morning, Emlyn went to the newsagent's in Castle Street to fetch a newspaper for himself and a woman's magazine for his mother, accompanied by his dog. He was coming out of the shop when Flora approached from the bakery and Waffles barked a greeting.

'Hello, Waffles,' she said, bending to make a fuss of him.

'Hello, Flora,' Emlyn said.

'Hello, Emlyn! You're taking Mum to a dinner dance tonight, aren't you?' she said, walking with him.

'Dinner dance?' He was startled by the question, and he stopped to look at her. 'Who told you that?'

'Mum did.'

'A dinner dance,' he said, scratching his forehead with the edge of his newspaper. Did they hold dinner dances at the Boat Inn? He very much doubted it – there wasn't the space, and Tad would surely have extolled the romance of dancing above the attractions of a river with midges. He realised now that it had been a mistake asking two long-married men where they would go for a date. How would they know? As Flora was still looking at him, waiting for an answer, he nodded. 'I am, indeed,' he said heartily.

'She's ever so excited,' Flora said. 'See you later, Emlyn!'

'See you, Flora!' He was surprised but happy to hear that Nancy was excited about going to a dinner dance with him. He thought the excitement would be all on his side.

Now of course it was tempered by the realisation he had to find a dinner dance to take her to. He turned around and walked to the red telephone box by the library, feeling in his pocket for change.

He opened the door, relieved to see that the telephone directory for Chester and North Wales was still there, chained up, and only a bit blackened around the edges where somebody had tried to light it. Quite recently too, from the smell.

He first looked up dance halls with increasingly sooty fingers, and then dancing and dinner dances, and then, in desperation, ballrooms.

To his relief he finally found just the thing, an illustrated advertisement for the Grosvenor Ballroom, chandeliers and all. Oddly enough, the couple dancing in the picture sported a top hat and a crinoline, but the message was clear enough – this was a 'classy joint', a phrase he had learned from his American visitor who had come for the festival the year before.

He picked up the black receiver, put his money in the slot and dialled the number.

Five minutes later, with the satisfied feeling of a mission successfully accomplished, he was on his way back home for the second time, and a few minutes after that he turned around again – on the same spot as previously – and hurried back to the telephone box to pick up his newspaper and his mother's magazine which he'd left on the charred directory.

He went straight to his mother's with the magazine, and because he was still feeling pleased with himself he told her about the dinner dance at the Grosvenor. Then he made them both a cup of tea and sat opposite her in good humour.

His mother looked at him thoughtfully over her china cup, in between sipping her tea.

Then she said, 'I don't want to put a dampener on things but have you asked Nancy about her husband yet?'

Emlyn paused with his cup halfway to his mouth. 'No.'

'No?'

Old Mrs Hughes reached out and took a few moments to steady herself by straightening a horse brass next to the fireplace that didn't need straightening. 'I don't like to say this to you, Emlyn,' she said turning back to him soberly, 'but be careful until you know what you're getting yourself into.'

I don't care, Emlyn wanted to say, but he felt this was an occasion that called for a certain amount of maturity, so instead he said, 'You're right, of course. I'll bring it up with her, just to be sure.'

'Good lad. Set your mind at rest. It's for the best, Em.'

Emlyn knew that it was more to set her mind at rest than his, but for the first time he wondered about Nancy's silence on the subject of her husband. To Emlyn, what mattered was that she was still young, in her thirties, lively and beautiful. She had a life to live.

And more to the point, he thought stubbornly, so have I.

Emlyn spent that afternoon washing his car, a black Rover 14 with a Viking head mascot. While it wasn't new, he'd looked after it well, one careful owner. Petrol rationing had seen to that.

He had his shirt-sleeves rolled up and a bucket of soapy water by his feet when his neighbour Mrs Evans's youngest, five-year-old Owen, who'd been playing hopscotch by himself, took it upon himself to lend a hand. Emlyn got another rag for him and set Owen to cleaning the bumper.

Like Harry, Owen had maintained his stocky appearance throughout rationing, and he washed away with enthusiasm, and when the job was finished, Emlyn let him sit in the driver's seat. Owen told him to hop in and Emlyn sat in the passenger seat and patiently listened to his running commentary about the imaginary trip to the seaside that Owen was taking them on.

As Tad was passing he waved at Owen, and came over to have a chat with Emlyn at the same time. Owen told him to hop in, too, so Tad sat in the back to join them on the visit to the imaginary beach, and Emlyn told him about his new plans for the evening, which, 'no thanks to you', didn't involve the Boat Inn at all.

That evening, Emlyn was in his black-and-white tiled bathroom getting frustrated because his normally obedient hair wouldn't behave itself, and he spent a long time wetting his comb to get it right.

As a result he got dressed in a rush and only after he had put his jacket on with something of a struggle and hooked his white silk scarf around his neck as a finishing touch, he realised the reason it was tight was that he'd lost his sleeves up the arms of the jacket because his cufflinks weren't fastened. With an impatient sigh he took the jacket, scarf and shirt off, fastened the fiddly links, and with a certain amount of force, put the shirt back on again by squeezing his hands through the cuffs. Finally he was ready.

'I'll do,' he told himself in the cheval glass once he'd got himself straight again, but it was false modesty really because he fancied for a moment that he bore a resemblance to Gregory Peck.

He left the house, got in his gleaming Rover and drove the very short distance to Nancy's house.

Nancy was looking out for him at the front window, and she opened the door like a vision. Her blonde hair was curled away from her face, her lips were red, and she was wearing a cream-coloured gown with a white fur wrap around her shoulders and a beaded evening bag dangling from her wrist.

'You look—' Emlyn began breathlessly on the doorstep, and found himself lost for words.

'Thanks, Emlyn,' Nancy said easily, and she turned to say goodbye to Flora. 'Behave yourself, won't you,' she said with a smile.

'Same to you,' Flora said, grinning, her gaze directed at Emlyn now.

Emlyn raised his hand, and hurried ahead of Nancy to the car so that he could hold the door open.

'This is nice,' Nancy said happily as she got in.

Emlyn went round to the driver's seat and they looked at each other in admiring surprise. It was very intimate and secluded in the confines of the Rover, just the two of them.

Emlyn started the engine.

'Oh look, there's Mai, watching!' Nancy said. 'I'll give her a wave!'

'Don't open the window, the glass will fall out,' Emlyn said quickly.

Nancy laughed. 'All right! Where are we going?'

'The Grosvenor Ballroom.'

Nancy whistled appreciatively under her breath.

As Emlyn turned right onto Mill Street, he wondered when would be a suitable time to ask about her husband.

Part of him felt reluctant, but now that his mother had put some doubt into his mind he realised that he had sensed some reticence in Nancy that until now he'd been content to ignore.

He didn't know why he let his mother bother him. I'm a grown man heading towards middle age, he told himself, but he only half believed it. Didn't matter. It was enough tonight to play the part of one.

'What are you thinking?' Nancy asked him.

He glanced at her ruefully. 'To be honest, I'm wondering if I'll ever really grow up.'

'I hope not,' she said and laughed. 'I like you as you are.'

He grinned. 'Do you?'

'You know I do. Mind you, you took your time asking me out. I'd almost given up hope.'

'Really?' he asked, blinking in surprise. 'I thought you'd say no.'

Nancy gave a delicious laugh.

He wanted to look at her and keep looking at her, but his eyes were fixed on the road. He couldn't believe they were talking like this, like the friends they always had been but all dressed up for a night out with each other.

She filled the car with the scent of talcum powder and hair-spray, and she kept her pale hands on the beaded evening bag resting on her lap, radiating a mysterious glamour.

As he drove through the small village of Johnstown with the New Inn pub on the left – nice little place, he'd enjoyed many a pint there – he asked her about her work in Cuthbert's seed factory and she asked him about his at the Milk Marketing Board, just small talk really, keeping it light, like a code to hide the subtext of their attraction.

It was a beautiful evening. The spring sky was streaked with turquoise clouds over the green hills and Emlyn felt he had never seen anything so lovely in his life.

They drove in silence for a while.

Nancy was the first to break it. 'How does your mother feel about you taking me out? Apart from approving of my white whites, I mean,' she asked casually as they approached the outskirts of the town.

'Quite happy on the whole, surprisingly,' he replied.

Nancy turned her head away from him and looked through the window. She picked up the little beaded bag from her lap, the fine chain strap jingling like Christmas, and unclipped the gilt clasp to open it. She looked inside for a moment and shut it decisively with a click. 'She doesn't think you're too good for me?'

'She doesn't think that, no,' he said, which happened to be true.

'I suppose she rather wants to know about Flora's father,' Nancy said.

And there it was, out in the open, without any effort on his part after all. His heart lurched. 'She has shown a certain amount of curiosity about the subject,' he admitted, dodging a rabbit that ran across their path. He gripped the steering wheel more tightly as it disappeared into the brambly hedge on the other side of the road. 'I suppose we all have.' It felt like the right thing to say but he knew that if the subject upset her, it would destroy the wonderful mood of the evening. 'But as far as I'm concerned,' he added firmly, 'it's your business and nobody else's.' He truly believed this.

They were in the town proper now, down roads of red-brick houses of various sizes and grandeur. At the lights, two sheepdogs were having a friendly fight on the pavement and a woman in a headscarf was pushing a coach pram chock-full of children towards a man who raised his trilby to her.

'The thing is,' Nancy began as they started off again. 'The thing is, Emlyn, you might change your mind about me this evening.'

To his surprise, her voice was high and trembling and he frowned and pulled into the side of the road. Bumping up onto the kerb, he stopped the car and turned to look into her troubled eyes. 'Now why on earth would I do that?' he asked, astonished that she would even think it.

She grabbed hold of the ends of his white silk scarf as if she were drowning in water up to her wet, desperate eyes. 'Because I've never been married. I thought he loved me but I found out very quickly that he already had a wife and he wasn't the man I thought he was. But by then I was expecting Flora.'

'Ah,' Emlyn said. His mild tone was deceptive. His mind was in a turmoil. It was shocking, what she was telling him, not a shadow of a doubt, and yet looking at her lovely tear-washed face he felt nothing but pain for her hurt.

'And when I came to live in the town, it was a fresh start, Emlyn,' she said sadly.

'Yes, I understand,' he said, nodding. He did, he understood it perfectly. He had never looked for a fresh start himself, it had been forced upon him when the farm was sold. Until then he'd always been perfectly happy with his lot, but planning the party and asking Nancy out had come to him like a gift, like a dazzling light in his life.

He'd always believed there were lessons in life that only came in useful after the event, and this was one of them. He understood what she meant. 'What about Flora?' he asked. 'Does she know about her father?'

'She met him once, when she was small. He was home on leave from the army and in some sort of trouble. I told him I never wanted to see him again, and I never have.' A tear rolled down her cheek, leaving a pale track in her face powder.

He caught her tear on the edge of his hand and handed her his handkerchief.

'What you've told me,' he began steadily, 'well, it makes no difference to anything as far as I can see. You've never spoken about your past, and I shan't mention a word to anyone about it, you know that, don't you?'

'Yes.' Nancy nodded, and gave a shuddering sigh of relief. She closed her eyes for a moment, and when she opened them again her lashes had left black smudges of mascara. 'Thanks, Emlyn.'

She said it in her usual way, casual and airy, as if she didn't have a trouble in the world, and he felt a deep rush of love for her that was so unexpected it took his breath away.

Nancy took her powder compact out of her little bag to repair her make-up, and Emlyn started the engine. It stuttered unwillingly for a moment, but the car lived up to its Viking motif and roused itself into action, and moments later they were on their way again.

24

While Nancy was out with Emlyn, Lauren, Garth and Rhiannon went around to Flora's, using the excuse that they had to work on their poems for the Coronation competition.

'I'm going back to my original idea,' Rhiannon said. 'To be fair, it's my only idea, but there's more scope in five verses than two. There's a bit about being brothers and the whole world forming one family. And saving the Queen from assassins.'

'Why do they leave out the exciting verses? I've only ever sung one.' Garth's confidence about praise poetry had entirely left him. He didn't have any ideas at all. He lay full length on the sofa and stared at the ceiling for inspiration.

'I wish Mr Jones hadn't said no limericks,' Lauren said, 'because it's put the idea in my head now.'

While they lounged around her front room, chewing their pencils and trying to think of something, *anything* that rhymed with 'Queen Elizabeth', Flora opened a bottle of pop. 'By the way, if you're wondering where my mother is, Emlyn's taken her to a dinner dance.'

'No!' Rhiannon exclaimed, tucking her pencil behind her ear. 'I thought he was taking her to the Boat for a drink!'

Flora shook her head. 'Dinner dance. Definitely. They

were that smart! Emlyn was wearing a white silk scarf with a fringe.'

'Tad saw him cleaning his car,' Lauren said.

While this point didn't seem strictly relevant because Emlyn cleaned his car every Saturday unless it was raining, it was also part of the overall picture.

'They might get married,' Rhiannon said breathlessly. 'They might ask us to be bridesmaids. You'll definitely be one, Flora.'

'I know,' Flora said. 'We'll be the bridesmaids and you, Garth, you can be pageboy.'

'I'm too old to be a pageboy. I'd rather be best man.'

'You can't be best man, you're not a man,' Flora pointed out. 'Don't worry, you can be something else, I'll make sure of it.'

'I'm not wearing velvet or buckles. I'd rather not be anything than wear those.'

In the town, everyone tended to turn up for weddings whether they were invited or not. They would stand at the lychgate with confetti and take it all in, the little bridesmaid's tears, the pageboy's embarrassment, the bride's dress, the groom's hangover.

Rhiannon laughed. 'Black patent shoes,' she said, 'and knickerbockers.'

Garth blushed.

'Sorry,' she said quickly. 'I was only joking. I didn't mean to hurt your feelings.'

'Too late. My feelings have shattered into a million pieces,' he said. 'There, that's poetic!'

They laughed at this and Garth laughed too.

'You could put it in the poem!'

'What did I say again?'

But they had forgotten the words, only knowing that it was funny, and returned to the intriguing subject of Nancy and Emlyn.

'Emlyn Kremlin will be rich one day because his mother sold the farm,' Rhiannon said, rolling onto her front on the rug and kicking her legs in a way she wasn't allowed to do at home.

'Yeah.' It was generally taken for a fact in Little Green Street that this statement was true.

'Emlyn's not rich yet because he works for the Milk Marketing Board. But everyone knows Old Mrs Hughes is the richest woman in town,' Garth insisted respectfully.

'Old Mrs Hughes doesn't act rich,' Flora said, because there didn't seem to be any obvious evidence for it.

'How do rich people act?' Rhiannon asked curiously.

'They buy a mansion and stocks and shares and a yacht and that kind of thing,' Garth said, knowledgeably encompassing the world's riches with a sweep of his arms.

'We could be nice to her and she might leave us some money.'

'I doubt it.' Lauren studied her bitten nails and curled them into her palm. 'When she dies, Emlyn will get all her money. If they marry, Old Mrs Hughes would be your mother-in-law, Flora.'

'No, she wouldn't,' Garth said, 'she'd be Nancy's mother-in-law. She'd be your grandmother-in-law, Flora. Have you got any other grandmothers?'

Flora shook her head. 'No. Mum fell out with her mum when she was pregnant with me and wanted to keep me.

If she hadn't, I'd have been taken by strangers and put in an orphanage.'

This was big news to them. They looked at Flora with respect.

'An orphanage,' Rhiannon said softly. 'That's awful.'

'I know. I'd have been an orphan.' Flora sat up and hugged her knees and rested her chin on them. Her eyes were bright. 'I don't care about Old Mrs Hughes's money, or anything like that,' she said. 'But if they get married,' she added wistfully, 'Emlyn would be my dad, and I'd quite like that.'

They were quiet for a moment.

'Aw, Flora,' Lauren said.

'I'm just saying *if*.' Flora jumped to her feet restlessly, as if she didn't dare to hope for it too much. 'Come on! Let's go out somewhere. Let's go into town.'

'We haven't done our poems yet.'

'Just write anything, like I did, and don't think about it. I want to go out now so I'm here when Mum and Emlyn come back, just in case they kiss.'

'I can't imagine that,' Rhiannon said with a shudder.

'Why not? It would only be like your mum and dad kissing.'

Rhiannon shook her head. 'They don't do that kind of thing.'

'They must have once, or how did they have you, then?'

'I mean they don't do that kind of thing now they're old. Uch! Let's change the subject, I don't like even think-ing about it.'

'Finish your poems so we can go out,' Flora said firmly, getting frustrated. She looked at the clock. 'I'll give you fifteen minutes and if you're not ready by then I'm going out without you and you'll all have to go home.'

They agreed that it was impossible to get anything to rhyme with Elizabeth or Coronation, and 'Queen' was much easier.

So by means of Flora's blackmail, encouragement and threats, they wrote their poems, and with the feeling that they deserved a reward for this achievement, they cut through the back of Flora's garden, over the fence, scrambled down the bank to the river to avoid any prying eyes, and headed into town.

25

Meanwhile, at the Grosvenor, Nancy tucked her hand in the crook of Emlyn's elbow as they were greeted solemnly by a bewhiskered and bemedalled doorman with gold epaulettes, who welcomed them into a glamorous world of high ceilings, gilded columns and piano music.

A lavish crystal chandelier sprinkled rainbows of light as they walked beneath it. Emlyn stopped and looked up. He observed to his delight that the chandelier was very much like the one in the illustration in the charred phone book.

He was enjoying the feeling of the rich red carpeting under the thin soles of his highly polished shoes. 'Wilton,' he told Nancy knowledgeably. 'The carpet, I mean. Quality.'

'It's wonderful, isn't it?' she said, smiling. 'I suppose you come here all the time.'

'I've never set foot in the place in my life before,' Emlyn said seriously. 'To be honest, I didn't know it existed. I asked Tad and Harry where to take you, and they told me the Boat Inn was romantic, except for the midges. But then I wanted something more special than that and I found this in the phone book.'

To his immense surprise, Nancy burst out laughing. She laughed so hard that her muscles went weak and her fur wrap slid down her bare shoulders and she had to cling on to him, and although he had no idea what she was laughing at, her laughter was contagious and he found himself laughing uncontrollably too.

'Oh, Emlyn,' Nancy said, recovering herself and adjusting her fur. 'You are funny! Midges!'

The manager was standing by a lectern with his hands clasped behind his back and he watched them with a restrained smile of his own. Leading them to a table with a perfect view of the dance-floor, he pulled out a chair for Nancy and brought them the menu of the evening.

' "Cream of parsnip soup, roast loin of pork with apple sauce, and stewed apples and custard",' Emlyn read out loud and looked up at her to see if she approved. But he needn't have worried. Nancy looked gloriously happy, as happy as he'd ever seen her, and the conversation they'd had in the car might never have been.

She tilted her head, speculating. 'So you told Tad and Harry we were going out.'

'I did. It saves time and gossip,' Emlyn said. 'Did you tell anyone apart from Flora?'

'No. But I will though, now that you have.'

Emlyn smiled and looked up as the band came in – Charlie Dacre and his Orchestra, according to the name emblazoned on the drums.

A spotlight lit up the musicians and Charlie Dacre began to sing softly into the microphone, as intimately as if he were singing in their ears. A waiter brought the bowls of parsnip soup, and as they ate, Emlyn and Nancy watched the first couples take to the dance-floor in a swirl of skirts and handsome partners.

'I feel as if I'm in a dream,' Emlyn said, watching them.

'Do you remember Tad saying at the first meeting that we were "uncertainly poised between catastrophe and a golden age"?'

'When he was being Churchill?'

'Yes. For a while that was who I thought Harry was going to the party as, but I don't remember ever seeing Churchill with a moustache. Anyway, what I was going to say was, I think tonight that the balance has firmly tipped towards the golden age, don't you?'

'Let's hope so,' Nancy said softly, and clinked her port and lemon against Emlyn's glass of stout.

The spotlights coloured the dance-floor in pools of pink and blue, silhouetting the dancers and their graceful steps.

The loin of pork came with the promised apple sauce and peas and potatoes. Emlyn hadn't had pork for ages because sausages and tripe were better value, but he realised now what he'd been missing out on and his mind went to the ox roast that the Ministry of Food had exempted from rationing for traditionalists. He thought of Harry's comment about the Wild West. 'Harry was confusing oxen with bison!' he said suddenly, out of the blue. And then, seeing Nancy's puzzled expression, he asked her, 'Have you got any views on his moustache?'

'Plenty,' Nancy said eagerly, leaning towards him. 'You should hear Mai on the subject! She'd even thought of shaving it off secretly.' Her eyes gleamed with conspiracy. 'But then that night at choir practice, they were thick as thieves, did you notice?'

'I saw him waggling his eyebrows at her,' Emlyn agreed.

'Giving each other secret looks which they hadn't done

for ages. It's as if she's suddenly seen the attraction of it. I must say, it looks better now it's got past that straggly phase. And he's trimmed it, so it doesn't catch food in the same way it used to.'

'Imagine if she'd shaved it off, and him so proud of it!' Emlyn agreed.

'Mai knows who he's going to be at the party, but she's not saying.'

'Mai not saying something? That'll be a first. We'll see how long it lasts.' He said it fondly because they both liked Mai and they knew what she was like.

He wasn't concentrating too hard on the conversation because the pudding of apples and custard was on the table in front of them and once the meal was finished they would get up and go over to the dance-floor and other diners would look at them in admiration, hopefully, at this well-dressed man with Nancy in his arms, her cream dress shimmering like a mirage.

Every time he thought about her in his arms, his heart rate accelerated with anticipation and a certain amount of nervousness as well, because he hadn't had much experience of dancing for the last few years. She would be a good dancer, he was sure of that. She had that air about her.

When the moment came he finished off his pint of stout for confidence, placed the glass down a little too heavily, stood and held his hand out to take hers.

It felt small and cool in his, and for a moment they swung their arms, happy as children, then they turned to each other and he was holding her close. He rested his face against her hair as they swayed to the music, and he heard her humming dreamily to the song 'In a Golden Coach (There's a Heart of Gold)'.

'I love this one, don't you?' she murmured, her breath warm on his cheek.

'Yes,' he said, knowing he would have said yes to anything.

After all these years, he was with her, he'd done it at last, and the reality was better than his dreams.

When the evening was over and the band had packed up and the tables were being stripped, they went out to the car, the last one in the car park, and looked up at the starry sky.

Instead of driving back through the town the way they'd come, Emlyn took the longer route deep into the country-side and along the vast majestic curve of the Horseshoe Pass above the dark valley.

He parked in a layby and they got out of the car, two people on the top of the world.

To the east they could see the sprawling, shimmering lights of the town they had left, and to the right, like rain-drops in the curve of a leaf, the shining town that was home.

Above them, the numberless stars pierced the black sky. A profound hush had fallen over the world, and they were alone, the only two people left to appreciate its wonder.

Emlyn realised he had had his arms around Nancy most of the evening. Now they felt empty without her and it was only natural that he should take her in his arms again. She snuggled up to him, and they began to dance gently on top of the mountain, her fur stole tickling his cheek, humming their own tune and finishing with a spin.

After that, he leant over and kissed her gently. When he did, he felt his whole body grow very big, cavernous, with its own stars and solar system and storms and glories, except for his mouth, warm and loving on hers.

26

Lauren, Flora, Garth and Rhiannon slunk like cats along the quiet streets of the sleepy town, looking for trouble and scared they would find it.

The railway station's lights were on, illuminating the cream and russet bridge over the railway where their fathers had welcomed the German choir to the town four years after the war. The light streamed into the river, lights shone from the houses, while the hills and trees were holes in the dark and Crow Castle was absorbed by the night.

'Tad would kill me if he could see me now,' Lauren whispered when they reached the Royal Arms, hiding by the empty barrels and watching every shadow spring to life into someone she knew. 'Where are we going, anyway?'

They looked at each other in the dark.

'We're going in there to steal drinks,' Flora decided.

Lauren groaned. 'We can't! Everyone knows us. They know where we live.'

Flora looked at Garth. 'What do you say, Garth? You're the expert at stealing drinks.'

'No I'm not! You make it sound as if I'm a profes-sional. That time with the shandy, I did it on impulse,' Garth said indignantly, 'save it going to waste. It was on the table, unclaimed.'

'It's still stealing,' Flora said mildly. 'Look, all you have to do is dash in and grab one off the table. Make sure it's full so we can share it.'

'It'll spill if it's full,' Rhiannon pointed out. 'It's a stupid idea anyway. I'm going home. My dad will be wondering where I am.'

It wouldn't be the same with just the three of them, they all felt that, but Garth felt it the most. 'All right. Wait here,' he said. 'I won't be a minute.'

He crossed the yard. The light burning over the door lit him up for a moment. He hesitated and then went in. The door closed behind him.

Waiting for him, the minutes passed until they felt he'd been gone for a long time. They began to imagine all manner of things happening to him, from the landlord, the police, Mrs Pugh woken from her forty winks.

'This is your fault, Flora.'

'I didn't think he'd do it,' Flora protested.

Suddenly in a burst of noise, the door flew open and Garth came flying out shouting: 'Quick! Run!'

He grabbed hold of Rhiannon's hand and pulled her down the street, Flora trailing behind and Lauren sprinting past them all; they were chased by the sound of their own feet slapping on the dark pavements; their cloudy breath streamed behind them like banners.

'I know who you are, boy!' the landlord threatened from the doorway, his voice bouncing after them down the street. 'I know where you live!'

They chased behind Lauren all the way to the back of Flora's, and doubled over by the fence to hide and catch their breath, waiting to be discovered and denounced.

After a few minutes of tremulous waiting, they were still alone, just the four of them, with the river behind them and ivy underfoot.

'Sorry about that,' Garth said formally to Rhiannon, his pulse still ricocheting in his veins. 'Instinct. Look what I've got!' He took a bottle out of his pocket.

They looked at it in astonishment.

'You're going to get into serious trouble,' Rhiannon said.

'I know,' he said with a trace of pride in his voice. He felt in his pockets, took out a pen knife and opened the cap. 'Who's going first?'

'You go,' Flora said.

'What is it?' Rhiannon asked.

'Some kind of – some kind of beer.'

'Is it black?'

'Black?' Flora said. 'Who'd want a drink that was black?' She took a gulp and shuddered. 'It *tastes* black,' she said, passing it to Lauren.

Lauren choked on it. 'It tastes green to me. Here you are, Garth.'

Garth put the bottle straight into his mouth without wiping it.

Rhiannon felt a pang of anxiety about germs as the drink bubbled down the neck of the bottle.

'Ahhh! That's good stuff,' Garth said grandly, like a connoisseur, and passed Rhiannon the bottle. 'Cheers!'

The drink was bitter and she felt it rush down her gullet and pressed her hand on her chest in the place where it stopped. It reappeared in a mushroom cloud of warmth in her brain, and for a moment she felt better. 'Yuck!' she said after a mouthful, shaking her head like a dog. 'I thought it would taste nicer, or why do people bother with drinking at all?'

For a moment Lauren felt suddenly small and fearful, skulking in back gardens drinking stolen beer that left a taste in the mouth and getting into mischief under the big sky over the black hills. They would get found out any moment and wrath would rain down on them, a sudden river surge would pick them up in retribution or forked lightning fry them or a stranger sneak up on them from the dark. But the night was deserted and silent.

Rhiannon was wiping her tongue on her sleeve to get the taste off it.

Garth pushed the bottle into the ferns, and they looked in separate directions pretending it hadn't happened.

Lauren said, 'What will happen to us in the future?' She could feel Rhiannon's eyes on her.

'I don't know,' Rhiannon said. 'I wonder that, too.'

'We'll be happy, that's what will happen,' Flora said. 'There's the party in a couple of weeks and everything.'

'Yes.' Lauren nodded. 'We will, won't we?' She looked for Crow Castle above the town, but it was invisible in the dark.

Suddenly, the night brightened and they saw that the kitchen light was switched on, creating a bright square of green grass on the night-black lawn.

'My mum must be back,' Flora said, looking over the fence.

'Is Emlyn with her?' Lauren asked, hiding.

Flora stood on tiptoe. 'I can't see him. But I can't see Mum either.'

'She'll ask us where we've been,' Rhiannon said.

'We'll say we've been out for fresh air,' Lauren said. 'Tad's always telling me to get fresh air, I don't know why, it's the only sort we've got.'

'We could go through the back door and pretend we've been there all along.'

'Writing poetry intently.'

'Didn't hear her come in.'

They would do anything to keep out of trouble.

They climbed over the fence and went warily in through the kitchen door.

Nancy came in just as they closed the door behind them.

'Oh, hello,' she said, draping her fur stole on the back of the chair. Her dress gleamed richly in the kitchen light. 'I was wondering where you were.'

'We've been out for fresh air,' Lauren explained, testing out the excuse.

'Fresh air's overrated, if you ask me,' Nancy said with a smile.

It was very hard to look at her without wondering whether Emlyn was sitting in the front room, bolt upright, waiting for her.

'Was the dance nice?' Flora asked, picking up the stole and wrapping it round her like a hug.

Nancy smiled. It started off as a small, secret smile and finished off as a delighted laugh. 'It was impossibly wonderful,' she said.

'Is he still here?'

'No!' Nancy laughed again. 'I invited him in but the light was still on in the bungalow, Old Mrs Hughes was making sure there was no hanky-panky.'

In the kitchen, barefoot and happy, she seemed younger than all of them put together. 'Thank you for keeping Flora company,' she said.

Garth pointed awkwardly towards the front room. 'We'll just get our homework. Poems.'

'Oh, the poems! Yes, Flora said you had to do one for the Coronation competition. It would be nice if you could recite them at the party, wouldn't it? Each of you in turn, your personal tributes to the Queen. Seeing as you've gone to so much trouble to write them.'

They nodded seriously, staring at the floor.

It was always shameful, Lauren felt, when someone thought the best of you and you didn't deserve it. They'd dashed those poems off just so that they could go into the town with Flora. To their mind it was just more homework that they would rather do without. They hadn't thought of it as writing a personal tribute to the Queen.

They collected their exercise books, evidence of their diligence, and said goodnight.

27

The following evening, Helen was sitting by the fire listening to the closing bars of *The Archers* theme tune. She stood up to switch the radio off and turned to Tad, determined to do it now, this minute, before she changed her mind and put it off a bit longer.

'There's something I've been meaning to talk to you about,' she said, tucking her hands into the pockets of her navy dress.

Tad looked up at her quickly and put aside his pen and crossword puzzle. 'Oh? What is it?'

'You know how my parents loved royal occasions,' she began, playing with the pearl earring in her earlobe and choosing her words carefully.

'Of course I do,' he said.

'It's always been rather a tradition of ours, you see.' She gave him a faint smile, glancing into Tad's solemn brown eyes. 'Anyway, the point is, I recently received a letter from my mother.'

Before she could say any more, Tad cut in quickly so as to get to the moral high ground. 'Is that so? I've been thinking, we must invite Dorothea to the party. She can sit next to Old Mrs Hughes. I don't know why it didn't occur to me sooner!'

It seemed to Helen that there was something artificially hearty in the way he said it. She moved in front of the fire, feeling the comforting warmth against the back of her legs in her nylon stockings, and gave a dry laugh. 'Sit next to Old Mrs Hughes? Yes, she'll love that,' she said. 'I'm not suggesting she should come here, Tad. She wants us to go there, to enjoy the atmosphere together as a family, to be in the very heart of things, where it's all happening.'

'But we can just as easily be together as a family here,' Tad said patiently. 'She'll understand. Tell her I've organised the party and she's welcome to join us.'

Helen stared at him. His eyes looked amber in the firelight. What had she hoped he'd say? She knew he loved her, but she also felt she was only a part of his life and that when they'd married, he'd fitted her into the space he had kept for a wife. Most things in Tad's life had a permanence, a history that he took for granted. But she had left her own history behind, and over the last few days she'd had a longing for the past and the sense that she'd given her heritage away too easily.

With a sigh, she sat down again, smoothing her navy dress over her knees.

'Oh, Tad,' she said hopelessly, 'I feel so miserable about everything.'

'Don't feel miserable, invite her,' Tad said with renewed enthusiasm. 'She might jump at the chance of a break! Look at it this way, if we went there it would only be for the day because of school, whereas if she comes here she can stay as long as she likes.'

'You don't understand.'

But Tad was on a roll as usual. 'Tell you what, you write her the invitation and get the spare room ready and I'll find out the train times. There we are, you see, it's easy enough once it's out in the open. Hey! Where are you going, Helen?'

'Bed. I've got a headache,' she said abruptly as she left the room, slamming the door hard behind her.

The following morning, as Helen was hanging out washing in the sunshine, Mai called to her over the fence.

'What have you decided about London, Helen? Only Harry was wondering. Casually, like.'

Helen propped up the clothes line and picked up her laundry basket from the lawn. 'We've invited her here instead.'

'Oh, have you?' Mai asked with a noticeable lack of enthusiasm. 'I suppose that will be nice for her. And has she accepted?'

'Not yet, I've only just written.'

'I suppose she'll be pleased to be asked, even if she says no. At least she'll know you're thinking of her.'

Helen bit her lip and looked towards the distant green hills. 'It's not much consolation, is it?' she said.

28

Now that they were courting, Emlyn and Nancy went walking in the lush green countryside around the town.

One warm evening they headed down the lane to look at the old farm again, Valley View, its white farmhouse set amidst a sprawl of outhouses and barns.

It was very quiet. A couple of red hens pecked in the yard, but there were no signs of life behind the net curtains. Emlyn leant on the wooden gate, lost in memories, feeling painfully nostalgic to be back. There was a word for that feeling in Welsh, *hiraeth*, a longing, a yearning for what had been.

Nancy leant on the gate next to him, her yellow dress fluttering in the breeze, her slender arm touching his. She was remembering, too. 'I was so nervous the first time I came here to visit Flora. I'd never been to the country before and I was scared of everything.'

'Were you?' Emlyn asked her curiously. 'What were you scared of?'

'The chickens, the cows, the corgis. Scared because I couldn't understand Flora as her accent was changing. I remember we came through this gate and I saw you in the barn, moving bales of hay. You were wearing a shirt and a black waistcoat and your trousers were tied with string around the waist.'

'You saw me in the barn?' Emlyn asked, tilting his head to look at her. 'I didn't know that.'

'No, you were too busy working, focused on the job. But you looked solid, and I felt right then that somehow it was all going to be all right.' She gave him a quick glance. 'Not just me and Flora, but everything.'

Emlyn nodded, and his mind went back to that day too. 'I came in for tea and saw you sitting by the table between Flora and my mother like a ray of sunshine,' he remembered.

'You wolfed your food down and then you rushed out again.'

Emlyn laughed. 'I wish now I'd dressed up for you,' he said, 'now I know you were looking.'

They walked for miles beyond the farm until their legs ached, going up to the top of the dazzling limestone Eglwyseg Cliffs. Panting for breath, they rested in the springy purple heather, lying next to each other and staring up at the clouds creeping across the blue sky.

'It feels as if we're floating,' Nancy said. She stretched out her arms on the scratchy heather to balance herself and reached for his hand.

Emlyn closed his fingers around hers and after a while he couldn't be sure that he was touching anything but the air.

'Nancy?'

'Yeah?'

Emlyn turned on his side to look at her, propping himself up on his elbow.

'What?' she prompted him.

'Oh . . .' He rushed the words all at once. 'I think

I might love you, I just wanted you to know that.' He looked at her shyly.

To his relief he was met with the loveliest smile.

Here in the mountains, nearer to the sky, an invisible blackbird sang a few clear notes on the breeze with a careless flourish. Emlyn found his mind following the sound, as if it was Nancy's reply.

'Do you?' she said at last. She didn't move as he nodded. She was staring at the clouds, relaxed and lazy. 'Well, I love you too, Emlyn. You mean the world to me.' She shielded her face with her forearm and squinted at him from its shadow.

He turned onto his stomach, folded his heather-scratched arms and rested his chin on them, watching her with a smile. 'Yeah, you and me, right? I've fancied you for ages,' he confessed.

Nancy lifted her head to look at him with wonder in her clear blue eyes. 'You, Emlyn,' she said fondly, 'are without doubt the loveliest, most respectful man I've ever met.'

They could have stayed there for ever that evening, but the breeze grew sharper and they watched the sky lower itself onto the hills and the colours in the valley below gradually fade after being too long in the sun.

Emlyn got to his feet, held out his hands to her and pulled her up. They walked over the bracken, disturbing busy flies, right towards the very edge of the escarpment.

From up here you could see the valley and the khaki, sheep-flecked fields. Down on the valley floor, eroded limestone rocks littered the ground like pebbles. To the right, the outskirts of the town tucked behind the hill on which Crow Castle stood. Emlyn stretched out his arms as though it was all his.

'Don't go too near the edge!' Nancy said, hanging back. Her voice didn't carry. With his arms still outstretched, he turned to her. She seemed a long way off from where he was standing, right at the limestone lip, invincible.

'Come here, Nancy!'

'No,' she called back, 'you come here.'

So he came back to her, bounding over the springy moss.

When he reached her he put his arms around her and they kissed through the strong mesh of her flying blonde hair. They kissed fiercely at first, and eased off, tenderly and with wonder. Her skin felt warm and through his chest he could feel her heart racing with anticipation.

She rested her head on his shoulder and he drew his finger along the parting that cleaved her hair.

'Nancy? Can I ask you something?'

She flicked away a fly that came close and lifted her head to look at him. 'What?'

'Will it always be like this?'

She was silent for a few moments. She couldn't lie to him, not up here under the honest sky. 'Like this, or similar,' she said and laughed.

He entwined his fingers in hers and kissed her hand.

Before they left for home, they faced each other and Emlyn carefully picked bits of scrubby grass from her yellow dress and bracken from her wind-tangled hair, and Nancy brushed him down from head to waist and from knees to feet. They walked back along the road with their arms around each other, their hips bumping, little knowing of the disruption to come.

29

A few days later, with three and a half weeks to go before the party, Tad, Emlyn and Harry were having a pint in the Hand before choir practice when a soldier strolled into the bar wearing a khaki uniform. They looked at the stranger over their pints with the civilian's respect for a military man.

He was thin and battle-scarred and he looked around the room, sharp and narrow-eyed, taking it all in as if he was still on alert for the enemy. Then, satisfied, he leant on the bar.

'What will it be?' Billy asked him.

'Pint of stout,' the stranger said. 'I'm just back from Korea.'

'Then it's on the house, my friend,' Billy said.

'Much obliged.'

Harry leant across the table. 'Did you hear that? On the house!' he repeated jealously under his breath. 'Scottish,' he added. 'I've got an ear for accents.'

'Scottish!' Tad marvelled. 'What's he doing here, I wonder, all this way from home? He looks as if he hasn't eaten for a week.'

Just then, the soldier began to cough. It was a terrible, full-chested, body-racking cough, like a miner's, doubling him over in a spasm which seemed to go on interminably.

The whole bar was silent, waiting respectfully for it to end.

Finally, the stranger straightened up and took a large grubby handkerchief out of his pocket, spat into it and folded it carefully away again.

Emlyn gave a violent shudder. 'Sorry. I'm squeamish about that kind of thing. It could be TB, you know. That's what my father died of.'

Tad and Harry knew the story of Emlyn's father from way back but they didn't mind hearing it again.

Emlyn gave a rueful grin at the memory and blew out his cheeks. 'He was taken to the Hospital for Incurables.'

'There's pessimistic,' Tad said, shaking his head. He felt it was something he'd said before, too. 'Imagine seeing that written above the gates when you're lying in the ambulance! It's enough to finish you off in despair.'

'Aye, imagine.' Emlyn's gaze drifted over to the soldier again. 'Funnily enough, it didn't finish him off, though. After a few months, they sent him home.'

'Cured?' Harry asked, although he knew the answer.

'No, no, he was still incurable but he thought he had a better chance if he got out of there. He slept in a tent behind the farm. He thought the fresh air would help his lungs.'

'Did it?' Tad queried obligingly.

'No. Pneumonia got him in the end. One of life's ironies.'

Emlyn's story made them feel they deserved another pint, for comfort, and Emlyn got to his feet and went to the bar. The soldier was talking to one of the regulars, and Billy was listening in, polishing the same glass absentmindedly.

'You're going to wear a hole in that, Billy,' Emlyn said to him. 'Same again, please, and one for the stranger.'

The stranger heard and turned to him with a salute. 'Much obliged,' he said again.

Emlyn nodded in acknowledgement. 'My pleasure.'

The man started to cough and Emlyn turned away quickly, because he didn't want to see that handkerchief make an appearance again. It was something he could quite happily live the rest of his life without seeing.

He took the pints back to the table. 'Now. Where were we?' he asked.

'We haven't moved. You were at the bar, Emlyn, getting them in. I was asking Tad whether he had heard from the mother-in-law yet, that's where *we* were at any rate.'

'Sarcasm, is it!' Emlyn said amiably. Then he grew serious again. 'It's talking about my father that's done it, it always takes me to another place and I can't always find my way back to the present that quickly. There's a cure for it now, of course.'

Tad and Harry looked at him.

'TB.'

'Yes,' Harry said, stroking his moustache. 'I expect the army will sort him out. I only hope he's not infectious. Anyway, Tad. Any news from London?'

'Not so far, but we've got the spare room ready for the mother-in-law.'

'Quite right. It'll do her good and I can't see her turning down a celebration full of true Welsh hospitality with the choir thrown in,' Emlyn said. 'There's not a person alive who would turn that down, in my opinion.' He looked back at the stranger again. The town's good name was founded on the fact that it Welcomed the World, and to illustrate this legendary hospitality, the soldier had several pints lined up in front of him now, casting amber shadows on the polished bar. He was being well looked after and getting louder.

'I bet he's got some stories to tell,' Harry said thoughtfully.

'Does Nancy Hall drink here?' they heard the soldier ask Billy.

Her name rang out among the hubbub of words and Emlyn felt an electric shock go through him, the way her lovely name came with such familiarity out of the soldier's mouth.

Wide-eyed, he sought Billy's keen, perceptive gaze.

'Yes,' the barman was saying mildly, changing his focus from Emlyn and back to the soldier again. 'She comes in now and then. You know her, do you?'

The old soldier laughed. 'I'll say I do. Nancy's my girl.'

Like the humming silence when a bomb dropped, there wasn't a sound to be heard in the bar. Harry looked nervously towards the door, expecting to see the corgi launch his assault.

Emlyn and Tad sat agog, trying to take the information in.

Harry relaxed again. He looked at them. 'What did he say?'

Emlyn gestured to Harry to shut up and listen.

'Funny,' Billy said to the soldier easily without missing a beat, 'she never mentioned you.'

The soldier gave a sly grin. 'That's women for you,' he replied, sliding his empty glass to one side and picking a fresh pint out of the line-up. 'Anyway, I want to surprise her. See what she's been getting up to while I've been away.'

Tad looked at Emlyn in alarm, because there was something nasty in the way the soldier said it.

'What's your name?' Billy asked. 'I didn't catch it.'

'Jimmy Green. Sergeant. Gloucestershire Regiment.'

'If I see her, I'll tell her you were here.'

Emlyn carried on sitting by the table with his hand around his pint, and everything about him was utterly still apart from his mind which was lively with alarm.

'No need, I'll—' The soldier began to cough again, putting his body and soul into it, and his lungs too, but it was harder to feel the same degree of sympathy for him this time round.

'Did you hear that, Emlyn?' Tad said softly. 'He says Nancy's his girl.'

'Of course I heard it, man,' Emlyn said irritably. 'Everyone did.'

'Lor, who'd have thought,' Harry said in disbelief. 'I wonder where he's been all this time?'

'Korea,' Tad said helpfully.

At that moment, Oswald came in, ducking under the doorway to avoid knocking his panama off.

He stood next to the soldier, holding his leather music bag, his thoughts on nothing more than getting a pint before he started playing.

The soldier laughed. 'Cold up there, are you?' he asked loudly, standing back, chuckling, and with a jerk of his head inviting people to laugh at Oswald with him.

Oswald wasn't very sociable at the best of times unless the subject was music. He looked down at the soldier with a frown of distaste. 'Not particularly,' he said.

'I'll tell you where's cold,' the soldier said, lighting up a cigarette that he plucked from behind his ear. 'Korea. Got a light on you?'

'No,' Oswald said, in a voice chilled by the altitude.

'I bet you thought it was hot out there, didn't you? It's not. It's perishing.'

'I've never thought any such thing,' Oswald said in an offended tone of voice. 'I have no opinions on the place at all. Excuse me.' He picked up his pint and went over to Tad's table.

'Ignoramus!' the soldier called after him.

Tad pulled up a stool for Oswald and they sat with their heads together and regarded their pints casting golden blurs on the polished table.

'Who on earth is that vulgar man?' Oswald asked, still in the same offended tone.

'Nancy's husband,' Harry whispered, and winked.

Oswald said firmly, 'I suggest you drop the wink, Harry, it doesn't suit you.'

'Yes, shame on you, Harry,' Emlyn said.

He would have liked to have told them there and then that he'd heard from Nancy's own mouth she'd never been married, but he'd promised not to. In any case, he wasn't at all sure how they would take it. Tad would be all right, he felt, because his heart was in the right place. But Harry could be pompous about these things. He and Mai had standing in the community and their righteous disapproval seemed to carry a lot more weight in some quarters than the friendly approval of the majority. He decided he'd keep quiet until he'd spoken to her.

'Korea,' Oswald said seriously to Emlyn. 'He's been

fighting the Communists.' He breathed in deeply through his nostrils, which whistled. 'He looks a ruffian, doesn't he.'

Emlyn glanced across at the soldier speculatively. 'I was handy with my fists, once.'

'Eh? When was that?' Harry asked. 'I've known you all my life and I've never seen you raise your fist in anger. Or sport, either, come to that.'

'Well, anyway, there's his cough,' Tad said consolingly. 'It's bound to hinder him a bit, Emlyn. You could probably out-run him if you had to.'

Harry shook his head, but he seemed to relish the thought.

Oswald glanced at the soldier and looked at his watch. 'He's not staying for choir practice, is he?'

'Maybe the music will calm him down,' Tad said hopefully. 'It might be just what he needs.'

'Nancy will be here soon,' Emlyn realised, checking the time for himself and jumping to his feet. 'I'd better go and tell her the town's got a visitor,' he said, grabbing his hat. 'If I'm not back, start without me.'

'Start what?' the soldier asked, catching the last bit of the conversation and grinning as he leant on the bar. 'He's in a bit of a hurry! I've stirred a hornets' nest, all right,' he said, watching Emlyn leave.

30

Emlyn ran all the way back to Little Green Street, jacket flying, and knocked on Nancy's door.

'It's open,' she called from the shady hallway.

As he opened the door, the sun shone in, lighting her up.

She was getting ready, putting her lipstick on in the hall mirror. Her yellow dress, patterned with red roses, shone like summer, and she turned to him happily. 'Oh, hello, Emlyn!' Her smile faded instantly when she saw his expression. 'What's up? What's happened?'

'I've come to tell you there's a soldier calling himself Jimmy Green here, in town, in the Hand.'

Nancy's eyes widened in alarm. 'No, don't say that! I don't believe you!'

'He's asking after you. Says you're his girl.'

'He's crazy! But how—?' Nancy took a deep breath and turned back to the mirror. She put her lipstick in her pocket and patted her blonde hair absently. 'All right,' she said, swallowing so hard that the saliva squeaked in her throat. 'Did you say anything to him?'

'No, I didn't speak to him. He's back from the Korean War. He was doing all the talking and having a right old time of it.'

Nancy sat on the stairs and pulled her yellow skirt tight around her knees. 'Yes, he's a talker all right,' she said bitterly. 'I don't understand. After all this time,' she said, her voice breaking in despair, 'why would he come back now? What are people going to say?' She covered her face with her hands, cracked and dusty from her work in the seed factory. Emlyn went to sit next to her. Through the frosted glass on the front door Emlyn could see dark shapes bobbing about on the road outside. His heart went out to her and he looked at her helplessly, wondering the same thing.

What are people going to say?

There was no glossing over the obvious claim this soldier had on her and Flora. But his plain-speaking mother's unquestioning acceptance of Nancy and Flora all those years ago had acted as a buffer between her and the town. Nancy was fun-loving, no doubt about it, but she was thoughtful, too, and that counted for a lot.

It was one thing to condemn an unmarried mother in theory, but quite another in practice, he consoled himself, especially when it was someone you knew and loved.

'Look, Nancy – the thing is, see—' Frustrated, he combed his fingers through his Brylcreemed quiff and it stuck out like prickles. 'You and me – this soldier—' he said, agitated. He squeezed his eyes shut to concentrate his thoughts. Then he turned to her and peeled her hands away from her lovely face to look into her blue, watery eyes. 'I don't know what's the matter with me,' he said, forcing a smile. 'I'm speaking Morse code in stops and starts.'

He settled his words in order and started again. It was easier now he was holding her. 'What I mean to say is, you've got me now. And I know that doesn't seem like much to you at the moment, but it's not just me, we've got the whole street behind us, and the choir, and the regulars at the Hand, and the congregation of the church.' He looked down between his feet at the runner on the stairs, the pattern of dark red swirls and curves between his polished shoes.

Nancy had always been, without knowing it, the sweetener on the grapefruit of his life. He was suddenly aware he was fighting for their future, and the adrenaline surged fiercely through his veins. He wasn't going to let it go readily, he would hold on to it as tightly as he could.

'All those committee meetings that you've sat through from the start, the yards of bunting, the preparation. How many times does something like this happen in a lifetime that we all come together of the same mind, for the same communal purpose, in glorious celebration? We won't let him spoil that. You're safe here, as safe as you've always been.'

Nancy was bending her head, resting her forehead on her knees.

Emlyn looked at her slim neck under the neat blonde curls, the pale curve of the bone at the top of her spine. He *would* protect her.

Nancy's voice was muffled by her flowery skirt. 'I'm not sure everybody will be as decent as you about me not being married. Mai, for instance.'

He felt a cool rush of logic like a mountain breeze on a hot day. He put his arm around her slender waist, and felt her trembling against him. 'Better not to be married,' he said a little too loudly, 'than to be married to him.'

And suddenly it became clear. He realised there was one single, outstanding solution to the whole problem. It was so stunningly obvious that he was surprised he hadn't thought of it before. 'Because,' he went on, speaking the words against her soft hair, 'it means you can marry me.'

He wasn't surprised to hear himself mention marriage. He'd been thinking about it since their kiss on the Horseshoe Pass.

Nancy didn't respond at first. She stayed curled up on the stairs, clutching her knees.

Emlyn straightened up and stared at her in confusion and love. He wondered whether she'd heard.

When she did stir, she uncurled herself and gazed at him, and all he could see were the translucent flecks in her startling blue eyes.

'Why, Emlyn?' she asked, perplexed.

'Well . . .' He could think of many pluses right off the top of his head, but he didn't want to bombard her with facts so he chose the best of them. 'Because I love you. Oh, Nancy!' he said quickly. 'Don't cry!'

'Emlyn.' She hugged her knees to her chest again as if she was about to lose them for ever. 'I love you,' she said, her voice muffled.

For want of anything better to do, he stroked her rocking back as though she was a baby and with his spare hand he felt frantically for his pocket handkerchief, clean, thank the Lord, to have it ready for when she emerged from her tears.

She came to herself eventually, snuffly and stuffed up, her eyes smudged and pink with tears, and clutched his hand.

He knew in that moment he would defend her to his dying breath. Aye, people would talk, no doubt, but before they did, he and Nancy would tell them and let them do with the truth what they wanted.

'It usually takes me ages to make a decision,' he said, marvelling.

But it was different now under the cold shadow of the soldier. He thought of him propping up the bar in the Hand, waiting for Nancy to arrive. 'Do you think if I had a civilised talk with Jimmy Green, man to man, so to speak, he'd go away?'

'I'm afraid only one of you would be civilised,' she said ruefully, wiping the tears from her face with the palms of her hands.

'Oh. Right.' A fresh thought niggled at him. 'And what about Flora?'

Nancy bit her lip. 'Apart from one visit when he stole her money box he doesn't want to know her.'

Emlyn shook his head because this seemed to him both very sad and a great source of relief. 'Right then. Let's deal with the immediate present. What shall we do about choir practice? Stay here or go? I told them to carry on without me if I didn't come back.'

Nancy pressed her knuckles against her mouth until they were pale and bloodless.

'Let's go,' she decided at last, 'and carry on as we normally do. Keep our chins up.' She smoothed her tear-damp skirt and looked at him, and saw what he looked like. She gave a crooked smile. 'You might want to borrow this comb, your hair's gone wild,' she said.

They got to their feet and looked in the mirror.

'My word, it has.' Emlyn, like Nancy, was pale and bedraggled after wrestling their problems. They didn't look their best. They looked lovelier than that.

He combed his quiff back into shape and she went to

the bathroom to wash her face and get, as she put it, presentable again. When they were ready to go out they looked at each other with the determined expression of two people ready to face a challenge.

Once they were outside in the cool evening, they saw Helen coming out of her house at the same time. Their front doors slammed in unison.

Helen waved a greeting. 'Mai's going to wait for us by the bridge. I wasn't going to come tonight, to teach Tad a lesson, but then I thought – what's the point? I'm not sure he'd notice whether I was there or not.'

'I'm glad you changed your mind,' Nancy said in her usual light-hearted way. 'The more the merrier because there will be ructions tonight. My very much ex has turned up.'

'What? Really? I thought—well, never mind,' Helen said, confused.

This was one of those times when Emlyn was glad of her English reserve. It had its limits, though, and Helen went to walk the other side of Nancy, hooking her arm in hers. 'What's he like, your ex?'

'Awful, you'll see. I haven't seen him yet. Emlyn has, though.'

'Go on, Emlyn, spill the beans.'

As they walked, Emlyn tried to paint a verbal picture of the soldier, starting with his most outstanding characteristic. 'He's got a cough that would frighten the cows,' he said. 'Seems jovial enough. Chatty. Good at putting them away and telling a yarn. But he has a bit of a side to him, sarcastic, like. Put Oswald's back up by commenting on his height.'

'Oswald hates that. As if he didn't know about it,' Helen said.

'Exactly.'

'Anything else?' Helen asked hopefully.

Emlyn's face was troubled. He thought about it for a moment as they turned into Castle Street. 'No, I don't think so.'

Just then, he saw Mai waving at them from the bridge and pointing at her watch. 'Hurry up!' she shouted over to them. 'We're going to be late! You've taken ages, you lot.'

They crossed the river and Mai chivvied them about their tardiness until they reached the Hand, so they put off telling her the news.

Once again, the bar was crowded and roaring with conversation.

'Is he here?' Helen asked Nancy, looking round.

Tad was standing by the piano with Oswald, looking at the piano score. Emlyn hurried over.

Oswald looked up. 'Did you see him outside?'

'No, has he gone?' Emlyn asked.

'Yes, but he wouldn't have gone very far. Billy refused to serve him any more on account of his being drunk. By the time he left he'd developed a curve to his step, walking crescent-shaped, he was. It took him three tries to get out of the door and even then it was touch and go. He had to feel his way out in the end. He's gone to look for a more convivial establishment, he said. Hello, Nancy,' he added pleasantly, to Emlyn's relief.

Good old Oswald.

'Right then, boys! Let's get started,' Oswald called out. He sat down at the piano and struck a chord resonantly.

Billy, anticipating a crowd, had brought in extra chairs from the dining room, so Helen and Nancy sat with six others at a table meant for two while Emlyn brought their drinks.

After having a word with Harry, Mai strode towards them, elbowing through the scrum like a short, imperious emperor, and confronted Nancy with her hands on her hips.

'You'll never guess, Nancy! Your soldier's been in,' she said gleefully. 'Your *soldier*!' she repeated with emphasis, putting her face so close to Nancy's that they were almost nose to nose. 'It must be like a miracle to you!' Her ever-searching gossip's eyes were gleaming with excitement. 'And he doesn't know about Emlyn yet. They've kept mum so far, but you know how people talk.'

'Do they, Mai?' Nancy asked. 'I hadn't realised.'

At that moment Oswald played the opening chords of the national anthem and the whole room got to its feet, so Mai's reply was lost in a wall of chests as the choir began to sing.

During the choir's break for refreshments, Emlyn joined Tad at the bar with a request.

'I would like you to call an Extraordinary Committee Meeting,' he said.

Tad was waving a ten-shilling note at Billy to get his attention.

'It's about – recent events.' He jerked his head towards the door that Jimmy Green had only recently felt his way through.

Tad momentarily forgot about ordering and rested his money arm on the bar. 'I see.'

'It's easier to tell everyone at once so that they all hear the same story, otherwise people only remember bits of it. Or imagine them.'

'You've got me on tenterhooks,' Tad said, and felt the ten-shilling note sliding out of his fingers. 'Thanks, Billy, same again! Right you are, then. I could tell you'd been thinking as soon as you walked in, Emlyn. You had that drained look about you. I know pondering takes it out of you.'

'I've a good mind to ask for a Scotch to recover from the insult.'

'Scotch, Emlyn?' the barman asked patiently.

But it reminded Emlyn too much of the soldier, and he shook his head.

Towards the end of the evening, when choir practice was over and everyone was relaxed and the soldier forgotten, they started to sing old songs for pleasure. In the middle of a song about a big saucepan and a little saucepan, a terrible, unearthly noise disturbed the harmony. It was somebody singing badly off-key.

'Good heavens!' Oswald cried, slamming down the piano lid. He jumped to his feet in alarm and pointed towards the window.

A hideous, twisted face leered at them, and under the white, flattened nose a tongue was smearing the glass like a slug. *'Eeeeeeeeee! Eeeeeeeeeee!'*

'It's him again,' Oswald said. 'I'd recognise that cap anywhere!'

The face disappeared and the noise stopped.

'Have a quick look, Oswald, in case he's fallen in the river,' Billy said.

'Fallen in the river?' Mai was both shocked and thrilled at the same time. 'Come on, Nancy,' she said, tugging her arm, 'don't you want to see if he's all right?'

Nancy flushed. 'Not particularly.'

Oswald opened the sash window and looked out. 'No, he's fine, he's sitting down under the windowsill.' He leant out a little further. 'I think he's nodded off.'

'Time, gentlemen, please, and ladies too,' Billy said, ringing the bell. 'We've had enough excitement for one evening. I thought it was Gogmagog for a minute, come down from Crow Castle.'

Picking up their coats and bags, Helen, Nancy and Mai left the Hand together on the warm, dark evening, followed along Castle Street by their three men. They were all keeping a keen eye out for Jimmy Green, the men because they were being cautious and Helen and Mai out of curiosity.

'I think we ought to have the Extraordinary Meeting after lunch,' Emlyn was saying, 'because people concentrate better when they're full.'

'Whenever you think, Emlyn,' Tad said. 'It's your meeting after all.'

'I hope there won't be shenanigans,' Mai said excitedly, lagging back to speak to her husband, 'don't you, Harry? Nothing like this has ever happened in this town before. And him, disturbing choir practice!'

'What do you mean, shenanigans?' Harry asked.

'It's untidy living, isn't it?' Mai began piously. 'Her past is catching up with her.'

'Keep your voice down, Mai, everyone's sleeping,' Harry reminded his wife in the hushed dark. 'It's gone ten. I heard

201

the church clock strike as we left the pub.' And as an after-thought, 'I wonder where he'll stay tonight?'

There was no need for him to say who.

It was impossible to know the answer to the question, so they walked the last bit of the way in an uncomfortable silence.

No doubt it was something that they would find out very soon.

31

Emlyn saw that the light in his mother's bungalow was still on when he got back from the Hand, and wishing everyone a good night, he tapped on the window to alert her before he opened the door and went inside, stepping over Waffles stretched out in the hall like a draft excluder.

The parlour was cosy with the warmth of the fire.

'You're a latecomer,' Old Mrs Hughes said, putting down her knitting. She reached for the poker and coaxed the remaining heat out of the glowing coals.

'I've got something to tell you.' Emlyn clasped his hands behind his back. 'I'm very fond of Nancy,' he began.

'There's formal!' She rested the poker on the brass fender. 'Why don't you sit down?'

'I can't. You mustn't interrupt me or I'll lose my train of thought. Now, Nancy had Flora, um, out of wedlock when she was nineteen years old. I know you'll be shocked by that, but the fellow was a womaniser and already married, which she didn't know about at the time. But for all that, he was reluctant to let her go. He was in the army, and away for long periods at a time and she moved here and moved on and has done her best to forget about him.'

'But he's come back now,' Old Mrs Hughes said astutely, staring at the fire.

'How did you know that? Have you seen him?'

'It's the obvious climax to the story, otherwise why tell it?'

'Fair point,' Emlyn conceded. 'But you're wrong about it being the climax. I've asked Nancy to marry me. There!'

Old Mrs Hughes picked up her knitting and placed the ball of wool in her lap. The clickety-click of the needles seemed to Emlyn like the workings of his mother's mind. Very soothing it was, and he waited for her judgement.

'Of course,' she said eventually, still knitting as she ravelled her thoughts, 'it would have been neater if she was a war widow. But Nancy never ever mentioned a husband when she came to visit Flora and she had plenty of chance to do so. And Flora never talked about her father to me at all. You remember, she wrote little notes to her mother constantly, they broke my heart, they did. And when Nancy first came to visit, and we met her at the station—' Old Mrs Hughes smiled to herself '—they rushed at each other like magnets, I thought they'd never let each other go.'

Emlyn was nodding at his mother's reminiscences.

'When I saw Nancy that first time,' Old Mrs Hughes continued, 'stepping off the train, my heart fell into my shoes, Emlyn. I thought, oh dear, she's a beauty and no mistake. I knew it couldn't be easy for her, looking as she did, and I could tell from the start she hadn't led a regular life. And then when Flora was settled and Nancy told me she wanted to move here, too, she never once mentioned family. It was always just the two of them. And I felt in my heart I knew the reason why.'

Emlyn looked at her hopelessly. 'People are going to talk, aren't they,' he said.

His mother's eyes were wise and troubled. 'Oh yes, there's no doubt about that, Em. But people behave differently during wartime; fear and hardship sees to that. I'm not making excuses, mind, but we all know how desperation feels and we have to cope with life as best we can. I can see you've made up your mind about where you stand. You haven't come to me for advice, have you?'

'No. But if I had?'

'I'd advise you to hold your head up high, and Nancy, too.'

'That's all?'

She looked up at him, her eyes gentle and her face creased with love. 'She makes life easy for you, Em, and you make it easy for her, and that's what matters. Hold fast to it. It's all I've ever wanted for you, because life is hard for everyone, like it or not, and we have to cherish what warmth and comfort we can get.'

Emlyn sat down at last, unaccountably moved by her words. He stared into the dying fire as it smouldered red, and they watched it against the ticking of the grandfather clock until the glowing ash turned grey.

After a good few minutes of companionable silence, he leant over and gratefully pressed his hand on his mother's and kissed her weather-worn cheek. He didn't have words to thank her, but as he looked at her kind face he knew he didn't need them.

'I'll be off then,' he said. 'Goodnight.' And with a smile, he headed off home.

32

Mai and Harry were early for the Extraordinary Committee Meeting because Mai wanted a chat with Helen around the dining table before it got started.

'I don't know why we're bothering with the meeting,' she said, busily pinning up her bun which had come loose in the excitement. 'It's pointless, if you ask me. We all know what's going to happen! Nancy's going to tell us she's going back to Liverpool with Jimmy Green and taking Flora. Mark my words! What else can she do?' she asked, her dark eyes gleaming.

Helen disagreed. 'I don't know, I think you're on the wrong tack, there. She didn't give me that impression. And what about Emlyn?'

'Exactly!' Mai said, folding her arms. 'Poor old Emlyn! He's got his reputation to think about, and his mother's, too. Best Nancy does the decent thing and leaves, because she's never going to live this down, not after we all witnessed Jimmy Green staggering against the window last night. Drunk as a lord, he was!'

'He certainly made a dreadful spectacle of himself,' Helen said. 'And all that screeching! I thought it was foxes, did you?'

'Foxes!' Harry laughed. 'You're a city girl, Helen, and no mistake! I'll tell you what that was – shell shock,' he said knowingly. 'It makes a soldier very unpredictable.'

'I suppose it does. Somehow that makes it worse. I hope Nancy will still be here for the party, though.'

'No, no, no. Better for her not to be, Helen,' Mai said. 'Just think, what if he comes and ruins it on purpose? He seemed the unpredictable type, as Harry says, and better if she takes him home, I think. Safer for all of us.'

'We'll miss her,' Helen said.

'Miss who?' Lauren asked, coming in to see if anyone had turned up yet.

'Nancy, if she leaves.'

Lauren looked anguished. 'Where's she going? Will Flora go, too?'

Mai and Helen looked at each other with a 'not in front of the children' expression just as Tad hurried in, checking the time.

'Oh, hello, Mai, what's happened to Emlyn and Nancy?'

He needn't have worried because they came into the Boardroom on the dot of two in real time, or five past by Tad's reckoning.

Nancy was biting her thumbnail nervously, and Emlyn looked unusually stern as he pulled out a chair for her.

'Right,' Tad said, getting straight to the point once they were settled. 'Emlyn has called this meeting to forestall any gossip.'

'Too late for that, Tad,' Harry said cheerfully, 'Mai's been at it like a town crier.'

'Yes. Well.' That was true enough, Tad thought, scratching the back of his neck awkwardly. 'Over to you, Emlyn.'

Emlyn stood up, smoothed his dark hair back and rolled his sleeves up neatly in a business-like manner. He glanced quickly at Nancy, cleared his throat and announced, 'I'll get straight to the point, I've asked Nancy to marry me and she's accepted.'

'Hey! Nobody told me about this,' Mai said indignantly.

'Be fair, I've just told you now,' Emlyn pointed out.

'Aren't you forgetting Jimmy Green?' Harry asked.

'Yes,' Mai said, backing her husband up. 'What about him? I don't understand, how can you get married? Does that mean you're a divorced woman, Nancy?' she asked suspiciously.

Nancy flushed and looked down at her hands. 'No.'

'Bigamy?' Mai asked eagerly.

'Steady on, Mai,' Emlyn cautioned.

'It's all right, Emlyn.' Nancy bit her lower lip. Looking straight at Mai she said softly, 'Jimmy Green and I were never married. He already had a wife at the time of our brief romance, who he neglected to tell me about.' The blush was fading from her cheeks and she looked pale.

'Sinful of him!' Mai exclaimed.

'Yes, it was, rather,' Nancy said, on the brink of tears. 'Anything else you want to know?'

'Plenty!' Mai said indignantly. 'How do you know that Mr Griffiths the minister will marry you, considering the circumstances? Have you spoken to him?'

Nancy shook her head.

Under the table, Emlyn took Nancy's hand and entwined his fingers in hers. 'Not yet,' he said. 'But he knows us well.'

'Still, what if he won't?' Mai persisted.

It seemed a good point. The committee members fleetingly met each other's gaze across the table and looked away again.

'And then there's Jimmy Green,' Mai went on. 'What

are we going to do about him? Staggering around the town drunk like that, it gives the place a bad name!'

'We're not going to do anything about him,' Tad said firmly, feeling he was on surer ground now. 'He's come as a visitor to the town, through no fault of anybody's as far as I can see. We have an international reputation for Welcoming the World, and whether we like it or not, that includes Jimmy Green, in my view. I think we can depend on him, as a British military man, to behave decently and leave well alone once he knows Emlyn intends to marry Nancy.'

'Behave decently? No chance! He made a terrible, uncivilised noise at choir practice,' Harry pointed out. 'He was wailing like a banshee.'

'What's a banshee?' Mai asked.

'It's a—' Harry began, stroking his moustache. 'Tad can explain it better than I can.'

Tad stood up again quickly before Mai asked him for a definition. Although he admired Emlyn for wanting to get things straight, announcing their marriage did seem a bit premature. They were already getting it in the neck from Mai. 'Right! Are there any more questions for Emlyn and Nancy before we bring the meeting to a close?'

'Yes!' Mai said with alacrity. 'I think the committee should vote that Emlyn and Nancy put all ideas of courting aside until they've sorted their affairs out.'

'Mai!' Helen said, outraged. 'That's nothing to do with you!'

But the reference to affairs was unfortunate and they looked at each other uncomfortably.

'Tad!' Helen appealed. 'Tell Mai it's none of her business. We're not voting on it!'

'No, no, of course we're not,' Tad said vaguely.

Emlyn's handsome face was tight with strain.

'There we are! That's your answer,' Tad said, relieved to be breaking the awkward silence. 'If there's nothing else, I'm bringing this meeting to a close.'

They all scrambled to their feet, leaving Emlyn and Nancy still sitting there.

'Short and sweet,' Harry said. 'I don't mean you, Mai.'

'I should hope not,' Mai grumbled, and Harry laughed.

33

With two weeks left until the Coronation, the committee members were decorating the street with bunting, tying it from lamp-post to lamp-post using Emlyn's wooden window-cleaning ladder.

Harry shared out Union Jacks that had been distributed to churches by the local council, and he went knocking at Garth's mother's door more out of courtesy than from any expectation that she would answer it.

But he could hear her carpet slippers shuffling along the hall, so he waited, and she opened the door a fraction and peered out at him anxiously.

'Hello, Barbara,' Harry said warmly. 'I've brought a couple of flags for you to put in your windows. You're looking well.'

To be honest, it was hard to tell just from the nose and one eye that he could see, and it was so long since he'd seen her close up that he couldn't precisely remember how she usually looked. She seemed to have a little colour in the one cheek he could see, which, except in cases of fever, he always took to be a sign of good health.

'Thank you, Harry,' she said, perfectly civilised, and opened the door properly. 'How's things?'

'Can't complain,' he said, and here the conversation seemed to come to a halt.

He handed her the two flags, and to be neighbourly he

unthinkingly said, 'Garth's getting tall, isn't he? Rhiannon said he was jumping off the bridge the other day with Paul Baker and Peter Thomas. Chip off the old block,' he chuckled, reminiscing. And he would have continued along these lines except that she interrupted him.

'Harry, I'm stopping you there. Garth wouldn't do that,' she said coldly.

Harry didn't like to be wrong about things. 'Rhiannon wouldn't tell me a lie. It was him, definitely. She watched him with her own eyes. He's growing up, isn't he! I remember—' Too late, he saw the effect his words were having on her.

Barbara Pugh slammed the door so hard that the door knocker rocked in the brass lion's head.

That needs a good polish, Harry thought, looking at it from only two inches away.

He knocked at the door again. Holding the letterbox open with his finger he called, 'Mrs Pugh? Barbara? Obviously a case of mistaken identity. My fault.'

He listened out but all he heard was the fading whisper of her slippers on the hall runner.

That's what you get for being neighbourly, he thought. He wished he'd kept quiet, now.

Garth got home from school that afternoon, tie adrift and a shoelace undone, to find his mother waiting for him by the empty hearth, white and rigid with anger.

Before he could say a word, she leapt at him and grabbed him by the arm, her voice shrill. 'How could you, after what happened to your father? How could you put me through it again?'

'What?' He dropped his school bag onto the rug, scared and baffled. 'What do you mean?'

'Jumping off the bridge! After you *promised* me.'

'Oh. That.' He wasn't really surprised she knew, although he wished she didn't. Word got round in a small town. 'I don't remember promising,' he said, frowning. 'Did I?'

'You promised me you were scared of the water, Garth,' she said in a deep, threatening voice that was more alarming than her shrill one.

'Yeah. I was, at first.' He noticed the Union Jacks lying folded neatly on the sofa. 'Where did they come from?'

'Harry Lloyd brought them.'

'Oh, right. Harry Lloyd told you.'

'And you needn't think I'm coming to the Coronation Party now,' she said bitterly. 'I wouldn't do a thing for you, after the pain you've caused me. I'm washing my hands of you.'

Garth knew from dismal experience that he had to be patient and wait it out. Her anger would subside sooner or later, and the turbulence would settle. In the meantime he stared at his scuffed school shoes while he waited, noticing one of his laces was frayed at the end, while her words came in waves as she told him that she had suffered enough with one loss and now he was risking her facing another and how could he? How *could* he?

Listening to her, he was suddenly struck by the sheer unfairness of it.

'Mam, listen – I'm still here though, aren't I,' he pointed out reasonably. 'I've done it lots of times and you haven't lost me.'

His mother resorted to the worst weapon at her disposal.

'I'm disappointed in you, Garth.'

Disappointed. He hated that word. In the past, when he was younger, that word would have made him cry. He wondered if that's what she was waiting for, for his repentant tears to act as a brake on her anger. But they wouldn't come. His eyes were dry and he felt unmoved. For the first time, he wasn't sad or frightened by his mother's emotions. He felt – slightly exasperated.

'Promise me,' she insisted wildly, 'that you'll never do anything like that again.'

He screwed his face up to corral his thoughts. 'I can't, really,' he said after a moment. 'I wouldn't like to break a promise to you, but I'm not like you any more, I'm not afraid of everything. And I'm not Dad, either. I'm a good swimmer, as it goes.'

'You're not him?' she said furiously. 'Hah! You're just like him!' The glass shade in the ceiling light rang with her anger, and all of a sudden, her venom subsided as if her anger had blown itself out. 'You're just like him,' she repeated, her voice breaking, as if it was something she was realising for the first time.

It was impossible for her to know how proud he felt when she said that.

And so I should be, he reasoned stubbornly, because I'm half him, anyway.

He thought he and his father would have enjoyed doing things together, if he'd lived. They would have had a lot in common by now. Eventually, they would have sung side by side in the choir. His father would have taught him how to fish.

And I, Garth thought bleakly, would have taught my father how to swim.

34

Nancy was making Welsh rarebit for her and Flora when there was an urgent knocking on the door.

'Who on earth—' she began, suddenly apprehensive. She just wanted to hide away and never go out again.

'I'll get it,' Flora said.

Nancy heard her daughter talking to someone, but the cheese was beginning to bubble and the toast was going brown, so she put the food on plates just as Flora was closing the door.

'It's only Garth. He's argued with his mother.'

'Oh dear, has he?' Nancy could hardly concentrate since Mai's virtuous condemnation. It had brought back the old feelings of shame and taken her to a time she thought she'd left behind for good.

She had regrets about her past, mostly for what should or could have been, but the good thing to come out of her relationship with Jimmy Green was Flora.

She would have liked, for Flora's sake, to have been able to tell her she had loved him once, and that she wished things had been different. She had a feeling now that they would never be rid of him. No matter where they went, he was sure to turn up one day for one reason or other – money, somewhere to stay, someone to blame.

Her mother had told her that men couldn't help

themselves, not in the same way that women could. She could hear her words coming at her in full volume: 'You've made your bed, now lie in it!'

Ridiculous! Wasn't that what had got her into trouble in the first place? Passion under the sheets to blot out the noise of the bombs.

Jimmy loved the army, because he could fight and kill legitimately and get paid for it, as he told her one night on a park bench, drunk. She was drunk too, and life had seemed a lark with him, walking on the dark side, playing at being grown-up, having fun.

And then she was pregnant. To her parents, it wasn't about how you felt but how things looked. Her father told Jimmy she'd make a good wife, she was a decent little worker, don't be too hard on her, as if he was selling a car and was in need of the money. A small wedding, just a few of them and down to the pub, her father said, talking to Jimmy man to man.

Jimmy said he wasn't going to be trapped like that, what did they take him for?

Her father told him to make an honest woman of her but Jimmy laughed in his face and said it was a bit late for that.

And then Jimmy's furious wife turned up at their door to 'have a word'.

It was the darkest day of her life. She was sent to a mother-and-baby home, where she worked from morning to night, the lowest of the low, a skivvy for the wealthy. All during the pregnancy, enduring harsh treatment and dark threats, she had known that she was going to keep the baby, come what may. It didn't matter that the baby was going to be part of Jimmy, the main thing was it would be hers.

And now, there was Emlyn.

Kind, warm, good-looking, good-scented, good-hearted Emlyn, everything she wanted in the world. Her life had changed for the better. And now she was dragging him down with her.

It wasn't fair that Jimmy had turned up now, after all these years.

How many times had she told Flora that life wasn't fair, and yet deep down she never really believed it.

'Aren't you going to eat that?' Flora asked her.

Nancy looked at her rarebit cooling on the plate. 'Yes, sorry. Of course.'

'Are you seeing Emlyn tonight?' Flora asked, as if she was picking up her thoughts.

'I'm not sure.'

Flora paused with her fork halfway to her mouth. 'What's wrong? You still want to marry him, don't you?' she asked suspiciously, narrowing her eyes.

Nancy laughed despite herself. 'Yes! Of course!'

Reassured, Flora carried on enjoying her food.

Nancy swallowed her toast with a heavy heart. She would have to tell her or someone else was going to pretty soon; and it probably would be Mai.

'Flora, do you remember your father, Jimmy Green?'

Flora fidgeted and screwed up her nose. 'Ye-es. A bit. He yelled at you. And you yelled at him. I remember the yelling.'

'Yeah. Well, look, I have news. The fact is he's turned up. He's staying in the town and—'

'And what?'

'And people might talk.'

Flora put her fork down and screwed up her nose. 'What do you mean? Talk about what? Do I have to go for tea with him or something?'

'Gosh, no.'

'What about Emlyn? Are you going to leave him now?'

'No, of course not!'

'So what then?' Flora demanded crossly, with a teen-ager's irritation.

'So what then?' Nancy repeated, surprised at the question.

'Jimmy Green's got nothing to do with us,' Flora said, wiping crumbs off her hands. 'He's basically a stranger, isn't he? Is he the reason you've been looking worried?'

Nancy looked at her daughter and nodded.

But 'So what then' seemed to sum it up, and she started to laugh. She felt as if Flora had taken a weight from her.

And never mind Mai.

35

It was just a week before the Coronation, now. In school assembly on the Monday they sang a hymn that Tad's uncle on his mother's side had composed.

As she sang, Lauren was proud of this connection between the anthem and her great-uncle. In Sunday School she used to think of hymns as coming out of nowhere that they knew of . . . except for hymn-books. She'd thought they came from some foggy distant past fully formed, same as the Bible; straight out of the humming mouth of God with no short-cuts. That Tad's uncle had come up with one – that even the headmaster had once said he was impressed by – well, it was something to be proud of.

Lauren took a deep breath and sang her great-uncle's hymn as loud as she could, swaying and singing to the music, going up on the balls of her feet to hit the high notes, making the music inside her body instead of it just coming out with her breath. With her father being a music teacher, that's how he'd taught her to sing.

By the side of her, Flora was whispering mischievously to Garth, and suddenly moved forwards and kneed the girl in front of her, who dropped right into a crouch, arms jerking for balance, making a human ripple that went through the rows of children right down to the front.

Flora nipped back into place and smiled at Lauren, and Lauren smiled back at her, still singing.

Flora didn't do very well in lessons, and she said she didn't care anyway, because she wanted to be a hairdresser. Rhiannon laughed at her for that, but an ambition was an ambition was the way Lauren looked at it.

She realised that Mr Jones was calling for their attention and the murmuring stopped under his commanding glare.

'Now then,' he said, in a voice full of wonder as he looked at them over the top of his glasses, 'I set a competition for the Coronation poem in praise of the Queen.'

Suddenly everyone in assembly was on the alert.

It seemed to Lauren to be a good sign that they had sung her great-uncle's hymn that day, because it didn't come around very often. Being a bard was in her blood. She held her breath and felt her heartbeat quicken like a drum roll.

'And what a selection we had!' Mr Jones said. 'Some with more spelling errors than others, but as this was poetry and not a spelling test, I didn't let that influence my judgement to any significant degree. I was looking for insight, emotion and majesty, and while a lot of poems contained two out of the three, there was only one stood out in its bold simplicity. Mrs Probert, have you got the crown ready?'

Mrs Probert had the crown on the chair next to her, on a seat of its own, and she picked it up reverently in both hands although it was light and made out of aluminium.

She stood up, and with a little bow presented it to Mr Jones. Mr Jones held it with his arms outstretched.

'This year's School Bard, and she should be proud of herself, is Flora Hall!'

Lauren had taken a step forward before realising her hideous mistake and stepping back again, hoping nobody had noticed.

Mrs Probert instigated the clapping, and as Lauren clapped too, she kept her eyes on Flora.

If she'd imagined Flora's reaction, hearing she'd won, she would have expected at the very least a beaming smile of triumphant pride, but Flora walked up on stage humbly with hunched shoulders as if she was approaching the gallows.

Mr Jones placed the crown on her head. 'Congratulations, Flora,' he said. 'Well deserved. It's yours for the whole year. Keep it safe, now.'

Flora walked back to her row pink with embarrassment, holding her head at a precarious angle to keep the crown balanced in place. Once she was back between Lauren and Garth, she took it off her head and stared at it in disbelief. It was embellished with glass jewels in a medieval style and she tilted it to the light so that the jewels glowed. 'Look at that,' she said in amazement at her good fortune. 'I can't believe it! I'm a poet, now.'

The last lesson of the day was history with Miss Dodd, a fierce spinster who was permanently cross. Flora wore the crown to walk home from school that afternoon. 'Why do we need to learn about history?' she asked plaintively, swinging her satchel. 'I hate looking back.'

'Do you? Why?' Garth asked with interest.

'I just do, that's all. I don't care about the Romans or any of that stuff. Why should I?'

'Yes, but – we can learn from the past,' Garth said, 'according to Miss Dodd.'

'Learn what?'

'I'm not sure.' He looked at Lauren. 'What are we supposed to learn from the past?'

'She didn't say. How to build roads, I think.'

'*I* like history,' Rhiannon said.

'That's because you're a swot.'

'I know!'

It was Monday afternoon, and they didn't have homework. They had the whole evening spreading out in front of them with all its glorious possibilities, and it made them feel happy and reckless. When they reached their street, Lauren said goodbye first, and then Rhiannon went up her path.

Flora and Garth carried on walking. She was about to say goodbye to him as they reached her house, when she saw a soldier sitting on her doorstep. His cap was tilted forwards and she couldn't make out his face. She saw the red light of his cigarette glow bright and then dim again and she heard a cough, deep and rumbling, followed by a throaty spit.

This was her father, Jimmy Green.

She remembered her mother's anxiety at the table and the awful scene the time he came to visit, and dread crept over her. The weight was like a heavy blanket, and suddenly she couldn't see properly. It was as if she was looking at him through a world speckled in black and white. The sensation filled her head and she felt strength going out of her knees. The last thing she heard before she hit the road was Garth calling her name.

'Flora!' The word was a roar.

When she opened her eyes again her eyelids felt heavy

but the snowstorm in her head had cleared and Garth was kneeling on the pavement next to her, holding her crown on his bony knees, his face bloodless as he looked anxiously into her eyes. 'Flora? Are you all right? You went down like a tree toppling.'

Flora sat up, dazed. She took the crown from him, the only prize she'd ever won in her life, and saw that it was dented. Her eyes filled with tears. She wasn't sure she was all right at all. Her cheek throbbed, her jaw and her ribs on one side radiated a bruised heat, and her hipbone sang with pain. She put her finger in her mouth, tenderly checking her teeth were still firm in their gums.

'Surprised to see me?' Jimmy Green asked with a chuckle, watching them with his thumbs hooked in his belt.

Flora struggled to get up. He looked a lot bigger when she was lying on the floor. 'How did you know where our house was?'

Her father winked and tapped the side of his nose. 'Ways and means,' he said. 'Ways and means. I asked the postman.'

Flora glanced at Garth, full of shame, but she was glad that he was there all the same. Every moment the three of them stood there seemed like a bad day unto itself. She had no idea what would happen next, and all she could do was wait.

'Where's your mother?' Her father expected an answer. 'What? Don't you know?'

Flora's mouth was dry. Her cheekbone, which had never given her any trouble before, which she'd never even *noticed* before, felt huge, and she touched it cautiously. 'She's at work.'

'At work, is she?' Her father seemed to think this over. He took another cigarette from behind his ear and lit it, looking at the white houses on the other side of the road and at the green hills behind them, and at the grey and crumbling castle perched above the town. 'What do you want to live here for? Anything happen here that's worth talking about? It's a dead-end kind of place. Singing in the pub! What are you supposed to do for fun?'

Flora shook her head.

'Have you got a key? Course you have.' He held out his hand, palm upwards, close to her face.

Flora flinched. She could smell the nicotine on his fingers. She looked helplessly at Garth.

Garth wasn't pale any more. He was flushed and he tucked his hands awkwardly into his trouser pockets. 'Flora's not going home, she's coming to my house. We've got homework. History,' he added defiantly.

Jimmy Green seemed to notice him for the first time, and he turned menacingly in order to give him his full attention and look him up and down. He didn't like what he saw. He didn't seem to like anything much at all. 'What's wrong with you that you can't do your homework yourself?' he sneered.

Out of the corner of her eye, Flora saw Waffles coming out of Old Mrs Hughes's house to do his afternoon rounds. But the corgi was immediately distracted from his mission by the unfamiliar smell of the soldier and changed course in order to investigate further.

He stopped a few feet away and growled deep in his chest.

Jimmy Green looked at him and laughed. 'Look at him!

He's a funny one! What happened to the rest of his legs? He looks as if he's standing in a hole.'

Protecting his herd as he'd been bred to do, Waffles charged at the soldier, nipping him around the ankles, and Jimmy Green danced in his boots, lifting his knees high to keep out of his way. Then he aimed a vicious kick at the corgi.

Little did he know that the corgi's whole genetic make-up was finely tuned towards dodging kicks. The soldier span round in a semicircle, cursing, but it was hard to make out the words above the barking. He gave up and walked briskly away with the lively dog snapping and weaving around his feet.

'Waffles!' Old Mrs Hughes was at her front door, come to find out what all the commotion was, and saw man and corgi hurrying up the street. 'What's the matter with that dog?'

'A soldier tried to kick him,' Garth said.

'What kind of a man kicks a dog? Who is he?'

'He's my dad,' Flora said sadly.

'I see,' Old Mrs Hughes said, craning her neck and trying to make out as much as she could of him before he turned onto the main road. 'He's still around then. Come in, you two, and have a biscuit. What's that you're holding, Flora? A crown, is it?'

Flora nodded and held it up sadly. 'It's for being this year's School Bard and now it's dented,' she said tearfully. 'And I've got to give it back next summer.'

'Let's have a look,' Old Mrs Hughes said, taking it from her and holding it up to the light. 'It's a beauty. And for poetry, too! Fancy! Oh, there, yes, I can see the dent now.

Don't worry about that, Emlyn will hammer it out for you. Come on in, then. Cup of tea?'

'Thank you, Old Mrs Hughes.'

They went into the parlour and sat down formally on the edge of the sofa, listening to Old Mrs Hughes boil the kettle and arrange a tray in the kitchen. She brought the tray out with the cups rattling musically in the saucers and the biscuits laid out neatly on a plate with a lace doily.

'Dig in,' she said.

As they dipped their biscuits in the hot tea, she said to Garth, 'Fair play to you, lad, for standing by her.'

Garth nodded, looking embarrassed as he transferred his soggy biscuit quickly to his mouth before the wet bit fell off.

'And Flora . . .'

'Yes?'

'You've been part of the family for a long time now, but hopefully, by the grace of God and the Methodist Church it will soon be official, and I don't think it's right for you to keep calling me Old Mrs Hughes.'

'Okay,' Flora nodded, cheering up at this turn of events. 'Shall I just call you Mrs Hughes then?'

'No, because your mother will be Mrs Hughes once she's married to Emlyn. Call me "Nain", like the number nine. It's grandmother in Welsh.'

Flora smiled shyly. 'Okay, Nain.'

'There we are!' the old lady said approvingly. 'That's better, isn't it? And mind you let everyone know.'

Garth picked up another biscuit. 'Can I call you Nain, too?'

'No, Garth, you can call me Old Mrs Hughes, same as always.'

'All right.'

After hot tea and two sugars, and a whole packet of Ginger Nuts, they left Old Mrs Hughes's to go home.

'I've got a nain,' Flora said happily, putting the dented crown back on until Emlyn came home to fix it.

'Yes, you have.' Garth looked at her carefully. 'How's your head?'

Flora felt her face and her ribs and her hip. 'I'm better, now.'

Waffles was coming round the corner, a powerhouse of energy with a satisfied air.

They made a fuss of him, which the dog accepted stoically.

'We'll be ready for him next time,' Garth said.

36

For the next few days, no matter where they all went, Jimmy Green showed up, until it started to seem as if there were several versions of him dotted strategically around the town. He was in the library talking too loudly, at the town hall causing a fuss, in the Royal Arms making a nuisance of himself. But worst of all, if it was sunny, he could be found sitting on the bench next to the war memorial in full uniform, telling tales of valour in return for a cigarette and claiming dubious acquaintanceship with the town's dead like a self-appointed battlefield guide.

When Tad went to see John Williams the barber again to have his hair smoothed, as he liked to put it, there was Jimmy Green coming out, all trimmed and cocky, with a little fringe of freshly cut hairs on his khaki collar.

'Despite myself, I gave him a free haircut,' John Williams said, sitting Tad down at the wash basin. 'He was telling me about Korea. He was a killing machine, he said, and I believe it. There's something ruthless about him, but I expect it's a wonderful quality in a soldier, even if he was disruptive at choir practice.' He turned the taps on, getting the temperature right before he started, and then he turned them off again so he could finish his train of thought. 'You know that noise he made outside the window – it made me shiver, I can tell you. It brought back memories of the time I took up the violin.'

Tad shivered too. 'Very similar,' he agreed.

'It's Emlyn and Nancy I feel sorry for. People are talking behind their backs. Imagine what he'll be like during the marriage service, if it ever happens! If anyone can find any just impediments, I bet you ten bob it will be him.' With that, he turned the taps on again and washed Tad's hair more thoroughly than it needed, to work off his indignation.

'He's very plausible, the stories he tells, and he's a hero in all of them,' Tad said to Helen when he got home, still trying to keep up the town's policy of welcome as well as he could whilst trying to keep an open mind. 'I've no doubt he's seen terrible things during his army career. Having said that, I'm not sure if we'll ever get rid of him. How's Nancy taking it?'

'It's upsetting her no end, although she's pretending everything's fine. You know what Mai's like.' Helen was reluctantly dusting Tad's grandmother's flamboyant Gaudy Welsh plates on the dresser.

It was exactly a week before Coronation Day. She hadn't heard back from her mother, and she was feeling increasingly uneasy about it. She swept the cloth inside a cup.

Just then, there was a rat-a-tat-tat on the door and Tad went to open it.

It was Mrs Evans's middle daughter Joanna, breathless, red hair bouncing in pigtails. She was pointing frantically towards the street. 'Mam says to tell you there's a phone call from London and the phone box by the library was ringing and Mam answered it and she says Helen is to ring this number.' She took a breath at last and handed Tad a piece of paper folded up small.

'Wait here, Joanna,' Tad said, 'and I'll find you a six-pence. Helen, have you got a sixpence?' he asked, handing her the folded piece of paper.

'Look in my purse,' she said, unfolding it. 'A London number? Joanna, did the person say anything else?'

'Just to ring this number,' Joanna repeated.

Just then, Mrs Evans appeared at the door with a pram. 'Did Joanna give you the message?'

'Yes, thank you, Mrs Evans. Do you know who it was who called?' Helen asked.

'Your mother's neighbour Cecil.' Mrs Evans raised her eyebrows meaningfully. 'Very posh. He asked you to ring him As Soon As. He didn't tell me anything else and I didn't ask, none of my business,' she ended virtuously.

'Thank you.' Helen turned to Tad very calmly. 'Have you got my purse?'

'It's here,' he said. 'Shall I come with you?'

Her lips tightened. 'You can please yourself,' she said without looking at him. 'You usually do. Here's your six-pence, Joanna. Thank you, Mrs Evans. I'm very grateful for the trouble you've gone through. Excuse me, please.' She squeezed past the pram and set off at a run, her heels clicking on the pavement.

Tad raised his hat to Mrs Evans in lieu of a goodbye and hurried after her.

Helen was already talking on the phone when Tad squeezed into the telephone kiosk alongside her. He smelled a strange sooty smell which he realised was coming from the charred directory and wondered why anyone would do such a thing.

Helen turned her head sharply away from him as if the sight of him repelled her. 'What did the doctor say?' she was asking Cecil the neighbour tremulously.

Tad tried to listen, his heart sinking as he stared at his wife's ear with its pearl earring half hidden by her fair hair.

'I see. I see,' she was saying. '"General debility". That sounds—Yes, I suppose you're right. No, of course not. I realise—Yes, I'll come. Of course I'll come. Tell her—tell her I'll see her very soon.'

Now she turned, tight-faced, to look at Tad, her eyes narrowed as if to reduce him into as small a space as possible.

He felt himself sinking out of the joy of the day into a new, dark, apprehensive world of guilt and blame.

Helen replaced the receiver. To get out, they revolved in the small space like two cogs and he pushed the heavy door open with his back and shoulders, stepping out and holding it open for her.

'What news?' he asked anxiously.

'Why would you care?' she asked bitterly, shrinking out of his reach and marching past him.

'I *do* care,' he protested, following her.

'Do you?' Helen started to run, her fair hair bobbing on her shoulders, her skirt clinging to her hips. As she ran across the bridge he heard the steam train pull into the railway station, and when she reached the other side of the bridge she turned down the small slip road that led to the ticket office.

'Stop her! Stop her!' Tad shouted to no one in particular but when he reached the platform, she was gone. He pressed his face against the smoky windows of the train carriages, cupping his hands round his eyes to see better, calling her name. 'Helen! Helen!'

'Thomas,' she said coldly from behind him, her skirt blowing in the draught. 'Do you always have to make such a spectacle of yourself?'

He spun round and saw she was clutching a railway timetable. 'I thought you were on it,' he said miserably, watching the train slide past at increasing speed in a cloud of smoke, at the same time registering with even greater misery that she'd called him by his given name.

'I shall leave first thing in the morning. I'm going home to pack. And I need to talk to Lauren.'

'And me,' he said, hurrying after her again. 'You can talk to me.'

'Oh? Why would I do that? You don't listen.'

'I do! I will!' he protested, and fell back, panting for breath, clutching his knees stiff-armed, watching her get smaller and smaller as the distance grew between them.

He heard someone chuckling nearby, and saw Jimmy Green sitting on the edge of a planter by the bridge.

'Trouble in paradise?' he taunted.

Back at the house, the kitchen was empty and the Board-room deserted. Tad could hear Helen in the bedroom talking to Lauren. Her voice was flat. Standing at the bottom of the stairs he tried to make out the conversation.

'It's not fair, Mum!' he heard his daughter cry. 'Don't go to London! What about us?'

'How do you think I feel?' Helen replied tearfully.

'I should have said yes as soon as she asked me, so that she'd have a special day to look forward to. I wanted to, and I didn't. If anything happens to her, I'll never forgive myself.'

Tad went back into the kitchen and turned in circles, looking at the table, the sink, the larder. He didn't know what he was doing or what he was meant to do, and in the end he filled the kettle and made two cups of tea with two spoons of sugar in each and took them upstairs for Helen and Lauren.

Helen was packing her case. The half-finished cardboard shield for her Britannia costume was propped up against the wall like a reproach.

He waited for her to say something, and when she didn't he put the cup and saucer quietly on the bedside table, and took the other one to Lauren's room.

Lauren was lying on her stomach on the bed, her face in the pillow, the floral curtains half shut. A slice of light divided the rug in two.

'I've brought you a cup of tea,' he said humbly from the doorway.

'I don't want it,' she said, her voice muffled.

'Right.' He went into the room and put it down on the bookcase.

Lauren turned over and sat up to a creak of bedsprings. Her face was puffy with tears. 'It's not fair, Tad!' she protested.

'I know it isn't.'

'I love Granny and everything, and I want her to be all right, but—'

'Yes.' His gaze drifted to the spines of her books,

Agatha Christie, Enid Blyton, a hymn-book and a children's encyclopaedia. That *but*. It was a very small word for life's contradictions.

But . . .

. . . there was the long-planned Coronation Party that they'd been looking forward to.

He thought of the red, white and blue striped dress that Lauren had made in the Boardroom with a pattern and pins, and the gentle homely rhythm of the sewing machine, her occasional frustrated outburst – broken needles, unpicking. He thought of her telling him cheerfully about Flora winning the bard's crown with disappointment in her eyes because her eyes spoke a language of their own.

'Your mother knows you've got school and we've only been given Tuesday off. I'm teaching and the party is my responsibility. I can't let people down.' He tried to avoid the thought that he was letting his wife down.

'But Tad – is Granny dying?'

Tad was hazy about the term 'general debility', but in his experience there were very few conditions that took a person in a matter of days. A heart attack or stroke was about it, he thought, and if it had been a heart attack or stroke, he was absolutely certain that the neighbour would have said so. 'No, I don't think so. I'm pretty sure she's not.'

'So why is Mum going there first thing in the morning?'

'Because if she doesn't, she'll be worrying. And Dorothea—yes, it must be lonely for her.' But then he felt a surge of self-justification. 'We did invite her to come to the party, you know. The spare room's all ready for her.'

'Didn't she want to come?'

'She didn't write back, so no, I don't think she did. She can see the real thing from her windows and she thought ours would be second-rate,' he said treacherously, because her use of the word *emulate* in her letter still hurt.

'Oh.'

Lauren frowned at the wall that separated the bedrooms as if she could see her mother packing her suitcase through it. She swung her legs off the bed and sat on the edge, next to him. 'Please could you pass me the cup of tea now?' she asked in a small voice. 'So Mum will go tomorrow by herself? And stay there for the Coronation? And she'll miss the party and we'll stay here without her, like we did when it was Granny's birthday?'

'That's right.' Put like that, it didn't sound good, he admitted that. 'But to make up for it,' he added, 'we'll go and see her in the summer holidays, and stay for a week. How does that sound?'

He had burned his bridges now, he knew that. The decision had been made, and he had been the one to make it. Oddly enough, he felt better for making it.

Going back to his own bedroom, he tapped on the door, although it was open.

Helen was sitting on the bed, looking towards the window. 'Go away.'

'Helen—'

'Don't say a word. I'm not leaving it too late this time,' she said furiously, 'not like I did with my father. I should have learned my lesson and followed my instincts. I should never have listened to you.'

He stood there for a moment, but she kept her back to him, and in the end he shrugged. Her decision, he thought miserably, giving up trying to talk.

He went back downstairs, put on his trilby and jacket and made his way to the Hand.

37

Tad woke up disorientated in the strangeness of the spare room in the middle of the night. He could hear banging and shouting and he had the immediate impression that it was still wartime.

He knelt on the bed to open the window, and as he looked out, he saw the houses along the street light up one by one, casting silhouettes on the windows.

The noise was coming from Emlyn's house. Illuminated by the porch light, Jimmy Green was hammering on Emlyn's door, cursing and bellowing with rage.

Tad hurried downstairs and, perceiving it to be an emergency, put his coat on over his long johns. He paused for a minute in the kitchen to wonder why he wasn't wearing his pyjamas. Then he remembered his bottomless thirst for oblivion in the Hand the night before.

He went out into the fresh night air and met Mai coming out of her house at the same time, her hair loosened from its bun for the night. She was dressed all in white like a ghost.

Harry was muttering to himself behind his gate, wearing his flamboyant paisley silk dressing gown which shimmered in the street light, and what looked like a small white hammock over his moustache. Normally Tad wouldn't be able to resist a comment, but this didn't seem a time for words.

'Any sign of Emlyn?' he asked.

'No. Nor Nancy, either.'

Harry and Tad looked at each other in the light of their porch, speculating.

'Perhaps lust has got the better of them.'

'Hush, Filthy!' Mai said from behind Harry, poking him with her finger.

'No, look, there he is, he's just coming out of the door now,' Tad said, 'in his blue pyjamas.'

'There's tactics,' Harry said admiringly. 'You can't fight a man if he's wearing pyjamas.'

'That's glasses, I think.'

In the porch, Emlyn was squinting at the soldier dancing around in front of him like a pugilist, his fists up, his shadow skittering on the path.

Tad buttoned his coat. 'I suppose we'd better go and help him, hadn't we.'

'I don't know. By the time we get there it'll all be over,' Harry said hopefully, holding on to his gate.

'Just a minute – is Emlyn wearing a hair-net?' Tad asked suddenly. He realised he ought to get one himself to keep his hair flat in the night because he was going through the Brylcreem at an alarming rate. He brought his thoughts back to the matter in hand. 'Come on, Harry. Come with me. We can sort him out between us.'

'What, hit him, you mean?' Harry asked.

'Better than that,' Tad said. 'We can reason with him.'

'Reason with him?' Mai snorted scornfully behind them. 'Useless!'

Tad ventured into the road on his own. He felt strangely light-headed, and realised he was possibly still a little under the influence. Listening to the soldier's threats to kill, he wondered if words, his weapon of choice, might prove inadequate in the circumstances.

Emlyn was still standing motionless on his doorstep in his blue pyjamas. Tad wondered if fear had frozen his old friend to the spot.

Flora's light went on and she looked out of her bedroom window, holding the net curtains aside.

Just then, Nancy's hall light lit up and she opened her front door, pulling her coat on over her nightdress. 'Jimmy!' she shouted, running to Emlyn's. 'Go home! Can't you please leave us alone? Go back to your wife!'

'Stay there, Nancy,' Emlyn cautioned.

'Nancy?' The soldier seemed to see her for the first time. 'Nancy!' he slurred. 'Come here, give us a kiss! Give us a kiss for old times' sake!'

'Leave her alone,' Emlyn warned him in a sudden rush of anger.

'Or what will you do?' Jimmy Green mocked him, putting his fists up again. 'Go on, take a swing if you're man enough!'

Emlyn finally made his move. He put his hands together, interlocking his fingers. It seemed for a moment to Tad that he was about to get down on his knees and plead for his life, but no – he raised his arms up high and with all his might he brought his two fists down on Jimmy Green's head like a club.

Jimmy seemed to kneel down as if in apology, and then sprawled on Emlyn's doorstep.

Emlyn stepped over him and walked with Nancy to her front door, where they stood talking in the light of the hall. After a few minutes, he clasped her shoulders reassuringly, and she went inside and closed the door.

When he went back, Jimmy was sitting on his doorstep, head in his hands.

'Goodnight,' Emlyn said politely. Moments later, his bedroom light went off and his house was in darkness.

Still adrift in the middle of the street, watching the action unfold, Tad's heart was racing with adrenaline. He contemplated helping Jimmy Green to his feet, which would be the neighbourly thing to do, but thought better of it, because he had enough on his plate.

He crossed back to Harry and Mai and they looked at each other over the hedge, shaking their heads in disbelief.

'Drunk!' Mai announced triumphantly, watching Jimmy Green weave his way along the street. 'It's shameful, that's what it is! Come on, Harry,' she said as she swept inside.

'In a minute,' Harry said, watching the lights go out in the houses. He turned his paisley collar up against the breeze and looked at Tad. 'Mai's right though, Tad. It's a shameful business. What are we going to do?'

'Sleep on it, that's my advice.'

Harry turned to go, and then turned back. 'Can I ask you something, Tad, man to man?' he said. 'Do you always wear underwear for bed?'

Tad, eye-level with Harry's moustache hammock, tried to think of a pithy remark in reply but decided on balance it could keep till the morning when his mind was sharp.

Going indoors, Tad was disappointed to find that the house was silent.

Helen hadn't witnessed his cavalry-like venture across the no-man's-land of Little Green Street armed with nothing but speech. And Lauren wasn't celebrating his heroic return from the jaws of danger. They hadn't even noticed he'd been gone. It seemed to sum up the day.

He poured himself a tumbler of water and went back to bed.

The following morning, Tad woke up in a panic and realised he was late for school. In the same state of panic, he went into their bedroom and saw the bed was made and the suitcase had gone. He dashed into Lauren's room. Her bed was a tangle of sheets, and he found her downstairs, eating Cornflakes.

'Has your mother gone?'

Lauren's hair was wild from the pillow. 'Yes, she caught the first train to London.'

'Did she say anything?'

Lauren thought about it for a long moment with one eye shut, as though trying to remember the very distant past. 'Such as?'

Tad sat down at the table. 'I don't know, really,' he said with a sigh. 'Well, that's that, I suppose.' He went back upstairs, pulled his clothes over his long johns in a hurry and came back down again. 'Don't be late yourself, mind,' he said.

As he walked to school, his head full of the fog of war and beer, he thought of Emlyn standing solid but alone in the porch in his blue pyjamas.

And then he thought of Helen hurrying to the station

by herself while he was asleep in the spare room. Both images troubled him greatly, in different ways.

He entered the schoolyard with a fretful sense of abandonment. He wondered uneasily if Emlyn and Helen had felt abandoned too.

38

Before she had left on the early train to London, Helen had written two letters as neatly as she could, which wasn't very neatly at all and evidence of her being in a rush. One was for Nancy and the other for Mai, explaining to both the reason for her absence.

Mai put the letter on the table for when Harry came home from work because she wanted his view on it before Rhiannon returned from harp lessons. 'What do you think?' she asked, handing him the letter with a cup of tea. 'She doesn't mention Tad. She's left him to go to London.'

'Looks like it,' Harry said, skim-reading it and folding it up again.

'"General debility",' Mai said suspiciously.

'Indeed.'

'Tad came back from school this afternoon looking very shabby. I wonder why he hasn't gone with her. What do you make of that? The least he could have done is gone with her. He's always had a self-centred streak.'

'He can hardly take time off work to see his mother-in-law, can he?' Harry said. 'He wouldn't even if it were his own mother, he's very diligent that way. You can't let a class of children loose with musical instruments. Imagine the discord! No, Mai, I don't make anything of it at all.'

Mai had noticed that Harry had an annoying tendency to take what she said at face value, when what she actually wanted was someone to dig a bit deeper with her. It was easier to dig with two so she persevered.

'And not only that, I feel as if Nancy and Emlyn are getting away with their dubious behaviour scot-free,' she pointed out, serving their meal of bacon and grilled tomatoes on toast.

'Not exactly scot-free – Scot included, more like,' Harry said, and laughed heartily at his own joke.

When Mai got it, she rolled her eyes and said crossly, 'It's no laughing matter.'

'No, I suppose it isn't. But be fair, Emlyn hasn't behaved dubiously at all. And as for Nancy – maybe she did have a wild side when she was a teenager, but didn't we all?'

'I didn't,' Mai said indignantly.

'What do you mean, you didn't?' Harry chuckled softly. 'I remember what we got up to in the ruins of Crow Castle after school. Of course, they weren't nearly so ruined then.' This was an assumption, as he hadn't been up there for years. Once he and Mai were married, there was no need to go, and now he was too unfit even if he did need to.

Mai did not respond. Harry ruffled his moustache with his fingers. He was having trouble with toast crumbs lost in the hairs of his upper lip, although he'd made sure to cut the toast up small. 'I wonder if we should ask Emlyn to give us a masterclass on his technique of subduing the enemy,' he said thoughtfully. 'He could have been a great asset in the last war, if we but knew it.'

'And him in his blue pyjamas,' Mai said.

'Tad in his long johns.'

They'd never seen each other in bedroom attire before and it had come as a bit of an eye-opener.

'How long do you think the soldier will stick around?' Mai asked.

'Hard to say. He seems to be enjoying himself. I worked with a man like that once, Dai Smith, do you remember him? I've never known anyone so irritating in my life, but if you pointed it out to him, to be helpful like, it only seemed to make him worse. He got satisfaction out of it.'

'Does he still work there now, Dai Smith?' Mai asked.

'No. He had a shock, he did, in the end.'

'Electrocuted?'

'No, he was sacked. Not for being annoying, it was something stationery-related. He tried to get the union on to it, and although they were positively enthusiastic at first, somewhere along the line they changed their tune about Dai and sided with the management. It was the first time in their history they'd done that, I heard later. But we can't sack Jimmy Green, more's the pity. If this was the Wild West, we could run him out of town,' he said nostalgically.

'We could report him to the police for being violent,' Mai said, serving up a dessert of tinned tangerines and evaporated milk.

Harry took a mouthful of tangerines to help him think about it. 'He hasn't been violent, though, has he? He hasn't laid a finger on anyone since he's been here, as far as we've heard. It's us. Waffles chased him out of the street and Emlyn floored him. If he wanted to, he could run *us* out of town.'

After tea on Thursday evening, five days before the Coronation, Mai went next door to fetch Helen's cakes, because she doubted they would be safe with Tad alone in the house. Sure enough, when she went into the kitchen

246

unannounced, Tad and Lauren were sitting at the table eating chocolate gateau.

'Caught you in the act!' Mai said, startling them both. 'Those are for the party! Helen warned me they might not be safe, and she was right.' She looked at the cake in the tin, or what was left of it. 'Is this the uncooked one?'

'No. Cooked,' Tad said with his mouth full. 'It won't keep. Help yourself to a slice.'

'No indeed!' Mai looked at the smooth chocolate butter-icing sprinkled liberally with vermicelli. Not only was the chocolate butter-icing spread thickly on the top of the cake but it was also all down the sides and running through the middle, too. 'Well, it's been started now and it's best when it's still fresh,' she reasoned. 'You can't serve it like that now. Go on then.'

She pulled up a chair and Tad got her a plate and a cake fork. 'Any news from Helen?'

Tad shook his head slowly.

'It's a terrible time for her mother to get ill, a week before the Coronation,' Mai said. 'I suppose she *is* actually ill, is she?'

'She had to call the doctor, so . . . It couldn't have happened at a worse time,' Tad agreed miserably.

'I don't know what to make of it all. I think I'll take a slice of this for Harry, if you don't mind. He can have it after choir practice.'

Tad breathed in a long, shuddering breath. 'Of course, Mai. Help yourself. The rest of the cakes are in the pantry. That's what you came for, isn't it?'

Mai leant over and cut a generous slice. 'And Helen's not coming back for the party, then?' she asked.

Tad shook his head again.

'Difficult for you,' Mai said. 'I'll take this now, before Harry grooms his moustache. He doesn't like to eat once he's combed it.'

Once she'd gone, silence settled on the kitchen again.

Tad looked at his daughter.

She was scraping the last of the chocolate butter-icing from her plate and saw him looking at her. 'Do you think Mum will be all right on her own with Granny?' she asked him.

Tad imagined Helen sitting next to her mother's bed and Dorothea sunk in the pillows, enduring her general debility like a martyr. The room would be gloomy and grey, the curtains drawn shut to dampen the sound of the jubilant crowds in the streets, and Helen would feel as far removed from it all as if she were in the North Pole.

'I hope so. I wish I could be with her. But the thing is, I've got choir practice tonight, school tomorrow, and on Saturday the final committee meeting before the party . . .'

'I know,' Lauren said in a small voice. 'I just wondered, that's all.'

Tad realised that Helen had adopted her mother's chill of late. He had always believed he could thaw her with his love, and he had done it proudly and joyfully throughout their marriage, at least for the most part. 'Excuse me,' he said, checking his watch with a start. 'I'd better get ready for choir practice.'

He went upstairs with no earthly idea what he was doing up there, except to avoid Lauren's questioning.

He looked at himself in the wardrobe mirror and squared his shoulders. His arguments for staying here for the Coronation remained the same as they had in the beginning when he'd found the letter. He was the instigator, the driving force, the chairman of the Coronation Party Committee, choirmaster, the power on the throne. He couldn't disappoint people, and he didn't want to be disappointed himself.

A pint in the company of Emlyn and Harry would sort him out, he thought, and he went back downstairs to put on his hat.

When Tad closed his back door, he saw Emlyn and Harry loitering by Harry's hedge, as if they were waiting for him, which was unusual.

Once they got moving they looked around a lot, like strangers who weren't quite sure where they were going. As they got close to the Hand, they were on home ground and walking so quickly it was almost a trot.

They got through the door of the bar with a feeling of relief that they'd avoided bumping into Jimmy Green.

The three men carried their pints to their usual table and clinked them together, survivors of an ordeal.

'That was some move you made on the soldier last night, Emlyn, fair play,' Harry said. 'Where did you learn that?'

'It's a well-known method of stopping a charging bull,' Emlyn said.

'It's not that well known, I've never heard of it. What's the technique, just so as I know?'

'You put your hands together like this, weaving your fingers through. That's right, like that. And then you bring them down, keeping your elbows straight.'

Harry tried it out and nearly knocked his pint over. 'Is it crucial, keeping the elbows straight?'

'Yes, you don't have to get so close to the horns.'

'Horns? Oh, right, yes.' Harry glanced at Tad. 'What's wrong with you? You're uncharacteristically silent on the subject.'

'I'm thinking about Helen.'

Tad had come to a grave decision. It was no use trying to fight it. His place was by his wife's side. He could imagine her sitting with her sick mother, alone and upset, and each time he thought about it the whole of his stomach muscles tensed up as he tried to take the plunge, part of him saying yes and part of him saying no.

He looked at Harry and Emlyn over his beer with sadness, because what he was about to tell them would disappoint them as much as it did him. He knew he was letting them down. Look at them, he thought. They looked so happy with their drinks in their hands, as if this night was like any other night.

'Listen, I've got something to say to you both. I know it will put a dampener on the next few days,' he began, 'but I've given it a lot of thought and I apologise in advance.'

Emlyn said quietly, 'Helen's mother's died, hasn't she?'

'What? Not to my knowledge. Who told you that?'

'I just assumed, from your expression.'

'No, that's not it at all, Emlyn. Although obviously yes, that would qualify as a dampener, no doubt about it. You gave me quite a turn there for a minute.'

'Are we supposed to keep guessing?' Emlyn asked.

'No,' Tad said irritably. He picked up his glass and put

it down again before Harry had a stab at it. 'Look, I'll get to the point. I'm afraid to break it to you like this, but I'm going to London to keep Helen company. She'll need me.'

'Oh. When?'

'Monday, after school. I'll be back for work as usual on Wednesday.' He waited to let his words sink in. So far, they hadn't made much of an impact. It could, he thought charitably, be down to shock.

Eventually, Emlyn observed, as if it had only just occurred to him, 'That means you're going to miss the Coronation Party.'

Tad nodded gravely. 'I'm afraid so.'

'Well! Can't be helped!' Harry said, unexpectedly cheerful, clapping his hands together. 'You're doing the right thing, and I'm very happy to volunteer to do the conducting of the national anthem in your absence, Tad, rest assured of that. As a matter of fact, I've been practising.'

'Have you?' Tad looked at him suspiciously. 'Why?'

'Just in case.'

'Just in case?' It was a stinger, to be honest, to know that they'd planned for this eventuality, and him so reliable. 'I thought you were taking it well.'

'No need to thank me.'

'I wasn't.'

Harry let this slide. 'As you won't be here on Tuesday, Tad, I'm going to let you into a secret about my fancy dress costume.' He paused for effect. 'I'm going as—'

'Charlie Chaplin?' Emlyn suggested quickly. 'Or Nancy says Oliver Hardy.'

'What have they got to do with the Coronation?' Harry asked. 'Oliver Hardy?'

'No need to get offended,' Emlyn said. 'She thought you had the shape for it.'

'I don't know why she would think that. No, I'm going as Adrian Boult.'

Emlyn looked at Tad, eyebrows raised. Tad shrugged.

'Never heard of him,' Tad said firmly. 'Who is he?'

'Philistines, both of you! Adrian Boult the conductor.'

'Which bus does he work on?' Emlyn asked with a wink.

'Has he got a moustache, then?'

'Of course he has! He not only conducted the music at the last coronation,' Harry said with great dignity, 'but at our last two musical festivals. Come on, you were there!'

'We only saw him from the back,' Tad said.

'I've made my own baton, too. Birch.'

'Ah! That's what you were doing in the garden, cutting down branches in your fancy dressing gown!' Tad said, pointing at him gleefully.

'Who told you that?'

'Helen and I were watching you through the bedroom window with our own eyes, fearing for your sanity.'

Harry folded his large arms and lowered his chins gravely. 'I can see I shall have to put up a bigger fence. I'll send you the bill for it, Tad.'

Tad waved to Billy for more drinks to mollify Harry and to soothe his own bruised feelings. Emlyn didn't seem to need mollifying or soothing, but he might if he left him out.

Back at the table with the beers, Tad said, 'I'll let the choir know tonight. You might as well have a go with them right away, Harry. I know you said you've been practising, but it's a different matter with voices.'

'Right you are. And as you won't be here,' Harry said, 'you might as well tell us what you were going to the party as. I know it involved a sword.'

Tad thought about his naval uniform with a pang. 'I was going as Prince Philip,' he said, 'Earl of Merioneth.'

'Ah!' Harry said. 'Hence the hair. I see it now.' He looked at Tad with sympathy, and patted his shoulder. 'Much as I appreciate being able to put my baton to good use, it's a shame you've got to miss it after all your hard work.'

'We'll do you proud,' Emlyn said. 'Don't worry about that.'

'I appreciate that, Emlyn,' Tad said gloomily.

Announcing the news to the choir in general wasn't as straightforward as Tad had expected. When the men congregated in their usual spot and he stood up to tell them, the regular drinkers stood up for the national anthem, as had become customary.

Tad turned to Harry to introduce him, but Harry had gone off looking for something that would act as a substitute baton, being wholly unprepared for this incredible turn of events.

Billy lent Harry a broken snooker cue, *pro tem*, and Tad went to stand with Emlyn and the rest of the tenors, lost in the crowd.

Although he sang with verve, his dream had faded, as dreams do in the light of reality.

39

On Friday, late afternoon, in the privacy of his sunlit bedroom, Tad got dressed up as Prince Philip, Earl of Merioneth, in the splendid naval uniform for the last time.

He put the stiff peaked cap on his head, held the magnificent sword in his hand and saluted himself, noticing how royally the gilt buttons gleamed and his sword shone.

He would have made a good Prince Philip, there was no doubt about it. But even if he'd stayed for the party, without Helen it wouldn't have been the same. Without her, nothing meant as much. He hadn't realised until now how much of what he did, he did for her, to impress her.

He had a feeling, as he looked at himself in the mirror, that this gesture, this sacrifice, was the kind that Prince Philip himself was likely to have made. He too would have been aware, on taking the princess to be his bride, of all the things he would be giving up along the way: his career, his sense of mischief, his freedom; and all out of devotion to her.

'I'm doing the right thing,' he reassured himself aloud.

Hearing him, Lauren came bursting into the bedroom. 'Who are you talking to? Oh, Tad!' she said in surprise. 'Are you going to wear it to go to London?'

For one glorious sunburst of a moment, Tad imagined doing just that, going to London on the train and becoming a Prince Philip impersonator. Changing his life entirely and never coming back.

'No,' he said. 'This was just for Little Green Street.'

She put her arms around him and hugged him tightly. 'You're a lovely Tad.'

For a moment, taken by surprise, he was silent.

'By the way, I've decided,' she said, looking up at him. 'I'm going to stay with Flora while you're away.'

He had been hoping she'd say Rhiannon, because the spectre of Jimmy Green was ever present in the town, but he'd been fair and given her the choice and she'd made it and he would respect it. 'Good.'

He waited for her to go downstairs, took his uniform off and put his everyday clothes back on. He wrapped the uniform up in the brown paper it had come in, and wrapped and tied the sword up with string.

'I'm off out for a bit, I won't be long,' he called to Lauren as he left the house.

As before, the mannequin stood guard outside the door of the army surplus store on Berwyn Street, camouflaged by netting. And as before, once Tad entered the musty shadows of the shop, he fancied he could smell danger, sweat and cordite ingrained in the noble soul of the place.

He put his packages down on the counter as Dennis Hill strolled through the shop, biceps bulging and blue eyes blazing. 'Sorry, no refunds,' he said sternly, pointing at the sign.

'No, I know,' Tad said, 'you told me that. It's just – I'm afraid I won't be needing the uniform for the party after all, and I thought it was better to give it you back so you can sell it on to somebody else if you get the chance.'

'Sorry to hear it.' Dennis's attitude changed instantly from foe to friend. 'If you don't want a refund, that's all right then,' he said, putting the packages on the bench. 'You know where it is if you change your mind. I'll only charge you storage.'

'Thank you,' Tad nodded. 'Appreciated.'

'The party's still on though, is it? Oswald said I could come along.'

'Yes, it's still on, and you'll be very welcome,' Tad said with a pang. 'I won't be there myself, I'm going to London on Monday. My wife needs me.'

Behind him he could hear whistling and his heart sank as a voice that was only too familiar disrupted the solemn gloom.

'What have we got here then?'

Tad braced himself. *Jimmy Green*. The man was everywhere.

The soldier was grinning, his cap at a jaunty angle, a cigarette behind his ear and his kit-bag over his shoulder. Recognising Tad, he sang 'Tra-la-la-la-la!' in a falsetto right in Tad's face, and grinned.

Tad nodded a curt greeting.

'Right then, Dennis,' Jimmy Green said in a familiar manner, thumping the counter and winking at Tad. 'Last chance, pal. I've got a Korean War issue compass, a souvenir wallet and an army field telephone. Any reasonable offer considered.'

'I was wondering when you'd turn up again. I said no, didn't I?' The proprietor's blue eyes glinted dangerously, a flash of colour amongst the khaki. He folded his arms and his regimental tattoo bulged on his bicep. 'Gloucestershire Regiment, right?'

The soldier thought about it carefully for a moment and then said warily, 'Yes?'

'Flown back from Korea early on medical grounds. That's what you told me.'

'That's right,' Jimmy Green said belligerently, 'and it's the blinding truth. It was on account of my chest, I swear. It's not my fault it turns out to be curable.'

'I thought you were due back in barracks last week.'

'What of it?' The soldier hesitated, narrowing his eyes. 'I'm taking some extra R and R, aren't I. Let's face it, I deserve a break, all I've been through.' He took the cigarette from behind his ear, tapped it on the counter, lit a match and stared at the tapering yellow flame. The cigarette glowed red. He took a drag, tipped his head back and blew a grey pillar of smoke towards the ceiling. 'And besides, I've heard there's a party here next week for the Coronation. I'd hate to miss a party. I like a bit of fun and even better, Nancy'll be there.' He grinned, and feigned a punch at Tad. 'I like my fun, don't I? I saw you watching me in the street in your long johns.' He laughed as Tad ducked, and turned to Dennis with a sneer. 'Thanks, pal, for nothing. I thought you were a mate.'

He left the shop and kicked the mannequin over on his way past, momentarily getting his boot tangled in the camouflage netting.

'Don't bother coming back!' Dennis yelled after him, going outside to pick up the mannequin.

'He's a troublemaker,' Tad said as they watched Jimmy

Green sauntering across Berwyn Street and disappear around the corner. There was something nasty in the way he'd mentioned the party, like a threat.

'Don't I know it. Men like him, they give the military a bad name,' Dennis said as they went back inside the shop. 'It's hard on Emlyn and Nancy too, so I heard.'

'You're right there.' Tad watched Dennis unwrap the naval uniform he'd brought back. 'But he has to go back to his barracks at some point, is that right?'

Dennis gave a dry laugh. 'You heard what he said. He's given himself extra R and R.'

Tad nodded knowledgeably, raised his hand and said goodbye. He was feeling depressed at this latest encounter; Jimmy Green seemed to have that effect on most people after a while. He could only imagine what Nancy was feeling. She'd lost her sparkle.

He got as far as Market Street and had the impression there was something he'd missed. He went over the conversation again. *You heard what he said. He's given himself extra R and R.*

Was that true? Tad wondered. Could a soldier grant himself extra rest and recuperation?

He turned around and walked back to Dennis's shop.

Dennis was happy to elaborate. 'He's AWOL, he is. He's a tough bloke but he's not blessed with brains,' he said.

That was something that hadn't occurred to Tad. 'Absent without leave?' he said thoughtfully. 'That's an offence, isn't it?'

'It's a *criminal* offence,' Dennis confirmed, hanging the jacket up on a rail.

'A criminal offence,' Tad repeated, scratching his head. 'Theoretically, just out of interest as a law-abiding citizen, what would one do about it?'

Dennis grinned, and his teeth were very white in the dim shop. 'Easy. Ask the police if there's a warrant out for his arrest. And if there is, you can tell them where to find him.'

Tad felt a surge of hope. As a course of action, it had a certain appeal, there was no denying it. 'And then what would happen?'

'He'll be put in detention and lose his rank.'

Tad rubbed his jaw thoughtfully and looked at Dennis. He thought of Nancy and Emlyn, and he had a sudden vision of Jimmy Green showing up at the party, causing more trouble for them both.

For a moment, he and Dennis looked at each other with a deep understanding.

'If you ask me, the town's better off without him,' Dennis said, unwrapping the ceremonial sword.

'I agree. You've been very helpful,' Tad said.

'My pleasure,' Dennis said sincerely, and shook his hand.

40

Tad went straight to Emlyn's house to talk to him about Jimmy. In his haste, he forgot to knock, and as he pushed open Emlyn's parlour door, Tad saw a flurry of black plumage.

Emlyn gave a loud shout of alarm and slammed the door shut. 'Get out!'

'Sorry!' Tad said, retreating quickly. 'Beg your pardon! I'll come back later!'

'Tad, is that you?'

'Yes,' Tad said warily from by the back door.

'Oh, that's all right then. Give me a minute to get changed. No, on second thoughts, come on in, or you won't have the opportunity to see it otherwise. Wait, wait! Right, I'm ready! Enter!'

Tad entered to find Emlyn posing majestically in front of the fireplace in a black suit polka-dotted with pearl buttons. Equally remarkably, he was wearing a matching hat with exuberant black ostrich feathers sweeping round in a curl under the weight of their own lavish extravagance, stopping short of his black quiff which had a marvellous gloss of its own.

Tad looked at him, dumbfounded. 'There's magnificent, Emlyn!' he said enviously.

Emlyn looked pleased. 'It's my funeral suit, really. You wouldn't believe it to look at it, would you?'

'Never!'

'I'm only giving you a preview because you won't be here. Even Nancy hasn't seen it. I'm hoping it will cheer her up.' Emlyn rubbed his jaw with the flat of his hand, his exuberance waning. 'She's not herself at the moment, Tad. It's Jimmy Green, it is.'

'That's why I'm here, I've got some news for you,' Tad said and he relayed the scene at the army surplus in detail.

Emlyn took his plumed hat off carefully and rested it on his knee. 'If it's true, that's a turn-up for the books. What are we going to do?'

'Tell Harry we'll discuss it over a pint later. Three heads are better than one, after all.'

Tad crossed the road home and saw Harry was deadheading the roses in his front garden that bloomed above the hedge like a magnificent bouquet. They had never looked more beautiful and the air was filled with their sweet perfume.

'You've done a grand job,' Tad said admiringly. 'They smell wonderful, too.'

'These are damask roses,' Harry said with an air of satisfaction. 'They'll last until the festival. I always like the garden to be at its best when the visitors come.' He mopped his damp face with his handkerchief. 'By the way, hope you don't mind me mentioning it, I was looking at your garden and couldn't help notice you need to do a bit of weeding before you leave.'

Tad looked at his flowerbeds and realised that Harry was right.

He spent an hour with his hoe and his gardening gloves, talking to Harry over the hedge about Jimmy Green.

When they stopped for a break Harry fetched his conductor's baton for Tad to see, and then showed Tad how to hold it properly so that it was like an extension of his arm.

It really was a very satisfactory instrument, Tad had to agree. Powerful, in fact.

Up until now, he hadn't mentioned Harry's conducting at choir practice. He had mostly been consumed by his own emotions on the night because he'd thought that nobody could get a tune out of the men like he could, and it turned out he'd been wrong. Which was a good thing, of course. 'It's got a lovely balance to it,' Tad said. 'It feels right and it certainly looks better than that broken snooker cue, although I must admit there was a good deal of elegance in the way you used it.'

'Don't thank me for that, thank Adrian Boult.'

'I wasn't thanking you as such, Harry. It was merely an observation.'

Just then, Mai came out of the house. 'I was just coming to look for you, Tad,' she said in a reprimanding tone of voice, wagging her finger at him. 'You haven't put your Union Jacks up in the window yet. You can't leave your windows empty, the only house in the street! People will think you're a republican! And I don't know what Helen would say. Any news from London, by the way?'

Tad shook his head and squinted in the sun.

'Does she know you're going to join her?'

'No. Even if I wrote to her, what with Sunday and the

bank holiday coming up I'll be there before the post, anyway.'

Mai turned to go into the house and then turned back again. 'Rhiannon says that Lauren's staying with Flora while you're away. I'm surprised at you, Tad, I really am, allowing that, what with all the goings-on over there and Nancy's soldier on the rampage.'

Tad and Harry opened their mouths at the same time to tell her about the plan, and caught each other's eye. It was very rare that they knew anything before Mai did, so this was a moment to be remembered.

'Haven't you heard?' Harry asked. 'We're getting the police onto him for going AWOL.'

For a moment, Mai was painfully torn between pretending it was something she already knew, and the strong urge to know more. Curiosity won. 'Come on in,' she said. 'I'll put the kettle on.'

In the meantime, Emlyn had gone round to Nancy's.

She was in the front room, standing on a chair, putting up a flag in the window. She pressed the drawing pin in with her thumb, and turned to him with a smile.

Emlyn held out his arms and she jumped into them.

'How's your day?'

'Better for seeing you.'

He lowered her to the floor and noticed she was wearing a pearl and diamond tiara in her curling blonde hair. He said admiringly, 'You look fancy.'

'Fancy Nancy.' She smiled, looking up at him. 'Your mother gave it to me. She used to wear it when she went with your father to the Farmers' Ball.'

'Yes, I remember.' Emlyn moved the chair to the other end of the bay window and secured the second flag with drawing pins.

The room was shady despite the sunshine which filtered through the Union Jacks that glowed in the window. This was convenient for Emlyn because he had the overwhelming urge to kiss her. He knew how much she'd suffered since Jimmy showed up and exposed her past to the town.

He held Nancy's sad and lovely face in his warm hands and he could hold off the news no longer. 'I've got something to tell you,' he said.

At quarter to eight that evening, Jimmy Green was in the Royal arguing with the barman when the three men went in to find him.

Harry put his hand on the man's shoulder. 'Hello, Jimmy.'

'Look who's here! The Three Stooges!' Jimmy said. He leant forward and said to Harry in a beery haze of alcohol, 'Be a pal and get us a drink.'

'Forget it.' The barman shook his head. 'I'm not serving him. He's had enough.'

'We've all had enough,' Emlyn said as Tad picked up the soldier's kit-bag.

'Shut up, you!' the soldier slurred, pointing his finger at Emlyn. 'You stole my Nancy.'

'She's not your Nancy,' Emlyn said, his voice dangerously cold. 'Come on, Jimmy. You're coming for a walk with us.'

'I don't want a walk. I want a beer.'

'Course you do,' Harry said sympathetically, putting his

beefy arm around Jimmy's shoulders and steering him towards the door. 'This way, that's right. Mind the step. Oops! You're all right, I've got you.'

Out on the road, the fresh air revived Jimmy and he blinked at them in confusion and looked around. 'Where're we going?'

Emlyn and Harry tightened their grip on his elbows and propelled him across the bridge. The whistle of the steam train echoed in the valley as it approached the station.

'You'll see.'

Tad felt for the one-way third-class ticket to Liverpool in his inside pocket, and they turned down the ramp where Idrys the porter was waiting for them. He tilted his cap at the sight of them. 'Evening.' He looked at the soldier with dislike.

They saw the train's bright headlights approaching along the track and it pulled alongside the platform with a deafening hiss.

'What's happening? What's going on?' Jimmy asked.

'You're going to Liverpool,' Tad said. 'Here's your ticket.'

Jimmy Green took the ticket and looked at it closely. 'Am I?' he asked in surprise. 'My wife's in Liverpool.'

'Lucky her!'

Idrys went to have a word with the guard and between them they bundled the soldier onto the train and tossed his kit-bag in after him.

The guard slammed the door shut and blew his whistle.

Emlyn, Harry, Tad and Idrys stood watching the train as it pulled away and disappeared into the distance.

There was one more thing left to do, and they walked to the telephone box outside the library. It seemed only right that Emlyn should make the call to the police. When Jimmy Green got off at the Liverpool Lime Street terminus he would find a reception committee waiting for him.

41

On Saturday afternoon, the house was quiet except for the ticking of the clock. Tad went upstairs to pack a small bag for his trip on Monday. It didn't take long.

He came back downstairs and glanced at the clock. He sighed with nostalgia. This time last week and for several weeks before that, he'd been full of excitement, getting the Boardroom ready, straightening his notepad, sharpening pencils, full of plans and agendas. Now he would miss the big event, and he felt empty with loss.

Lauren came dashing into the house, hanging on to the door handle. 'Oh! There you are!'

'Here I am,' he agreed.

'I've just come to tell you I'm going to Flora's.'

'I thought you were at Flora's already.'

'I was, but I came to see if you were all right.'

Tad wanted to confess that he was not the slightest bit all right. He wanted to ask her to keep him company and not to ever leave him. He wanted her to cheer him up somehow, anyhow, but instead he said with a smile, 'I am perfectly content, thank you. You enjoy yourself.'

'Thanks, Tad,' she said happily. Off she went, slamming the door.

Tad went into the Boardroom and sat at the mahogany dining-room table, looking at the empty chairs and listening to the silence. He covered his face with his hands.

Staring into the warm darkness of his palms, he heard the kitchen door open again and he looked up quickly, trying to fix the smile back on his face before Lauren caught him moping.

Then Emlyn and Nancy came in for the committee meeting as if nothing had changed and he jumped to his feet with alacrity. 'I forgot to cancel the meeting!' he said, dismayed at his own ineptitude. 'Hello, Emlyn and Nancy, nice of you to come but there's no meeting tonight because—oh, here's Harry, too, and Mai. I was just explaining—'

Now Lauren was back with Flora, Rhiannon and Garth, the four of them looking at him, eager and expectant as they crowded around him.

Flora nudged Lauren. 'Go on, then! Hand it over!'

'I'm going to, Flora, give me a minute! Tad, we made you something to wear in London,' Lauren said, putting a small bulging paper bag on the table in front of him.

Tad opened the paper bag and looked inside. He pulled out a tie, made of cotton, in familiar red, white and blue striped fabric, scraps of which he'd seen scattered around the house for days. He stroked it, speechless, turned it over, saw what a lovely job they'd made of it and draped it around his neck. 'Beautiful!' he said, looking down at himself.

'It's the same as our dresses that we're going to wear,' Flora explained.

'I've got one identical,' Garth told him.

'There's handsome,' Tad whispered, moved beyond speech.

'We've made you some cakes to eat on the train,' Harry said. 'Mai? What have we done with them?'

'We?' Mai asked with asperity, putting a small sandwich tin down in front of Tad.

'Fair do's, I was working in a supervisory capacity, and the tin is mine at any rate,' Harry told him as Tad opened it. Nestled together on a bed of greaseproof paper were four brightly coloured iced cakes.

Tad nodded, eyes shining, and replaced the lid carefully. 'I shall enjoy them very much.'

'Here you go.' Emlyn laid down a package about three foot long. 'You'll be wanting these when your mother-in-law takes a turn for the better.'

Inside were three Union Jacks, with the Queen's image printed in the centre. 'Thanks, Emlyn and Nancy,' Tad said and, as he waved a flag over the table, the gesture made him remember what it all stood for. He felt the faint stirrings of anticipation again. It struck him for the first time, despite the way he was feeling, that it wasn't all over at all. He would still be celebrating the Coronation even though he would be in a different place from this one. 'Thank you,' he said hoarsely, getting to his feet.

They looked at him expectantly, waiting for him to continue and possibly make a speech.

But Tad turned away, shook his head and rubbed his face with his sleeve.

'You know,' Harry said, breaking the silence, 'this day will go down in history as the day Tad was speechless. I'll never forget it. It's going in my diary.'

'They'll probably make it a bank holiday,' Emlyn agreed. 'Mention it in Parliament.'

'Anyway, in this interval before Tad finds his tongue again, let's give him three cheers. Hip hip!'

'Hooray!'
'Hip hip!'
'Hooray!'
'Hip hip!'
'Hooray!'
'Shortest meeting we've ever had,' Harry said, and they headed for the door.

42

On Monday afternoon after school, with the three Coronation Union Jacks tied onto his small suitcase and wearing his trilby and best jacket, Tad noticed everything with a new appreciation. He had never seen Little Green Street look lovelier. The lively red, white and blue bunting fluttered gaily, pictures of the young Queen smiled out from the windows, the hedges were trimmed, the lawns were cropped, the gardens were bright with blooms and the heady scent of Harry's damask roses wafted over him on the breeze.

He walked briskly so as not to be late catching the train, and when he reached the bridge he saw the black-painted planters in Castle Street were joyfully filled with purple petunias, yellow pansies and red geraniums. Above his head a profusion of flags from all around the world snapped and danced a welcome. This town is a picture, he thought proudly.

Despite his hurry, he stopped to look down at the black, froth-adorned river, with its tumbling, ageless energy. And then he looked up towards the hill. Its greenness was faded in the morning light, and mist topped the ruins of Crow Castle like a crown.

He knew that when he came back, everything would be different. The whole street would have had an experience without him, one that he couldn't share, and he would listen to the stories eagerly with an outsider's ears, knowing the experience would, for him, only ever be second-hand.

Disappointment weighed heavily on him.

He already felt a longing, a homesickness in his heart.

He heard the whistle of the distant train as it approached the station, and he squared his shoulders, tightened his grip on his small suitcase and crossed the road. At the ticket office he bought one return ticket, second class.

In his imagination, he'd been alone in the railway carriage, but in reality, the service was surprisingly busy. He chose a compartment that contained a man hidden behind a newspaper and an elderly couple who were dressed for a funeral. The man was wearing a black top hat and his wife was wearing black silk.

Tad tipped his hat and greeted them cordially. They looked at him with some resentment. Rather put off, he stepped back onto the man with the newspaper's shoes. He apologised, the man flicked the newspaper in a gesture that wasn't hard to translate, and Tad sat down with his suitcase on his knees, trying to take up as little room as possible.

However, the rolled-up flags took up more space than he expected, so he turned his suitcase sideways and that way the flags rested against his shoulder.

The funereal couple scowled.

Tad glanced at the newspaper that the man was reading. 'Coronation Countdown!' read the leader. It was a compulsion with him to read anything that was put in front of him, and his gaze kept drifting to the headlines. From personal experience he knew how annoying it was to have somebody read words free that one had paid for oneself, so he adjusted his angle of sight and noticed the elderly lady was whispering to her husband. As his gaze met hers, she hid her whispers behind her hand without ever taking her eyes off him.

Tad smiled politely, hoping to make a favourable impression, and then he began to wonder why on earth he wanted to impress two people that he didn't know. He had always wanted to be liked, that was the trouble, and not just trouble but a failing, some would say. For a long time, he'd assumed it was the same for everybody, but some people, like Mai for instance, put being liked quite low on the list. Mai preferred to be informative.

Harry didn't seem to see any need to be liked, either. He'd insult a man as soon as look at him. Harry's weak spot was that he always wanted to be right.

Tad wondered if he himself always wanted to be right, but he concluded he didn't, because he usually was.

Emlyn, now . . . he was younger than the rest of them, of course, and he'd had a different kind of life. He'd lost his father young – for a moment, the sign above the Hospital for Incurables flashed into Tad's mind as if he'd seen it with his own eyes – and at that young age he'd taken over running the farm with hard work and then sold it with little fuss, or so it seemed.

In the years that Tad had known Emlyn, he had been self-effacing. He never said much about his job at the Milk Marketing Board, good or bad. There was his well-tended quiff, of course, which revealed a certain amount of vanity, but he couldn't hold that against the man. 'Drat!' Tad exclaimed aloud, suddenly reminded of something.

The elderly couple stiffened.

He'd forgotten to ask him how to source a hair-net before he left. It had completely slipped his mind. I expect they have hair-nets in London as well as home, he told himself doubtfully.

He thought about Emlyn's hope that he could marry Nancy. Influenced by Mai and Harry's sanctimonious doubts that the minister would marry them, Emlyn hadn't been able to bring himself to approach him yet. It was a shame, because he and Nancy made a good couple, it was obvious to anyone.

Tad looked through the window and saw that they were coming into Ruabon Junction, where he had to change trains.

He left the carriage as discreetly as he could without ever seeing anything of the man behind the newspaper apart from his fingers, while at the same time feeling he'd seen far too much of the couple in mourning. With a sense of relief, he changed platforms and waited for the London train.

When it came, he found that it was equally as busy in second class. Eventually he found a carriage with some space in it, which was mainly due to two of the young occupants sitting on the other two young occupants' knees.

He slid open the door: 'May I?' and sat in the seat nearest the corridor, looking away from the courting couples out of tact.

'Going to the Coronation, are you?' one of the girls asked him cheerfully, bouncing from her boyfriend's lap onto the seat next to him so that he found himself rising momentarily before sinking back down again.

'My mother-in-law's not well and we're going to keep her company, my wife and I,' Tad explained.

'Is that so? Only I saw you had flags. We've got flags, too. Show him our flags, Bert.'

Bert seemed intent on bringing the conversation to an end by means of his lips, so as he kissed his girlfriend Tad swiftly averted his gaze and went back to looking at the corridor again.

People walked back and forth, looking for a carriage with enough space, and to his surprise he saw the mourning couple pass by. Even more surprisingly, they stopped dead when they saw him, slid the door open and greeted him like an old friend.

'Fancy seeing you here! Have you got room for two more?'

'Plenty of space for two little ones,' the friendly girl said.

'Small world,' the man with the top hat said to Tad.

'Very small,' Tad agreed with a certain degree of bafflement. Somehow or other, in the course of changing trains, the elderly couple seemed to have taken on a personality change.

He wondered if he'd undergone a personality change himself because he'd lost all interest in finding out whose funeral it was and now saw the elderly couple as intruders. With an ill-disguised huff, he put his small suitcase with the large flags on the luggage rack above his head, folded his arms and watched the countryside beyond the corridor slide by.

Presently, he started to feel hungry and he remembered Mai's fancy cakes packed neatly in Harry's sandwich box tucked away in the case. He wondered what Harry would be doing, and checked the time on his watch. Last-minute preparations, he thought, conducting Rhiannon on the harp with his baton in preparation for the following day.

The lady in black bent forward to get his attention. 'We're going to Auntie's funeral,' she said to him, just as if he'd asked.

'Oh, that's—' 'nice' didn't seem to quite fit the occasion, so he substituted '—respectful.'

'Yes. I expect you're wondering how she died, aren't you?'

It was perceptive of her, because it was something Tad always wondered about when he heard that sort of bad news, in a purely superstitious sort of way. 'It wasn't of "general debility" was it, by any chance?'

'Is that something that's going around?' the man in the top hat asked with a worried look.

'No,' the woman said firmly, not to be diverted. 'It was mumps.' She lowered her chin and inflated her face and became alarmingly transformed into a mumps sufferer. Then she deflated and became her normal self again.

Tad stared at her in astonishment; it was quite a party trick. He glanced at the couples sitting by the window to see if they'd been watching, but they were lolling happily against each other to the rhythm of the train and seemed to have fallen asleep.

Sleep was an appealing way to pass the time, and Tad closed his eyes, feeling comfortable, warm and isolated. He wondered idly whether he'd had mumps as a boy, and he was still working his way through his childhood illnesses in alphabetical order when he nodded off.

43

Tad woke up at Paddington with a dry mouth. The other occupants got off before him and he had the feeling of being totally lost and abandoned without his companions. He got off the train light-headed, and the station was a world of busyness and unceasing din.

Following signs for the Underground station, he caught himself looking into the faces of the people who jostled past him, as though he was expecting to see someone he knew. Back home, he knew everyone and at the same time was known by them, but here in the capital he was a stranger, anonymous, and the realisation was a shock to his sense of self. No one even returned his glance.

When he was young, in his soapbox days, Tad had imagined himself as a great orator, making his mark on the city. He'd been fearless then, or that's how he remembered it, but he knew it was a lot easier to be fearless when one was young. He'd imagined going into politics, or failing that, becoming ordained and energetically preaching about the truths he'd discovered in his short life.

After his time in the pit he'd gone into teaching instead, holding on to the same vision of influencing people for the better, although he hadn't made much of an impression on the children, he was the first to admit. They seemed to tolerate him, and humour him sometimes, and over time he'd settled for that.

He looked at the other passengers on the platform and tried to copy their everyday nonchalance, but when the Underground train entered the station it nearly blew his hat off and he couldn't imagine how people coped with the noise day in, day out.

He eventually emerged at Oxford Circus. Workmen were checking the barriers along the procession route, flags were stretched across the road, window displays were filled with royal colours and velvet cushions edged with gold. Just like home, he thought affectionately, although admittedly on a larger scale.

He walked down towards Marble Arch, at the western-most end of Oxford Street, where Dorothea lived.

His mother-in-law had a grand address, and he had found quite early on in his marriage that that kind of thing, location, mattered a lot to Dorothea.

Her flat was at the very top of an old Georgian building, above offices and a large department store. Seen from the outside, the windows dwindled in size the further up you looked, like a wedding cake.

The entrance for residents was inset to the left of the department store windows. The breeze had sent a sheet of newspaper scuttling against the shabby blue door, and before he pressed the bell, Tad picked up the newspaper out of neatness, folded it up as small as he could get it, and put it in his pocket. He was feeling nervous and playing for time. He wasn't sure what kind of reception he'd get, coming at this late hour.

Here goes.

He pressed Dorothea's apartment number with his thumb, and waited. It hadn't made a sound so he began to wonder whether it was working or not. He hovered his thumb over it again while images flashed through his mind: hospitals, doctors with grave faces, Helen too heartbroken to speak.

The speaker crackled. 'Yes? Who is it?'

The voice sounded very energetic, which threw him in the circumstances. 'Dorothea?'

'This is she,' his mother-in-law said stiffly. 'Who's that?'

'It is I, Tad,' he announced, as formally as if he were speaking a foreign language.

'It's your husband,' he heard her say off-speaker, as it were. Then the connection went dead.

Tad looked at the shabby blue door and waited for something to happen. Against the roar of the traffic he heard a distant, tumbling noise which echoed in the hallway as it grew nearer, and changed to the sound of approaching footsteps.

The door opened. It was his wife.

'Tad! What on earth are you doing here?' Helen asked, glancing down at his case with the flags tied to it.

'I was worried about you,' Tad said truthfully.

Helen looked confused. 'But what about the party? Is Lauren with you?'

'No, she's staying at Nancy's. How is your mother?'

'Oh, she's fine now. She was just lonely and upset, that's all.'

Tad stepped back, confused. 'She's fine?' he asked. 'Not ill with general debility? Why didn't you let me know?'

'Oh.' Helen shrugged, as if considering it for the first time. 'I didn't think it mattered to you that much.'

Tad looked at her incredulously. 'How can you say that?

Lauren and I have been worrying ever since you left because we hadn't heard from you. We thought the worst.' A black top hat and a whisper of black silk flashed into his mind.

Helen shrugged again, with a little less conviction this time. 'You had your own business to see to with the party and everything,' she said, as if his life was nothing to do with her at all. She glanced up the stairwell and then back at him, trying for a smile. 'Anyway, you're here now. Come on up.'

He climbed the stairs and entered the small apartment, dotted profusely with *objets d'art* and elegant porcelain ladies in crinolines, and saw Dorothea sitting by the window with a distant expression, dabbing her mouth with an embroidered handkerchief.

Tad took his hat off, put his suitcase down and stepped forward to shake hands with her.

She returned his handshake wearily with the reproachful eyes of a bloodhound.

'How are you feeling?' he asked, noticing the glass of sherry on the occasional table next to her.

She patted her neat waves. 'As well as you can imagine.'

'You've recovered from your general debility, I take it?' he asked politely. 'Or was it specific debility? It wasn't clear.'

'Sarcastic as ever, I see,' she countered.

Tad was offended. While he had certainly felt sarcastic, he had only let her hear the merest glimmer of it, he'd made sure of that.

'Sherry?' Helen asked him.

He didn't want a sherry, but as there was nothing he

did want, other than to be told to go home, he nodded his head.

'Lauren not with you, I don't suppose?' Dorothea asked.

'She's in Left Luggage at Paddington.'

'Tad!' Helen exclaimed indignantly. 'That, Mother, was a joke.'

'I don't need a joke explained to me. I know a joke when I hear one,' Dorothea said, strongly implying she hadn't heard one yet.

'Sit down,' Helen said to Tad irritably, handing him the glass.

Tad sat.

Dorothea carried on telling Helen a story she'd apparently been halfway through before he'd interrupted, about her troublesome neighbours and their noisy daughters who she could hear through the wall.

Tad sipped his drink, and regressed in his mind to the age of ten, when his mother would talk to friends on the street and he would stand there holding her shopping basket and believing he was about to die of boredom if he had to listen to any more stories of people who knew people who'd offended, snubbed, or inadvertently ignored other people, none of whom he knew. He could feel his life trickling pointlessly away. He'd never felt more depressed.

At home, he would be doing things now.

And even if he was doing nothing, at least he would be doing it in his own home. He glanced at Dorothea, who had come to the end of the interminable complaint about the neighbours and seemed to be waiting for a response from him.

'You don't even care, do you?' she asked him crossly after a few moments' silence.

'To be fair, I wasn't paying attention,' he said. 'I didn't realise you were talking to me.'

He was about to carry on in this vein when he remembered, too late, that communication with Dorothea was very different from the way he communicated with his friends, where insults and gentle mockery were the norm. One only spoke formally to strangers and officials. Even then, it wasn't necessary to be formal if they seemed to be on the same wavelength as you.

'Would you like to take your suitcase to the guest room?' Dorothea asked him coldly.

He was about to tell her that, no thanks very much, it could wait, when he saw Helen giving him a nod.

'There's nothing I'd like better,' he said, picking up his case.

He followed Helen into the guest room.

Helen closed the door and leant against it, as if she was expecting him to rush her and escape. 'What is *wrong* with you?' she asked him furiously.

'What do you mean?'

'You're being horrible to my mother, Thomas, and you know it.'

There it was again, her rare, unwelcome use of his given name. 'Horrible, am I? I've travelled all this way and what thanks do I get? None from her, suffering very lightly from general debility, if at all. I don't know why I came.'

'I don't know why you came, either, when you obviously didn't want to. My mother and I have had a chance to talk, for a change. Now it's all gone wrong again! We were having a nice time together.'

'Were you?' It hadn't occurred to Tad that this was possible. 'But I thought you needed me,' he said.

Helen laughed briefly, through her nose.

Tad put his suitcase on a chair by the dressing table and squeezed his temples. 'I can't do anything right,' he said, baffled. 'What can I do?' he asked her desperately. 'How can I make things better?'

Helen folded her arms and looked at him. 'I'll tell you what you can do. Try to be sociable, keep your thoughts to yourself and Don't Say a Word. Or is that too much to ask?' And without waiting for a reply, Helen went back to join her mother.

44

In Little Green Street, on Coronation Day, Lauren and Flora were wearing their Coronation dresses and looking through Tad's notes in the kitchen, studying the lists of what everyone had promised to bring.

'We can tick them off as they come,' Lauren said. 'I hope there'll be enough food, with the choir.'

'Not all of them are staying to eat.'

'We'll have to have everything laid out before they come. They'll be hungry after singing, they'll want to dig right in.'

There was a knock on the door and Harry said jovially, 'Good morning, girls! We've come for your table!'

Lauren and Flora gathered up their things with great excitement, because the day was here at last, after all this time of looking forward to it, a bit like Christmas. Having sent off their kitchen table, they went into the Boardroom and sat each end of the polished table. 'I'm making cucumber sandwiches, what are you making?'

'Tinned salmon and watercress.'

'I love tinned salmon, do you?'

'Mum is making a savoury cheese pie. She's got three or four cakes, and a chocolate cake for Harry. It's all he talked about in the committee meetings. He suffered terribly from missing chocolate when it was sweet rationing.'

'Yes, Tad underlined it so we wouldn't forget. Chocolate cake. See? I wonder what he's doing now?'

Flora put her pen down and propped her chin on her hand. 'I can't imagine Tad in London,' she said.

Lauren laughed. 'He'll be the same there as he is here, except smaller.' Her laughter dwindled to a smile and then faded altogether. 'I hope they're all right.'

'He liked the tie, didn't he.'

'Yes. He'll be wearing it today.' She bit her lip and glanced at Flora.

Flora wrote something down, tore the page out of the notebook, balled it up and threw it at Lauren as if they were in school. Lauren caught it and smoothed the note out on the table. She smiled. *Don't worry*, it said.

Emlyn and Harry positioned the tables in the middle of the street. They were trying to get them straight. They eventually concluded after much shifting back and forth that the tables were fine as they were but the street had a curve to it that they hadn't been aware of before. They gave themselves a break and revisited the discussion about who was going to propose the loyal toast, and with what.

'I thought we decided tea,' Harry said. 'Although Tad disagreed.'

'Absolutely, but it wasn't Tad who disagreed, it was me,' Emlyn told him. 'Look in the minutes.'

'Don't get worked up, old boy, I knew it was one of you.'

Emlyn frowned. 'I don't know how you can get us mixed up, Harry, I'm younger than he is,' he said, sitting casually on the corner of the table and rolling his shirt-sleeves back up. 'Anyway, Mai was the only one voting for tea, if you remember.'

'True. Mai worries a lot about the evils of drink.'

'Aye, but she's forgetting about the pleasure it gives,' Emlyn said passionately. 'And to be honest, I think it's the pleasure that's the important thing. Anyway, before you interrupted me I was about to tell you that I have a quantity of well-matured sloe gin in my shed. I always make a lot more than I can drink when it's a good berry year, and we've had quite a few good berry years in a row so they've accumulated. It's grand stuff. We used to drink it a lot on the farm, to keep out the cold, and it's good for you, too. Healthy. You can't drink it in large quantities, mind, but for a loyal toast, you can't beat it.'

Harry's small eyes lit up. 'I hope you're not expecting me to take your word for that, Emlyn.' He rubbed his hands together and grinned.

'Wouldn't dream of it,' Emlyn replied seriously. 'Come to the shed and have a quick sample. If you don't like it, there's always the tea to fall back on.'

They crossed the road and went down the side of Emlyn's house, straight to his garden shed.

In Emlyn's neat shed, the walls were adorned with tools of varying sizes. Emlyn took a bottle out of a wooden crate and held it up to the light of the window. The red glow reflected on his shirt, giving him a festive look. 'Now this one,' he said, 'is sweetened with honey. It's not got the same taste as sugar but until rationing came to an end it was a decent enough substitute. Gives it more of a garnet colour, rather than ruby, see?'

On his workbench he had a couple of small metal beakers, and he poured a measure in each. '*Iechyd da*. Good health.'

Harry sipped at the drink cautiously as if it was cough mixture, but then his face brightened. 'Lor, that's good stuff!' he said. 'I can taste the honey, but I'm not sure I would have noticed if I hadn't looked for it.'

'It's all right though, isn't it?' Emlyn said happily, reaching down for another bottle. Again, he held it up to the light, his face warmed by its rosy glow. 'Now try this one, sweetened with syrup. Finish that up first though or you won't notice the difference.'

'Now,' Harry said, smacking his lips like a connoisseur as he tried one from the second bottle, 'this one tastes more subtle, in my opinion, but keeping the wonderful tartness of sloes. The flavour is more retiring.' He blinked. 'Strong stuff, though.'

'Well? What do you say? Are we sticking to tea, or shall we make an occasion of it?'

Harry didn't bother answering, because the choice was obvious. 'We'll need glasses. Where on earth can we get a lot of little glasses from at the last minute?'

'Hang on.' Emlyn tilted his head in thought. 'I've seen some somewhere just recently. Where was it now? Just a minute, it's coming to me. I know where! It was in the Methodist Church!'

'Eh?' Harry exclaimed. 'What would the Methodist Church be doing with glasses? They're supposed to be teetotal!'

'I mean the ones we use for communion.'

Harry looked swiftly up at the roof of the shed for signs of heavenly displeasure. 'Isn't using communion glasses for sloe gin sacrilege?' he asked, keeping his voice down.

'I don't see why it should be. Think about it, Harry. In the Scriptures, the Lord turned water into wine when they ran out at the wedding, which makes a strong case for alcohol, and an even stronger case against water at celebrations, which includes tea, in my opinion. Ours must be the only religion where you get wine every Sunday, like it or not, even though the pubs are shut.'

'I've never thought of it like that.' Harry looked at Emlyn with respect in his eyes. 'That's a powerful argument you've just made,' he said. 'I might try that out on Mai one day.'

'I'll go and ask Mr Griffiths if we can borrow the glasses for the loyal toast. There's no harm in asking, and if he says no we'll think of another idea. If the worst comes to the worst, we could use egg cups.'

'Egg cups? It doesn't seem to strike the right note, drinking a loyal toast out of egg cups, especially as ours are brown and shaped like hens. Off you go, good luck to you, and I'll start collecting the chairs.'

Mai was in her bedroom trying to get into the white lace bridal gown. Her bottom half was in it, no problem at all, more or less, but the top half, revealing her salmon-pink corset, wouldn't fasten up at all.

'I don't understand it,' she said to Rhiannon. 'It almost fitted a couple of weeks ago. Near as, anyway. I've been cutting down, too, on sugar but it's all those cakes I've been making for Harry. Try again!'

'No!' Rhiannon gave up, sat on the bed with a sulky bounce and folded her arms. 'There's no point in trying again because it just won't close and that's that.'

'I don't like your defeatist attitude one bit,' Mai said crossly. 'It's not how we brought you up.'

'It's not my fault! I thought you were going to wear a cloak to hide the gap. That's what you said.'

'I haven't got a cloak, have I? Helen was going to make a panel to fit it. Quick! Go round to hers and ask Lauren if she left a panel for me.'

Freedom! Rhiannon hurried next door and did a double-take in the kitchen when she saw four empty chairs grouped around an invisible table.

'Anyone home?' she called.

'We're in here, Rhiannon,' Lauren said.

'Oh, hello, Mam sent me to ask if your mam left a panel for her because her wedding dress for the Coronation Party won't do up.'

Lauren opened the lid of the sewing basket and shook her head. 'No. Did she promise?'

'I don't know.'

'How big is the gap?' Flora asked.

'About—' Rhiannon held her hands out, palms facing each other, like a fisherman describing his catch '—this big. She might have some fabric of her own somewhere I don't know about. Let's go and ask.'

The three girls went to Rhiannon's and found Mai sitting on the bed in the wedding dress looking as glum as a jilted bride. 'Well?' she asked hopelessly, seeing they were empty-handed.

'No, nothing,' Rhiannon said.

'I know,' Lauren said, suddenly inspired, 'you could wear my mother's outfit.'

Mai perked up. 'What is it?'

'Britannia, like on the penny. Mum's made a shield out of cardboard. And she's got a pitchfork for a trident.'

Mai's mouth turned down. 'And what's the dress like?'

'It's just a sheet wrapped around her and tied with a knot up here on the shoulder. It looks lovely, though.'

'A sheet? I'm not wearing a sheet. I'd rather not wear anything.' Mai slumped again.

This was quite an alarming statement.

Mai got off the bed and for the first time, Lauren and Flora saw the V of the back of the dress revealing her underwear and exchanged troubled glances.

Mai crouched down to look through her fabric chest for something that would cover her up, and the gap in her gown stretched wider than ever. 'Harry said I could wear a cloak, but I haven't got a cloak,' she said regretfully.

'My mum's got a cape,' Flora said helpfully. 'It's sort of white fur.'

'White fur? Ermine, is it?' Mai asked, brightening up. 'Will you ask Nancy, please, if I could just borrow it for today? Don't forget to say please and tell her I would be awfully grateful.'

In a rush, the three girls ran across the road, bypassing the long row of tables to get to Flora's on this emergency mission for Mai.

Nancy was in the kitchen wearing her pink dressing gown and curlers in her hair, and the air was warm and sweet with baking. She was beautiful and welcoming, cutting sandwiches on the larder hatch as Flora explained their mission.

'My white fur cape? No, it's not ermine,' Nancy laughed, wiping her hands on her apron.

'Her dress doesn't even get close to fastening up and she said she'd be awfully grateful if she could borrow it,' Rhiannon added.

'Did she? I expect she would. You know, she hasn't been very nice about Emlyn and me, and the whole Jimmy Green thing.' Nancy said it mildly, as if it didn't matter to her anyway, but the fact she'd mentioned it at all showed that it did.

'I know,' Rhiannon said apologetically. 'My mother's always been a martyr to gossip.'

'That's probably because she's never been the subject of it,' Nancy said in that same mild tone. 'Ah well. It's not your fault. Wait here, I'll fetch it for you.'

She brought the white fur cape down in a fabric bag and gave it to Flora, who couldn't resist taking it out and trying it on before handing it over.

Lauren and Rhiannon stroked it admiringly.

'It's so soft,' Flora said. 'Why don't you wear it, Mum?'

Nancy hesitated for a moment. 'It's for special occasions,' she said.

'Please can I have it when you don't want it any more?'

'Of course,' Nancy laughed. 'Now off you go, put Mai out of her misery.'

The three girls ran back to Mai's with the cape.

Up in her bedroom, Mai took it out of the garment bag and rubbed her cheek against the fur. She put it around her shoulders and fastened it with the little diamanté clasp at the neck. 'There's regal!' She looked at herself in the mirror front on, and then over her shoulder more critically. 'Can you see a gap, girls?'

'No, no gap,' they chorused with relief because they themselves had plenty of things to do.

The coloured bunting tapped against the window as if reminding them of the occasion.

The crisis was averted.

The countdown to the party had begun.

45

When Emlyn got to the Methodist Church for the glasses, he found Mr Griffiths the minister kneeling in the quiet, holy hush in front of a small Bakelite television buzzing with static. It was set upon a table dressed with a purple cloth.

Mr Griffiths was a wise man afflicted by a stammer on occasion, except when he was singing or being theological. He was a member of the choir and had witnessed the drunken soldier when he'd interrupted the singing with his supernatural screech. He also knew that Nancy and Emlyn were courting and he'd been wondering what he would do about it if they approached him on the question of marriage.

But on Coronation Day he had other things on his mind and he greeted Emlyn with great relief. 'E-Emlyn! You're a sight for sore eyes! D-dashed if I can do anything with it,' he said. 'I understand the weather isn't what one would hope for in London, but it's not blizzard conditions, surely?'

Emlyn looked at the busy, crackling screen. 'It needs an aerial, I expect,' he said knowledgeably.

Mr Griffiths polished his glasses with his handkerchief. 'Oh dear. And what would that look like?' he asked despairingly. 'The only thing it came with was that little hat stand.'

Emlyn scratched the back of his neck thoughtfully and looked at the little hat stand. 'Yes, that'll be the aerial,' he said, 'hidden under your bowler. I expect your hat was blocking the airwaves.'

'Well, I never!' Mr Griffiths got to his feet, rubbed his knees, and examined his bowler hat on the inside.

Meanwhile, Emlyn took the minister's place, knelt down and turned the knobs. Very much like a radio, the television whistled, hissed and whined, until suddenly, miraculously, a very English voice said clearly: 'People lining the streets . . .' And to prove it, there was a long shot of crowds clustered around the statue of Eros in Piccadilly Circus. 'Quickly! Come and see!' he cried.

The minister tossed his hat to one side and both men slid into the very front pew to watch history unfold in the streets of London.

'S-so many people, they look like little ants,' Mr Griffiths said, marvelling.

'Tad's in that lot somewhere. Funny if we saw him.'

'Oh, look, the umbrellas are going up! What's the weather like here, Emlyn?'

'It's fine,' Emlyn said. 'Quite warm, in fact, with just a little breeze.'

'Perfect,' the minister said happily. 'You know, I was praying for a miracle and then you turned up. Thank you.'

Emlyn realised there was no better time to ask a favour than this. 'Actually, Mr Griffiths, I've come to ask a favour. We'd like to borrow your communion glasses for the loyal toast.'

Mr Griffiths's eyes widened momentarily with a preacher's doubt. He picked up a hymn-book and shut his eyes for inspiration. Then he opened them again, hearing the voice of Richard Dimbleby on the television.

Emlyn read the minister's expressions one by one and watched him reach a conclusion.

Mr Griffiths cleared his throat. 'The way I see it is, theologically speaking, the Queen is head of the Church, and so in effect, you'll be toasting the head of the Church with her own glasses. In light of that, I can't, in all fairness, see any objections at all. I'll need them back for the service next Sunday, mind.'

'Of course.'

'What are you toasting her in?'

'Sloe gin.'

'Very fitting. If there's any left over, I could find it a good home.' He chuckled and went to the vestry for the glasses. He brought them out on their circular, tiered oak stand, which he handed to Emlyn carefully. 'All the best for today,' he said.

'All the best to you, Mr Griffiths. And God save the Queen!'

46

Tad had woken up in Dorothea's flat in London on Coronation Day with a panicky sense of dislocation. Like a ship's compass, he liked to sleep pointing north and he opened his eyes to get his bearings, wondering if it was morning yet. A grey light seeped in through the windows. Next to him, under the blankets, he saw his wife's tangled fair hair as she lay curled away from him. He groaned quietly at the total horribleness of the situation.

He inched out of bed, ducked under the closed curtain and opened the window. From here, he could see Marble Arch. A constant trickle of people were already heading for Hyde Park Corner. He leant out and looked straight down. Lines of heads bordered the pavement along Oxford Street like strings of beads. He wondered what time those people had got up, dawn, maybe, claiming their places by the barriers so they would have a good view of the procession.

He had the overwhelming urge to join the enterprising crowd and get the most out of the occasion while he was here. It would be easy enough to leave the apartment and go out into the street to soak in the Coronation atmosphere.

He went round to Helen's side of the bed and said her name softly.

In response, she stirred for a moment, looked at him from under her eyelashes. 'What is it?'

'I'm going for a walk.'

'Don't be too long, will you, Mother's got plans,' she said anxiously, and pulled the sheet over her head.

Tad got dressed quickly and put on his Coronation tie, jammed his trilby on his head, grabbed his raincoat and made up his mind to make the best of things.

He tiptoed to the door carrying his shoes in his hand, and went quietly down the stairs, sitting on the bottom step to put them on. Moments later, he was outside in Oxford Street, Mayfair, with a heady sense of recklessness.

Suddenly he stopped and raised his head – he could smell coffee. Looking around, he saw a young man selling hot drinks from a van on the corner, and Tad bought one, along with a souvenir newspaper. 'You're up early,' he said.

'Been up all night,' the young man said cheerfully. 'I tell you, the whole of London is camping out, nobody wants to miss anything. I was down the Embankment at six this morning for the Lord Mayor's procession in his State Coach, with his pikemen and musketeers. There's a sight to lift the spirits! There's nothing quite as smart as a pikeman, don't you think? I got moved on from the Mall. Too busy.'

Tad was startled. 'Too busy? Already? My word! That was an early start for the Lord Mayor, surely? The ceremony doesn't start until eleven o'clock!'

'He won't be complaining, don't you worry. He's got a ringside seat, in the dry. Where did you spend the night?'

'At my mother-in-law's,' Tad confessed, 'drinking sherry and being sociable by keeping quiet, as my wife instructed.'

The lad laughed.

It started to drizzle again and Tad pulled his hat brim

down a little lower and tucked his souvenir newspaper inside his coat to keep it dry. He sipped his coffee, enjoying being one of the crowd under a sky that was low with cloud. Everybody was undoubtedly cheerful under their plastic rain macs, despite the weather. He marvelled, realising there was something extraordinary to be said for being here, and being part of it, for being able to stake his claim on this memory for the rest of his life: *I was there!* He finished his coffee, pushed his way through the crowds and headed back to Dorothea's flat, feeling lighter than he had in days. He wondered if he could talk them into going to Westminster with him.

He pressed the bell and Helen answered sharply through the intercom's metallic voice. 'Tad! Where have you been?'

'To buy a newspaper,' he said. The door clicked and he pushed it open and went upstairs.

Dorothea was sitting very straight at the dining table, dressed in navy, her dark hair neat against her head. She had a notebook in front of her, and looked stern, as if she was about to put him in detention.

'Good morning,' he said.

'Good morning, Thomas. I was just explaining to Helen our timetable for the day,' Dorothea said briskly.

'Oh, right.' Tad wanted to be scornful about a timetable, but at the same time he thought it was an excellent idea and just the kind of thing that he himself would do. 'I'm listening!'

Dorothea consulted her notebook. 'At ten o'clock, we're going to go next door to watch the proceedings on Cecil's television.' She tapped the page with her pen.

'Once the Coronation service is over, we'll have lunch together, and at two fifty-five we will come back here and look out of the window so we can watch the procession go past. How does that suit you?'

'A television, lunch, and a bird's eye view of the procession?' he said, taken aback by her planning. 'That's wonderful!'

Dorothea gave him one of her sudden, rare smiles, and as their eyes met her face lifted with happiness. 'I'm so pleased. Now that you're back, let's have breakfast. Poached eggs on toast.'

Tad smiled back, opened his newspaper and looked at it in a desultory way. It wasn't often that he pleased his mother-in-law, he realised, but maybe that was because he'd never tried to before. He had only thought about the strength of his own bitter disappointment at missing the Coronation Party with all the plans he'd made. He realised for the first time that her disappointment would have been equally acute, because she had made plans, too. Rather good ones, as it happened.

Beneath the gaze of the porcelain ladies he had a feeling of being unusually well-behaved.

He glanced at Helen for approval, but she was slicing bread for the toast. He stared at her for a long time, knowing she must be aware of him, but she didn't look back.

47

In Little Green Street, Mai and Nancy covered the tables with freshly ironed sheets for tablecloths, and stretched long runners of red crêpe paper down the middle.

Lauren, in her stripy Coronation dress, was all ready to tick the food off the list as it arrived, but so many things arrived all at once from different houses that it was impossible to keep track.

Old Mrs Hughes, wearing a yellow knitted crown to keep her ears warm, was bringing out quantities of pickles in jars: black pickled walnuts, purple red cabbage, golden pickled onions, indigo pickled beetroots, all of which doubled conveniently as paperweights to hold the red crêpe paper in place.

Nancy, still in her dressing gown with curlers in her hair, was bringing out plates of tinned salmon and watercress sandwiches covered in a damp muslin cloth to keep them fresh.

Mrs Evans, whose younger children were camping under the table, hidden by the sheets, had made a quantity of pilchard pasties, with the pastry folded up like an envelope, as illustrated in the Ministry of Food-approved recipe.

And Mai, in wedding dress, fur cape and apron, was carrying out a vast bowl of Coronation Chicken.

Mai said to Lauren, looking at her over her shoulder,

'Make sure you tick my Coronation Chicken off the list. It's got two boiled chickens in it. I hope it will be enough.'

'Tick my pilchard pasties off too, while you're at it,' Mrs Evans said.

'Pilchard pasties . . .' Lauren said, scrolling down the list with her pen.

Garth came over carrying a platter, his Coronation tie flapping over his shoulder in the breeze. 'Chicken rolls in golden breadcrumbs,' he said breathlessly, unwrapping the greaseproof paper to reveal them.

'That's kind of your mother,' Mai said, patting his arm. 'Will we see her at all, Garth?'

'Maybe,' he said. 'We're saving a seat for her at the bottom of the table.'

Mai made a sound of displeasure. 'Are you? I was going to sit there,' she said. 'And Harry is going to sit at the other end.'

'But we promised her,' Lauren pointed out. 'It's so that she can go home quickly if she wants to.'

'I don't remember that being decided in the committee,' Mai said, trying to take the notebook. They had a brief tug-of-war. 'Show me where it says.'

'It's not in the book, but she won't come if she can't sit there,' Garth said. 'I know it.'

'You and Harry can sit together at the top of the table like the King and Queen,' Lauren said in a moment of inspiration.

'You mean the Duke of Edinburgh and the Queen,' Mai corrected her.

'Sorry, yes.'

'But he's not going as the Duke of Edinburgh, is he.

He's going as—' Mai clasped her hand over her mouth and caught herself just in time. 'Sorry, can't tell you, it's a secret. Oh, there he is! He's just revealed himself! Fancy!'

They looked at Harry hurrying over in his suit, looking like no one other than himself. He was clapping his hands at them in a businesslike manner. 'Quick, quick! Keep moving! There's no time for talking!'

'We're not talking, we're having a discussion,' Mai said. 'They promised Barbara she could sit at the bottom of the table when I was going to sit there. It's not even in the minutes!'

Harry turned his head quickly, as if he was catching a fleeting thought as it flew by. 'Let her sit there, Mai, where she feels safe,' he said happily.

'My mother's made chicken rolls,' Garth told him, 'in golden breadcrumbs.'

'Lovely! Put them at the top of the table by me,' Harry said. 'I'll keep an eye on them.'

'Harry Lloyd!' Mai said indignantly as they went back to the house. 'The table's getting very crowded up your end.'

'All the more reason for you to sit there too,' Harry said with a wink.

When they were out of earshot, Garth said, 'Quick! Give me your paper and pen so I can reserve the place for my mother.'

'That Mai!' Lauren said indignantly.

'I know. She thinks she really is the Queen. Have you seen Flora yet?'

'Yes, she's in Rhiannon's front room, both of them scared to death with nerves because Rhiannon doesn't want to play the national anthem and Flora doesn't want to read her bardic poem. They just want to enjoy themselves, really, and have fun.'

'Think how the Queen's feeling,' Garth said. 'I bet she can't wait for afterwards, when she takes her crown off, puts her nightie on and cuddles up with her corgi.'

It was a startling and comforting image, and they started to laugh.

Emlyn was coming out of his house carrying a small rosewood occasional table. He set it up on the pavement in front of his Rover, and went back into the house again.

He came back out carrying a wooden crate that jingled musically with bottles, and put it under the table.

Finally, he returned with a little oak stand that held a lot of small glasses, and placed it on top.

Just then, a car drove up and parked at the end of the street, and Oswald, Dennis Hill, John the barber and Billy got out, carrying violin cases.

'Like gangsters,' Garth said enviously, 'come to make a rumpus.'

The four of them rested their violins on Tad's wall, went back to the car and returned with crates of beer which they put next to Emlyn's table.

'Caught in the act!' Mai said, flying across the road and confronting them like an avenging angel. 'Put those back in the car! This is a teetotal celebration!'

Dennis straightened up from behind the table and looked at Mai quizzically, biceps bulging, blue eyes gleaming, and held out his hand to introduce himself.

'Dennis Hill,' he said in his strong, deep voice.

Mai giggled and fluttered her hand coyly to her throat. 'You boys!' she said, and she dropped her anti-alcohol protest and got down to the serious business of accumulating knowledge. 'I'm Mai. Who do you belong to, Dennis? Where do you live? Have you got a wife?'

In the meantime, Emlyn and Harry were discussing the timing of the loyal toast. Harry had bought a book on *Etiquette for the Modern Gentleman*, which said it should come after the entrée and before dessert, followed by the national anthem.

'That means that the choir won't be singing the national anthem until after they've eaten,' Emlyn pointed out. 'And not all of them are staying. Some of them are going to church to watch the television set.'

Harry looked at his etiquette book resentfully. 'Waste of money,' he said.

'At least it's got the words for the toast in it, hasn't it?'

'Yes. "The Queen".'

'That's it? "The Queen"? You could have worked that out for yourself.'

'I know. I'm going to be rushed off my feet,' Harry said, 'doing the toast and then conducting.'

'Why don't I do the toast,' Emlyn offered. Seeing that Harry was about to object, he added, 'Or I could conduct, I don't mind either way.'

'You do the toast,' Harry quickly conceded. 'Do you want me to write it down?'

'I think I can remember it, thank you. Now that's sorted, we'd better get changed.' Emlyn looked at his watch. 'We've got ten minutes.'

Harry frowned. 'I've already changed.'

'Are you sure? You look the same as usual to me.'

'I'm Sir Adrian Boult?' Harry reminded him. 'The world-famous conductor? With a moustache?'

'Oh, yes. Adrian—yes, I remember now.' And he went home to get dressed up as the Pearly King.

48

Tad, Helen and Dorothea went to the neighbour's flat at ten o'clock on the dot and were welcomed by Cecil, a very tall man, equally as tall as Oswald by Tad's estimation, who was wearing a formal suit and a red bow-tie. He had perfectly round, black-framed glasses, which marked him out as an intellectual.

Dorothea introduced Tad as Thomas.

'Come in, come in and take a seat, Thomas,' Cecil said warmly. 'I do love your Union Jack tie.' Out of the corner of his mouth he said to Dorothea, 'Number eleven is coming in later.' Then he looked directly at Tad, lenses flashing, and mouthed *children*, in explanation.

The curtains were closed, shutting out the dim glare of the gloomy morning. Cecil had arranged a row of elaborate gilded chairs with velvet cushions in a semicircle around the television set, and a young man called Benjamin, delicate-looking, with a lock of black hair that fell over one eye, was helping him with hospitality.

Cecil smiled at the young man. 'Champagne, please, Benjamin!'

Tad raised his eyebrows in surprise and checked his watch for reassurance. But his watch confirmed the worst – it was only five minutes past ten, Tad time. He had never in his life had alcohol this early in the day and he fully expected Dorothea and Helen to have their eyebrows raised too – but on the contrary, they were looking expectantly towards Benjamin who was removing the gold foil from a bottle of Bollinger.

Tad lowered his eyebrows to their normal position and resolved to enjoy it. For all he knew, it was customary in London to drink champagne just after breakfast.

The champagne cork popped, the bubbles sighed, the drink whispered into the crystal champagne saucers and Cecil handed them a glass each. 'A little refresher before the service starts,' he said. 'Bottoms up!' With one arm in the air, holding up his own drink, he turned up the sound on the television set.

Tad stared at the screen in fascination. Looking at the crowds, he was perfectly sure he had never seen so many people gathered together in one place in his whole life. There were hundreds, thousands of them, and he felt he'd only previously caught a glimmer of the magnitude of what was unfolding. That all those people had gathered together in one mind to pay allegiance to a monarch they had never met, and probably never would, stood for something remarkably good and noble about the human race, in his view.

He was still holding his glass by its delicate stem and he looked at the restless riot of bubbles in his crystal saucer with the feeling that he was about to cross the threshold into hedonism. He sipped cautiously and felt the bubbles fizz on his tongue. 'Oh my!' he said appreciatively.

Cecil heard and gave him a fond smile. 'You know, Thomas, you remind me of someone,' he said. He snapped his fingers in the air several times and then said, 'No, it's no use. It will come to me, don't you worry.'

Tad was still embracing the policy, outlined by his wife, of being sociable by keeping quiet, otherwise in normal circumstances he would have started guessing in order to jog Cecil's memory. As it was, he settled on feeling proud that he reminded Cecil of someone he knew. He liked Cecil. He wondered if he should start wearing a bow-tie himself, combining playfulness with elegance. He imagined returning to Little Green Street as a different person altogether, as a quiet man called Thomas who wore a top hat and a red bow-tie. With a distant smile, he wondered what they were doing now, and whether they were thinking about him, too.

On the screen, carriages full of kings and queens, assorted dignitaries, viceroys and presidents from all over the world were funnelling into Westminster Abbey.

Outside the building, crowds were gathering.

And inside, Cecil topped up the glasses.

49

In Little Green Street, Emlyn was dressing in his Pearly King outfit. He arranged his hat carefully so that it didn't interfere with his quiff, and then adjusted it once more so that the black ostrich feathers didn't tickle his face, and studied himself square on in the cheval glass. The pearl buttons caught the light in the most extraordinary manner. He nodded at himself, feeling pleased.

This costume had brought him an enormous amount of luck, because without the planning of it he would never have found the courage to ask Nancy out, and certainly he would never have had the confidence to ask her to marry him. It was no exaggeration to say that it had changed his life. He felt strangely nervous about going out in public in it, though.

But then he thought about Harry, whose costume consisted of a moustache and a baton. At least he himself was making an effort. It hadn't taken any effort on Harry's part to grow a moustache, except for having to put up with a little scorn and a periodic ambush by Waffles, which he ought to have expected.

'Right, then,' he said aloud, and he galloped downstairs, black plumes bobbing, and went next door to call on Nancy.

Flora answered the door in her red, white and blue

striped dress and stared at him, speechless, taking him in from hat to foot.

'Hello,' he said to break the spell. 'Is Nancy in?'

'Front room,' she said, pointing as she let him in.

'I'm nearly ready, Emlyn,' Nancy said, with her back to him.

She was brushing out her blonde curls and she turned to look at him with a smile that took his breath away. Her dress was a deep purple, and he had never seen anyone more beautiful in his life.

'Hello, Nancy.'

'You look handsome,' she said softly, coming close to him and resting her fingers lightly on his pearly sleeve.

Emlyn felt all his courage coming back. 'And so do you.'

'Thank you,' she said, putting on the pearl and diamond tiara that Old Mrs Hughes had given her.

Arm-in-arm, they headed down the path to the occasional table positioned in front of Emlyn's shiny car, and he started filling the glasses with sloe gin for the loyal toast. He turned to count how many people had gathered by the table, but as they kept moving around, he decided it was easier just to fill all the glasses up for now.

Nancy went over to the table to help Mrs Evans distribute orange juice for the children, and she took one into Harry's for Rhiannon, who had decided to play the harp in the front room where no one could see her.

When everybody had a drink of some kind in their hands, Old Mrs Hughes rang her brass bell in the shape of a Welsh lady to get their attention, and when everyone had settled down and he had the full attention of the crowd, Emlyn stood on Tad's wall. 'Ladies and gentlemen, boys and girls, I would like to propose a toast to the Queen on her Coronation Day. Please raise your glasses to: The Queen!'

They responded, calling out, 'The Queen!' and drank the sloe gin.

Then Emlyn jumped off the wall, and Mai gestured wildly from her path to Rhiannon, who was looking out of the window and then disappeared, and moments later came the opening notes of the national anthem on the harp, and Harry stood poised with his baton, and the choir began to sing.

Their voices were a soaring celebration of homage and harmony in the pure air, accompanied by the tumbling thrum of the river and the trilling birds. The sound drifted on the breeze from the valley and soared towards the green hills.

And all the people in Little Green Street joined in because they had been listening to them in choir practice for weeks and knew all the words. On this day of all days, the words were special, and as they sang Lauren noticed a lone figure wearing a grey dress coming up the road from Garth's house.

She nudged Garth. 'It's your mum!'

'I know,' he said in amazement.

They watched his mother walk towards them and Lauren realised she was singing, too.

She had a beautiful voice, high, soprano, and instinctively the choir and all the guests began to sing more softly, so they could hear Barbara's voice soaring joyfully and bravely as she continued her long walk back to the fold: '. . . *to sing with heart and voice, God save the Queen!*'

When the anthem came to an end and they stopped singing, the music seemed to hang in the air above them in a shimmer of sound.

Garth walked the last few yards with his mother and led her to the promised place at the bottom of the table, with her name written on the 'Reserved' sign.

When they all sat down, Flora, with the bard's crown on her head, the recent dent smoothed out by Emlyn, stayed standing to recite her poem, holding the sheet of paper in front of her face, although she knew it by heart.

When she reached the end, Harry said, 'Hear, hear!'

Flora replied, 'Phew!'

Rhiannon hurried out of her house looking flustered and came to sit in the seat Lauren had kept for her. 'Was I all right playing?'

'Beautiful!'

'I was so nervous I got some notes wrong.'

'I didn't notice.'

'Look at me! I'm still shaking!'

Harry went round the tables to say hello to Barbara, and Emlyn handed her a little glass of sloe gin because she'd missed the toast. Seeing there was plenty left, Mai picked up a fresh glass for herself too while she was saying hello, and Nancy handed round the sandwiches.

Joanna and Owen emerged from under the table on their hands and knees because their secret camp was encroached on by legs, and wore their paper crowns lopsided, happily distracted by food.

Going back to sit at the head of the table, next to Harry, Mai had a good view of everyone, which was a mistake because she didn't seem to like what she saw.

'The choir's brought beer,' she told Nancy disapprovingly. 'I hope the alcohol won't lead to bad behaviour.'

Nancy laughed, and pointed to Mai's glass. 'What do you think that is?' she asked.

'Communion wine,' Mai said firmly. 'There's no alcohol in it, it's from the Methodist Church. Thanks for the cape, by the way. I like your tiara. I don't suppose it's real, is it?'

'It doesn't matter whether it is or not, it's pretty.'

'I suppose that's one way of looking at it,' Mai said doubtfully. 'Where did you come by it?'

'It belongs to Old Mrs Hughes, she wore it for the Farmers' Ball. Why isn't Harry wearing fancy dress? I thought he'd be the first to jump at the chance.'

'He is, he's Sir Adrian Boult the conductor. That's why he's got a baton.'

'Oh, I thought the baton was just for the choir. And is Sir Adrian Boult famous?'

'Quite famous.' Mai screwed her nose up for a moment because Harry was getting up from the table in such a hurry that he knocked his chair over and she was afraid it was a sign that he'd had too much stout.

Then she saw the corgi patrolling the tables. He was studying Harry with that determined, focused look in his eyes.

'It's the moustache,' Mai went on, reaching for a cheese butterfly. 'It explains everything, and holds the Adrian Boult look together. I'll be glad when he shaves it off, to be honest, although he is very fond of it. He pampers it something awful, in private.'

'Pampers what?' Harry asked, sitting down again.

Mai changed the subject. 'Emlyn's looking smart. Did you sew the buttons on for him, Nancy?'

'No, his mother did.'

'I see. And where are you going to live when you get married? Yours, or his?'

Nancy smiled. 'We haven't decided yet.' She stretched out her leg and stroked Emlyn's ankle with her foot.

'Well, I suggest . . .' Mai was saying, and her suggestion was lost in the babble of voices and a trellis-work of hands reaching for the plentiful food.

50

In Cecil's drawing-room in London, the Coronation service had started, and Benjamin had put the champagne back in the ice bucket for the duration.

Tad was feeling exceptionally comfortable and slightly giddy on the velvet and gilt chair, and he watched the solemn proceedings in a bit of a dream, but following Cecil's example he stood up when the people in Westminster Abbey – more formally known as the Abbey Church of St Peter – stood up, and sat when they knelt, because Cecil had made it clear to them before the service that kneeling didn't agree with his trousers.

He listened to the archbishop saying, 'Sirs, I here present unto you Queen Elizabeth, your undoubted Queen: Wherefore all you who are come this day to do your homage and service, are you willing to do the same?'

And Tad, Helen, Cecil, Benjamin and Dorothea said together in a state of excitement in Cecil's drawing-room, 'God save Queen Elizabeth!'

The trumpets sounded, and Tad settled back in his chair mesmerised by the archbishop's solemn words. Then it was the crowning itself, and he was jerked back to the present by Cecil and Benjamin shouting, 'GOD SAVE THE QUEEN!'

'Queen,' said Dorothea, waking up with a start.

The windowpanes vibrated behind the velvet drapes as

the cannons sounded in Hyde Park, and a flurry of pigeons flapped startled from the roof and made a graceful circuit around Marble Arch.

It wasn't until the Duke of Edinburgh, Earl of Merioneth, ascended the steps to the Queen's throne that Tad sat forward and gave the television his full attention, his head suddenly perfectly clear. It was the most touching thing he had ever seen.

Prince Philip humbly took off his crown and knelt down in front of his wife.

There was total silence in the Abbey as the Queen took her husband's hands in hers.

In a clear voice, he looked up at her and said, 'I, Philip, Duke of Edinburgh, do become your liege man of life and limb, and of earthly worship; and faith and truth I will bear unto you, to live and die, against all manner of folks. So help me God.' Getting to his feet again after this enormous promise, Prince Philip touched his wife's crown and bent forward to kiss her cheek.

Tad's eyes blurred with tears at the power and love of his words and he squeezed his eyes shut to save them spilling down his cheeks and betraying his feelings.

After a moment he glanced at Helen, who was staring at the screen wistfully with her chin resting on her fist. He wondered what she was thinking.

The choir was singing the anthems and then, when they fell quiet, the drums beat and the trumpets sounded, and Cecil waved his arms at them. 'God save Queen Elizabeth! Long live Queen Elizabeth! May the Queen live for ever!' they shouted with gusto in the elegant room.

They sat with heads bowed through the wonderfully

familiar communion service, and Cecil sprinkled in a few 'Amens' in the appropriate places, and some inappropriate ones. When it was finally all over the five of them stood up to sing the national anthem with a great deal of verve, which stemmed from the feeling of having been personally involved in something quite out of their experience.

Cecil had ordered in food from Fortnum & Mason, already arranged on silver trays, and there was a knock on the door as the troublesome neighbours from number eleven turned up promptly with two young daughters in party dresses, not much younger than Lauren, Tad estimated. He stood up to stretch his legs and went over to look out of the window at the crowds.

Dorothea came up behind him with her notebook. 'Refreshing service, wasn't it?' she asked him pleasantly.

Refreshing? The poet in Tad had many words in his head a lot more majestic than 'refreshing', but, feeling his wife's eyes on him, he smiled and nodded instead of quibbling.

Dorothea checked her notes and glanced at the clock. 'Nothing is going to happen now until two fifty-five precisely, when the head of the procession is due to walk past, with the Queen arriving at three-forty. Come and eat, to pass the time.'

Cecil instructed Benjamin to fill his glass again. 'Thomas, it's just come to me! You've got the look of the Duke of Edinburgh about you. I expect everyone tells you that,' he said.

Tad smiled modestly and nodded. It didn't seem necessary to tell Cecil that nobody had told him that except he himself. He really was the most discerning of people, he thought warmly.

The girls, Jane and Sara, sat cross-legged on the floor in front of the television, watching their hero of the day, little Prince Charles, who the BBC had spotlighted watching his mother's crowning in varying poses with a certain endearing restlessness. 'He's so darling!'

'He's such a sweetie!'

'We cheered when we saw him, did you?' they asked Benjamin, who was handing them a canapé each.

'He's our little prince!'

'We toasted him in fizzy lemonade!'

'That little chap will be crowned King one day,' Benjamin said, eating the last canapé himself.

Tad raised his glass. He was enjoying himself far more than he'd expected. Even the noisy neighbours from number eleven, who seemed to him to be a perfectly ordinary and unassuming family, were very friendly and although he would have liked to, he could find no fault in the occasion at all.

At two forty-five, Dorothea, Tad and Helen went back to Dorothea's flat. Tad remembered the three Union Jacks that Emlyn had given him, and the iced cakes from Harry and Mai. He went to the bedroom to fetch them out of his bag.

As Dorothea opened the windows, a roar like distant thunder rolled over the city, increasing in intensity in a tidal wave of sound. Leaning out, they could hear drumming and trumpets and marching, faintly at first but coming ever closer along the park's East Carriage Drive. The crowds in the streets began to chant: 'We want the Queen!' as they waved flags, pennants, hats and the cardboard periscopes bought to see over the heads of the Royal Air Force airmen lining the route from Oxford Street all the way to the Haymarket. The soundwaves rolled up the side of the building and Tad, Dorothea and Helen waved their flags joyfully.

In Tad's mind, partly because he'd watched it on the television set and partly because of the dull drizzle, the Coronation had been a black and white event. But now he was seeing everything in full, dazzling colour as the gold State Coach came into Oxford Street gleaming like a sunrise. The red of the Royal Guards' tunics and the white coats of the horses were bright against the damp grey street, and as they passed, Tad caught a glimpse of a white-gloved hand at the window and he joined in the crescendo of cheers that rose up from the street below. And when to his surprise Dorothea started singing along with the crowd, Tad joined in, beating his hands against his leg to the rhythm of the marching bands:

> 'It's the soldiers of the Queen, my lads,
> Who've been, my lads,
> Who've seen, my lads,
> In the fight for England's glory, lads,
> When we've had to show them what we mean.
> And when we say we've always won,
> And when they ask us how it's done,
> We'll proudly point to ev'ry one of England's
>   soldiers of the Queen!'

51

Back in Little Green Street, under the turquoise and grey sky, the children were being taken home to bed, and Harry and Emlyn were moving the chairs and tables back to the houses so people would have something to eat their breakfast off the next day.

The choir members were lapsing into song, and on the garden walls, the empty bottles of stout and sloe gin were outnumbering the full ones. Mr Griffiths came with his wife after watching the Coronation on the television, and Dennis Hill, Oswald, John the Barber and Billy took their violins out and, nodding the signal, they started to play.

Garth, Barbara, Emlyn and Nancy were tapping in time to the jaunty music. Nancy was wearing Emlyn's hat with the black plumes, and Emlyn was wearing the tiara around his quiff. They looked carelessly happy.

Mai was looking carelessly happy, too, in her wedding dress.

Outside in the twilight, in the absence of chairs, the men moved the bottles to the rosewood table in front of Emlyn's car and all the neighbours were resting on their garden walls.

Rhiannon sat next to Lauren because their house had a hedge instead of a wall, and with two strong notes in G, the fiddlers played a folk tune that followed the joyful dance steps of their fathers.

Harry beat his foot on the pavement and his face rested on his chins as comfy as a neck brace. He picked up the rhythm with his baton, and Lauren and Flora began to clap. All the solid men of the choir clapped along under the turquoise and grey sky.

Garth, with his striped tie fastened around his head and his shirt collar undone, danced towards Lauren, bowing formally and taking her hand.

Happy at being claimed, Lauren skipped into the circle and suddenly, giggling, kicking, tripping, stepping, breathless and happy, Flora, Rhiannon and all the women were dancing, holding hands with Garth's mother Barbara, Nancy with Emlyn's Pearly King hat coming down over her eyes, and Mai swaying from foot to foot.

With a gleam in her eye, Mai lifted her aggressive Welsh chin and held out her hands to Oswald, who scooted her sideways so fast that she shrieked.

As they danced, the darkness spread gradually upwards from the Dee, blackening the gardens and absorbing the trees and the people. Only the dark blue sky over the hills stayed bright.

In the darkness, Harry put aside the clapping and disappeared into his white house, coming out shortly afterwards with the communion tray tinkling with clean glasses, and a fresh bottle of Emlyn's sloe gin tucked under his arm.

'Quick, Mai, I can't manage,' he shouted irritably but he was excited by his own hospitality and poured a measure of the garnet liquid into every glass – letting the girls take one too, to show what a good host he was. '*Iechyd da!*' he shouted. 'Good health!'

Billy from the Hand held up one of the little glasses to

examine it in the street light. 'I'll bet you anything these are communion glasses from the Methodist Church,' he said perceptively enough until he drank it.

Lauren was wearing Old Mrs Hughes's knitted crown. The sloe gin scorched ferociously, sweet as toffee, and she sucked the cool night air down her throat in the hope of swallowing the evening whole. The world had relaxed its hold on them that day and become warm and generous. The music and laughter and clapping lifted from the small street in the small valley and diffused up into the vast dark universe above the hills.

'What's Mam doing?' Rhiannon said, tugging Lauren's arm.

Mai was parting the little crowd with her arms as though she was swimming breaststroke along the street.

'Um . . .' Lauren let her explanation trail away into the minims because she wasn't sure herself.

Mai made a space for herself with great confidence, and at the promise of a new spectacle the neighbours obediently formed a ragged circle around her, Emlyn, Nancy, Mrs Evans, Barbara, Harry, Garth.

'Kay Palinka!' Mai commanded. 'I mean, play "Kalinka"!' and the musicians obligingly tucked their violins back under their chins.

Garth and Emlyn started to clap, beating Harry to it, because despite his moustache and baton, he wasn't the only one who could clap in time.

Lauren and Flora, sitting on the wall to catch their breath, started to clap too.

Mai's dancing came as a bit of a surprise to everyone – powerful and energetic, she was as lively as an eel.

The musicians increased the tempo and Mai started to twirl around on the spot, giving the occasional kick, something she'd learnt from the Cossacks when they came to stay for the music festival. Her lace wedding dress caught the breeze, her fur cape floated from the diamanté fastening, and Harry gave an appreciative wolf whistle.

Enjoying herself, Mai kicked off her shoes – one just missed Oswald and the other fell off the kerb – and danced breathlessly at the centre of one large clapping circle, her bun coming undone, her brown hair flying loose, hair grips dangling. She was exhilarated, happy, and as Lauren clapped she looked at Rhiannon briefly, expecting her at any minute to start dancing too.

Rhiannon's lips were parted as she stared at her mother.

No wonder; they'd seen a lot of folk dancing over the years and this was as good as any, because it was difficult to sustain a pirouette for any length of time. And yet Mai didn't stop.

The harder they clapped, the faster she moved. It seemed as if the clapping was powering her, making her dance more vigorously, with sharp turns of her head that flicked her hair into a blur. She twirled faster and faster – and then suddenly she vanished from the circle of people, just like that, leaving an empty arena of dark street with neighbours clapping.

The fiddlers stopped playing with a discordant scrape and looked at each other in confusion, as though they had clapped Mai Lloyd off the face of the earth.

Harry strode onto the pavement to look over his short green hedge, cursing. Its leaves glowed bright green in the lights from his house. 'Dash it all!' he said crossly. The hedge was intact, but it was trembling, and after a moment Mai got to her feet and appeared from behind it, pale, shocked and covered in petals.

'What did you do that for?' Harry demanded crossly, his hands on his waist. 'Look what you've done to my damask roses!'

As if she'd done it on purpose, Lauren thought, feeling the laughter rise in her chest. She cupped her hand over her mouth and exchanged wide, excited eyes with Rhiannon.

Flora pinched her nose and her laughter came through as a snort.

'Stupid place to put a hedge, Harry,' Emlyn said, deadpan, patting his back.

Mai staggered diagonally onto the grey concrete path with her hands held out as if she didn't quite trust the ground to stay still. Apart from the wedding dress, she was unrecognisable. The cape had twisted round, giving her a furry white bib and her long, tumbling hair barely hid the gaping back. A terrible change had come over her; she looked as if something awful had happened to her behind that hedge.

After a moment's indecision, Harry followed her into the kitchen, still cross about his roses, and slammed the door.

Back outside it was hard to know who started laughing first, because all the men had come under her disapproving scrutiny during the day because of the beer, and now it took them a while to recover.

When they finally did, it was Old Mrs Hughes who summed it up best for all of them. 'Mai, of all people!' she said happily, wiping tears of laughter away. 'She's got her come-uppance all right, after all her airs and graces! Drunk as a lord, and her so proper! I'll tell you something, though, I'll never forget her dancing as long as I live.'

'Are you all right, Rhiannon?' Lauren asked because it was awful being shown up by one's mother.

'I'm not sure. Let's go for a walk,' Rhiannon said. 'They're always going on at me to behave but nothing I do is ever going to be as bad as that. Are you coming, Flora?'

'Yes,' Flora grinned.

Garth hesitated. He was standing with his hands in his pockets, looking at his mother. His love for her vied with his eagerness to join them.

'You go, son,' Barbara said kindly. 'I'll just go in to see Mai, check if she's all right.'

For a moment he hesitated and then he smiled and gave the slightest nod of his head. 'See you later then,' he said.

The four friends walked to the bridge in the growing dark, arm-in-arm like a human chain, then down to the river path where the steps were inset into the wall. The sleeping ducks woke up from their nests in the reeds, protesting at their intruding voices, and settled down again.

They climbed down to the flat grey rocks, lay down feeling the residual warmth of the day, and spreadeagled themselves like starfish.

Above them, the stars glittered in the darkening sky.

'This has been the longest day in the world,' Lauren said, 'and this morning when we were worrying about everything, it seems like weeks ago now. But it's gone quickly, too.'

Their words were almost lost against the tumbling water.

'Do you think your mother enjoyed it?' Flora asked Garth.

'I think so,' he said thoughtfully. 'I think she could see what she'd missed. I'm glad she came, or she wouldn't have believed it.'

'Just think! All these weeks that we've been planning it, and now it's over,' Lauren said.

Rhiannon grunted. 'All that worrying I did about playing the harp for the choir.'

'And me being scared stiff of reading my poem,' Flora agreed. 'It wasn't that hard, after all.'

'And me, wondering whether my mother was going to come or not.'

'And my mam worrying that her wedding dress wouldn't do up,' Rhiannon added indignantly. 'I was so embarrassed. Honestly, when she disappeared—'

'And we couldn't understand it—'

'Aw, Rhiannon, don't worry, Tad embarrasses me all the time.'

'Has he ever been drunk in public though?'

'Not in public, but probably in Little Green Street, especially at Christmas when there's brandy in the white sauce and Christmas pudding and mince pies and everything.' Lauren watched the moon slide out from behind a cloud. 'I can feel the whole world turning, can you? I wonder what the Queen is doing now?'

'Tucking Prince Charles and Princess Anne up in bed.'

'And then doing the same as us, I expect. Lying down like a starfish on the carpet in Buckingham Palace, thinking how long the day was from start to finish, and at the same time, how quickly it all went.'

'And knowing all their guests are on their way back to their homes.'

'Their villages.'

'Their towns.'

'Their countries.'

'All over the world.'

Rhiannon stood up and smoothed the skirt of her dress, and one by one, Flora, Garth and Lauren stood up and stretched as if they'd been asleep for a long time.

They climbed back up to the river path, and headed home too.

52

Coronation Day was over.

Dorothea walked with them down the stairs and stood by the door to say goodbye. Helen kissed her cheek, and Tad shook her hand.

'I've thoroughly enjoyed myself,' he told her.

She gave him another of her rare smiles, and it warmed his heart. 'I'm so pleased,' she said. 'And, Thomas,' she added as he turned to go, 'don't be a stranger.'

'I won't,' he said sincerely.

Tad and Helen joined the crowds in the streets that evening, battling their way to Paddington Station. They were held up at a barrier in the Edgware Road by two policemen, who were letting people through in large groups. Tad, liberated from Mayfair rules, started talking to three men his own age whose damp overcoats he was squashed up against and who were trying to get to Euston. They were going all the way back to Belfast on the Coronation Express, which would get them home the following morning.

'I never!' Tad said, marvelling at the thought of the marathon journey ahead of them. He told the men where he was from, which happy coincidence, they realised, made them neighbours, with only the Irish Sea between them, all the time keeping a tight grip on Helen's arm to save losing her in the throng, and he was glad he had because the barriers were opened just then and in the sudden surge his trilby got knocked off his head.

To his dismay, he saw it tumble over the crowd and then quickly lost sight of it, but there was nothing to be done.

The crowd gradually thinned out, and although it had stopped raining and the day had brightened considerably the air was damp and heavy.

When they got to Paddington, he stopped to check his wallet for his ticket and realised that Helen was staring at him strangely, with a half-smile on her pale lips. 'What is it?' he asked her, bracing himself for criticism. She had barely said a word to him all this time.

'Your hair's all wet. You look like Tad again,' she said, and then her voice was lost in the hiss of steam.

He patted his hand over his head, and sure enough, to his dismay, the familiar kinks and crinkles were back. In his mind he could hear Prince Philip saying, 'Your liege man of life and limb,' with steady conviction and confidence, but the kinship he'd had with him was fading now he was Tad again.

Their GWR train was waiting alongside the platform with its heraldic imagery of a golden lion astride a driving wheel, and they climbed on board and found an empty carriage. He let Helen choose the seat, and sat next to her because that way he wouldn't have to notice whether she was avoiding his eyes.

It wasn't long before their carriage filled up, the morose passengers quiet, their happiness exhausted, sitting too close with their coats smelling of damp.

Tad's memories of the day came back to him in a series

of images: Prince Philip kneeling before the Queen, the archbishop's sonorous tones, the gathering of solemn and robed peers, coronets being taken off and put back on again, the small boy in the Abbey watching with his aunt and grandmother, with only the faintest subliminal knowledge that one day this would all be for him, the triumphant volley of the Royal Gun Salute from Hyde Park and the Tower, the military bands and fanfare of trumpets, the delicate crystal stem in his fingers and champagne on his tongue, the blinding dazzle of colour and pageantry, the golden State Coach lighting up the wet grey streets like sunrise, troops marching in step, hundreds of them, men and women, arms swinging in perfect time to that stirring music, the ebb and surge of constant cheering from the crowd.

Through half-closed eyes, his head rolling with the rhythm of the train, Tad watched the countryside go by, and the stations of Slough and High Wycombe.

He wondered how Little Green Street was managing without him as he left the day's triumph behind. He wondered whether the party had gone well and if not, how long it would take them to forgive him.

Tad and Helen got off the train in the early hours of Wednesday morning, their only company in the deserted moonlit town a black cat who walked alongside them for a few yards and slunk away through a garden gate.

Tad felt as if he had been away for a long time, a traveller who had seen many wondrous things. At the same time he was very glad to be home. He had no doubt that Little Green Street would be tucked in bed and fast asleep, the houses white and luminous in the dark. So it was a surprise to see lights on in Harry's upstairs window, and Emlyn's, too.

He noticed to his dismay that at the bottom of Emlyn's drive was a small table covered in empty bottles glistening under the street light. A piece of crêpe paper, grey in the dark, flapped listlessly over their wall. He stopped dead – he could hear singing coming from one of the houses in the dark.

As they walked down their path to the front door, Helen said softly, 'Look at Harry's roses!'

The flower heads were bare and bowed, and the soil beneath them was lost under a bed of petals.

'Armageddon!' Tad whispered, shocked.

They went into the kitchen, and he put their bags down, wondering what they would find. Lauren had left them a note on the table so he studied it for clues: *Welcome home. See you tomorrow. The party was great.*

Tad read it twice, as if it was written in code, and passed it to Helen. 'What do you make of that?'

'Nothing, really. I'm glad she had a good time. Do you want a cup of tea before bed?'

'Yes, let's have one,' he said, not because he was thirsty but because she'd offered and it was something to share. They were behaving like people who'd known each other well a long time ago, and had forgotten why.

While the kettle was boiling, he went quickly upstairs in the hope that Lauren was awake in bed and waiting to fill them in on the day's events, but the door of the room was open and her bed was tidily made.

He went back down. Helen pushed a cup of tea across

the table towards him and propped her chin on her fist. She tilted her head thoughtfully. 'You're very quiet,' she said. 'It's not like you.'

'Quiet?' Tad was feeling out of sorts now he was back. 'I thought that's what you wanted, Helen.' He hadn't meant to say it, but there it was, his resentment making itself known.

She frowned. 'I told you to stop talking when you arrived yesterday because you seemed intent on upsetting my mother.'

'At the time I felt she'd got us to go there under false pretences of having general debility.'

'Not me, she didn't. I *wanted* to go there, once she'd asked.'

Tad stared at her in surprise. 'Did you? You didn't say.'

'Yes, I did. You didn't listen. I think you'd have preferred it if she had been dying, wouldn't you? It would have made you look noble and dutiful.'

'No! That's a terrible thing to say, Helen!'

'Instead, you had a good time. You enjoyed yourself. And don't give me that look – I've lived my life your way for seventeen years and for once, just once, you've had to do something my way and you did it with bad grace.'

'You've lived your life *my* way?' Tad asked incredulously, slamming his hands on the red tablecloth. 'You've come to chapel with me, have you? You've sung at choir practice? You've learned the language?'

'I've *lived* here!' Helen's voice rose shrilly. 'In this backwater! Sharing the bloody collective consciousness of the town whether I've wanted to or not!'

He stared at her in shock. He'd never seen this side of

her before. He felt her cautious guard had been ripped away, revealing the anger beneath.

'Why didn't you tell me that was how you felt?'

'What's the point? You can't talk in a civilised way, without shouting.'

'Shouting?' Suddenly aware he *was* shouting, Tad fell quiet and gripped a clump of hair in his hand. She'd seen him for what he was, and he felt raw and ashamed.

'You're impossible. I'm going to bed,' Helen said abruptly. She left the tea on the table, undrunk, and ran upstairs. He heard the bedroom door slam.

Resting his head on his folded arms, Tad miserably replayed the conversation in his head. He analysed it, looking for reasons why it wasn't all his fault. If she'd said that she wanted to go to London . . . But she *had* said it.

And it was also true that he'd been resentful at discovering Dorothea was perfectly well after all.

But he *had* enjoyed himself, she was right about that too. He'd enjoyed it more than he could ever have imagined. Dorothea, Cecil, Benjamin, the champagne, the procession, he was proud that he'd been there and he would never, ever forget it. The experience was part of him now, the kind of thing that he could talk about to friends; and when he'd exhausted them with it, to acquaintances and strangers too.

And he was truly glad that Dorothea wasn't ill. They had bonded in a way he'd never imagined, and he felt things would be different between them from now on.

He went upstairs intending to tell Helen all these things, but the light was off and she was sleeping. He crept to the bathroom. It would have to wait until morning, when he would put things right.

Tad got up for school a few hours later feeling as if he'd been awake all night battling with self-reproach. As he left the house he saw that the crêpe paper had gone from their wall, whether blown by the breeze or picked up by a passer-by he wasn't sure. The table with the bottles on by Emlyn's house had been put away.

He couldn't detect any other signs of life in the street. From Nancy's windows, the Queen greeted him, her gloved hand raised. He hoped the girls had gone to school and weren't still asleep in a state of chaos.

He glanced at his watch, and for only the second time in his career, he saw he was going to be late.

53

Harry's shrill alarm clock woke Mai up that morning and she found herself lying on top of the bed clothes in a state of depressed confusion. Her head was throbbing and she had a strange, fruity taste in her mouth.

Next to her, Harry was on his back under the covers with his mouth slightly open and his moustache hammock quivering with snores. As the alarm penetrated his dreams, he swallowed a snort and threw his arms wide. Keeping his eyes shut, he reached instinctively for the clock and pressed the button that shut it off.

Mai saw to her shock that not only did she still have the wedding dress on from the day before, but it had leaves and twigs caught up in the lace.

She propelled herself into a sitting position by means of her elbows and became aware of a huge gap in her memory where the evening should have been. The instant panic of loss galvanised her, and she recognised it as the same feeling she had when she'd mislaid her purse or her keys, except without the urge to hunt for it. She was finding it difficult to move.

Dried out and feverish, Mai rested the back of her hand against her hot forehead and wondered if she'd contracted malaria, transmitted from the East by Jimmy Green. Then she noticed her bare feet. They were dusty, as if she'd been dancing with no shoes on.

After always priding herself on her good memory, which had kept her in good stead all these years, she forced herself to concentrate on what she could remember of the night before. There was the Coronation Party, raucous singing, violins – dancing! She recalled her shoe flying off . . . 'Harry! Wake up!'

'I am awake.' He opened one eye and looked at her crossly. 'What? What is it?'

Mai had the unsettling memory that he'd been deeply disapproving of her the night before. 'What happened last night?'

'Ha! Don't you remember?' He propped himself on his elbow to look at her. 'You got drunk and fell over the hedge onto my roses. Ruined the garden. There's not a petal left on any of them.'

'Do you think . . . did anyone notice?' she asked him hopefully.

'Oh yes, they noticed all right,' Harry said. 'You were the star turn, and no mistake.' He looked at the alarm clock again, threw back the covers and sat on the edge of the bed. 'How's your hangover?'

'Hangover?' Mai had the faint recollection of Old Mrs Hughes telling her to go easy on the sloe gin, and in a playful response she'd pulled Old Mrs Hughes's knitted crown down over her eyes. She groaned.

'I'll get you an aspirin,' Harry said, putting on his dressing gown to go downstairs.

Mai got out of bed too and found the floor was unsteady underfoot. Catching sight of herself in the mirror, she looked terribly mad and unkempt and she felt a pathetic need for Harry's reassurance.

Downstairs, Harry was sitting at the kitchen table, starting on a slice of chocolate cake for breakfast. The kettle was boiling. Nancy's white fur cape was hanging on the back of the chair with bits of privet caught in it.

She remembered all the things she'd said about Nancy behind her back, and some to her face. 'What am I going to do?' Mai groaned again in shame. 'Did Rhiannon see me?' she asked fearfully, trying to comb the twigs from the fur with her fingers.

'Yes, and she stayed at Nancy's last night, on the grounds you were a bad influence.' Harry didn't say it unkindly, because the chocolate cake was restoring his good humour, but it was rather novel to be able to reproach his wife for a change. 'What a do!' he exclaimed cheerfully. 'We surpassed ourselves in our celebrations and no mistake!'

Mai held on to the table to steady herself. There was something strange about it. A fresh unreality hit her. 'Harry! This isn't ours. Where's our table gone?'

'Somebody will have it,' he said logically, getting up to make the tea and wiping cake crumbs from his moustache. 'We couldn't tell one from the other in the dark. As long as we had one each for the morning, that was our thinking.' He found a little brown jar of aspirin in the cupboard, took out the cotton-wool plug and shook out two, which he dropped into Mai's palm. He poured her a glass of water and watched speculatively as she drank it down. 'I don't know if you're ever going to get out of that frock, Mai, after that struggle we had last night – we couldn't get it up or down,' he said. 'I might have to cut you free with the scissors. Or shall I get Nancy in to help you before she goes to work?'

'No!' Mai had a faint memory of Nancy being kind and gentle with her, and while she knew she should be grateful, it now made her feel worse. 'No,' she repeated. 'Just cut me out of it and throw it away. I never want to set eyes on it again as long as I live.'

The kitchen door opened and Rhiannon came in wearing her school uniform. She looked at her mother with her nose held high in disapproval. Without a word she went upstairs and they heard the water running in the bathroom wash basin.

Harry took the scissors out of the kitchen drawer and Mai turned round, wanting to die to get it all over and done with. She felt the waistband of the dress give way and she turned back to him, pale and ill, gripping the shawl collar of his dressing gown desperately. 'What am I going to do, Harry? And me with my reputation to think of?'

He blew his cheeks out. 'It's too late now to worry about your reputation,' he said, trying to smooth her unkempt hair and releasing a sprinkle of hair grips and a leaf. 'It'll be all over the town by now. After all these years of you being holier-than-thou, people are going to make the most of it and you can't blame them. Don't worry,' he said consolingly. 'I dare say you'll live it down eventually.'

Eventually. Mai, who had spent her life gossiping, was now the subject of it and it didn't feel nice. Her doom-laden thoughts beat in her skull like a gong and she whimpered pitifully.

'Go and have a rest, love,' Harry said, patting her head.

'Yes, I think I will.' Clutching the wedding dress, she went back upstairs, glad of the darkened bedroom, and tried to sleep.

54

Emlyn was ready for work and feeling relieved that he'd had the foresight the previous day to leave one bottle of sloe gin safely in the shed for Mr Griffiths.

He had something important to ask him, and while the minister was very keen on hell-fire in the pulpit, he was compassion itself in day-to-day life and he'd enjoyed himself no end the night before, so Emlyn was encouraged.

He brought in his rosewood table, and wiped off the dew. He counted the quantity of empty bottles and realised he'd never been happier in his life.

What a party! He felt as if he'd been smiling all night, and he was still smiling now.

Nancy had been the best-dressed woman in the street, no question, and although he and Harry had got into a heated argument quite late on about whose the best costume was, and despite Harry's protestations that he'd put a lot of effort into growing his moustache, the general feeling of the assembled partygoers had been that, as a rule, facial hair grew regardless of whether one put effort into it or not and so Emlyn's costume won, hands down.

Emlyn wondered whether Harry would keep the moustache, or whether now, in the cold light of day, it would be a harsh reminder of the night Mai spun out of control.

He chuckled to himself and decided to have a quick

look at Harry's garden on his way to work to admire the damage.

But the other thing that was making him happy was Nancy. Not only was she beautiful, she was kind. Emlyn knew the white fur cape that Mai was wearing belonged to Nancy, and that she'd intended to wear it herself. And therefore, when Mai had reappeared, horribly transformed, on the other side of the hedge, it wouldn't have been surprising if Nancy had reacted in exactly the same way about the cape as Harry had about his roses – with blood-stirring indignation. She would have been entitled to. There was no doubt that many or even most of the rumours about Nancy over the years had been started by Mai, and that there was a certain amount of snobbery in the way that Mai felt Nancy was 'enjoying herself' too much in life, as if the alternative, not enjoying oneself, was morally superior. So it was a perfect opportunity, if she'd been that way inclined, for Nancy to make the most of Mai's downfall.

But she hadn't done that at all. She'd just gone into Mai's kitchen after her, to see if she was all right and to make her a coffee.

Emlyn fastened the knot in his tie with the comfortable feeling that he was a very lucky man.

As he left the house and crossed the road to Harry's to look at his roses, Harry came out of his front door carrying his briefcase and he and Emlyn stood together and regarded the damage like two mourners at a graveside. Emlyn muttered words of sympathy and Harry gripped his briefcase more tightly, shaking his head and puffing his cheeks. 'Dew, Emlyn. She made short work of them and

I was hoping the blooms would last until the festival visitors came. They're a sorry sight now, aren't they.'

'Unsalvageable. How's Mai today?'

'Shabby,' Harry said, lowering his chins. He gave Emlyn a sideways glance.

Emlyn sucked in his cheeks.

Harry was having difficulty keeping a straight face too. They held it in and walked as quickly as they could to the end of the road, where they guffawed with laughter.

For a moment the memory of the sheer fun of the party lifted them buoyantly into this new day.

'See you later,' they said in unison, still chuckling as they parted ways.

55

That morning, Lauren, Flora, Garth and Rhiannon had plenty to talk about on their way to school.

Rhiannon had unfortunately seen a different side to her mother, one that she'd never realised existed. 'And you'll never believe it, she was still wearing the wedding dress this morning,' she said. 'She looked as if she'd been drawn through a hedge backwards.'

'To be fair, she had,' Flora pointed out, swinging her satchel.

'Seeing your mother dancing in the street drunk made the whole day for my mother, to be honest,' Garth added, to cheer her up. 'Someone worse off than herself, and the scandal of it, too. I mean, if it helps.'

'It doesn't,' Rhiannon said. 'She's ruined her reputation.'

'That's just the kind of thing that Mai would say,' Lauren teased, and Rhiannon chased her all along the main road and over the canal until they collapsed, breathless and laughing, by the school gates.

At school assembly that day, after they'd sung the hymn, Mr Jones the headmaster read the notices. Lauren listened half-heartedly to the plans for sports day, netball practice was taking place at the same time as the football tournament, articles for the school newsletter were welcomed by the editor, classes were continuing as normal, and the

International Musical Festival was taking place at the end of term, volunteers to put their names on the list on the noticeboard.

'This,' Mr Jones said, introducing an unfamiliar enthusiasm into the boring recital of the notices, 'is going to be a particularly special musical festival for us because Her Majesty Queen Elizabeth, well-known for her knowledge and love of music, is coming to Wales to see it for herself – and so soon after the Coronation, too!' He looked at them over the black frames of his spectacles.

'As you know,' he continued, 'every year it is customary for the Youth Message of Peace to be read by a pupil from a local school. This year, it is the turn of our school and I have decided that the pupil reading the Peace Message will be—' He paused, adjusted his glasses to the bridge of his nose and consulted the sheet of paper in his hand '—Lauren Jones.'

Lauren was watching Garth flick a screwed-up piece of paper at the supply teacher, who batted the air as if it were a wasp.

Flora nudged her. 'It's you!'

Lauren looked up, alarmed and flustered. 'Do I have to go up or what?'

'Yes, go on, quick, hurry!'

Lauren started to edge along the row, nimbly avoiding the feet of those trying to trip her up on the way, and at the same time the headmaster left the stage, gown draped around him and his neck bent at an angle like a vulture, so Flora grabbed Lauren's shirt and jerked her back.

'Thanks a lot, Flora, I nearly made a fool of myself,'

Lauren said indignantly but it was a half-hearted protestation because she was laughing too and mostly she was thinking, I've been chosen to read the Peace Message!

Her first instinct was that she couldn't wait to tell Tad. But then she had a better idea – she would surprise him.

Rhiannon was full of excitement. 'The Queen might hear you reading it! We'll wave and give her flowers! And she might see my dad and think he's – what's his name again? I keep forgetting.'

'Andrew Bolton, or something like that,' Garth said confidently.

'Yes, him, and she might accidentally talk to him, if he's still being him by then.'

It was all very exciting. Lauren had always been proud of the festival because of the smallness of the town and the boldness of its belief. Every year, they welcomed visitors into their homes, and into their hearts, to share music and hospitality, optimism and peace.

And it was wonderful to think they could give that same Welsh welcome to the Queen too.

56

On Thursday, early evening, Tad was sitting in the front room with the light on because the picture of Her Majesty in the window was casting a shade. He was reading a thank-you speech that the Queen had broadcast on the evening of the Coronation and which was reported in *The Times* in full and which brought tears to his eyes:

'When I spoke to you last, at Christmas, I asked you all, whatever your religion, to pray for me on the day of my Coronation – to pray that God would give me wisdom and strength to carry out the promises that I should then be making.

'Throughout this memorable day I have been uplifted and sustained by the knowledge that your thoughts and prayers were with me. I have been aware all the time that my peoples, spread far and wide throughout every continent and ocean in the world, were united to support me in the task to which I have now been dedicated with such solemnity.

'Many thousands of you came to London from all parts of the Commonwealth and Empire to join in the ceremony . . .'

Tad sat up a little straighter in his armchair, and continued reading.

'... but I have been conscious too of the millions of others who have shared in it by means of wireless or television in their homes.

'All of you, near or far, have been united in one purpose. It is hard for me to find words in which to tell you of the strength which this knowledge has given me ...

'In this resolve I have my husband to support me. He shares all my ideals and all my affection for you. Then, although my experience is so short and my task so new, I have in my parents and grandparents an example which I can follow with certainty and with confidence ...

'Parliamentary institutions, with their free speech and respect for the rights of minorities, and the inspiration of a broad tolerance in thought and expression – all this we conceive to be a precious part of our way of life and outlook ...

'As this day draws to its close, I know that my abiding memory of it will be, not only the solemnity and beauty of the ceremony, but the inspiration of your loyalty and affection. I thank you all from a full heart. God bless you all.'

'Fair play to her,' Tad said to himself, moved to tears.

In the pub that evening, Tad, Emlyn and Harry oiled their throats with ale in preparation for singing, and discussed the impending royal visit to the town.

Harry had got it on good authority from Idrys at the station that the royal party was not, as had been believed, arriving by train, but leaving by it.

'Obviously, and I don't think anybody's going to disagree

with me here, it makes sense for us to keep our Coronation bunting up for the royal visit, and that way our international visitors can share in the experience, too,' Harry said. He put his arm around Tad's shoulder. 'Tad, you know Her Majesty well. How will she feel about that? Is she likely to call in on you while she's in the neighbourhood?'

Tad had put up with a lot of teasing since he got back. In the privacy of the compost heap at the bottom of the garden, he had practised an accurate and vivid recital of his London experience while being mindful of keeping just this side of showing off. But nobody seemed interested in hearing the details of watching the royal procession from, as Emlyn put it, a pigeon's perspective. They were a lot keener on talking about Mai's wonderfully scandalous Coronation experience in Little Green Street.

Tad had first heard about it on Wednesday after work during the sorting out of the kitchen tables, when they had carried them all out into the street for an identification parade so that their owners could claim them in the clear light of day.

The story of Mai's demolition of the rose garden was told with badly disguised hilarity. But he also listened with quiet respect to the story of Barbara's miraculous musical return from the wasteland of her grief. And heard from Harry and Emlyn, when no one was listening, about Dennis Hill's large repertoire of rugby songs in dubious taste that they'd sung well into the night.

Tad wanted to be disapproving, especially as they'd asked Dennis to join the choir on the spot without consulting him, but on the other hand he liked Dennis and he hadn't sung a dubious rugby song since he was a young man, when he'd had a bit of a repertoire of his own.

If he'd been in charge, he would have made sure that everyone had the right tables to take home with them at the end of the day, but nobody was impressed when he pointed this out, and on Wednesday Harry had gone so far as to call him an old spoilsport. As Tad had carried his own table back into the house, he wondered if this was how Helen felt; outshone and misunderstood.

And worse was to come.

Emlyn looked up at them from his pint and said, 'By the way, I've got an announcement.' He smoothed back his dark quiff and gave a sigh of satisfaction. 'Nancy and I are getting married in four weeks' time.'

'What? When was that decided?' Tad asked.

'Don't worry, Tad, you don't have to do anything,' Emlyn said soothingly, misunderstanding his alarm.

'I'm not worrying, I'm just asking.'

'Oh, right then. Nancy and I went to see Mr Griffiths earlier this evening and we've decided that we'd like to tie the knot before the visitors come.'

Harry smoothed his moustache thoughtfully. 'So Nancy's past didn't trouble the minister in a theological sense?'

'No, it didn't trouble him in any sense. He was with us on Tuesday night, enjoying himself. Ironically it was Mai's behaviour at the party that helped to get things straight in his mind. He quoted John, Chapter 8. "He that is without sin among you, let him first cast a stone." Actually, Harry, you might want to share that with Mai, because it might cheer her up regarding her own recent fall, not from grace exactly but over the hedge.'

Tad grinned.

'Anyway,' Emlyn went on, 'we're going to have a small wedding with the reception held here in the Hand and Billy is organising chicken and chips.'

'Who are you having for best man, Emlyn?' Harry asked as Tad was himself preparing to accept the role.

Emlyn lifted his glass. 'The way I look at it, it's hard to choose between the two of you so I've decided in all fairness not to have one.'

'What?' Harry and Tad said in unison and glanced at each other, feeling snubbed.

'Who's going to deliver the best man's speech?' Tad asked.

'No speeches, although I intend to thank my mother for sewing all those buttons on my Pearly King costume, because without her, well, you know.'

'It beats me how a suit with buttons on could exert so much influence over you,' Harry said, looking grumpy as he stroked his moustache. 'Very superficial, I call it. I thought you had more strength of character than that.'

'I suppose Old Mrs Hughes is cutting all the buttons off again now,' Tad said and thought fleetingly of his naval officer's uniform in Dennis Hill's shop.

'True, and it broke my heart to watch because I'd had half a mind to get married in that suit,' Emlyn said, 'but with the buttons it's a bit flash for a solemn occasion. And I'll need it back to normal for the Male Voice Choir competition, anyway.'

'A bit flash!' Tad saw the perfect opener. 'If you want to see flash, you should have seen the Coronation coach! All gold and pulled by white horses! And as you can't get more high church than the Coronation—'

'Any thoughts on bridesmaids, Emlyn?' Harry cut in, as though Tad hadn't spoken.

'Just Flora. We're keeping it low key.'

'Rhiannon was hoping . . . well, never mind. If that's what you want.'

'You've got it all sorted,' Tad said, disappointed he was not playing a key part, or any part at all. 'I suppose we will be allowed in the church, will we, on the day? Or is it so low key that you're scrimping on the congregation too? Keeping the numbers down?'

Debatable though it was to his mind, Little Green Street seemed to believe it could manage perfectly well without him and he felt that the certainties of his life were, like the ruins of Crow Castle, crumbling around him.

'Don't let paranoia get the better of you, Tad,' Emlyn said, laughing. 'Everyone is welcome. We want some volume to the hymn-singing, there's nothing worse than an apologetic, timidly voiced congregation, in my view. Here's Oswald! Oswald, have you got those hymns for my wedding? "Love Divine, All Loves Excelling", you don't mind us having a quick practice, do you, Tad?'

Tad looked desolately into the foam lacing his empty glass. 'Don't talk to me about love,' he said, and he went to get the drinks in.

57

Emlyn and Nancy's wedding took place on a sunny Saturday at the end of June in the quiet, wood-lined simplicity of the Methodist Church.

Bride, groom, Old Mrs Hughes and Flora all sat together in the front pew, and Mr Griffiths w-welcomed them all, and from then on stirred the silence with his ringing eloquence.

'Nancy looks beautiful, doesn't she,' Helen whispered to Mai as the bride and groom stood up.

Nancy was wearing a ballerina-length ivory dress with rustling petticoats that she'd bought on a trip to Browns of Chester with Helen. It flared from the pink sash at her waist, and she was holding a bouquet of pink and white roses, tied with ribbon.

Mai took the bouquet personally and fanned herself with her hymn-book. 'Very unfeeling, I call it, to choose roses,' she whispered to Helen. 'I can't bear the scent any more. Bad memories.'

Helen grinned and glanced at Tad to see if he'd heard. His hair was brushed back, coarse and lively, and his eyes were half closed in semi-prayer. He never closed them completely in church in case he missed anything.

During the marriage service he threw in an 'Amen' here and there as the spirit moved him, just as Cecil had in London.

When Nancy and Emlyn were saying the vows, Helen's eyes filled with tears. She'd never understood why people cried at weddings because, after all, it was a celebration of love and a time for rejoicing. But now, with her new-found insight into the loneliness that marriage could bring, the promises that Nancy and Emlyn were making to each other moved her with their courage and certainty, their voices clear and sure.

Nancy's blonde hair was pinned back and her cheeks were flushed as she held out her hand for Emlyn to put the gold ring on her finger. His gaze connected with hers, and they both broke into smiles which so affected Mr Griffiths spiritually that he accidentally closed his black leather-bound service book and lost his place, and spent a few moments finding it again.

Old Mrs Hughes, who had long given up the idea of getting Emlyn off her hands, cried noisily into a voluminous handkerchief embroidered with her late husband's initials, and every time she blew her nose the blue silk roses adorning her large hat quivered as if with their own emotion.

Flora, wearing pink and holding the two bouquets, looked utterly happy, in a way she'd never looked before.

Garth was standing with his mother. He had his finger in a black hymn-book and was staring straight ahead with a faint smile on his face, listening. His freckles looked very dark against his pale skin.

The last hymn they sang was 'How Great Thou Art', and although Garth held the hymn-book for his mother to share, he didn't look at it himself – he didn't need to. He was singing strong and deep in a voice that no one had heard before, swaying forward and upwards on the balls of his feet. He held on to the final note long after everyone else had stopped.

Tad decided, first chance he got, to ask him to join the choir.

With Garth's 'Amen' still in their ears, Nancy, Emlyn, Old Mrs Hughes and Flora gaily processed out into the summer air in a cloud of confetti.

58

The week before the International Musical Festival, Helen was polishing a shine into the dining-room table. The Boardroom had been demoted to the dining room again now that the committee meetings had finished. She folded up her duster and sat in Tad's chair, imagining the committee members were sitting around the table with clasped hands and attentive expressions.

The first item on the agenda would be Tad himself.

Ever since London, things hadn't been right between them and she didn't know what to do about it. Mai's imaginary voice, humbler than usual since her downfall – although you would have to know her well to be able to tell the difference – wondered if Helen had considered offering an apology to Tad and the committee for calling the town a backwater.

What would you call it? she wanted to ask.

But the words had been fired by the furnace of anger rather than reason. Compared with London, it *was* a backwater. Whenever she got off the train in Paddington to the noise, the steam, the heat, the crowds, she would feel a thrill and breathe it in, smog and all: 'I'm home!'

But the truth was, when she returned to the town from anywhere, she also fell into a featherbed of pleasure at seeing the streets, the green hills, the wide river again. She wanted to stretch her arms out to it, embrace it and shout: 'I'm home!'

She realised it was perfectly possible to belong in both places, and it was a good feeling knowing that. The imaginary Harry looked at her gravely across the table, stroking his moustache. 'Don't mind me asking, but what's home got to do with anything? It's Tad himself that's the problem. He's been too quiet since he got back, we can all see that.'

'That's because I've hurt his feelings.'

'Why don't you tell him that?' Nancy would say lightly.

Why don't I tell him that? Helen had always tried to hide her emotions. She let Tad be emotional for her, while she herself kept it all inside. 'The one time I told him what I really thought, look where it got me,' she would tell Nancy.

And Nancy would smile. She'd say, 'I know, let's go for a drink at the Hand and forget all about it.'

The irony of it! During the years that Helen had known her, Nancy had been loudly and buoyantly cheerful. But now that her joy was genuine, instead of celebrating her good fortune in a wild and giddy way, she was quietly and serenely happy.

Unlike me, Helen thought.

That evening, at the kitchen table, Lauren finished her dessert of tinned apricots and evaporated milk and put her spoon down. She was desperate to go out into the bunting-bright town and walk around under the pale sky, below the majestic ruins of Crow Castle, where the green, humped hills of Barber's Hill, Bryniau-bach and Pen-y-Coed curled, waiting for the visitors to arrive.

After tea, Tad went out to the front garden. Harry was hoeing the soil around his roses to get rid of the weeds. 'I don't know how the Queen and Prince Philip are going to fit all of Wales in in just two days.'

'And for one of those days she'll be in the south of the country,' Tad said. 'But the point is that she's coming, and I'm not prepared to quibble about the duration because she'll be seeing the best of our town and that's what counts in terms of deep national significance, if you ask me.'

'And we did give her that Wendy house, Y Bwthyn Bach, to play in when she was little, styled in the manner of a Welsh cottage, so she'll feel perfectly at home. Also,' he added, 'she might hear us sing.'

'No, she won't.' Tad had already checked the programme and he'd accepted this disappointment stoically although he couldn't think of anything nicer than knowing she was listening.

'What a shame. Sir Adrian Boult is not coming, either. He's exhausted from the Coronation and taking a break.' Harry was more disappointed by this than anything else.

'Talking of Adrian Boult, how long are you keeping that moustache for, Harry? It's not a permanent fixture, is it?'

'Don't you start,' Harry grumbled. He straightened up and rubbed the small of his back. 'Look, I don't suppose there's any chance you would let me conduct the choir at the festival, is there?'

Tad was feeling different about things since the rift with

Helen. Certain things had become less important to him recently, himself included.

A month ago he would have got very worked up and indignant at the suggestion, whereas now, certain things seemed to have faded into insignificance. To his surprise his place in the world was nowhere near as important as he'd once believed, and it was taking him time to get used to it. 'Let me think about it,' he said.

Harry looked at him with concern. 'Are you feeling all right? You're not sickening for something, are you?'

The unexpected show of sympathy gave Tad a strong desire to unburden himself and he asked hesitantly, 'Do you think I'm an unreasonable man?'

'On occasion, yes, undoubtedly,' Harry said.

'And how about Helen? Do you imagine she could be unreasonable?'

'What sort of question is that? We're all unreasonable at times, and for the most peculiar reasons. Take Mai, for instance. Well, on second thoughts, you don't want twice the trouble, so it's probably best to leave Mai where she is.'

But because Tad had promised to think about letting him conduct, Harry tried to console him. 'Anyway, rest assured this atmosphere between you and Helen will all blow over in time. These things do, you know.'

59

CROESO! WELCOME!
VELKOMMEN! ISTEN HOZTA! HOS GELDINIZ!
WITAMY! BIENVENUE! WILLKOMMEN! FÁILTE!
SHALOM! WELKOM! BENVENUTO! VÍTÁME VÁS!
WALES WELCOMES THE WORLD!

Flags from different countries flounced in the breeze above the wide stone bridge that crossed the Dee, and the overcrowded hanging baskets burst with colour, dripping blooms down the black lamp-posts of a small town in a green valley.

In the town, houses of all sizes, from stucco-clad mansions to Tudor halls, red-brick farmhouses to stone detached cottages, bungalows to blocks of flats, all of them, from the grandest to the smallest, had beds prepared with laundered sheets and soft, plump pillows, ready for the visitors to arrive.

To be greeted in one's own tongue and to see your national flag flying in a strange land must be a wonderful thing.

But a clean bed in a warm house at the end of a long journey . . . that was a welcome.

On Sunday the fifth of July, the residents of Little Green Street were loitering purposefully in their front gardens waiting for their visitors when a cream and green coach drove up, the hazy sunlight bouncing off it like spray. A cardboard sign taped on the windscreen said: *Frederiksborg Folkedansere, DENMARK.*

'The visitors are here!' Lauren stared at her flattened, fattened shape in the coach's paintwork as it came to a stop. The coach's air brakes hissed, churning out dirty heat against their bare summer legs.

Inside the coach everyone was standing and reaching into the luggage racks, gathering possessions.

The folk dancers from Denmark congregated in the street around their luggage, stretching and smiling and looking around at the green hills. Tall, tanned and good-looking, they seemed not only a different nationality but a different species; even better than they'd dreamt. A giggle caught high in Lauren's chest.

'Oh, wow,' Flora said.

Lauren felt her heart triple-bounce against her ribcage, full of instant love for the visitors.

'Oh, they're gorgeous,' Rhiannon said weakly, flopping against Lauren.

Two lads caught the girls in the slow sweep of their gaze. The plainer one winked.

'He winked at *you*, Lauren,' Flora said, nudging her.

'Now we just need a short one for Rhiannon,' Lauren said.

'Or stilts.'

Rhiannon was looking at the Danish girls. 'Look at them,' she said sorrowfully, 'they're all so beautiful!'

'They probably get bored, seeing beautiful girls all the time,' Flora said knowledgeably.

Mrs Hugh Pugh from the Hospitality Committee came

out of the coach last carrying a clipboard, smart in a silky summer dress which inflated as she stepped down and floated back to earth. She shook hands with Tad.

They had Ole staying with them.

'*Velkommen*,' Lauren said.

'You speak Danish?'

'No. Only that.'

He grinned. Lauren grinned back. She knew that soon their town would be hot and loud with strange, elusive languages that you wished you understood and almost did. *Croeso, velkommen*, welcome, she thought.

That evening they were having lamb chops for supper and Lauren could hear Tad's voice rumbling from the dining room as he spoke to Ole.

Ole stood up politely as Lauren took the plates in. He was taller than she was and the ceiling seemed to lower a foot or two around them. Right up close she could see that his tanned nose was peeling and his lips were chapped but he was still the most gorgeous boy she'd ever seen.

The oven timer buzzed and Lauren excused herself as her mother called her back into the kitchen.

'Ole seems very nice, doesn't he,' her mother said softly, tucking her hands into her blue striped oven gloves. 'Drain the carrots, will you, and we'll be ready.'

Lauren took the carrots in and watched the food steaming on the table.

'Do help yourself to potatoes, Ole,' her mother said quickly, but although Ole had the serving spoon in his hand he had lost interest in the food and was deep in conversation with her father.

'Mrs Hugh Pugh said that the Germans would be competing. They shouldn't *be* allowed here,' Ole said sternly, 'after starting a war.'

Tad put his cutlery down with a clatter and tucked his napkin into his shirt for safekeeping. 'No, no, no!' he said quickly, 'you don't understand! That's the whole point! This is *exactly* where they should be!' The passion shone in his brown eyes. 'Let me tell you something, Ole,' Tad said seriously, sitting forward in his chair. 'The year of the third International Eisteddfod, four years ago, there wasn't a house in the town that hadn't lost someone, friends, brothers, cousins in the war, not one. But we heard the news that the Luebeck Choir was coming over from Germany to sing. Brave of them, that's how I see it now. We'd invited the world, you see.' He rubbed his hand along his jaw. 'Anyhow,' he said, 'it wasn't an easy journey. Europe was damaged beyond imagining. They'd had difficulty getting passports and they had to get their money on the black market.'

'But they came?' Ole asked.

'Yes, they did. They came by rail right here into this station. We waited on the platform to meet them. When the doors opened and out they stepped, young men and women, carrying small suitcases, I could see the look on their faces. They looked—' Tad fell silent as he remembered '—scared,' he finished. He cleared his throat. 'Our wives kissed them in welcome.'

Lauren watched his hand move to his heart and she realised with dismay that her father was tearful.

'At the festival,' Tad continued, 'Hywel Roberts had the task of introducing the choirs, and his brother had been killed in Germany on the last day of the war. There was an audience of several thousand, mind, and you could hear a pin drop as Hywel went onto the stage. But Hywel was up to the job, you see, and we needn't have worried. He asked us, with his usual quiet confidence, to join him in greeting "our friends from West Germany". Friends . . .' Tad shook his head. 'You never heard such applause. The Luebeck Choir couldn't sing for a few minutes, and I don't blame them . . . I tell you, that was a day.'

Tad's eyes were intense with fervour. 'You see, Ole, in this town during festival week, music overcomes enmity, because a world that sings is blessed.'

He fell silent, then he suddenly noticed the table and all the waiting food and he remembered the laws of hospitality. 'Help yourself,' he said, spreading his arms, 'enjoy it, there's plenty.' His smile was kind.

60

On Tuesday, the first day of the festival, the town was draped with banners and fluttering with Union Jacks for the royal visit to come.

Lauren, Flora, Rhiannon and Garth walked to Abbey Road to cheer as the whole of the noisy, colourful parade of competitors made its way past the red-brick chapels and the white-housed streets of the small town, led by a Chinese dragon who pranced playfully with the red Welsh dragon as they danced over the stone bridge. They were followed by a male-voice choir from Israel and spinning dancers from Egypt; Turks with boots and skirts and daggers; Kurds with dazzling smiles; ringleted dancers from Northern Ireland; Sri Lankan girls with jewelled faces; and the Indian Heritage dancers with headdresses bright as peacocks close behind. Russians and Bosnians, Americans and Vietnamese, Palestinians and Israelis joined together in friendship, and the song and drumming, the music and the singing were drowned by the cheers of the people lining the streets.

The festival field smelled of crushed grass as Tad, Emlyn and Harry strolled around the tents, and the canvas sails of the huge marquee rose up and caught the wind as though it could sail away any moment.

The international folk-dancing competitions were taking place, and on the open-air stage in front of the Royal

Pavilion, Japanese drummers wearing blue martial arts suits and wide black bandanas were beating out rapid rhythms. There was plenty to do beyond watching the music – drink tea or coffee, eat cakes at the food stalls, study the craft exhibits or lie on the grass to sunbathe.

Through the speakers, a lively folk melody was accompanied by the thud and tap of feet on the stage, and as was customary, the hosts were there to cheer for their visitors.

The people of Little Green Street were going to watch the Frederiksborg folk dancers. They entered the huge, earthy tent and in the canvas-tainted humidity they waited for the competition to begin.

Against the vast backdrop of flowers, Ole and their new friends from Denmark walked onto the stage and moments later they were skipping, spiralling, arms linked, kicking rhythmically, celebrating courtship, marriage, heartbreak and divorce.

Bird shadows flew across the canopy and, from outside in the open air, overlaid against the listening crowd, children squealed, their voices leaping and falling as though on elastic.

At the end of the dances Lauren, Flora and Rhiannon jumped to their feet to applaud. Turning around, Tad saw Helen and Nancy a few rows back, talking intently as they clapped the visitors.

'What do you think they're talking about?' Tad asked Emlyn, nudging him.

'Us, probably,' Emlyn said happily.

Back outside, Emlyn looked around at the colourful groups of competitors in their brightly embroidered jackets with pom-poms and bows.

'I wish I was foreign,' he said as he listened to the Babel of tongues he didn't understand.

'To the visitors we are foreign,' Harry pointed out.

'True enough,' Tad agreed. 'I'm foreign to my own wife.' Yehudi Menuhin was coming in a few days to play his violin and Tad was wondering now if it was too late to take it up himself as a way of getting out of the house.

The three men passed a van nestled in the grass selling tea and biscuits, and decided to go back and join the short queue for refreshments to have a break from strolling. Harry was tapping his leg with his concert programme in time to the music when suddenly he stopped and let out a loud gasp of astonishment. He grabbed his friends in a frenzy of excitement. 'Look! Over there! It's him! It's Sir Adrian Boult!'

The famous conductor was indeed mingling in the flow of the crowd, deep in conversation with Jack Rhys Roberts, the festival chairman. On hearing Harry say his name, he looked enquiringly in their direction and Harry opened his arms wide as if he was greeting his long-lost brother.

Emlyn cautioned him with a hand on his arm. 'Steady on now!'

But there was no stopping Harry. He lumbered over and greeted his hero with great warmth and bonhomie. 'I expect I look familiar to you!' he said as an opener.

'I beg your pardon?' Sir Adrian Boult replied, politely enough.

Tad groaned as Harry suddenly roared with joyful laughter – a nervous reaction, no doubt, but startling all the same.

'Hahaha! I know what you're thinking! It's like looking

in the mirror, isn't it. You and me and the moustache!' Harry said. He put his tongue under his upper lip to give his facial hair more prominence.

'Have we met before?' the conductor asked, looking confused.

'Every morning in the bathroom when we get up! Watch this! Watch!' Harry started waving his finger right in front of the conductor's eyes like a hypnotist whilst humming the national anthem. 'Do you see it now?'

With an expression of dawning panic, Sir Adrian Boult did a smart about-turn in the direction he'd just come from, with Jack Rhys Roberts hurrying after him.

Harry watched them go, perplexed. Reluctantly he turned back to join Tad and Emlyn in the queue for tea. 'Did you see that? Snubbed, I was.'

'He thought you were a madman,' Emlyn said, 'waving your finger at him like that.'

Tad agreed. 'To be fair, when you were standing right next to him there was no resemblance whatsoever. He's bald. And you made two of him. At least.'

'But the moustache—'

'Yes. Just the moustache.'

Harry was unwilling to let it go at that and he continued to look hopefully into the crowd. 'He's probably got a ticket for the whole week. He might have got it complimentary. He'll be wanting to say hello to the Queen, tomorrow, seeing as they go back a few years.' He turned to Tad, and the small features on his large face were hopeful. 'I know this is a big thing to ask, but you did promise you'd think about letting me conduct. What do you say, Tad?'

As Tad shuffled forwards in the queue, he realised he'd been anticipating this moment from the very day in the Hand in April when Harry, cold-eyed, first asked him who'd decided Tad should be the conductor.

He'd held tightly on to his position at the time, because it seemed important to him to be in charge. Now, as he looked beyond the bright, noisy hubbub of the festival field towards the calm green hills and the blue summer sky, he realised how very small his role was in the scheme of things. He was a speck, a dot, a fleck and nothing more, and the knowledge freed him to be generous.

He looked at Harry's broad shoulders, squared optimistically under his straining jacket as he hoped still to impress his hero.

'Yes,' Tad said. 'Fair play, Harry. You should conduct.'

Harry's face lit up. 'Great, then! Thanks, Tad,' he said, and finding himself at the counter at last, in a gesture of largesse, he paid for the teas.

61

Lauren needed peace to practise the Peace Message. On Tuesday night after they had eaten, she pulled the hood up on her coat and headed up the road, over the canal and towards Lower Alder Farm. In the evening light the farm buildings looked mysterious and limitless. She listened to the prolonged double-barking of a dog carrying through the cooling air.

As she walked uphill, the blood pulsed in her veins, and as she passed the farm she saw a light in the window and imagined the farmer's wife looking out at her and seeing a mysterious hooded figure pass, alone and fearless.

She climbed to a steady rhythm, listening to the suck and blow of her breath. Her eyes scanned shadow-filled dips and loose-lying stones that in her mind were skulls and bones. The hill became steeper. Up above her, the ruins of Crow Castle hunched black and conspiratorial against the evening sky. She grasped handfuls of grass to scramble up the last incline, hands closing on gorse and sheep droppings, and then she was at the top, rubbing her hands on her jeans and catching her breath, looking down on the town.

She sat on the grass and leant back comfortably against a stone wall out of the wind and unfolded the page. It felt as if it was the most important thing she'd ever done. She read the words over and over with passion, conviction and from the heart. When she was satisfied she had memorised it and that it sounded the way she wanted it to, she folded the sheet up and put it back in her pocket.

The next day, Lauren had told her parents they had to be at the festival ground at four o'clock in the afternoon.

At quarter to four, Tad and Helen were walking along the canal to the festival field. Straight ahead of them, like hills in winter, the tents of the festival ground glowed white under the summer sun.

Music drifted to them on the breeze, the notes falling gently out of the sky. The distant church clock chimed.

Tad and Helen walked along the path in silence, ducking under overhanging branches. Neither had anything to say that was trivial enough, and the important things were too big to talk about. Words lodged like lumps in their hearts. A horse was pulling a narrowboat along the leafy tow-path, plodding and jingling, his head lifting and falling with every ringing step. As Helen turned to admire it an overhanging branch caught in her hair and as she freed herself she cried out suddenly, 'Oh! My pearl earring! Tad!'

They crouched down to search for it on the path and by the roots of the trees on the bank. The tow-path had seemed uniform grey as they'd walked along, but on their hands and knees, close up it was a confusing mosaic of stones and pebbles, seeds and leaves.

On all fours, Tad cautiously felt along the fringe of grass by the water's edge. He was aware that time was passing, but he very much wanted to find the earring for her. It seemed to matter to them both very much that he did. 'It may have bounced into the canal,' he realised in dismay, looking down into the pea-green water.

'But we have to find it! You gave them to me on our wedding day,' she said, her voice high and tight with tears as if she'd lost some good and true part of him. Tad knew they'd always been important to her, and he was glad they were important to her still. As he reached for what turned out to be a pebble, he noticed it was almost four. He straightened up and dusted the gravel from the knees of his trousers. 'I'm afraid we're going to have to leave it for now. We'll come and look for it on the way back. I'm sure we'll find it again.' His gaze met hers and for a moment neither of them moved.

Helen's pale blue eyes were blurred with tears. 'But what if we *don't* find it?' she asked him desperately. 'What then?'

He'd wondered that himself. 'I'll buy you another pair, bigger,' he reassured her, taking the question at face value. 'I'll get you the finest pair I can find. Come on.'

He was relieved there was still a promise he could make to her that staked a flag in the future.

The music was louder now. Tad and Helen hurried over the humpback bridge to the festival ground, worrying because the lost pearl had made them late.

As they entered the ground they heard over the loud-speakers: 'And reading the Message of Peace and Goodwill from the Youth of the Town – Lauren Jones!'

Tad knew how far it was to the entrance, and that it was guarded fiercely by the volunteer stewards, who practised their power as seriously as if they were being paid.

'Quick,' he said to Helen like a hero in a film, grabbing

her hand tightly, 'follow me,' and they high-stepped over a cat's cradle of guy ropes. Tad uprooted a tent peg as large as a skewer for an ox, and held up the flap.

Helen crawled under the flap with Tad following her and they emerged self-consciously at the back, behind the clapping crowd, just in time.

A long way away on the stage, surrounded by the floral decorations, Lauren looked like a miniature version of herself in her school uniform with her wild hair clipped back.

Tad wanted to scoop her up high and hoist her on his shoulders and run with her to safety.

But she didn't need him. She cleared her throat and her voice was strong and clear.

Lauren spoke about friendship and reconciliation, and about conflict being the punishment people imposed on themselves; about coming together in harmony through music, and the blessing of peace. As she spoke, her words were full of suffering and hope. She was speaking to the whole world, to the crowds on the festival ground, to the audience in the marquee, and to her father, standing wild-haired with her mother at the very back, hoping they'd heard.

As Lauren walked off the stage to join her classmates, Helen looked around the tent with a frown, as if the world had unexpectedly changed. She thought of Lauren's words about reconciliation and then she turned to Tad and reached for his hand.

'Forgive me, Tad,' she said in a small voice. 'Shh, please don't say anything yet, just listen. I told you what I'd given up for you but I was being unfair. It's nothing compared with what you've given me. And you missed the party which meant so much to you and I never thanked you for that. I know I ruined things and I'm sorry for that.'

'Ruined things?' Tad ran his hand through his dark, bushy hair. He thought about it for a moment and shook his head. 'No, you didn't ruin things, Helen. I spent Coronation Day with you, where I wanted to be.'

She looked into his brown eyes and put her palm gently against his warm cheek. '*Caru ti*,' she whispered.

His gaze softened, and he broke into a wide smile. 'And I love you, too,' he replied, and he kissed her.

Tad, who preached about peace in his own home, felt the cold of their solitude rekindle into the warmth of love. 'Your Welsh is coming on a treat,' he said, taking her arm, and before the audience settled, he and Helen strolled nonchalantly to the exit and emerged from the steamy tent into the mountain-cooled air.

Tad began to hum, and unable to contain himself he burst into song: '"But this I know, the skies will fill with rapture! And myriad, myriad human voices sing!" The power of words, Helen. I'll write a poem about it.' It was the most he'd said to her in a while, in weeks, it felt like.

She hugged him. '*Now* you're back,' she said with a smile.

62

The Male Voice Choir competition took place on Thursday in the packed, hot tent on the green meadow in the valley. Up on stage, the Dee Male Voice Choir in their best suits, with Tad and Emlyn in the tenor section and Garth between them, men who knew each other like family, sang their anthems and their love songs. Harry conducted them majestically, easing, teasing, taming their voices with the commanding power of his baton.

In the front row of the audience sat Helen, Nancy, Old Mrs Hughes, Barbara, Mai, Rhiannon, Flora and Lauren. When the choir bowed, they roared fit to inflate the pavilion roof, and their rendition of the national anthem moved the audience to tears.

The following day, July the tenth, the Queen and Prince Philip were arriving in the town.

Old Mrs Hughes had taken a flask, her knitting and a chair to the festival ground early and bagged them all a place right on top of the grassy bank so that they would get a good view of the royal party as they walked by. Now Emlyn and Nancy were sunning themselves on the multicoloured picnic blanket that she had made for them as a wedding present, talking about the competition.

'You know something, Harry?' Emlyn said. 'We would

have won yesterday, if only the Rossendale Male Voice Choir hadn't been better than us.'

'For the second year running, too,' Harry pointed out. 'But fair play, they were good, I admit,' he conceded. He was sitting on an old cushion he'd brought along, to save getting damp. He fidgeted, trying to get comfortable. 'Hey, swap cushions with me, Mai, will you,' he said. 'This one's got no stuffing in it.'

'Daft thing, of course it's got stuffing, you've squashed it, that's all.'

Tad was lying on the grass with Helen resting against his chest in her bluebell-blue dress. She felt warm and comfortable in his arms. 'We might win next year,' he said cheerfully.

'I'll sell you my baton if you like, Tad,' Harry said.

'It's second-hand now, mind.' And then, like distant thunder, Tad heard a thrilling crescendo of cheering that was familiar to him.

'She's coming!' Helen said, scrambling to her feet. They ran down the grassy bank to join the crowd, and moments later, there she was, Her Majesty Queen Elizabeth the Second, coming towards them, a delicate figure carrying a large bouquet and waving to the cheering people on the other side of the route. Prince Philip, Earl of Merioneth, was walking behind her in his naval uniform, his buttons bright, and braid shimmering, and his peaked cap perfectly straight on his smooth hair.

Seeing him, Tad had a sudden revelation. It wasn't important to be the figurehead, he realised; it was more important to be the support, the strength and mainstay. 'God save the Queen!' he shouted, overwhelmed by the moment, his teacher's voice booming over the crowd. The Queen turned towards them with a quick, shy smile, so close they could have touched her.

Tad bowed in homage.

As he straightened, Prince Philip gave him a brief look of acknowledgement before walking by.

The scent of the blossom from the Queen's bouquet remained with them, and the day seemed so easy, so perfect. The group of friends lingered in the pleasure of the afternoon with the sun on their faces, the women sitting on their cardigans and the men on the grass, listening to the cheering as it undulated out of the ground and along Abbey Road, following the royal party all the way to the station, where the royal train was waiting.

Emlyn lay back and looked at the sky, his black hair furrowed from the comb.

Tad propped himself up on one elbow and narrowed his eyes to tell them about his philosophical epiphany. 'It's like the difference between a wedding and a marriage.'

Emlyn lifted his head. 'What is?'

'The Coronation and the reign. The Coronation is like the wedding ceremony and the reign is like the marriage. No doubt there will be trials and difficulties in her life, but we, her subjects, will remain constant in our love and support to the end.'

'On the subject of subjects, Tad, tell her to stay longer next time she comes,' Harry said, smoothing his moustache. 'Tell her we'll show her the town.'

Helen laughed. 'We'll take her to the Hand.'

'You can have a sloe gin with her, Mai,' Nancy said with a wink.

Mai fanned herself at the thought. 'Get away! No, indeed!'

Emlyn looked at Tad. 'Just think,' he said, 'she might be there already, waiting for us to join her.'

'Having a drink with Adrian Boult.'

'Better not disappoint her, then,' Harry said, and the group of friends got up off the grass, brushed themselves down and started to walk.

Acknowledgements

With warmest thanks to Joel, because there has been a lot of trust involved in the last few months and I really appreciate that, and to Clare Bowron and Eugenie Todd for sorting out loose ends in triple time.

It wouldn't have got off the ground without Judith Murdoch, my agent, who happily for me knows a good thing when she sees it and I'm lucky to have her.